phnom penh noir

phnom penh noir

Roland Joffé James Grady
John Burdett Christopher G. Moore
Kosal Khiev Prabda Yoon
Bopha Phorn Giancarlo Narciso
Christopher West Richard Rubenstein
Suong Mak Andrew Nette
Bob Bergin Neil Wilford
Christopher Minko

Edited by Christopher G. Moore

Heaven Lake Press

Distributed in Thailand by:
Asia Document Bureau Ltd.
P.O. Box 1029
Nana Post Office
Bangkok 10112 Thailand
Fax: (662) 260-4578
www.heavenlakepress.com
email: editorial@heavenlakepress.com

All rights reserved
Book copyright © 2012 Asia Document Bureau Ltd.
Individual story copyright © 2012 the authors: *Hearts and Minds* by Roland Joffé, *The Fires of Forever* by James Grady, *Love and Death at Angkor* by John Burdett, *Reunion* by Christopher G. Moore, *Broken Chains* by Kosal Khiev, *Darkness Is Faster Than the Speed of Light* by Prabda Yoon, *Dark Truths* by Bopha Phorn, *Play with Fire: A Sergio Biancardi Mystery* by Giancarlo Narciso, *Orders* by Christopher West, *Sabbatical Term* by Richard Rubenstein, *Hell in the City* by Suong Mak, *Khmer Riche* by Andrew Nette, *A Coven of Snakes* by Bob Bergin, *Rebirth* by Neil Wilford, "Buckets of Blood," "Prison of Sobriety," "The Ying," "Bangkok Tattoo," "Don't Go Away," "Mango Madness / Monsoon Sadness," "Where'd Ya Go," "Phnom Penh," and "Tango Traffic Tango" by Christopher Minko

First published in Thailand in 2012
by Heaven Lake Press

Cover photograph: Channa Siv © 2012
Jacket design: K. Jiamsomboon

ISBN 978-616-7503-15-8

For Christopher Minko

Contents

Introduction	vii
Hearts and Minds by Roland Joffé	1
The Fires of Forever by James Grady	47
Love and Death at Angkor by John Burdett	77
Reunion by Christopher G. Moore	113
Broken Chains by Kosal Khiev	149
Darkness Is Faster Than the Speed of Light by Prabda Yoon	155
Dark Truths by Bopha Phorn	163
Play with Fire: A Sergio Biancardi Mystery by Giancarlo Narciso	187
Orders by Christopher West	219
Sabbatical Term by Richard Rubenstein	241
Hell in the City by Suong Mak	269
Khmer Riche by Andrew Nette	299
A Coven of Snakes by Bob Bergin	327
Rebirth by Neil Wilford	361
KROM: Songs from the Noir by Christopher Minko	371

Introduction

Many anthologies have inspired writers and publishers to gather "noir" stories about a city. The history of Phnom Penh qualifies it to be placed at the top of any list of cities deserving of a noir anthology. What other city in modern times was emptied of all of its people at gunpoint, abandoned, and left as a ghost town? When the Khmer Rouge arrived on April 17, 1975, they evacuated Phnom Penh. The Khmer Rouge experiment aimed for a radical societal transformation down a notoriously bloody trail, one that left almost no family untouched.

The entrance of the Khmer Rouge into Phnom Penh, a key moment in history, was famously depicted in the iconic film *The Killing Fields*. It is appropriate that Roland Joffé, the director of *The Killing Fields*, is one of the contributors to this anthology.

After the Khmer Rouge marched into Phnom Penh, a reign of terror descending into genocide and war crimes followed for the next four long years as the country was turned into a vast gulag and slaughterhouse. It is difficult to imagine a darker period in the lives of Cambodians. Time moves on, and it has done in Cambodia, but Phnom Penh continues to offer the contradiction of renewal and noir.

As the editor of *Phnom Penh Noir*, I invited a select group of writers and artists to provide their take on the genre as a lens for viewing Cambodian life. Readers who

Introduction

relish a journey into the dark side of life discovered noir long ago. Most anthologies with "noir" in the title are collections of short stories. While short fiction is central to the genre, music, lyrics, photographs, and paintings also are important sources of creativity inspired by the concept of noir. In searching for the right mix of authors, I asked myself the question—why not expand the book's view of the noir landscape to include other types of creative artists?

That is just what I've done in this anthology. The reader will discover a wide variety of approaches and perspectives here. The idea of a collective of writers and artists seeking to realize the full range of possibilities of noir has led to a cultural journey through one of Southeast Asia's most interesting countries, one shackled by the burden of history.

In *Phnom Penh Noir* the writers and artists include famous names such as Roland Joffé, John Burdett, and James Grady as well as less well-known names internationally such as Suong Mak, Bopha Phorn, Kosal Khiev, and Christopher Minko's band KROM. Western writers and artists and Cambodian writers and artists are the midwives who have delivered Phnom Penh into the world of noir literature.

Their collective vision is fired by dark images—of powerful, influential figures, gangsters, fraudsters, shady foreigners, crooked NGOs, corrupt officials, and the streets of Phnom Penh. A literary and artistic movement to openly question the past, upend received wisdom, and examine the nature of power, fairness, authority, and justice has taken root in many places around the world, and Southeast Asia is no exception. *Phnom Penh Noir* is an example of the growth of this broad-based literary and artistic movement.

Noir has no one-size-fits-all definition. The term is used to describe the moody atmosphere of certain films, fiction, paintings, photographs, and music. What is that mood? As an artistic expression, the unifying theme revolves around those suffering injustice and unfairness, ordinary people driven into a corner as they watch their hopes, dreams, and lives evaporate without a trace.

In the realm of fiction noir presents the possibility of examining the roles of Truth and Morality as they shape and influence our lives. Think of Truth and Morality as twin rails of a single railroad track. In noir fiction there is a running theme that the builders and designers of that track have in mind, a system that delivers people to a certain kind of destination. The end of the line comes in the form of an ignominious death and oblivion, or a close call with these existential outcomes.

We live in a time of great distrust, and we disagree about who should be given the responsibility to build our societies, who will maintain what has been built, and who will restrain the self-interest of the builders. We are loaded into boxcars and, for better or worse, sent on a journey along the tracks laid down by others. Noir fiction gives a sense that we aren't masters of our own destiny and questions the official position that taking those tracks is in our best interest.

In the best of noir we find people who have chosen sides, one side electing to create "sacred" beliefs that unify its members and that define Truth and Morality as having timeless, changeless meanings. On the other side are people who view Truth as tentative, testable, and revisable through experiments and statistical analysis, and believe that when and where Morality diverges from truth, it should also be, as a matter of principle, always open to change to reflect revised information and knowledge.

Introduction

Both groups—the absolutists keen on the sacred, and the tentative revisionists—claim noir as a genre that supports their own vision of this track-building venture. The absolutists read the bleak darkness of noir as the environment where just deserts demand punishment for anyone who, by his or her actions or thoughts, has turned away from Truth and Morality. Such noir characters are caught in a web of desperation and destruction because of heresy or disbelief.

The revisionists read noir stories a different way: as parables of the illusions, manipulations, and distortions that the builders of Truth and Reality design into the rail track system to make certain the train arrives on time and where they want the goods delivered. Fictional characters in a noir story who challenge or resist the official version of Truth and Morality are punished by being thrown into a state of despair and hopelessness from which there is no escape.

In *Phnom Penh Noir* the stories and lyrics can be understood from either point of view. What makes this collection unique is the backdrop of the Khmer Rouge and the Killing Fields that arose during their rule. Truth and Morality play out in each story. The characters find themselves at the terminus of the track, sometimes confused, perplexed, and sometimes recognizing for the first time the forces that have brought them to the end of the line.

The best noir narratives are expert hackers that probe and finally plunder our fear vault. Noir storytellers find the combination to that safe, open the door, and release all those eternal monsters we fear most. At the same time the masters of noir abandon us to our fate without so much as offering a key to the exit door.

Channa Siv's cover photograph of Phnom Penh evokes the streets of the city at night. A haunting image that transmits the loneliness of the metropolis and takes us back in time to think of a large city that not long ago forced its inhabitants into the countryside.

The black thread of noir runs deep through Kosal Khiev's personal story, coloring his vision of the world. He joins the vitality of a rap artist with the soul of a poet to produce incredible emotional velocity and force. The power of his poetry transforms his experience into the stuff of art.

With Christopher Minko's KROM, the band mixes Khmer and English in songs like "Ying," "Phnom Penh," and "Tango Traffic." The lyrics ring true as pure cries from the heart. Like Kosal Khiev, Christopher Minko and KROM can be viewed as part of an ancient line of ballad singers. They belong to the tradition of creative artists who traveled from village to village, bringing along their musical instruments and lyrics, telling stories through their songs. These are folk tales as black as night. While this book's readers don't have the benefit of Sophea's voice ringing clean, liquid, and clear like a troubadour, or Christopher Minko's voice with its haunting, elegant, and soulful depth, or the felt rhythms of Kosal's rap poetry, we hope you will seek out their music once you've read the lyrics presented here.

Whether the medium is prose, lyrics, or the cover photograph, *Phnom Penh Noir* is constructed to transport you straight into the heartland of Khmer noir. These creative artists are offering up a hardscrabble noir hymnbook. There is no way out. No escape. No hero who rides to the rescue.

The voices, the lyrics, the images—our hope is that they will linger long after you put this book to rest on your bookshelf. And that you will have a perspective to guide you on your future journeys through worlds

Introduction

of lost souls struggling to find personal freedom and dignity.

Warning: *Phnom Penh Noir* offers you a ride down a dark road. A door is open. It is up to you whether to get in and take the ride. It will be an experience you won't forget. When you finish the book, you may realize that we are all on the same road, the same journey, headed for the same end, and we share the dream that there is a pot of gold of one kind or another at the end of the rainbow. If you keep this shared experience in mind, perhaps you can better understand and draw some meaning out of the lives of those who are of the post-Killing Fields generation.

The Khmer Rouge era is fading from memory. Many of the new generation know little of what happened. *Phnom Penh Noir* is a testament to those who lived through that period and those who came afterward, a book to bridge those who were there and those who can only travel there through literature and art.

Noir wakes us up from the mass delusion of mass culture, from the greed, brutality, and cruelty. By looking at the underbelly of society, you start to understand that society has become all underbelly. Thugs, con men, fast talkers, smiling hit men, people on the make, shills, and prisoners are in the back of the car you just got in.

The driver?

You be the judge.

The writers and artists included here offer you a passport not just through time and space but inside a cultural dimension where it's clear that people were traumatized by an overwhelming evil force. You have been issued a visa for the journey. It's a multi-entry visa. You can travel in and out as many times as you wish. But do understand that once you enter the space occupied by *Phnom Penh Noir*, you've entered a place that you may never quite leave.

Christopher G. Moore
Bangkok
October 30, 2012

Hearts and Minds
Roland Joffé

His name is Simon Cowel, and the slight sinking sensation in his stomach tells him he has just fallen in love. He tries to censor the thought by concentrating on his surroundings rather than on Carla Saenz. That's not easy. And before he knows it, Simon is peeking at her again, through the press of bodies that fills the bar.

Carla Saenz is thirty and has the kind of beauty that makes her life an effortless glide. The kind of beauty that makes even the most mundane of her actions, the least interesting of her observations, seem profoundly and breathlessly exciting. Carla is tall and athletic, her eyes are aquamarine, and her slight astigmatism convinces those who find themselves the focus of her unwavering gaze that they are special, even extraordinary. Carla is doing PR for WOMB, the World Organization of Mothers and Babies, a swaggeringly rich NGO with its Southeast Asian base in Cambodia—Phnom Penh, to be precise. Carla's hair is chestnut, and like everything else about her, luxuriant and, well, elegant. Her boyfriend of the moment is Carney Bilsor, who is an attaché to something or other, or someone or other, at the US Embassy.

This evening in the Blue Diamond bar, Carla is, as usual, the center of an adoring group of males. Simon has to shift slightly to the left to keep her in his line of vision. At this precise moment Carney pushes through the throng and kisses Carla on her full, deliciously full, lips. Inwardly, Simon shudders with jealousy and longing. In an act of heroic denial, he tears his gaze away from Carla and heads for the restroom.

It's Friday night, and the Blue Diamond bar and the uneven pavement outside it are crammed with the tight-bodied young princes and princesses of Phnom Penh's NGO community. With their loud voices and their drinking, they remind Simon of the crowd at one of those wine bars in the city of London, with dim lights and sawdust on the floor, where young bankers with blond hair and newly minted degrees sink endless bottles of Pinot Noir.

Banking had been Simon's world. A world of bodies and bonuses, each seeming to lead to the inevitable perfection of the other. More accurately, it should be said, the world of banking was Simon's intended destination until he met Janet Pollard. Janet was striking, with black hair and huge dark eyes. Banking and its attendant behaviors, as Simon soon found out, were very much in Janet's line of sight, not as a destination but as a target. Sleeping with Janet, as Simon also soon discovered, involved embracing her ideas as well as her body.

Unluckily for Simon, his will proved weaker than hers. Before he had completed his first anniversary with Janet, and concurrently his final year of reading English at the University of Edinburgh, Simon's fiscally robust plans for the future had sunk under Janet's relentless and witheringly scornful salvos. Into the ensuing vacuum in Simon's ambitions, Janet tirelessly injected proposals of her own, proposals that included both the moral improvement of the hapless Simon and the social improvement of what Janet called the "EN's!!!" as in "Emergent Nations!!!"—a phrase, in enunciation, invariably punctuated with many exclamation marks.

So, by the alchemy of Janet's forceful character and her athletic and satisfying sexuality, Simon's desire for the good life was transmuted into a more generalized ambition to "do something with an NGO." What that something would be, however, was never quite clear until Janet, lying naked and sweaty one Sunday morning after sex, turned the pages of a Sunday color supplement to reveal a photo of Angelina Jolie sitting in a decaying sampan somewhere in Cambodia, looking soulfully at what appeared to be a newly hatched Louis Vuitton handbag. Janet's resulting eruption of indignation, in its molten state, envisaged the utter annihilation of that actress and her snobby handbag, and upon cooling, solidified unyieldingly around the conviction that Cambodia itself must be saved. Since Janet herself was embarking on a career in the theatre, this saving was to be implemented, as far as possible, by Simon. So it was that after finishing university Simon found himself working as an intern with GRAIN—the agricultural NGO was opening a field office in Battambang in Cambodia—while Janet stayed behind to appear in a production of William Shakespeare's *Titus Andronicus* at the Edinburgh Festival. Perhaps it was the talk of a London transfer that blinded Janet to the irony that this particular production was funded by a grant from the Barclays bank.

Janet resolutely intended, at some stage, to join Simon in Cambodia, but the subsequent West End transfer of *Titus* made the timing issue moot. Now, as Simon pissed disconsolately into the ochre bowl in the surprisingly trendily decorated toilet of the Blue Diamond, he had been, he reflected, in Cambodia, on his own, for seven months. In recent weeks more alone than he wished. About three months ago Janet's communications had been shot through with the mention of a certain "Mickey." Mickey was an actor—according to Janet, a "super-talented" actor. Mickey was helping her with her development as an actress.

To Simon's increasingly desperate inquiries as to what this "training" involved, Janet replied with evasions based on the fact that Simon was, one, too pragmatic to understand and, two, so far away as to be of no use if he did. Since that particular aspect of their situation had been brought about by Janet's own actions, Simon ended the conversation feeling hard done by. The feeling grew into epic bitterness when in a later call Janet confessed she was both in love and, as she put it, in "deepest shit" as Mickey had impregnated her—against her will, she assured Simon, because the last thing in the world she wanted was to get pregnant. Simon acidly observed, though, before hanging up, that that hadn't stopped her from letting Mickey do what was needed to achieve precisely that end.

Their relationship slid rapidly from ghastly to unbearable. Finally, Simon told Janet to fuck off—though to be fair, this was after she had asked Simon whether he would step in to the breach as father to her unborn infant. The super-talented Mickey, it turned out, was married. Further, he felt honor bound to return home and give his marriage a chance. Janet broke this news to Simon in between heart-wrenching sobs and protestations of suicide. She rang off, then rang back an hour later to say she realized that Simon and she shared a bond that was unbreakable and to beg him for his forgiveness.

After Simon had terminated the call in some confusion, he lay on his bed in the Colonial Villa shared by GRAIN's junior staff and stared at the shadows thrown on the white ceiling of his bedroom by the palm trees in the villa's well-tended garden. To his surprise, as the tide of anger retreated, he found himself feeling sorry for Janet. For reasons that were unclear to him, he even began to feel guilty. After all, he was the male in the relationship, he thought to himself, and technically he had left poor Janet on her own. He fell into an uneasy and exhausted sleep.

When he woke, finding himself staring at the same eerily moving shadows, he decided that the only thing to do was to invite Janet to come and join him in Phnom Penh, until such time as she could find her bearings. He got out of bed and spent at least three hours composing an email to that effect. Eventually he decided that an email was too cold a communication and made another expensive phone call to Janet. She didn't pick up, and Simon spent the next few hours torturing himself with the possibility that his hardness of heart had resulted in her suicide. In fact, as Janet rather brutally told him some time later, she had failed to answer the phone because she was in bed with Mickey, who had decided after the briefest return to his wife that being with Janet was what he really wanted. After this confession Janet in turn forgot her special bond with Simon and decided that life with Mickey was the only one possible for her future happiness. She asked Simon not to call her again.

The Khmers who worked in nominally important positions at GRAIN coped with the fallout over the next few days, as Simon reeled between extreme self-pity and a dull generalized anger at life. After Simon had left the office at the end of each workless day, Thach Soun, his skinny assistant, would neatly stack the unfilled-in USAID forms that lay scattered on Simon's desk and then pad softly down the mahogany boards of the corridor to an office at the far end. This office, barely big enough for a person to squeeze between wall and desk, belonged to Sally Cullen, the AFOD, or Assistant Field Officer, Disbursements. Without a word, Soun would deposit Simon's blank paperwork on a corner of Sally's desk; then, pursing his lips in mock disapproval but offering a sympathetic smile with his eyes, he would pad off again into the evening gloom.

Sally was the engine of GRAIN'S Cambodian operations. Hard-working and committed, she was good at everything she touched, and she particularly touched the hearts of the Cambodians with whom she came into contact. Any unfinished business, any form filing, any proposals, invoicing, report, dossier, or any other form of work that involved sitting in a cramped office outside normal hours found its way into Sally's fat but capable hands. Sally was never ill, never unsmiling, and in some way known only to herself, never behind with her inhuman multiplicity of tasks. Without her GRAIN would have slowly submerged beneath the mounds of paper that descend endlessly on an NGO in giant flakes of bureaucratic dandruff. Human nature being what it is, Sally was rarely rewarded, even with faint praise, for the burden she so willingly lifted from the shoulders of her co-workers—or "co-shirkers," as Soun, with his remarkable English, dubbed them. No, the most that anyone would say about the heroic Sally was that she had truly politeness-defying body odor.

Sally was relentlessly, unrequitedly, and unexpressedly in love with Simon. By this time in her life, in her early thirties, she was quite used to her loves being unrequited. Sally had become a self-taught and hungry expert in all the tiny delights and slights that flare briefly but, oddly enough, pleasurably, in the otherwise gloomy corridors of unrequited love. Unrequited love kept Sally emotionally fulfilled. For her it was like being immersed in an endless comic book, full of meaningful glances and balloons encapsulating thoughts too powerful to be uttered. Sally was born to be a mother, and if it seemed cruel to her that nature should have made that task so hard to achieve, Sally gave no sign of it. She duly thanked her kindly god before going to sleep for the benefits he had bestowed on her, and she found room in her capacious heart to care deeply for those whom she saw as less blessed than she was.

It was while taking over Simon's uncompleted responsibilities that Sally made a shocking discovery. It was half past ten at night. Outside her open window *cyclo-pousse* drivers trilled their bells as they passed, whilst their wealthier cousins lay on the seats of their motor rickshaws and chatted. The night was otherwise hot and still as Sally sat at her desk. Above her head a ceiling fan rotated silently as the AC was, as usual, off, and sweat beaded at Sally's temples. She was silently comparing two sets of files, and what they revealed was making her feel sick. Wiping sweat from her eyes, she leant back in her chair and tried to calm herself by listening to the familiar noises outside. After a time she began, with soothingly automatic gestures, to tidy her desk. When only the two offending files remained, she sighed and then placed them carefully in her desk drawer. She then stood up, closed the window of her cubbyhole, and headed off to the Blue Diamond to get drunk.

It is in that state that Simon finds her. He is on his way back to the bar after taking a turn around the block to try to clear his head of the confused whirl of emotions that Carla Saenz has set in motion. This, and the fact that they have both had rather a lot to drink, may help account for what happens next.

"Hi, Sal," Simon says, unconsciously avoiding sitting downwind of the large fan that swivels on a stand behind her.

"Oh, Si!" is all Sally can mutter, before, to her horror, tears begin to stream down her fat cheeks.

At that moment a burst of laughter ripples from the group by the door. Carla and Carney Bilsor are at its center. Simon tears his gaze away from the group to find Sally staring at him with watery, accusatory eyes.

"There's something I have to tell you," she says.

Simon barely hears. His eyes are on the group around Carla and Carney.

"Something . . . I have to tell you." Sally repeats. "It's not very nice."

Simon turns to look at her. "Are you all right?" he asks, confronting the large and protuberant eyes fixed so intently on him.

"Rather awful . . . in fact."

She stops, losing confidence.

"Oh." Simon feigns interest. He notices Carney leave the group and head toward the large green Toyota four-wheel drive with its diplomatic plates. Green for the Embassy, white for the NGOs, Simon notes to himself pointlessly. He turns back toward Sally, who, standing now, is still staring intently at him.

"Sal, what is it?"

What she has discovered is so deeply unsettling, and her feelings for Simon are so strong, that Sally is at a loss as to how to begin.

"I love you—that's the first thing you'd better know," she blurts out. Then she looks at him in horror. "Oh,

God!" she says. She looks deeply unhappy. "I didn't mean that. I mean I do mean it, but I shouldn't have said it."

"I see," replies Simon, though he doesn't. He's wondering if Carla will stay long enough at the Diamond for him to chat to her. Usually she doesn't stay long after Carney leaves.

"What I'm trying to say is ..." says Sally, uncomfortably. "What I have to say doesn't mean I don't . . . Oh, God! I've fallen in love with you."

She feels that she is sliding down a quickly crumbling slope.

"Why?" asks Simon absently. "Why would you do that?"

Carla has settled down at the bar. She catches Simon's look.

"I can't help it." Sally says. "I don't know why."

This truth sounds lame to her, so she adds, "I think you're rather special."

Simon can't help responding to that. He doesn't feel special at all at this particular moment.

"Thanks, Sal," he says.

Sally stares at him. She wants to tell him about the discovery she made in the GRAIN office, but she seems to be sliding faster and faster down the crumbling slope, and fear of frightening Simon off is swamping her need to warn him of danger.

"I want to sleep with you," she says, surprising herself. "Shall we? Not really sleep . . ." Her confusion is mounting. "Have sex . . . I mean . . . not sleep."

Simon is taken aback. Sally misinterprets his look and grabs him in a desperate bear hug, pressing her lips against his and trying to worm her tongue into his mouth. Simon wonders if this is a dream. Sally takes his surprise for approval and pushes her tongue deep into his mouth. Simon is aware that conversation in the bar has waned and hopes Carla isn't watching. Sally's breasts are pressing against him. His arms are pinioned. He wriggles in her grip as their hips grind together.

"Oh, Simon!" she sighs.

She moves back so she can look at him. He is the first male she has kissed in passion, and she likes it. "Oh, God, Simon, I'm wet!" she says, the slope crumbling endlessly beneath her. "Oh, Si, dear Si! All I needed was a push..."

She examines his face tenderly. After a moment it hits her that what she is seeing is not desire; it's disgust. Too late Simon realizes what his face has revealed. Now he stands there awkwardly, unsure of how to repair the hurt. Her face is reddening, his rejection wounding her deeply.

She murmurs, "It's all right. I'm just a bit drunk... I'd better get back to the Villa. No, don't. I'm all right. Really. Don't need any help."

Sally, true to her noble view of human beings, now translates Simon's awkwardness into concern for her. He is concerned—concerned that Carla has noted the scene, concerned that he is cutting an awkward figure, and, somewhere deep inside, concerned that Sally is hurting and he doesn't have the simple skills to salve her badly grazed feelings. So when she turns on her heel and makes her way into the patchy shadows of the street, he stands there watching her stumble off, feeling like an idiot and uncomfortably dissatisfied with himself for caring more about his discomfort than hers.

He feels a hand on his shoulder. He turns and finds himself staring squarely into the wide-set and very green eyes of Carla Saenz. It would be unfair to say that his mood lightens, but it changes, as irrevocably as a kaleidoscope changes with a simple twist.

Sally steers herself in between the potholes that dot the pavement. Her eyes are a bit blurred with tears and drink. A *cyclo-pousse* slows by her side, touting politely for trade. She waves him away. True to her upbringing, she expects a mildly emphatic divine rebuke for this uncharacteristic brusqueness. So when she steps into the road and is hit by the huge Lexus four-wheel drive that swerves silently round the corner, her last conscious thought is that her Father above has acted with unusual firmness.

She lies in the road. One leg is twisted underneath her at an odd angle. It seems to her that it must belong to someone else. She is aware of figures crowding around her, and as they fade away into a soft, cloying blackness, Sally realizes that one of the figures is Samantha Jane Roberts, GRAIN's boisterous director. Samantha's voice modulates from irritation to concern, but Sally doesn't hear. Before the darkness steals her ability to see, Sally does, however, notice the finely cut baguette diamonds that encircle Samantha's perfumed wrist.

Samantha Jane Roberts bends over Sally. She is still breathing, but her body, lying on the tarmac, seems in an oddly disorganized heap. Her eyes are closed, but her lips are moving. Samantha Jane Roberts leans in close, and what Sally mumbles gives Samantha Jane Roberts a powerful jolt of panic because what Samantha Jane Roberts hears is "double dipping."

Samantha bends over Sally, who is no longer mumbling but instead emitting a long, low groan of pain that penetrates the inner prison of Samantha Jane Roberts's fears and prompts her to phone the Calmette Hospital for an ambulance. Samantha Jane Roberts congratulates herself for her foresight in taking out medical insurance for her staff. If Sally's injury is as bad as she suspects, she will have to be flown to Bangkok. As that thought strikes her, so too does she become aware of the advantage of Sally's being well out of the way for the next few days, or even weeks, while Samantha Jane Roberts attends to what she suspects may be a major and dangerous situation. "Double dipping" can only refer to one thing, and if Sally is right, then some major and exquisite footwork will be needed, and at once.

The ambulance arrives after a slow half an hour. Sally does not recover consciousness, and the crowd that has gathered around her prostrate body are talking amongst themselves, quietly admiring the motherly way that Samantha Jane Roberts cradles Sally's slack body, mistaking the look of concentration on Samantha Jane's face for pity. Oh, pity there is in Samantha Jane Roberts's feelings for Sally, but equally she is planning. Planning how to avert what might be an impending disaster and to convert what her father would call a "stumble" into a leap forward, to bigger and better things.

It's raining at Pochentong airport, and the helicopter that will take Sally to the hospital in Bangkok squats on the warm, wet tarmac, its blades flashing and its steel-colored strobes giving the raindrops the glisten of diamonds. Sally barely stirs as she is lifted on her gurney into the belly of the helicopter. Thach Soun, clutching his hastily packed little suitcase, follows her inside. He has been elected by Samantha Jane Roberts to accompany Sally to Bangkok, to keep an eye on her and attend to her well-being. He's glad to do this service for Sally, and to leave behind the two little rooms he rents in a shared apartment near the sports arena, for what he hopes will be no more than a couple of nights. Thach Soun peers through the window as the helicopter lifts off and Pochentong slips away and out of view. After a moment he turns to Sally and, reaching across, takes hold of her clammy hand.

Samantha Jane Roberts stands in the rain on the tarmac, watching the helicopter flail its way into the gray night sky. The tarmac glistens wetly in the moist, warm air. Samantha Jane Roberts walks across it to where the big Lexus waits. Samantha examines it. Not a mark. All that damage done to Sally, and there isn't a mark on the shiny stainless steel bars that project from the front of the luxury four-wheel drive. Samantha Jane Roberts sighs heavily and then clambers, in her ungainly way, into the comfortable leather womb of the vehicle's interior. She tells Phireak, her drowsy chauffeur, to take her to the GRAIN offices. She won't be sleeping much tonight, she thinks to herself in frustration.

No one in the Blue Diamond is aware of the drama that has played out a few streets away, least of all Simon and Carla Saenz. They are dealing with some complex and engaging chemical and emotional reactions of their own. Simon is wrestling with Carla's penetrating intelligence. Having a conversation with her makes him feel like an ungainly seal waddling down a beach studded with razor blades. These come in the form of mercilessly interrogative and unsmiling "Whys," asked whenever he expresses a hastily crafted opinion about this or that aspect of Cambodia. Now Simon's flow of improvised opinions is drying up, something that Carla seems to sense with almost cruel glee. Fighting the paralyzing undertow of her level gaze, Simon is reduced to offering comments about the wonders of Angkor Wat. The grandeur of its conception, the height and breadth of its walls, its original and vast network of waterways. Eventually he stops babbling and looks at Carla breathlessly.

After a short pause, during which he very much wants to lean forward and kiss her, she says, "I think a certain amount of corruption is acceptable, don't you?"

"Well..." he responds, "I think it depends on what you mean by 'a certain amount.'"

She shakes her head. He can't help but be aware of the fullness of her lips.

"Imagine," she says, "that a man attacks you. You know that if you hit him too hard, he will die, but if you don't hit him hard enough, he will kill you."

Her widely spaced eyes seem to smile at him, and the sensual curve of her mouth reminds him of the merciless smile of the Khmer emperor Jayavarman, carved into a giant stone face on the corner of the temple at Bayon.

"Well... I'll have to judge my hit carefully," Simon replies thoughtfully.

"That's not the point," she says bluntly. "The point is the intention. A good one: to save yourself from attack. No one will judge you for miscalculating the force of your hit. They will judge you by your intention."

He feels there is a flaw in this analysis, but she goes on in her almost mocking way.

"There is a gardener at the Embassy." The way she says "the Embassy" implies it is that of the United States, but she does not say so specifically. "This gardener has been fired for taking a commission from his ... er, underlings. But his aunt is in hospital, in Battambang. Without those commissions he wouldn't be able to pay for her treatment."

She pauses as if waiting for him to answer. He fills in the silence.

"I think that's a case of extenuating circumstances..."

She smiles at him with her green, feline eyes, certain she has scored her point.

She says, "Morality, like beauty, is just a matter of taste."

Later he discovers that recently she has been listening avidly on her iPhone to a series of podcasts called "Philosophy's Bootstraps." He can't work out if she truly understands what she hears or simply stores up phrases for effect—or does it really come to the same thing, given philosophy's malleability?

"All certainties are, how do you say . . . platitudes?" She nods as though agreeing with herself. "We just kid ourselves that life makes . . . moral sense. But it doesn't"—her eyes hold his—". . . just because we want it to."

The next half hour—or is it two hours?—passes rapidly. Carla asks Simon if he is married. Rather shocked, Simon asks her why. Does he look married? Carla doesn't answer directly, just laughs gently, and he ends up by telling her all the convoluted circumstances of his presence in Phnom Penh. They are sitting down by this time. Simon has downed four Cuba Libres; Carla hasn't touched her Blue Diamond Dawns. Two of the creamy white cocktails sit on the table between them. Carla reveals that she has been married twice, both "mistakes."

"One was a writer. I believed in his talent. I had great plans for us. The other was a good man, but . . . both mistakes."

Her words trailing off, she stares at her white drinks as though she's surprised to see them. In the half-light Simon thinks he can see tears in her eyes.

"So, size matters," she concludes suddenly, looking up from the drinks, her abrupt smile now, to Simon, distractingly, mischievously seductive. "Size matters, whatever people say."

Simon shifts uneasily in his creaky rattan chair. He is getting used to the way in which she never appears to be saying quite what she means. He wonders if part of her power over him is the way in which she leaves him scrambling for half-submerged subtexts, while wondering, concurrently, if they might not be just the barely glimpsed, shark-shaped shadows of his growing desire to fuck her.

She takes a long swig of her creamy cocktail. When she puts it down, her full lips glisten with coconut cream. Simon is finding the slight sheen of sweat on her forehead, and the dark patches on the silk blouse under her arms, more and more excitingly suggestive. As though reading his mind, Carla puts her hand on his bare arm. Simon's stomach churns with delight and anxiety. She puts a little pressure into her touch, as though reassuring him. He realizes how white her skin is. He has a sudden vision of her naked and white, limbs jumbled and spread, under the contrasting brown of his fluidly contorting body.

Not much is said as they walk away from the Blue Diamond into the patchy yellow light of the boulevard. Unwittingly, they traverse the site of Sally's accident. They step, innocently, over the little dark pool of Sally's blood and walk toward the pinhead glitter of lights that decorate the colonial facade of the Hotel Le Royal. In front of the hotel there is a little park laid out in the French provincial style. They meander through it. Simon feels absurdly happy. He feels that all of life has conspired, in some wonderfully complex set of fractal coincidences, to bring him here to Cambodia, at this instant, to walk by Carla's side.

Carla sits on a bench. Then after a moment her body seems to sag and she looks vulnerable and touching. Simon sits next to her, close, but not as close to her as he wishes.

"It's over between me and Carney," she says quietly. "Done."

Simon can't think of anything to say. Carla touches his arm again, with a wistful shake of her head.

"So you are the first to know, apart from me and him," she says.

Simon clears his throat.

"What happened?" he says ineptly.

"Love was there and then it wasn't," she replies. "That's how it happens. We pretend that love withers because we're too embarrassed to admit it simply dies. In fact it dies in an instant—there one moment, gone the next."

She is staring at her shoes—Gucci loafers—with the same air of surprise she displayed in the Blue Diamond, staring at her coconut cream cocktails.

"I am not Colombian, you know? Maybe that's my problem. I'm Ukrainian. My mother left my father when I was nine. We emigrated to Colombia . . . Bogotá. It was a mistake. She had meant to go to Brazil. We were poor . . . very poor. I saw how it works. The poor work for money, and money works for the rich. I saw how it works."

She's going to add something, Simon thinks, but she stops herself and they sit in silence.

Eventually, staring at the twinkling lights on the facade of Le Royal, she says, "Carney's father was here, staying here, at Le Royal. We went for dinner last night before he left. He told Carney that he was disappointed in Carney's generation."

She sniffs, then continues.

"His father said, 'Carney, you don't have any standards. You hold others to high standards, but you don't hold any of your own.'"

She imitates what are presumably Carney's father's nasal New England vowels. It's a clever imitation, sharply observed, Simon notes to himself.

"Carney says that his father is wrong. But I know his father is right. About Carney . . . and about me. I remembered about that gardener at the Embassy, who was fired . . . And the love dies, right there at the table. Nothing to do about it, is there?"

Simon finds himself wondering what Sally's warm heart would make of all this. But he pushes the thought away. Carla rises.

"I need a man to sweep me away," she says. "All women do. That's why we get so furious with what's on offer."

"I suppose," responds Simon, "that the Ukraine must be rather a cruel place."

She shoots him a curiously inquiring smile.

"Touché!" she says.

He gets up, desire for her coiling and uncoiling itself throughout his body.

After a moment she says, "I might need your help with something."

"Might?" he queries.

"Yes. I am . . . how do you say? Putting toes in the water."

"What sort of help?"

"Maybe breaking some rules a little?"

"How does one break rules 'a little'?"

He should have known better than to expect a direct answer to that. Carla's narrowed eyes suggest that she's having the same thought. She watches a motor rickshaw coast toward them. She waves it to a stop. She turns to Simon and, putting her hand on his shoulder, looks at him again with those narrowed, assessing green eyes.

Taking his hand, she presses a folded square of paper into it. She kisses him on the cheek and then climbs into the rickshaw. The soft bubbling of the engine hides what she says to the driver. He follows the rickshaw with his eyes as it drives off. It circles the oblong drive of the little park, and he watches it glide away through shadows. He can make Carla out in the back of the little machine, but she doesn't look back at him or wave.

Later, regretting that snatched goodnight, Simon stares out of his open window, trying to find solace in the moonlit order of the French garden that surrounds GRAIN's villa. GRAIN possesses two villas, both built in the early 1930s, one as an office and one as a residence. On the window ledge in front of Simon lies the piece of paper, now unfolded, that Carla has pressed into his palm. It depicts a small statue, described by the caption beneath as "Statue of Vishvakarman, C12. Rare. Gold." Simon wonders what on earth Carla intended this scrap of paper to signify.

Later still, Simon sits alone in the dark, on his large bed, in his large room with its too large, elderly, mahogany furniture. He sifts anxiously through his jumbled emotions. CNN flickers silently on his laptop. This room, with its hint of some dark, secret history, makes him feel unreal, like a time traveler who has forgotten where and in which eon his journey began. Just before he goes to sleep, Simon realizes that for the first time in days he is not wondering about Janet. Wondering about Janet has now been replaced with wondering about Carla.

At about this time, as she lies in bed in a modern hospital near the Bangkok airport, Sally's left hand begins to tremble. Alarmed, Thach Soun, who has been sitting patiently in an upright chair by her bed, calls a night nurse. Fearing this trembling might indicate a seizure, the night nurse calls a staff doctor. The doctor examines the results of the brain scan that Sally was given on her arrival. He purses his lips.

"Are you a relative?" he asks Thach in heavily accented English.

"No, I am a friend," Thach replies. He was about to say "just a friend" but stopped himself because he realized that being a friend to Sally was at this moment far too important to be qualified by a "just."

"There is hematoma, here in the parietal lobe. It may subside. It may not. We must wait and watch."

The doctor leaves, and Thach Soun settles down again in his hard chair by the unconscious Sally's bed. He watches as the lights of passing cars make yellow bars that travel across the white ceiling.

Meanwhile in Phnom Penh the lights are burning in the Director's office at GRAIN'S headquarters—GHQ, the English staffers like to call it, in a parody of the British secret service's listening post in the UK countryside. Samantha Jane Roberts is sitting unhappily at her desk. The color has drained out of Samantha Jane Roberts's world. She feels the way she felt when she was thirteen and learned that she had failed her French exam, even though she had so carefully cribbed the answers from dorky Jane Birdsall. That failed exam meant that Samantha Jane Roberts had lost her chance of attending a swish private girls' school far away from the dull manufacturing town of Bundon, Ontario, where her father, to her everlasting shame, owned a one-armed bandit franchise. Tommy Roberts loved his profession, loved the regular way in which the slot machines milked the punters and gave him something for almost nothing. The "something" that

Tommy's machines delivered had enabled him to marry above his station in life.

For a time, and while Tommy was young and handsome, that marriage had worked tolerably well. But as Samantha arrived, Tommy began to develop a paunch and his hairline receded, as though his energy was flowing from it to his enlarging belly. The marriage emptied of passion, and his wife, Samantha's mother, filled the ensuing space with regrets. The foremost amongst these was that she had made a vile mistake in her marriage, and that life was at best untrustworthy and at worst cruel.

Samantha Jane inherited much of her mother's angry despondency, but in her case it was shot through with her father's robust delight in beating the odds. It was this volatile but effective set of perceptions that drove Samantha Jane Roberts to be both eminently suited and eminently successful at "shearing sheep," as her father put it, while holding fast to her mother's view that there was nothing more durable than a double string of pearls, or a diamond pendant, to stop others looking down their noses at one. And because being looked at "down a nose" was a fate of unendurable bleakness, to be avoided no matter what, considerable energy was justified in being spent on acquiring items of jewellery and other modes of self-ornamentation that offered protection from that bleak, inhumanely bleak, fate.

Samantha Jane Roberts's mother once, and unforgettably, accused her of harboring her father's criminal nature. This cut Samantha Jane Roberts to the quick and played a large part in her decision to engage in charitable works and to surround herself with the good on her way to joining the great. Now she is a talented administrator as well as a supremely and covertly manipulative leader, and the board of GRAIN count themselves lucky to have secured her services for their well-intentioned and effective international aid programs.

Not quite as lucky as Samantha Jane Roberts counts herself, on her up days, when the enterprising and freewheeling spirit of her now deceased father is playing merry hell with the organization of her inner value system. Though it has to be said in her defense that there have been many days when the moralizing spirit of her mother has spread a viral gloom in Samantha Jane Roberts's soul, quite extinguishing her father's manic self-satisfaction. Samantha Jane Roberts is, in short, under her polished, capable exterior, a battleground for the violently opposed spirits of her deceased parents. If others were to realize it, her inner conflict would undoubtedly elicit their sympathy. But of course, letting others know of her plight is not within the capabilities of Samantha Jane Roberts's emotional makeup, so she suffers alone behind her smoothly machined exterior, and the world looks on and applauds.

A soft cooing and the rustle of wings bring Samantha Jane Roberts out of her reverie. Dawn has woken the doves that nest in the eaves, and this is the first time that she has heard that sound—early rising not being one of Samantha Jane Roberts's habits. Bright yellow slices of sunlight spread across the dark mahogany planks of the floor. A gecko darts across the white wall and then freezes at some unseen fear. Samantha Jane Roberts notices that she is aimlessly twisting her baguette diamond bracelet around her tanned wrist. She takes the bracelet off and lays it on the desk in front of her. Briefly she imagines presenting it to a tearful and grateful Sally, in a strange farewell-cum-awards-ceremony.

Samantha Jane Roberts is not feeling particularly good about what she is about to do, but this momentary sympathy is quickly replaced by annoyance at Sally for having put Samantha Jane Roberts in this difficult position. Why did the silly cow have to pry into things that didn't concern her? That kind of prying is disrespectful and treacherous and deserves the treatment it is about to get!

Samantha Jane Roberts rubs her eyes and surveys the paperwork—Sally's fate—spread out on her desk. Realizing that it will soon be time for Ser Moen, her Cambodian accountant, to arrive for work, Samantha Jane Roberts settles down to the task ahead: tinkering with reality. She has inherited her father's mathematical skills, and quite soon, and with satisfying deftness, Samantha Jane Roberts has transformed good-natured Sally into a vile, self-serving, heartlessly opportunistic little thief.

At about this time, in Bangkok, Sally opens her eyes. She has no idea where she is and begins to panic. It takes all of Thach Soun's gentle but persuasive strength to calm her down. Sally wants to get back to her work in Phnom Penh immediately, and it is only after Thach Soun makes her look at her bruised face and bandaged head in a mirror that she agrees to take a sedative and rest. It's quite clear to Thach Soun that Sally is highly confused and has no memory of events after about a week before the accident. He decides to let her sleep a little and then, after seeing how she is, to telephone Samantha Jane Roberts and let her know the exact state of her valued AFOD.

By the time Simon arrives at GRAIN'S office, news of Sally's accident has filtered through the building, leaving everyone feeling uneasy and the Cambodians despondent. Meanwhile Samantha Jane Roberts has whipped herself into a frenzy of indignation over Sally's theft. Ser Moen, who, like all the Cambodian staff at GRAIN, loves Sally and is fighting back tears, confirms that indeed, according to the evidence Samantha Jane Roberts has presented her with, it seems that Sally has been stealing a not inconsiderable sum of money. How much money has yet to be established.

"I can't believe it . . ." Samantha Jane keeps saying. "The cunning little bitch! I can't believe it."

Simon can't quite believe it either.

"It seems out of character," he mutters.

But his faith in human nature has taken a knock recently, so he's open to the possibility that Sally might have taken him in.

"She took us all in. My God!" says Samantha Jane Roberts plaintively. "All of us. You too, Simon! God, she was a smooth little operator, if she took you in! My God!"

This compliment to Simon's perceptiveness, and the uncanny way it both echoes and contradicts his self-doubt, wins him over, on the surface at least.

"Smooth operator indeed." He nods wisely, and then, enjoying this feeling of complicit wisdom, adds, "Very smooth."

"And that BO!" exclaims Samantha Jane Roberts. "Why the fuck did we all put up with it?" suggesting by this that, in comparison to their saintly forbearance, Sally's betrayal can barely be considered the act of a human being.

With an injunction to utter confidentiality, Samantha Jane Roberts waves Ser Moen back into her adjoining cubbyhole—apart from Sally's, the smallest office in the villa. After Ser Moen has left and closed the door, Samantha Jane Roberts turns to Simon.

"What shall we do, Si?" She is suppressing the desire to cry. "What shall we do? If this leaks, GRAIN could blow apart."

Simon nods in agreement. Samantha Jane Roberts takes a deep breath and then leans back in her chair with an exhausted sigh.

"The coffee machine's broken." Simon says irrelevantly.

"What?"

"The machine . . . I mean, I should send Thach Soun out for a latte . . . if you want one."

"Soun's in Bangkok with Sally," says Samantha Jane Roberts. "It wasn't really allowed by the Air Ambulance rules, but . . . well . . ."

She rolls her eyes, suggesting that a bit of personally expensive bribery, though adding to her martyrdom, at least solved that issue.

"Sure you don't want something?" asks Simon solicitously.

Samantha Jane Roberts regards him with glistening eyes.

"Of course the interests of the clients must come first," she says after a pause. "Mustn't they . . . come first?"

"They must," Simon echoes.

"This will require some management, Simon," says Samantha Jane Roberts.

Simon can't help but notice that, beneath their watery glisten, there is something quite wolverine peering out of Samantha Jane Roberts's brown eyes.

"I have a bad feeling," Samantha Jane Roberts continues, "that she might try to pin this on us."

"On us?" Simon is startled.

"Well, you're looking after the clinic at Kompong Som. That's where the irregularities are."

"Irregularities?" Simon asks, puzzled—and now undeservedly worried that he is in some way implicated.

"Don't worry. It's all cleared up. I'm just bringing you into the loop. Sally will have to be fired, of course. I shall be making the announcement later this afternoon."

"I see."

Simon clears his throat.

Samantha Jane Roberts sighs and gives Simon a wan smile that is at once conspiratorial and recruiting.

"After the initial shock she'll probably try to shift the blame."

"Well, there'll be an inquiry, I would imagine."

"Absolutely!" Samantha Jane Roberts says convincingly. "And Si, I want you to be part of it. You and I. This needs to be handled sensitively and with . . . subtlety."

"Yes . . ." Simon nods.

"OK, then?"

Now that she has Simon where she wants him, Samantha Jane Roberts bends her eyes toward the papers on her desk. Simon takes the cue and heads to the door.

"Si?"

He stops, his hand on the door handle.

"Yes?"

"Thank you. It's good at a time like this to . . . good to . . ."

She takes a deep breath as one controlling her hurt.

"Good to know I have one person at least, I can trust."

"Yes ... of course. Good."

He gives her a manly glance, conveying that, with him at least, her back is covered, and then he leaves.

Before he has closed the door, Samantha Jane Roberts is sifting through various ways of avoiding any form of inquiry, however small.

Back in his first floor office Simon stares down into the peaceful courtyard of the Buddhist temple next door. Two monks in orange and saffron robes are sitting on a bench, chatting softly and drinking tea. An elderly woman is crossing the courtyard with a small mobile flower stall. The monks break off their chat to watch, in quiet delight, the passing bevy of red, yellow, and blue flowers. Green parrots have a brief, if raucous, parliamentary moment amongst the heavy dark gray leaves of the banyan tree that shelters the silent monks.

Simon looks at the peaceful scene in irritation. If only that was the real Cambodia, he thinks to himself, simple and accessible, whereas the real Cambodia is complicated and dark. He turns and sits at his desk. After a moment he pulls out the paper that, last night, Carla pressed into his hand. The photograph stares back at him inscrutably: "Statue of Vishvakarman, C12. Rare. Gold." He stares at it. He can't be sure, but he thinks it smells faintly of Balenciaga's Le Dix, Carla's perfume.

He snaps out of his reverie to wonder how Sally is. His pleasant first floor office seems dismal, and in spite of its mahogany floor and swish Italian leather furniture, he feels sad at the thought of Sally bedridden in some impersonal Bangkok hospital. He decides that he should order some flowers for her. Then the thought strikes him that this might be construed as being disloyal to Samantha; it might even suggest to the suspicious mind that he is in some way colluding with Sally's crime, if crime there is. He remembers Sally's sweaty embrace and the stricken glance she had given him before she wandered off into the darkness of Phnom Penh. Abruptly Simon decides to send the flowers and damn the consequences.

A few hours later, in Bangkok, Sally regains consciousness, and the first thing she sees is a serenely beautiful arrangement of pale yellow orchids in a square jade-gray porcelain container. A beam of light rims the translucent beauty of the flowers and the waxy green of their narrow leaves. The second thing Sally sees is the loving and concerned face of Thach Soun—a face that breaks into a warm smile with a fondness in the eyes that dilutes the fear that creeps into Sally's bowels when she realizes where she is.

"Soun?" she whispers.

He waits, patient and welcoming.

"Is this Bangkok?" Her voice is hoarse.

He nods. She clears her throat.

"Why am I here? I don't understand."

Very gently Thach Soun tells her about the accident. She looks at him in amazement. She notices a calendar on the wall, decorated with red and gold dragons.

"Is it really May?"

He nods, letting the awareness of the date sink in.

"Have I been here since April?" she asks.

The fear in her voice causes him to pat her hand gently.

"No. You were brought here last night."

She absorbs that. She turns it over in her mind. Her eyes rest on the orchids in their jade colored pot. Thach Soun follows her gaze.

"From Bong Simon. He is most concerned."

Sally puts her hand to her mouth. She blushes as her memory rushes back. Thach Soun sits quietly by her side. Sally is remembering it all. Eventually Soun's peaceful smile and stillness draw the memories out. Sally talks. She is telling herself as much as telling him, but she tells it all. She tells of looking through Simon's papers, of checking the funding proposals from Canada, Australia, and the UK. Then she stops, fearful that she might be inadvertently incriminating Simon. Soun sits by her side, nodding once or twice. She can't even be sure he is listening or whether he is listening but not understanding. Her thinking is still fuzzy. Eventually, worn out and embarrassed, she dozes off again.

Once he is certain that she is asleep, Thach Soun goes into the corridor and telephones Ser Moen in Phnom Penh. Ser Moen fills him in on what she knows, especially what Samantha Jane Roberts is about to announce to the assembled GRAIN staff later in the afternoon. When she has finished, Thach says nothing. Ser Moen listens to him breathing down the phone. Eventually he speaks.

"Get Bong Roberts to call me here."

"Yes. As you ask . . . What are you going to do?"

"Thank you, Ngaeng Moen, for your kind help," is all he says in reply.

The call comes fifteen minutes later.

"How is Sally?" Samantha Jane Roberts's voice is filled with breathy concern. "Has she recovered consciousness?"

"Yes, Chumtea Roberts."

Samantha Jane Roberts is eager for more.

"Is she . . . I mean . . . does she, er . . .?"

Samantha Jane Roberts's eagerness is muddling her ability to play the role of Concerned Boss With Weighty Problem.

Thach Soun replies, "Her memory is . . . tattered, Chumtea."

He is proud of the English he is learning online.

"Tattered?" Her tone is sharp.

"Chumtea, she could not remember anything after April fifteen," he tells her, hoping his use of the past tense means he will have avoided breaking the Buddhist prohibition on lying.

Hearts and Minds

Samantha Jane Roberts tries hard but fails to suppress her eagerness.

"Nothing since April? Nothing? Does she remember the accident?"

Thach Soun with his usual equanimity replies, "Chumtea, she remembered nothing. Nothing after April."

"She doesn't remember the accident? Or what she was doing before then?"

"As I said, Chumtea," Thach replies evenly, "her memory is tattered."

Samantha Jane Roberts twists the baguette bracelet around her plump, tanned wrist. She is in an uncomfortable turmoil. If Sally truly doesn't remember anything, then there is no need to unravel the double dipping—triple dipping, in truth—that has served Samantha Jane Roberts so well up to now. Because, while it's true, she thinks to herself, that sacrificing Sally will save Samantha Jane Roberts's skin, equally, drawing attention to any form of misappropriation at GRAIN will make it very difficult, certainly for the foreseeable future, for Samantha Jane Roberts to continue, as her father might put it, to "rig the fruit." On the other hand, there is no guarantee that Sally's memory won't return at some time in the future, with dire consequences for Samantha Jane Roberts and the financial eggs she has so snugly nested in Singapore's best banks. Then there is the risk of disgrace to be considered. A public disgrace, which no amount of Cartier necklaces or Bulgari baguette bracelets would be able to eradicate.

For the next hour the ghosts of Samantha Jane Roberts's parents restlessly fight it out in her mind. With only an hour left till the meeting of the GRAIN staff, Samantha Jane Roberts's parents are still no nearer a solution, and she decides to call the meeting off until the next day—both the parental ghosts in her head agreeing at least that a good night's sleep will do no harm.

The evenings begin early in the Orient. In the sterile peace of the hospital in Bangkok, Thach Soun watches Sally solicitously as she tries to swallow some noodle soup. His iPhone (a number one fake, with a double SIM card) trills the short birdcall that signals a text. Thach Soun glances at it. The text, from Ser Moen, simply says, "Meeting was postponed!" Thach Soun smiles and, nodding at Sally, slips through the airtight door into the neon light of the corridor.

Ser Moen picks up immediately.

"Is it done, Ngaeng Moen?" he ask softly.

"I have the figures," she replies. "It is a big sum of money. A whole family might live on this for a lifetime." She pauses. Then she adds for emphasis, "A business might be set up with this sum of money. Investments, property..."

"Yes, so I imagine, Ngaeng," is all Thach Soun offers in response.

In Phnom Penh Ser Moen sits in her cubicle after the call, considering what businesses could be set up with nearly half a million dollars, what miseries could be eliminated, what luxuries enjoyed, what medical treatments accomplished. She has an idea of what Thach Soun's plan might be, but she has to acknowledge that she has mixed feelings about it. Her reverie is interrupted by Samantha Jane Roberts, who bustles in asking brusquely for the "Sally papers." Ser Moen hands them over and watches as Samantha Jane Roberts stuffs then deep inside her Louis Vuitton bag (bought after seeing the very same Angelina Jolie advertisement that had so enraged Simon's girlfriend Janet Cullen a year or so ago).

"Just want to check all this, the figures. Can't afford errors, can we?" Samantha Jane Roberts says rudely.

So stressed is Samantha Jane Roberts, usually a stickler for protocol, that she doesn't say goodnight to Ser Moen as she leaves. But that's not her worst mistake. Her worst mistake is confusing Ser Moen's polite smile for subservience. What Samantha Jane Roberts does not notice, therefore, is that the files she has crammed so swiftly into her brown Vuitton are scans of the evidence she has prepared against Sally and not the originals. Originals which are now safely stored, with other sundry evidence, under lock and key in Ser Moen's desk.

Some hours later Simon is sitting in a suite on the top floor of a boutique villa hotel a few minutes' stroll from the gilded spires and pagodas of the Royal Palace. The room has a beamed ceiling and ornately patterned tile floors. Outside is a pool surrounded by a dense mini-jungle of palm and banana trees, amongst which educated tourists sunbathe on hardwood recliners or loll under the lights in the sultry evening air as they learn about Cambodian history from glossily illustrated guidebooks. Simon is here to meet a Monsieur Nim—Cassandra Nim, to be precise. The meeting was arranged earlier in the afternoon and Simon agreed to it, his misgivings melting away under the persuasive gaze of Carla Saenz's catlike green eyes.

Carla and Simon met for an afternoon latte at the Tourist Centre on the banks of the broad, powerful but slow Mekong River. The Tourist Centre is a modern construction of glass and white-painted concrete surrounded on two sides by white umbrellas, under which one can sweat in the heat whilst avoiding the harsh rays of the sun. Out of the corner of his eyes Simon watched black and gray barges and an odd array of shabby, ungainly tour boats parade up and down the dark silted river. The tour boats looked dangerously top-heavy, as though they might overbalance at any moment—appropriate, Simon cynically thought to himself; many things overbalance in Cambodia. Carla was wearing a loosely cut gray silk blouse that clearly showed the shape of her firm breasts with their full, pointed nipples. Her skin was extremely white; she did all she could to avoid tanning in the hot sun. Normally Simon found skin of this extreme whiteness off-putting, but Carla's skin seemed almost creamy, with the smooth full texture of the flesh of an arum lily.

"I told you it was a crime, darling," she said.

"It's more like twelve crimes . . ." he replied, not quite daring to add "darling" to his sentence.

She laughed lightly by way of reply.

"Are you afraid to do it?"

"No. It's just that . . . well . . . I was thinking about what Carney Bilsor's father said about standards."

"What do you mean?"

"I thought you said he was right?"

"Oh, he is. Look . . ." She waved her hand around at the crowded terrace. "No one here has standards . . . but they have new Range Rovers and disposable incomes."

"Those things aren't incompatible."

Carla laughed. Her teeth were even and very white against the pink of her cupid lips.

"You'll love Koh Samui," she said.

"I'll hate Koh Samui."

"You said you've never been there."

"I haven't been there, but I know I'll hate it."

"No you won't, darling," she teased. "You'll love it."

"How do you know?"

He knew what she was going to reply, but he wanted to hear it said. He wanted to hear the words—see the words—issue from that beautiful sensual face with its intelligent, knowing eyes.

"I know because, darling, after . . . our little crime, I'll be there with you, all weekend. Just you, me, and a tropical island."

He wanted more. He needed her to say more. She stared at him with that slightly mocking expression that filled him with a curious mix of desire and dread.

"Because I shall let . . . you . . . taste . . ."

Her eyes held his.

"Taste?"

She nodded solemnly, but also teasingly. Not for the first time, Simon wondered how she did that.

"Taste what?" he said again, basking unreservedly now in the flirtatious sensuality of the moment.

"Me . . ." she said.

Before he could get his breath back, she leant forward and dug her spoon into the puddle of melting ice cream in its glass bowl. Then, putting the spoon in her mouth, she slowly sucked the ice cream off it. Her eyes never left his, but somehow her gaze diffused, as if she were no longer in the present moment but giving herself over utterly, unreservedly to some longed-for sensation.

So it was that Simon walked, alone, as had been arranged, through the patchily lit, uneven streets, through the deserted market and along the empty, potholed lanes behind the Royal Palace, whose white walls glowed eerily in the light of an almost full moon. Who knows what might have happened if Samantha Jane Roberts had not called him at this very moment on his mobile, but she did.

"Si?"

Her voice was breathy, and Simon wondered if she was dunk.

"Si . . . I've been going over this Sally business."

"Is that why you put off the meeting this afternoon?"

Samantha Jane Roberts did not reply directly.

"I think, for her sake, she should be asked to move on, with minimum . . . er, profile," she offered.

"Move on?"

"Be asked to leave, yes."

"Be fired, you mean?"

There was a silence on the end of the line, then . . .

"Yes, if that's the way you want to put it."

Something began to uncurl itself inside Simon.

"Fired without an inquiry?" he asked. "What if she's not guilty?"

"Why? Are you on her side?" Samantha Jane Roberts said testily. Then, unable to stop herself, she added, "You aren't above suspicion yourself, you know, Simon. Dirt sticks even to the innocent. It's better for all of us that this ends quickly . . ."

"And quietly?" he said.

Samantha Jane Roberts's anger crackled down the phone. "Ser Moen's been over the figures. It's all quite clear!"

"Ser Moen will do whatever you tell her," Simon replied, much to his own surprise, committing, like Samantha Jane Roberts, the mistake of underestimating the quiet Cambodian accountant.

"Well, we'll deal with this in the morning!" snapped Samantha Jane Roberts. "I have no wish to go into it at this time of night," she added, forgetting that she was the one who had phoned Simon.

She angrily cut the connection.

Simon walked on down the deserted lane. He had booked his ticket to Koh Samui, but the lissome thoughts of the coming weekend were now darkened by Samantha

Hearts and Minds

Jane Roberts's call. He walked on in silence. Two cats streaked across the road, making him jump, and he realized that he had walked a few paces past the gate of the hotel. He retraced his steps and went in, unobserved, as had been agreed.

And now here Simon is, in the suite that Cassandra Nim has hired under an assumed name. Not that this was necessary. No one in Phnom Penh without a death wish would cross Cassandra Nim in any way. Physically Nim is slight, and badly long-sighted. His hair is black and oiled. He wears badly made suits from Hong Kong but is worth many fortunes. As with many very rich people, Cassandra Nim never feels quite rich enough, and no detail that might add or subtract from his wealth is ever overlooked by his decisive and cruel brain.

The lights in the suite are dimmed. Only one light above the table where Simon sits illuminates the small, solid gold statue of Vishvakarman that lies in front of Simon on a dark red velvet cloth. On the table eleven other statues of similar size and similar workmanship and precious metal can also be seen, laid out in an oblong wooden box.

"It is very beautiful and very old. Twelfth century. The era of Cambodia's greatness, when our empire stretched across half of Southeast Asia," Cassandra Nim murmurs in his dry monotone. "The others are equally beautiful, though disguised," he adds, his lips pursing in a grim smile.

Indeed the other eleven statues have been dipped in cheap bronze, mounted on cheap wooden bases, and look like any cheap souvenir that a tourist might buy, right down to the badly printed brass plaque that says "Phnom Penh," set slightly skewed on each red-stained base.

Simon turns the little gold statue over in his hand, admiring its beauty, the almost sad expression on its face, and the perfection of form and movement in its raised arms and the bend of its dancing legs.

"You travel to Bangkok every month. An item like this will raise no suspicion," Cassandra Nim is saying in his even voice.

Simon isn't really listening. Aware of this unaccustomed inattention, Cassandra Nim raises his voice a level.

"Of course payment will be on delivery, in dollars in any bank account you care to suggest. A set of twelve gold statues of this age is inestimable in value," he continues, watching Simon twist the ancient gold ornament around in the lamplight.

"Shouldn't these stay here in Cambodia?" Simon suddenly asks.

Cassandra Nim forgives this rude breach of etiquette and smiles at Simon. A warning smile, Simon might know, if he had studied the mores of Cambodia with more care.

"This country does not treasure its past," Cassandra Nim says smoothly. "Objects like this are wasted here. Better they are kept in the collection of a foreigner that loves them, no?"

As Simon does not respond, Cassandra Nim adds, "Here people care about power, and the money that feeds it. People here do not care about the past."

"They don't?" says Simon.

The directness of his question breaks another eggshell rule of Cambodian etiquette. Again Nim smiles his warning smile.

"Perhaps it is better for all concerned that we think of the practicalities of delivery and not worry about arcane issues of archeological value," he says in his tuneless way.

"Mlle. Saenz says you will be a worthy courier."

"Does she?"

"Indeed. Tea?"

Cassandra Nim gestures to an earthenware pot that sits surrounded by its offspring of little handle-less cups. The gesture blinds him to the sudden flush of anger that wells up in Simon. Pieces of a puzzle are fitting together in Simon's head at lightning speed—pieces of a puzzle that make him feel physically sick.

Cassandra Nim pours a small cup of tea, pushes it toward Simon, and then takes a bronzed statue out of its box and places it before the young Englishman.

At this exact moment Simon is seized with the immutable conviction that Sally is innocent. He is certain of it. He can't rationalize why; it is just something he knows for a certainty. And the more he is certain of it, the more he is sure that he is out of his depth. And the more he becomes aware of how out of his depth he is, the angrier he gets. It's as though all the angers that have lain deep inside him since his early teens are welling up in a great lava wave of rage that boils with the sudden scalding fear of his own utter worthlessness.

"I don't want to do this!" he almost shouts. "Thank you, but no. What do you think I am?"

Simon's fury and the bluntness of this question are landing him in a danger from which his ignorance cannot shield him. Cassandra Nim's own anger and embarrassment manifest themselves in a smile of extreme gentleness.

"This is theft," says Simon. "It's unforgivable that you would steal from your own country, and I won't help you do it," he adds, breaking the last rules of Khmer propriety. "And don't smile like that—I'm sorry, but it's grotesque!"

He stands to leave. Nim rises too, his smile fixedly in place.

"I take it, Bong Simon, that you will not be going to Koh Samui?" he asks.

Simon feels for his ticket and, pulling it out of his back trouser pocket, crumples it and then throws it as a deformed little ball onto the table.

"Not on your dime!" are the last words he says as he lets himself out of the suite.

M. Cassandra Nim mutters to himself in French as he packs away his treasures. He is not worrying about the million or so dollars that this sale might net him; that can be attended to later. No, M. Cassandra Nim is determining how to avenge the insults Simon has heaped upon him.

The rules of interpersonal behavior in Cambodia, as elsewhere in Southeast Asia, are as rigidly precise as the mechanical movement of an expensive Swiss watch. Disturbing the smooth interactions of this movement, in even a slight way, is felt by Cambodians as a deadly insult. An insult that results in public loss of face is doubly deadly. Loss of face is what M. Nim must now undergo with the buyer of his statues, along with Carla Saenz and his bodyguard, Heng Chey, who, hidden in the shadows of the bedroom adjoining the elegant salon, could not have avoided witnessing the whole messy incident.

Now Cassandra Nim, having packed up his statues, takes a deep breath and decides on his next move. It doesn't take him long because added to his loss of face is a greater problem that must be solved: the clumsy barang, Simon, knows too much, much too much. After a pause

39

he steps into the bedroom to issue instructions to his ex-Khmer Rouge bodyguard. Being a naturally cautious man, Cassandra Nim shuts the door to the bedroom carefully behind him.

A few minutes later he watches Heng Chey let himself out through a discreet side gate. Assured that his bodyguard has left unseen, Cassandra Nim packs the box of disguised gold statues away in a holdall and prepares for his own unseen departure. For a moment he dwells on the problem of Carla Saenz: what she knows and what her relationship with the clumsy barang might be. After a short rumination he dismisses any thoughts of danger. He has damning evidence of Carla Saenz using the diplomatic bag of a certain embassy to smuggle out the artifacts of another, smaller dealer. Enough evidence to merit expulsion or even, with his influence, a long term in prison. No, Carla Saenz will not be a problem.

Simon strides back along the route he followed so carefully on his way to the hotel. He barely notices his surroundings or the almost inhuman emptiness of the deserted marketplace. His anger has barely subsided. He is thinking about how to prove Sally's innocence. He feels his life, his future life at least, depends on it. He imagines himself striding into Samantha Jane's office, full of exuberant righteousness. He wonders what he will say to Carla. He will go to Koh Samui at the weekend, but on a ticket he has paid for. These thoughts and the larger-than-life role he sees himself playing in both situations make him laugh out loud—maybe the first real laugh he has enjoyed in all the months he has been in Phnom Penh.

In Bangkok the almost noiseless whisper of the air conditioning is interrupted by Sally's sudden cry. Thach

Soun, dozing in a chair by the side of the bed, tries to calm her.

"I have to call Simon!" she says urgently. "I have a bad feeling about him."

Thach Soun finds her mobile. Sally presses the speed dial. She has never called Simon on her mobile, but the rules of unrequited love are strict about possessing the phone number of one's beloved, and Sally is a slave to those rules. The phone rings but is not answered.

In Phnom Penh Simon crosses an empty boulevard and then cuts down a small, half-lit side street. He barely notices the motorbike with its dark rider that appears by his side. Thinking he is being offered a ride, Simon waves the bike away while fumbling for his phone, which is emitting its weird *Star Trek* ring. The phone is stuck in his pocket, and in the struggle to get it out he fails to notice that the motorcyclist has dismounted and is standing in front of him—and that his own path is further blocked by a disheveled old Toyota truck.

Simon has almost freed the phone when, without warning, the motorcyclist lunges forward and hits him hard in the chest. Simon stops in amazement, and the man hits him again, another blow just below his sternum. Aside from the force of the blows, Simon feels no pain, but his knees buckle under him. He feels a sudden wetness on his chest. He looks at his hands and without emotion he sees blood. He looks up into a pair of expressionless eyes. Below those eyes is a smile that, like Carla's, reminds him of the carved smile on the huge stone face of King Jayavarman's statue at Bayon. Before he slips away into blackness, Simon wonders if that is the smile that so many Cambodians saw on the faces of their Khmer Rouge masters.

Simon dies soundlessly. Heng Chey's expert knife has severed his aorta, and a final twist has ruptured both chambers of Simon's battered heart. A few minutes later the rusting Toyota, bearing Simon's body, drives away, bumping over the deserted, potholed road and heading to the country butcher's shop where the barang's body will be separated into many small pieces, before being scattered like some ancient human sacrifice into the mud of an unknown and distant rice paddy.

The next morning in the Bangkok hospital, Thach Soun gently takes the much recovered Sally through the events of the last couple of days. He finds that everything she says confirms her innocence, and a couple more telephone calls to Ser Moen convinces him that the orchestration of the double dipping has been conducted by Samantha Jane Roberts and a complicit accountant at a large and reputable international accounting firm. The scheme is breathtakingly simple and has much to do with the way in which charitable giving is often a generous impulse that is rarely followed up with further involvement. In short a number of GRAIN'S projects in Cambodia—clinics, agricultural schemes, and a technical school—have been paid for three times over by donors from as far afield as Canada, Australia, and the UK, believing that they are the sole donors, and the accounts have been rendered to the various boards and watchdog committees supporting that assumption.

At the close of Thach Soun's last conversation with her, Ser Moen advances a plan of her own. It involves, amongst other schemes, importing Range Rovers, now the rage in fashionable circles in Phnom Penh, and setting up a luxury jungle resort on an island off the coast that the vehicles could be ferried out to for "Jungle Vacations." Fifteen percent of proceeds would seed investment for local rural development.

"Guaranteed income!" Ser Moen concludes breathlessly.

Thach Soun bids her his usual gentle goodbye. Then he explains to a nervous Sally that he will be returning to Phnom Penh for a couple of days, but that she is being left in good hands.

By four o'clock that afternoon in Phnom Penh, Simon's non-appearance is causing a stir. The police have been alerted, though no one in the GRAIN office is aware that Cassandra Nim has done some alerting of his own, and even the most wholehearted searching by the gendarmerie is unlikely to uncover anything of much use to the investigation. Amidst the hubbub of speculation Thach Soun, Ser Moen, and Samantha Jane Roberts have a closeted and deeply uncomfortable meeting in the boardroom at GRAIN, the erstwhile dining room of the villa.

"It is a very thoughtful and clever scheme, Bong Roberts..."

Thach is summing up, polite as ever, to a white-faced Samantha Jane.

"And the very considerable funds it has generated..." He pauses, enjoying for a moment the total attention he has generated from these two intelligent women. "Those funds will be used after a full and open discussion, here in the office, with the local staff, and as part of an open competition, fully disclosed, to the benefit of the rural workers it was intended for."

Samantha Jane Roberts looks at him with artificial composure. He smiles at her sweetly.

Hearts and Minds

"After agreement is reached, Bong Roberts will gracefully and with our full gratitude for her excellent work . . . retire." Thach Soun taps the box of evidence in front of him. "And on that day this box will be discreetly burnt in the incinerator of a selected temple."

Samantha Jane Roberts wrestles with the vertiginous sensation that her whole grasp on reality has been upended, but after a moment she signs the admission of guilt that Thach and Ser Moen have prepared for her. She watches helplessly as Thach Soun puts the signed paper in the box along with the other evidence of her misdeeds.

After Samantha Jane Roberts has left them, Thach Soun turns to his compatriot.

"I am sorry Ngaeng, but no Range Rovers . . . No resort. Those things can look after themselves, if they have merit."

Ser Moen replies with a little bow.

"You are not surprised, I think?"

"No . . ."

He rises and gives her a gentle look.

"I was a monk, Ngaeng. I learned to love the ten precepts. It is a shame to dishonor what we love, don't you think?"

They look at each other for a moment and then exchange smiles. The happy twinkle in Thach Soun's eyes is matched, after a moment, by that in Ser Moen's.

Later that day, in Koh Samui, Carla gets news of Simon's disappearance. From M. Cassandra Nim she receives only a curt text through a local untraceable SIM. "Normal business to resume when appropriate," is all it says.

Carla sighs and then regards with approval her long white legs, stretched out before her on the recliner. She sips a Mai Tai and considers her future. She does not think about Simon. An unhappy childhood has taught her not to dwell upon pain, and to her Simon is already becoming a ghost, joining what she with her accustomed honesty would readily admit is a long line of others.

Some months later, and a day or two after Samantha Jane Roberts's tearful but honored departure, Sally is sitting outside the wooden house on its slender stilts that belongs to Thach Soun's elderly parents. Rice is being harvested, and the villagers are tired but elated with the size of the harvest. In the distance temple bells ring, children scamper about laughing, and pigs snuffle under the banana plants. These pleasurable noises, however, cannot camouflage the hardness of rural life that is etched into the faces of any villager above the age of twenty.

"This is what we need to change," Thach Soun is saying. "Working in factories is not the answer, but this village life is too hard. It was a problem in 1970 and it is a problem now."

Sally nods.

Thach Soun looks at her. The setting sun brings out the yellow of her blond hair.

"Many people come to Cambodia with strange hearts," he says, "and some come with good hearts. And those with good hearts we need . . . and love."

They don't say much more that evening. There is not much more to be said.

Roland Joffé

Roland Joffé is a film director. He was born in England in 1945.

The Fires of Forever
James Grady

Last night I dreamt I got out of Phnom Penh alive.

My dream surfaces as a gossamer morning in our bedroom. I'm alone. The dream flows to outside the cottage we rent in the neighborhood that Phnom Penh's savvy citizens call NGO-ville. A golf cart-like tuk-tuk waits for me. Takes me past an apartment building whose concrete blockhouse décor is the envy of thousands of Cambodians and a few foreign junkies who live in shacks with corrugated aluminum roofs that tropical rains love to bombard. In my dream a golden-eye sun burns high in swampy air that smells of dinosaur-fed engines and dust. Always in this city there is the dust.

My dream has no sound. Not then. No metallic buzz of motorcycles racing like angry bees through jammed streets. No cries of sidewalk vendors selling everything from fruit I can't identify to butchered raw meat swarming with black flies. No 1970s American rock 'n' roll blasts from the bars along the Tonlé Sap riverfront, and even in the dream I'm grateful for that. How many times can you hear an entombed-in-Paris rocker growl *Don't ask why, but show him the way to the next whiskey bar, the next little girl,* before you go mad?

Buddhist monks in orange robes glide through my dream. I see all the old familiar places I've been in the decade since I was twenty-six and stumbled off the plane from post-9/11 America. In my dream I know that I'm *finally* getting out of here.

If Larkin doesn't kill me first.

Larkin's not in my dream. My dream is beyond Larkin. Beyond everyone, I think—then I know that's a lie: Makara is at the heart of all my dreams.

But as I ride my dream tuk-tuk down Mao *Tse-tung* Boulevard, past the North Korean embassy that is the most sought-after posting by grim servants of that no-personal-passion-allowed Orwellian empire, what I notice and simply accept is that no one has a face. Not my tuk-tuk driver. Not the Buddhist monks. Not the street vendors. Not the sunburned tourists getting on that allegedly air-conditioned bus to go sightseeing at the pile of skulls in the Killing Fields for an inoculation of ignoble history that lets them justify their trip here and the coming night in bars where blowjobs from smooth-skinned black-haired beauties are always only a few dollars more.

With the effortless transitions that dreams allow, I'm in a taxi on my way to Phnom Penh's airport, past chain-link fenced factories where Khmer locals sweat out an "official living wage" assembling brand-name clothing for American malls and cyber-shopping carts. The taxi's rear-view mirror miraculously shows my best friend Phil's bar that he's turned into a shrine to the Hollywood superstar who's the second-most beautiful woman in the world. I smile. The taxi's rolled-up window captures my reflection. I have no face.

The dream lets me hear my scream.

But tonight is no dream.

Tonight I'm going to my best friend Phil's whiskey bar shrine to the second-most beautiful woman in the world.

Tonight I'm going to face Larkin.

Tonight the most beautiful woman in the world is Makara.

The triumph of her beauty comes from the sheer brilliance shining through her incongruous cobalt blue eyes.

"What did you see when you walked over to my table at BackStreets?" I asked this morning as we stood in our bedroom and she helped me decide which shirt best hid the .45 automatic I'd tucked in my pants near my spine for tonight's meeting with Larkin.

Her midnight hair shook.

"I wish you had a smaller gun."

"I've got what I've got," I said. "The night we met, what did you see?"

A smile rose to her lips. "I saw you appreciating all of me."

"Not just another barang hoping to convince the beautiful bar hostess to come back into the game for a pile of dollars?"

"What you wanted from me has never been for sale." Her body molded to me as her arms snaked up my chest, around my neck. "What you get with that is everything else."

Then her lips pillowed mine and opened with a taste of our morning coffee.

The throwaway cell phone marked with yellow tape vibrated its MESSAGE buzz on our bedside table. Makara was gone from my arms and reading the text message before the third buzz.

"Jorani says Derek grabbed it." She frowned. "He should have waited until the last minute this afternoon."

"He took the chance he got."

"Now it's the chance we have. Nothing else changes."

"Are you sure Derek and Jorani will trust me for the pass-off?"

Makara shrugged. "You're the barang everybody trusts."

"Maybe I'm more than that."

Her head shook. "You are exactly who you are. That's why I love you."

The ceiling fan stirred the air above us like a helicopter from a long-gone war.

My laptop beeped as an email hit the in-box. Odds were that the email was from a local non-governmental organization that had contracted me to write a grant funding proposal for their nonprofit goal of keeping their foreign staff comfortably employed trying to save the world, or at least making this Southeast Asian smear of it a better place. I was far enough along on the proposal to know the data needed to decorate the muscular prose I distilled and parroted back from the grant applications. I used this year's corporate buzzwords like slashes of a samurai's sword. *Management by objective*—as if there were some other desirable way to manage. *Indigenous evaluated empowerment*—a shape defined by available and perhaps relevant statistics. *Results-based paradigms*—making *what happens when* fit what you predicted.

Makara said, "We must live in this day."

She untied the belt on the blue Hong Kong silk robe I'd bought to match her eyes from a vendor at Central Market on the day three weeks ago that Makara had told me about Jorani, the seventeen-year-old country girl who worked as a prostitute at the BackStreets bar Makara refused to give up managing.

"We can't rely on me just staying home," Makara would argue.

"I need my own money," she'd say.

"I need my own eyes on the world," said her voice that had grown up in refugee camps the UN built to help Cambodia repopulate Phnom Penh after its ghost years.

"I need to be me," was what Makara eventually always said.

And I needed her.

Then that day three weeks ago, she said, "Jorani is in love."

You know when your beloved has more to say.

All I could do was ask, "So?"

"Love is never enough," answered Makara.

Making me work for it. Buy into it.

"And there's never enough without love," I reminded her.

Makara shrugged. "You say you'd like to leave Phnom Penh."

"You say you'll never go."

"I'd like to see snow," she said. "I want you to be happy. As long as here is here."

My heart pounded in my chest. "So if we could come back ..."

"Before we can come back, we have to be able to go. You earn big money for Phnom Penh, but just okay dollars for the rest of the world. Even if we bring all we have together, we cannot afford to go anywhere else."

She frowned. "I could learn the rules in your America."

"Always before it was *never ever*. Why is it *maybe* now?"

The Fires of Forever

"Afterwards, it would be good for us to get away for a while."

And there it was. She would leave with me *if* we had to go and *if* we could afford it and *if* we would come back someday.

Maybe I could make someday into never. Maybe I could make us into something more than the magic of Phnom Penh.

I said, "Tell me about Jorani."

What mattered was the part of Jorani's story called Derek, a twenty-four-year-old gamer who'd gotten out of his parents' basement to work for a brand-name clothing company whose executives live in suburbs outside New York City, where their mistresses and showrooms and corporate suites are and the workers who make their wares aren't.

Derek was an information technology drone to the executives, good enough to get on the payroll, geeky enough to never get out of IT. They figured they could trust him with the IT ops in their Cambodian factory. Besides, their local enforcer, Nhean, would keep an eye on this kid who kept the offshore IT from crashing while his cool bosses in NYC donated dollars to America First campaigns that elected politicians who knew how to keep Uncle Sam and the Do-Gooders from screwing up the whole system.

Derek spent his first six months "in country" spending every dime he made on all the bar girls who'd let him do all the rather ordinary things he'd dreamed of doing with all the American girls who'd never looked at him, *let alone* ... Just when Derek thought he'd finally done it all, he met Jorani. They fell into California fantasies.

But Derek knew how to read the zeros on his and Jorani's spreadsheet.

"What does he want?" I asked.

Makara answered: "Start-up capital."

"What's he got?"

"Source code."

I didn't want to know but heard myself say, "What's that?"

"Source code is computers' religion. Source code for a big hedge fund runs a zillion calculations a day. Tells the computers when to buy or sell a stock and does the deal in microseconds. The computer system for Derek's clothing company on the edge of our city is networked into all its big stockholders. Derek hacked into the network of a stockholding hedge fund and got to its source code.

"Hijacking someone's source code lets you program it so your computer gets a few seconds' heads-up to take advantage of what the hedge fund's computer is about to do. Or you could flat-out rig the hedge fund buy-sell and make yourself a huge fortune. Or bankrupt the hedge fund. A multi-billion-dollar coup without spilling a drop of blood."

"That's not our can-do. What do the lovers want from us?"

"They don't have a clue who to sell the source code to."

"And we do?"

Makara shrugged. "Derek can copy the source code onto a flash drive. He says sending it over the Internet will leave a trail. That means a hand-to-hand transfer."

"Swiss accounts and cell phones for instant payoffs," came out of me.

Cloud lips pressed mine.

"I knew you'd be great at this."

And she said, "Anybody who'd pay for this has to be big, like the Yakuza or a Chinese government business,

The Fires of Forever

one of the Triads. Or the hedge fund's competition in New York. The new Brothers Circle mob. Any potential end-user buyer ..."

She shuddered for both of us.

Said: "We need a broker with a bankroll to front our end with Derek and Jorani. We go wholesale and out. The broker buys all. How he unloads it is all on him."

We reasoned through Phnom Penh to three names in less than an hour.

Billy Wu: Lean and Ivy League, flashy, in Phnom Penh for the long haul. Owned a little of this, a lot of that; loans could be arranged. Hosted Chinese hotshots from the Mainland and Hong Kong and San Diego, mining and timber execs from Australia. Wu liked to bring his guests to BackStreets because Makara let only respectable prostitutes work there. Plus he had a crush on her. Who didn't?

Paulson: American. Ran an NGO for his public face. Was a respected fixer. Word was, Paulson also ran the recycled/stolen NGO hardware racket. He worked with freelance girls who sold their customers ganja or more that they bought from whoever Paulson told them to, and in return Paulson got those girls close to visiting big money. Paulson sometimes led his female allies to BackStreets. As long as he didn't push the regulars out or make trouble, Makara kept out of his way. Paulson was gay, so he merely admired Makara. He'd paid me well to write a grant funding request to a reputable American foundation, and I'd said yes because the project did much of the good it promised. We knew each other, and he knew that I knew enough.

Larkin: Claimed to be British, sounded Russian. Wore linen sports jackets in case of air conditioning, like a cautious lizard. The linen also hid his guns. He let me buy him a club soda one night in Phil's bar because he knew I knew the sanity of such respect. If you had rough trouble, you went to Larkin. If your trouble was Larkin, you went away. Heroin trans-shippers paid Larkin protection taxes or lost profits in pools of blood. Working on an NGO grant, I'd stumbled across a New York law firm that listed Larkin as "consultant on retainer." In this city sweating sex, no one ever knew Larkin to indulge. His internal source code ran its calculus solo.

"Has to be him," said Makara. "Billy Wu would take too long to put it together. More time equals more risk. Paulson's not big enough or tough enough.

"And it has to be you that does the hand-to-hand."

Makara brushed my cheek.

"Larkin'd take me off and take the source code without a blink. But taking out a barang is just enough of a problem that it's not worth it, so he'd do business with us straight. If we're careful."

"And lucky," I said.

This morning she stood in her untied blue silk robe, said: "Do you feel lucky?"

A Cambodian chess set waited on a bedroom table beyond her. Only it's not chess; it's Ouk. The rules are different from the ones where I was born. Here, pawns start two rows out from the royalty players and are almost as powerful as the queen. Makara wins without mercy. Of late she's been scolding me to "see all the pieces on the board."

"In Ouk," she says, "every moment has its play. Every piece has its power and follows its own nature. Luck is only you seeing all that when it's your turn."

Makara's cobalt blue eyes naturally saw *all that* with such clarity that I never got why she built a home shrine where she'd burn incense and *sampeah* to an ebony Buddha.

And this morning she'd said: "Do you feel lucky?"

Standing there, wearing only her loosened blue silk robe.

"I'm lucky to be here with you now," I said.

She let the blue robe fall to the floor.

Cupped my face with her soft-as-a-flame palms.

"Now never lasts," she said. Kissed *oh* kissed me. Said: "Now lasts forever."

I lost all my fears and forbearance in our fire.

Until that afternoon when the sun made long shadows in the streets and the heat of the day softened toward the warmth of the night. Tourists wondered about dinner and *after*. Factory line workers still had hours to go on their day shifts while the clean shirts in the factory's air-conditioned offices went home. And as I dressed to leave, I remembered Tantar the elephant.

"He's gone from out in front of Wat Phnom, where tourists got their pictures taken with him, fed him bananas, got rides on him for a few bucks more. Four different NGOs complained enough to the city governor and the Forest Administration that Tantar's owner has stopped bringing him around."

"Someone paid someone," said Makara as she brushed her black hair.

"Tantar'd been there before the Khmer Rouge." I tied my shoes. "Somehow got out of the city during the ghost days. Afterwards got found and brought back here to do what he did. But years of sidewalk bricks under his feet, infections, bone decay …"

"This turn of his is gone," said Makara. "Don't forget your gun."

She walked me to our door. Held both my hands and said our silly ritual of love: "I see you."

"I see you," came my words, just as they had that night years ago, or was it yesterday, when we'd met in a bar where everyone else showed only their faceless phantoms.

Unlike in my dream, I had to walk from the street outside our house to one of the main boulevards to find a tuk-tuk. Throwaway cell phones wrapped in different-colored tapes filled both of my front pants pockets while my own cell phone rode buttoned in my shirt above my heart, the shirt I wore untucked over the pistol pressed against my spine.

Wat Phnom, where tourists come and Tantar wasn't, is where I'd chosen to meet Derek for the pass-off. I had the tuk-tuk drop me off down the block. Strolled back along the stone sidewalk under trees' green clouds, just another barang in a blue and white Hawaiian shirt looking for enlightenment or at least a worth-an-email image of a temple devoted to that.

This Phnom Penh breathed peace. A fullness of quiet. You could feel the river run.

You could lose yourself there.

The burn-scarred street boy sold me a green foil pack of mint gum, gave the pickpocket crew working this strip the nod to leave me alone. He didn't want to lose a local customer, not when there were tourists to boost. I used unwrapping a stick of gum to scan the scene. Saw no cop eyes. No vampire shadows.

Saw Derek striding toward me.

Sandy-haired, stout, with eyeglasses that screamed *keyboard smart*, Derek didn't stand out in this late afternoon stream of tourists whose chatter sounded of Germany or maybe Holland, even though beside him with equal seriousness hiked a black-haired, jeans, and T-shirt dressed Cambodian woman.

Oh no, he didn't!
Oh yes, he did.
Walked up to me clasping Jorani's hand like dawn might not come.
"I know I broke the rules!" he blurted.
"This was supposed to be a brush pass, you alone, and ... Take a stick of gum."
"What?"
I thrust the green foil pack toward him: "Take a stick of gum!"
"Oh, *no thanks*, I don't—"
"Take a damn stick of gum so we've got a reason to be standing here!"
"Oh."
And he did. Luckily, he was slow about unwrapping it.
I held the pack toward the black-haired girl, whispered, "None for you."
Jorani gave me fierce eyes I didn't know she had.
"Whatever together comes."
As her English seemed to be doing, even though she'd mangled the message: *Derek and I are together whatever comes.*
"Now," I said, "all three of us are *together*, so we better hope we've got enough gum to explain that if somebody sees us and somebody cares."
I slid the minty stick of gum into my mouth, told Derek: "Save your wrapper."
He hissed: "It's Nhean!"
Don't swirl your head to look! Whisper. "Where?"
"I don't know, back at the factory!"
Do. Not. Kill. Your. Partner.
Derek said: "I hacked and downloaded, got through the day and was walking out cool and calm after work,

just like we planned, *but there he was!* On the prowl! Not on the factory floor like normal! Up in our offices! I got out of there, called Jorani to be sure she was safe, and she figured she'd come to protect me, help, and this way's okay 'cause it looks like we're just here because we're lovers."

The wat behind him preached patience.

"What do you think Nhean knows?"

"I don't know if he knows anything or not, but there he was!"

"Everybody's somewhere, you idiot. What matters is why."

All I had to do was walk away. These two would be fucked. We'd need to throw Larkin big dollars for his time and trouble. But then Makara and I would be out of this speeding crime car with only Derek and Jorani's splatter on our karma. Derek and Jorani would roll over on us with the first push, but no law could make much of a case, and if the corporate bosses went off the books, Larkin was on our side. All I had to do was walk away.

"Where's the flash drive?" I said.

"In my pants pocket."

Over Derek's shoulder I saw a burly bronzed man on crutches with only one leg swinging our direction. A white handkerchief fluttered on the bottom of his left stump.

Last Chance Nigel. Australian. Pensioner living more like a big shot than he'd ever dreamed. Drunk all the time. Dragged himself to rentable girls in every bar on his way to death. Most Phnom Penh expats knew him by sight and smell, and even through the fog of his day's first drunk, he knew who he saw if they'd been around as long as me.

"Stick your hand with the gum wrapper in your pocket," I told Derek. "Get the flash drive. Bring it out and pass it to me with the gum wrapper."

The flash drive and crumpled wrappers filled my right fist.

Nigel swung closer on his crutches. The fluttering white handkerchief wrapping his stump looked stained with blood. Or something.

Derek hissed: "Now what?"

"Give me a *thanks for the gum* nod and go."

"Wh ... where?"

"I don't ... Go home and fuck. If someone's going to get you, it's a better way to go than most, and if you get a call saying you're rich, you might as well be celebrating."

Then I peeled the wrapper off a second stick of gum, slid it into my mouth and jawed it into a minty wet pulp with its brother. Kept the wrapper visible in my left grasp as I walked toward a green plastic litter barrel maintained by an NGO client. I put the wrapper in my left hand together with the wrapper from Derek in my right fist. Palmed the flash drive. Let my imperceptibly heavier heart-side closed hand fall to my side as I opened my right fist above the litter barrel. Shiny foil floated free into that green maw.

And I walked away.

Stuffed both fists into my pants pockets like I'd seen on a technologically antique Bob Dylan album cover for sale at Central Market, complete with a bullet hole.

My hands came out of my pants pockets five steps later, and because I'd *obviously* learned it was more comfortable, I put what must have been just the pack of gum in my right shirt pocket, buttoned the flap.

I rode a tuk-tuk to the Raffles hotel, walked inside, through the lobby, out a side door, dodged through the crowd at a sidewalk food cart, smelled curried fish *amok*, slid into a taxi as it emptied out two Japanese businessmen. The taxi sped away, dropped me three blocks from Phil's bar.

The bleeding-eye sun showed me no one on my trail.

This early, only a half dozen customers lingered inside Phil's bar when I walked through the glass bead curtain filling the doorway. Four men nursed beers at a table far from the glass beads that the spirits of their ancestors might peer through. One of them worked at an NGO that had run into trouble with the last grant my writing had won for them. Neither of us wanted to be near trouble, so we ignored our acquaintanceship. A sixty-something married American couple perched on stools by the glass beads entrance, staring at each other with that nervous horror of knowing you've said too much. I tipped the bar hostess enough to get what I wanted, but not so much as to make her worry. Five break-your-heart bar girls ignored me as they worked their way through dinner at one of the round tables. They knew I was Phil's friend and with Makara, so they saved their efforts for the night's first wave of gettable customers who'd soon stalk in from the dark.

The music was dinner-hour off in this saloon. The lights were turned up, revealing the bar as a shrine with walls covered by hundreds of pictures and posters and cut-out framed news stories about *her*, the second most beautiful woman in the world.

Waves of auburn hair caressed her shoulders. She sported cheekbones and lush lips to rival Makara, plus heavier curves and longer, sleekly muscled legs that always struck a power pose in the posters from her twenty-some movies. On that wall hung a movie poster where she's a betrayed assassin. The poster over there showed her as an honest cop in a corrupt city. There was the killer wife movie that won her an Oscar. In that one she was a comedy's casino heist *artiste*. There a wronged mom on the run. A zombie hunter with a secret. A lawyer scammed by a killer she must defend. A jewel thief. A journalist who shot more bullets than words to get justice. On and on. The woman worked. Her roles showed no man could break her. I don't watch many movies; Phnom Penh reality is as cinematic as the pirated DVDs for sale in its streets. In my favorite movie of hers, she stars as a spy who discovers her master is insane.

Phil looked up from what he was working on at the end of the bar. Sent me a smile with all we'd shared over the years.

"Whoa, my man! Come seize the moment!"

Walking to him, I checked over his shoulder. The back door was still there.

"*Seize the moment?* Is that what we're doing?"

I leaned on the bar.

Phil pulsed energy. I once feared I'd lose him, but then Phil realized that keeping the bond of our years strong meant weaving us together with Makara. And he did. She liked him, worried about him, said: "He's trapped in a dream."

"We're all trapped somewhere," I'd argued. "His life—good sex, lives like a rich man, runs his bar like a king. He's got it all, and us, too."

"But he's waiting for some dream to come true. And it won't."

"Mine did," I'd whispered to her. "This is Phnom Penh. You never know."

"Check it out," Phil said at the bar that held the black wood, glass-framed color download he spun around for me to see: *her* at a red carpet event, melting the camera with a ruby smile and a long, bare white leg striding out of a simple, slinky black gown.

"I know you think she's *only* the second most beautiful woman in the world," said Phil. "But look at her! Makes your mouth go dry. Want a beer?"

"Not now."

I scanned the barroom. Saw no other searching eyes.

"And the world doesn't even know what I—what *we* know about her, right?"

That bar girl with the rhinestone clip in her hair—she's new. Who …? *Oh*, right. The hostess's daughter, learning the game so she can take over the family job slot when her hoping-for-grandkids mom retires.

"Forget about how cosmic she looks, right?" continued Phil, his eyes full of his latest photo. "She comes here couple years back for a *get-some-press* fashion shoot, groks the scene, has the savvy smarts and the soul, man, the *soul* to dump dollars into a few NGOs who actually deliver. Talk about good karma—and she does it on the q.t. Plus she adopts a baby girl out of the orphanage that she supports. Takes her homeside. That's one girl who won't grow up for guys like us to fuck, and it's all because of her."

"Where do you think I should hang this?" he added.

A fat white-haired man wearing a brought-from-home shirt made in a factory outside of town clatters through the glass beads for tonight's party.

My eyes follow Phil's.

"Wonder where her actor husband was in that shot."

"I cropped him out. Do you think that *Nat krou* out by Kilometer 6 can really transmute consciousness? Me into his body, him to like, Nowhereville. Or even nirvana. Hell, give the guy a break."

"No."

Phil didn't believe in that magic either, or he'd be out the glass beads. Once he grokked what he had to and could do, *my man* knew no hesitation. One night as he tended bar, a tourist from Dallas who'd failed to get it up with the girl he'd paid for started knocking back bourbons, prepping for consolation ratification with his fists on the first hapless fool he'd find. The instant Phil recognized that negative energy, he smashed a scotch bottle over the Texan's head, dragged the unconscious guy out front, dumped him in a taxi, and used the bully's own bucks to pay the fare to his hotel and calm our cops.

Phil said: "Are you going to tell me what's wrong, why you're here *alone*—or should I tell you *again* about that one time I saw her standing on the street here, all zen?"

"I'm meeting Larkin. Here. Business."

"My brother, I did not think you were that way."

"We are."

"*We?*"

"Makara. Me."

Phil cocked his head to focus an insight through his nightly stone.

Said: "Life's all about what you get for what you do."

"We're getting out of here," I said.

"*We* being *you* and *Makara*. Thought she wanted to never go."

"It's part of the deal. We can always come back."

"Sure." Sorrow deadened his voice. "I'll still be here."

The hollow inside his tough-guy voice moved my heart, so on the spot I made up: "We know we need you to watch our backs. That means you get a cut," I said.

The ten percent dollar figure I quoted him was five times what the average Cambodian family lived on for a year.

"Whatever is whatever, and you always been the fair one of us." His stoned stone eyes misted. Blinked clear. "*Wow.* I guess tonight is the big time. What's happening?"

"I need friendly eyes on my back *right now.*"

"What we do. You got my back, I got yours. And Makara's. What's the deal?"

"The less you know, the better. Tonight, here, soon, it's the exchange."

"A heads-up would have been cool."

"Something else. I need you to get behind me, take a .45 out of my waistband."

"For real?"

"I just went through another guy breaking agreed-to rules. I know how I felt. And I'm a restrained guy. Larkin's not. So I'm not breaking his no-guns rule."

Phil looked at me. He's a year older. Other than that, we're much the same.

He said: "Larkin'll come strapped."

"No doubt. But I'm playing it straight."

"He could go cowboy."

"Not here. Not with you behind the bar."

"And if he does, I've got your gun that he doesn't know about."

"You do what you've got to do," was all I could ask.

"Shit."

He walked around the bar so I stood between him and the room. No one saw what I felt: him sliding the war surplus 1911 Colt .45 automatic out of my pants.

"Born in the motherfucking USA," he said. "We got the gun we gave the world."

Phil stands beside me. Now his light blue shirt is untucked.

"Fuck reality," he said. "I feel like I could shoot her husband from here."

Phil frowned at the glass beads entryway.

"What's up with that guy?"

Nhean. A muscle man, short even by Khmer standards and clearly pissed off about that. He carried some kind of semi-cop badge. His family owned a piece of the factory that employed him as its enforcer. The same factory Derek had ripped off.

"Oh, fuck."

Phil gave me a look. Moved so he'd have my back in case of Nhean.

The enforcer marched right up to bark at me: "You call?"

"*What?*"

"Some barang man call my cell phone. Say he know where union organizers meeting. Say meet him here right away. Come alone. In here, you the alone barang."

"Not for you," I said. "You should know that, knowing me and what I'd feel okay to sell. It's some other guy. Maybe you're too early. Or too late."

He had to buy that truth. Moved down the bar to wait alone for his contact.

Would Larkin buy that Phnom Penh was this small of a town?

"Let me give you one last chance, my friend," said the man who had my back.

"I saw Last Chance today. He still needs crutches."

"Use my back door. You can still get out of this."

"I've been trying to get out of this before it got me for years," I told him. "Now I figure the best way out is to dive in as deep as I can."

"Don't give me my three-bong-hits fucking cosmic bullshit," said Phil, not even knowing the Nhean problem. "Are you sure this is smart?"

"No," I said.

And then I grokked it: I'm not that smart.

"See all the pieces on the board."

Envision our panicked Derek and Jorani. Hope they used the safe cell phones to call Makara, who talked them down from the edge. Then see her figure that if the dragon Nhean, who guarded what we'd stolen, was hunting, give him something else to hunt.

But if you're steering a dragon, why send him to … *Yes!* Larkin's nature was savage, but when he saw Nhean, not knowing the *why* of a dragon on the scene would keep Larkin cautious, conservative. And that gave me another wisp of protection. I could hear her say: *"Make the most of every move and make every move matter."*

Makara had paid some barang stranger to phone Nhean, say what she wanted, and forget it. Or spun her pawn into some elaborate, maybe political-activism prank.

She had my back. Knew I'd tough it out for us no matter what.

Standing in the bar with me, Phil said, "What now?"

"I gotta pick my spot."

I lied. I already had.

"Should I start the party?" asked Phil.

"Why not?"

The Fires of Forever

He walked back behind the bar. I walked into the jumble of empty round tables. I sat at table that was just a quick run to the back exit. Thought about it. Got up, sat at the next table. Considered its unobstructed view of the glass beads.

"DUN-DUNH, DUN-DUNH" boomed electric guitars from the sound system speakers on every wall as Phil flipped the toggle switch for the music—1970s or 1980s Americana, *of course*, this song from a dead junkie's purple haze. Blackness slammed the barroom with the second guitar chord. White strobes machine-gunned through swirling rainbows of red and green and orange lights.

You could see people and chairs and tables and glistening bottles behind the bar, but only as changing-colors images caught in strobe flashes of white light. Everyone moved in snapshots like a jerky old-time movie. Only not silent—all around boomed a soundtrack of rock music from the last century. Still, at any of the tables or booths, you could hear your companion saying *yes, no, what, how much, I'm from*.

In the strobing rock blare, I moved to a third table. Looked right, saw the empty booth with its wall photo of the second most beautiful woman in the world dressed as a cunning temptress from a guy-gal *noir* homage movie set in the fabled 1950s, a color press kit photo that showed her long leg clad in a black stocking clipped to a black garter belt heavenwards under her skirt. She was smiling. Phnom Penh was too hot for Makara to enjoy wearing a black garter belt and stockings. But we were leaving.

Sitting amidst the blind-to-bright strobe flashes at the third table, I stroked my shirt pocket. Brought the pack of gum and the flash drive to my lap. No one noticed. Derek had used a flash drive with a plastic protective holster for the plug-in end. I dumped the last sticks of gum out of their green foil pack and slid in the flash drive—a nice fit. I covered my mouth, coughed, and filled my fist with what my chewing had transformed. That gooey wet wad smushed onto the foil pack. No one saw my hands go deep under the round table and stick the gum pack/flash drive to its yucky bottom. My palm trembled beneath the stuck-on packet for a whole song. It held. Like I knew it would.

Then I claimed the booth with the black-garter belt photo of the second most beautiful woman in the world.

Heartbeat flashes of white strobes revealed images in the swirling color darkness.

The dragon Nhean coiled on a barstool.

Ghostly strobe light mirrored off the front door curtain of glass beads.

A bar girl on the stage rocked out to a dead man's music like she was on TV.

Two French-looking vagabonds promenaded into the bar.

Dragon Nhean lit a cigarette.

My buddy Phil stood watch behind the bar.

A white-haired fat man found his way to a table.

Dragon Nhean closed one ear over a cell phone.

Glass beads swayed behind a pale lizard in a linen sports jacket.

Larkin.

I kept my hands flat on the booth's table and my eyes on the flashes of him. Standing there. Taking it all in. Spotting Nhean.

The bar girl with the rhinestone hair clip scurried toward me, giggling.

But I paid the bar hostess to make sure I was left alone and got this booth and—

And the bar girl with the rhinestone hair clip that sparkles with the strobe lights is at my booth, her eager hands pulling me.

Larkin paid her. Long before I showed up.

She stood me outside the booth and laughed like we were playing a game. Ran her hands over my chest and back, pulled my shirt up high as she spun me around. Flashes of strobe light showed my bare flesh unsullied by any steel. She dropped to her knees in front of me. Her rhinestones sparkled. Her hands ran over my pockets, found the cell phones. She laughed and still on her knees pulled them out and waved them high to the beat of the blaring rock music before she put them aside on the booth's table. She pushed my pant legs up past my calves, pulled down my thin cotton socks in the black sneaker-like shoes I'd worn because they made it easy to run. She found nothing. After a *just-playing* stroke of her finger to my groin, she was on her feet in high heels whose clicks on the floor were drowned under the rock music as she sashayed back to the glass beads.

I sat in my booth. Left the tape-wrapped cell phones on the table. Rhinestone girl missed my personal phone in my shirt pocket, but when Larkin got close enough to see its bulge, he'd know what it was and not care. My hands pressed flat on the table, visible and still in the strobe flashes.

He came to me in beats of *seen*.

Moving from the glass beads.

Walking through the now more populated round tables.

Looming beside my booth.

Sitting across from me, so close the spinning color lights—*orange, red, blue, green*—lit his face between bright strobe flashes.

"Alan Cain."

"Here for you."

"No," he said. "You're here for yourself. And Makara."

He smiled. "Should I get the flash drive before or after I shoot you?"

"Shoot me and your popularity will go way down."

"Yes, she would realize that."

"Shoot me," I said, "and you won't find a fucking thing you want on me."

Heartbeat flashes of strobe lights.

"Well," he said, "you are here after all. And after all this, I don't and won't care about you. Or her. Just our business that we all want to stay quiet."

Don't tell me who your end-user buyer is!

I said: "Here's how it works. You call the Swiss bank. Transfer our fee into that numbered account. Then we wait. When I get confirmation of that transfer on my cell phone, I'll transfer it to another account and from there it'll vanish. When I get a text message that all the money is clear, you get the flash drive."

"You hid it in this room," said Larkin. "I won't leave here without it."

"Then let's do the deal."

Behind Larkin, the dragon Nhean hurried off his bar stool and through the glass beads curtain as if he'd gotten another cell phone inducement—one timed five minutes after my scheduled rendezvous time with the never-late Larkin.

Larkin held a cell phone between us as he dialed a Swiss bank where dawn was now lighting that cold-mountains sky. Snow, maybe in Switzerland there'd be snow. Larkin entered all the right commands, crooked his thumb above the last button, set his eyes on me.

I nodded.

His thumb hit send.

"Proud Mary" blared out of the loudspeakers.

Flashing white strobes lit the two of us staring at each other in the booth.

My green taped cell phone vibrated on the table.

I checked the call: a text. Tapped in a reply. Hit send. Set the phone down.

Thumping bass drums and clapping hands claimed, "We will rock you."

My blue taped cell phone buzzed.

Two text messages. Makara: our twenty-five percent transferred so many times it was home free and clear. Derek: confirming his seventy-five percent hit his system. Who knew what he'd do with it? Who cared?

"Where?" said Larkin before I could set down my second cell phone.

"That white-haired fat tourist those two bar girls are working on—it's stuck underneath their table. With gum."

He face sneered disgust.

In the strobe light flashes, I see:

Larkin stands as the music blares "Under My Thumb."

Phil isn't behind the bar. *He must have gone for position on Larkin, in case.*

Larkin looms by the white-haired man's table.

Not saying a word as the bar girls hustle their confused customer away to some safer corner of darkness.

Larkin sits. Revulsion flickers on his face as his hands crawl the grimy underside of the barroom table and ... he smiles.

Gives me a nod as he sits there facing me, his back to the glass beads.

Phil staccato flows toward where Larkin sits in blaring music and strobing lights.

Even Phil sees Larkin put something inside his linen jacket.

Larkin catches my puzzled brow in a strobe flash.

Phil whirls in front of the sitting lizard, points—

BANG! The .45's cannon roar explodes through the Rolling Stones song.

Bedlam amidst the rainbow swirling white strobe flashing darkness. Customers crash away from the gunshot sound everybody knows isn't in that Rolling Stones song and this is Phnom Penh: *Get out the fucking door fast!*

Phil whirls away from having his hands inside Larkin's linen jacket.

Larkin slumps in the chair as a red fountain flows from his third eye.

Phil stretches toward me his hand he took from under Larkin's jacket and—

What?

Slumping against the booth, chin on my chest. Down there looks sticky wet. *Gurgling, I'm gurgling.* My head rises/flops against the booth and up to my right. I see dark spray has splattered the black garter belt movie picture of the second most beautiful woman in the world, crimson tears run down that glass, and look: There's Phil, my best friend Phil, scooping the two cell phones off the table—*smart if there's going to be some sort of trouble, better to hide them*—and I can't move my arms to help and he lifts my right arm from my side, drops it on the table like a slab of meat in a sidewalk butcher stall. Puts my .45 beside my hand that *darn it* just won't work. In flashes of strobe light and the roar of my heart thundering louder than the rock music I realize he had grabbed Larkin's gun from under the linen jacket and then left it in that dead man's hand.

After he used it to shoot me.

Now there's enough apparent evidence for our cops, who'll want to close the books on this, no other forthcoming witnesses, barang trouble, with Phil's story of how Larkin and I shot it out *who the fuck knows why*. Phil doesn't know, but he's too smart not to have also grabbed what he saw Larkin stick in his pocket.

"You're right," says Phil: "Makara is the most beautiful woman in the world."

And in the whirling strobing roar I envision him crying with her that he did what he could, instinctively saved this flash drive out of their mutual tragedy, what is it? She has the fortune from Larkin and *now—then—still* she has something to sell. Billy Wu and someone to watch over her. And as a cosmic crimson mouth sucks in everything, I realize that my turn is gone and I'm getting out of Phnom Penh.

James Grady

James Grady's first novel became Robert Redford's movie *Three Days of the Condor* and gave Grady a career with scores of novels and short stories as well as stints as a U.S. Senate aide, an international investigative reporter, and a Hollywood writer. Grady lives in Washington, D.C.

Love and Death at Angkor
John Burdett

> *C'est parce qu'il possède ces conditions d'érotisme que je m'acharnai dans le mal.*
> —Jean Genet, *Journal du Voleur*

1.

"Some guys have all the luck."

I uttered this cliché not so much on behalf of my own thwarted libido, but to comfort my good friend Jeff. To be sure, I'd felt a serious twinge or two myself when the Swedish girl passed by—what man with a single red corpuscle remaining in his blood wouldn't have?—but I can't claim it was the *coup de foudre*, the bolt of lightning as the French say. I'm not sure I seriously believed in such a thing until I took Jeff on a jaunt to Angkor.

An old school friend I'd not seen for a decade, Jeff had decided all of a sudden to visit me in Bangkok, where I'd set up as a struggling novelist, journalist, and, if absolutely necessary, tour guide (red light districts not excluded). Since he was unlikely to have the time or funds ever to visit Southeast Asia again—especially not with the way the economy was going back in depressed and depressing England—he'd committed to the full Southeast Asian tour of Laos (Luang Prabang and the Plain of Jars),

Burma (Mandalay and the pagodas), Malaysia (Penang and Tioman Island), Thailand (the islands, the beaches, and my Bangkok), the Philippines (Boracay Beach), and, last but not least, Cambodia (Angkor).

He was a good-looking guy—about five ten, slim, flat stomach, pale skin, curly hair still near-black at thirty-two. But he had an obvious weakness which women sensed instantly: he was a sucker for them and way too sensitive for psychic survival in a cruel world. If one may adapt a vulgar phrase, it was not merely his brains he kept in his dick, but his heart as well. He fell. Oh, he fell, over and over again—and they despised him for it. In fact, to be perfectly clear, I should reveal that the reason he had taken a sabbatical from his job as university librarian, at some godforsaken degree factory somewhere in the British Midlands, was to convalesce from yet another affair gone tragically wrong. (A fellow librarian, a cute-to-die-for trainee, according to him, had worshiped him as her mentor with heart and body until a maths lecturer took her to lunch—you know the kind of thing.)

I confess my first instinct was to apply some Bangkok Penicillin: when a man is confronted by as many as a hundred beautiful, charming, instantly available girls for seven nights on end (I insisted, though he groaned: "It's Soi Cowboy again tonight, mate, and we *are* going to the Pink Pussy, and you *are* going to pay the bar fines of at least two, and you *are* going to take them to the short-time hotel across the street), it's a little difficult to maintain the romantic delusion of soul-mate-and-lover-for-life. But I had to relent after the first week. You see, the game fellow *did* take a girl out from time to time—once he even took two—and *did* take them to the hotel, and *did* have some wild Dionysian nights. And the next morning he would be sick as a parrot—miserable as hell, as if he'd drunk two bottles of Mekong rice whiskey instead of a teetotaler having the time of his life at an orgy.

He was staying with me at my condo in downtown Krung Thep, which he used as a base of regional exploration, so I could not avoid an eyeful of Late Romantic male anguish at its most pathetic. I remembered his literary adolescence, for that was the peak of our friendship: he was Lawrencian to the marrow, could recite whole pages from *Women in Love*, *Lady Chatterley*, *Sons and Lovers*—and the poems. Oh, the poems! It really is great writing, and had I been a frustrated Edwardian, I might have fallen for it myself.

For Jeff, it seemed, was an erotically displaced person. He had come to the Far East hoping for, even expecting, as a kind of karmic compensation for the loss of the cute librarian, one of those beach romances where the male and female leads are irresistibly drawn together from a distance of a mile or more of sand and sea under a tropical sky (a couple of piña coladas, shared literary/musical/fine arts tastes, one more lurid sunset, and Bob's your uncle—or should I say *coup de foudre*?).

Perhaps it was cruel of me to insist that he take a ringside seat at—even become a player in—that other, more commercial erotic theatre in which Asia has specialized since the first Vedas? I meant well, I really did, and I've seen the cure work fifty times since I've been out here, but when I saw what it was doing to poor Jeff, I relented and, by way of redeeming any abuse of friendship of which I might have been guilty, agreed to accompany him to Angkor in Cambodia on the last leg of his exciting, wonderful, but, until then, unsatisfying Oriental adventure.

Which is where the Swedish girl came in. We'd clocked her for about a minute on the main street at Siem

Reap the day before and could not be sure at first that she *was* Swedish; say rather that she had "Stockholm blond bombshell" embedded in every curve. And she had the sweetest smile, not at all over-confident or arrogant, or fetching, or feminist-aggressive. Jeff could never resist the perfected natural.

I thought nothing more of it, and neither, I think, did Jeff, on the basis that we were unlikely to see her again.

Then the fatal miracle occurred. He saw her sitting alone at one of the coffee shops in downtown Siem Reap, reading from a slim volume entitled—you've guessed it—*The Selected Poems of D.H. Lawrence*. He sat at a table nearby (he said); he achieved eye contact; and he proceeded to impress her by quoting the first lines of *The Ship of Death*:

*Now it is autumn and the falling fruit
and the long journey towards oblivion.*

*The apples falling like great drops of dew
to bruise themselves an exit from themselves.*

*And it is time to go, to bid farewell
to one's own self, and find an exit
from the fallen self.*

Then, on the brink of conquest, came, as he put it, "the *de rigueur* kick in the goolies." A short, squat, balding bloke in his mid-forties (with a long, disgusting slick of gray hair interrupting the otherwise barren pate), had appeared from nowhere, sat next to her, and kissed her on the cheek. That was not the moment when the venom hit the bloodstream, however; that came a nanosecond later when she looked at the new arrival with something so horrific from Jeff's point of view that he almost puked into his latte: adoration bordering on—no, not *bordering on* but the thing itself—pure unmistakable worship. *Pure worship*. The girl of his dreams, who read D.H.L. and who had no need to worship anyone at all except the woman in the mirror after she showered—somehow that squat aging dwarf had given *her* the *coup de foudre*. And he didn't seem particularly proud of his conquest. That's how it appeared to Jeff at that moment, anyway.

To be polite, Jeff supposed, the girl, whose name he still did not know, nodded in his direction and told the Enemy how the stranger was a Lawrence fan and knew that very special poem by heart. That the Enemy turned to smile at him with a kind of collusion did not help; Jeff had, as a basic reflex of psychic survival, convinced himself that the Enemy was one of those semi-literate apes with hydraulic cocks who could make a female anything swoon once he had her horizontal. Now that last defense was blown when the Enemy said: "My favourite line from that miraculous poem is:

Build then the ship of death, for you must take the longest journey, to oblivion.

And die the death, the long and painful death that lies between the old self and the new."

2.

Jeff related his mini-adventure in a comical tone of self-mockery the next morning while we were sitting on a terrace sipping our coffees and planning our third day at Angkor. After all, even he was not capable of serious heartache over a woman in whose company he had spent less than five minutes and whose character was entirely unknown to him. Siem Reap, by the way, is the business side of the vast Angkor complex; the town where you stay, eat, hire cabs or tuk-tuks, buy marijuana, seek medical attention for upset stomachs and other, peculiarly local, ailments (a friend of mine was bitten by a one-armed monkey at Bayon temple and needed rabies shots), and—if you are so inclined—get laid with an obliging and inexpensive local. It is a perfect foil for the incredible jungle temples which stretch over an area the size of Manhattan and where limestone pillars two yards in diameter are slowly being strangled by tree-sized creepers, giant Buddhas ride monster serpents all the way to nirvana, and the Milky Way itself is vicariously twisted and churned to produce what we Westerners childishly imagine to be the universe.

That I was a born skeptic in such matters, or thought I was, has not prevented me from visiting the place more than twenty times. I'm not an expert—that would take a lifetime—but over the years I've learned quite a lot about it. Jeff, the erudite librarian, was amused that for once he had to sit and listen while *I* lectured *him* on the astrological plan on which the entire city is laid out, and in particular the occult powers which are invoked, trapped, and focused by the great, dark, sinister, irresistible Wat itself. It's the biggest temple on earth, but I was particularly fond—if that is not too diminutive a term—of Banteay Srey, aka the Citadel of Women, which is not Buddhist at all but almost provocatively Hindu. I took a personal pleasure in explaining that women of that time exerted power by drawing on their womanhood instead of twisting themselves into second-rate men.

I was in full flight, describing the erotic carvings and the deeper significance that the inner path ascribes to sexual energy, the science of its use particularly in Tantra—when I saw him turn pale. He had momentarily gazed down from the terrace and across the street to where, by accident, was situated the very café in which he had almost fallen in love the day before. I didn't need him to tell me that she was down there. Irritated—was this guy ever going to even *consider* growing up?—I stopped and followed the line of his sight. She was there all right, sitting with a straight-backed elegance, wearing one of those light cotton frocks which are so airy that the slightest gust can make heart-stopping revelations—the chief of which being that she was not wearing a bra and that her breasts were in the order of perfect: shape, firmness, size, proportion, the lot. I didn't spend much time on them, though, because the company she was keeping was even more intriguing. I had no difficulty recognizing the villain of Jeff's story of the day before. If anything, Jeff had erred somewhat on the side of generosity in his description. The short bald fellow was also cursed with those floppy asymmetrical lips and sloping shoulders that are such convincing evidence of decadent genes that the most saintly of curriculum vitae would not shake your conviction that the inhabitant of that body was terminally depraved.

He and his stunning conquest (if that's really what she was—already I had my doubts) were not alone, though. At the head of the table sat an Indian woman in a flowing sari, about forty years old, with streaks of gray in her jet black hair, two young women about the same age as the Swede—not quite at her level of twenty-something female perfection, but exceptionally attractive nonetheless—a couple of pretty young Thai men, and another man, about my age, who struck me as American, perhaps because he looked strikingly clean-cut in the way of the New World, as if that bright, fresh face had no direct connection with the lower organs but was perhaps sustained by Wi-Fi contact with a more moral network. I had the distinct impression that it was the Indian woman who was head of the group. Even the aging roué deferred to her, the girls nodded with groveling eagerness at everything she said, and the American gave bright smiles whenever their eyes met. The Thais behaved exactly as Thais do in the presence of a spiritual superior. They seemed to agree with everything she was saying.

I was just about to turn back to Jeff, when another member of the group arrived with a tray of coffees and sat down at the end of the table, opposite the Hindu woman. Now I was seriously hooked, because I recognized him. He was Khmer. This I knew for sure because I'd seen him in the uniform of a guard at Angkor Wat, complete with gun and badge. He had even once checked our tourist passes as we strode across the bridge over the lake-sized moat.

I turned to Jeff with a frown, but Jeff wasn't there, only his body was. In the very brief moment when I had turned away, the Swedish girl had looked up at our balcony, seen Jeff, and waved in a chummy way. Jeff waved back with obscene eagerness. Now she mimed *Why don't you join us?* At the same time her ugly friend looked up and, his sloppy lips twisting into a genuinely charming smile, just as if Jeff were a long-lost relation, also mimed, *Please come and join us.* Then, seeing me, he semaphored that I should come too.

I withdrew from the edge of the balcony, looked at Jeff, and shook my head.

Allow me a word of advice. I've been in the East a long time. Generally, I've been treated with legendary kindness and hospitality—but there have been some dangerous moments when I've realized that even small mistakes can be fatal. I didn't like the look of that group. In fact, the hairs on the back of my neck were standing on end, and a cold shiver shook me in the tropical heat. I wanted to forbid Jeff to go down there, but I saw from his face that I would need a small army to prevent it. The only strategy was to make excuses for myself. If he got into trouble, at least I would be free and able to sound the alarm. I didn't say that, of course. You can't warn starry-eyed newcomers without producing evidence.

"Look, Jeff," said I, "I'm not feeling particularly sociable at the moment. You go, mate. I'll see you back at the hotel later."

He shrugged, said something cutting about my ability to relate only to brothel society, and was off. I watched from the terrace when he appeared on the street, beaming all over his sunburned face. The group greeted him like a long-lost friend. I beckoned the Khmer waiter, who I'd clocked a couple of times and who had clocked me back. I hardly needed to utter the word *ganja*. He grinned, disappeared, returned in less than two minutes with a small package which he discreetly dropped into my lap. I discreetly handed him a rolled-up ten dollar note, and that was my day taken care of. I decided to spend the morning shopping for illegal DVDs and then to raise my level of consciousness in Angkor itself and take a motorbike taxi to my favorite temple, Banteay Srey. I must have known something like this was going to happen because I'd brought king-size Rizlas, some cigarettes, and a butane lighter with me.

Before I left the café, my candy man, the waiter, brought me the local English-language newspaper. I glanced at the headline without much interest. It seemed a relic thief had been shot by the guards the night before.

This was a common enough event. Everyone knew that the guards had orders to shoot on sight anyone found anywhere without permission in the vast temple complexes after curfew, but from time to time some unfortunate Khmer desperado bought it, as they say. I felt sorry for the corpse with the hole in its head and the miserable sagging face characteristic of violent death. A lot has changed since the swashbuckling days of the original sandstone burglar, that daring young man who was one day to become France's Minister of Culture, André Malraux, who lopped off a few Buddha heads and shipped them out on a bullock cart in broad daylight, no doubt whistling the Marseillaise as he went.

3.

The problem with the Citadel of Women—the only problem as far as I am concerned—is that its exquisite beauty, almost on a miniature scale compared with the rest of the temples, is simply irresistible even to those who have no taste for Hindu architecture. It is said the carvings are so meticulous in detail they might have been wrought by a goldsmith. Consequently, there are always a bunch of tour groups ogling every erotic curve in the exquisite reliefs, and popping in and out of the innermost sanctum, the holy of holies, to stroke Shiva's smooth—and enormous—granite linga. In other words, even in wild Cambodia it is not the best place to smoke a joint. Therefore, when I said just now that I decided to take a motorbike to Banteay Srey that afternoon, what I actually meant was that I would get off the bike about two hundred yards from the temple and climb up a small hump of hill into the jungle, from which vantage point I could gaze with weed-assisted insight on the antics of Shiva and his most obliging shakti Uma—frozen in colored quartz by a craftsman of genius—without fear of being nabbed by a guard and forced to pay a modest bribe. It wasn't the bribe that bothered me so much as the threat of having my dreamtime interrupted by the barbaric forces of law and order.

So there I was, behind my favorite banyan tree under the declining sun, taking a long, contemplative toke and quietly thanking Buddha for the chance of solitude, when—imagine my surprise—a private minivan stopped on the road and out trooped—you've guessed?

The Indian woman led the way, followed by the Khmer guard, the girls, and the older man, with Jeff in the rear. No sign of the American or the Thais. When the group reached the temple, the Indian woman made a point of taking Jeff in her charge with a rather charming grasp of his arm and began lecturing him, I suppose—I couldn't hear what she said—on the most erotic of the base reliefs, while the others stood around, apparently familiar with the tour. Jeff's introduction took no more than a few minutes, however, and seemed to be the extension of a lecture the Indian woman had been giving him in the van. Then, to my extreme discomfort, the woman in the sari said something to the Khmer guard, who nodded and led the group up my hill, apparently headed straight for me. I immediately slipped to the other side of the great tree, just in time to watch them pass on the way to the top.

"And this is where it all took place," the Indian woman said.

I was not surprised that she owned one of those top-of-the-range Oxford accents that native Brits—even the royals—rarely sport these days.

They were passing close enough for me to reach out and touch them when the guru in the sari said: "We sometimes make the analogy with pranayama—you know, the science of breath. Just as air, when concentrated, can become an irresistible power—those awful pneumatic drills they use to break up concrete are a good example—so the same can be done with sexual energy. The difference, of course, is that with sexual energy we are dealing with a living force, indeed the life force itself."

She paused for breath.

"But for the full effect you need the geomantic assistance of a magical location. There aren't any on earth as good as this. That's why that dynasty of master wizards, the Jayavarmans, built their city here—in honor of their women, especially their mothers."

She gripped Jeff's forearm.

"Imagine, if you can, not merely a perfect temple, which is to say a functioning machine capable of raising us to heaven, but a whole city—a city bigger than the plague-ridden noisome metropolises of Britain and France at that time; the biggest city on earth, bigger than imperial Rome at its height—where every citizen from the divine monarch to the lowest slave enjoyed the sublime privilege of submitting to the living laws of the gods instead of the dead laws of man."

She controlled her rapture with a shudder.

"The earth forces are simply stupendous," she added, as if assessing a new variety of lotus bloom. "Unfortunately, we cannot use the temple itself—except at night after the curfew."

She nodded respectfully toward the tame Khmer guard.

She stopped speaking, no doubt from the effort of climbing the hill, and when she started again, the group was too far away for me to distinguish her words. I could see that something rather extreme had happened to Jeff, though. He seemed to be in a most extraordinary state of excitement.

When the group had reached a point where no one down below could possibly see them—except me, of course—they sat in a circle. But they did not sit around the guru in the sari; they sat around the three young women, with the most beautiful—that blond Stockholm bombshell—in the middle. The Indian woman stopped talking. The three girls stood up. At a command from the woman, Jeff also stood up. The two girls on either side of the Swede quickly removed all her clothing, consisting, to be exact, of the loose cotton dress and a pair of panties. She slipped off the sandals herself. An electric charge shook the whole of Jeff's body and the same thing seemed to happen to the naked girl, who now was supported on the shoulders of her sisters. Jeff sank to his knees and with the reverence of a saint for his god—or goddess—began to lick the area around her vagina, which she eagerly made accessible by parting her thighs.

4.

"Hi, Jeff," I said. "How was your day?"

It was about six-thirty in the evening, just before dark. I'd not expected him back so soon—or at all. I assumed he'd finally found the erotic adventure that he'd come to the East for and—well, who knew what violent change of path and identity that might entail? Not that it was quite the same Jeff who came back to me that night. For a start he was feverish as hell and could hardly look at me. To economize, we were sharing a room in a three-star hotel-cum-boarding house on the outskirts of the town, which made a degree of intimacy inevitable, whether we wanted it or not. Jeff understood that he could not avoid my eyes for the rest of the evening.

"Something happened," he said. "You should have come. Or maybe not."

I raised my eyebrows.

"I had sex with her," he blurted. "The most amazing, bone-shaking, mind-opening, terrifying—"

I raised a hand.

"The earth moved? I thought that only happened to Hemingway?"

"Fuck Hemingway."

Then he stared at me full face. He was badly sunburned, which added to the drama of his expression. His black hair was a mass of curls and sweat, his long thin arms were lobster red—but it was his eyes that scared me.

"Come here," I said.

I was lying on my bed. He obeyed. I held his hand.

"Let's say you have had the most amazing experience known to man. Let's assume that. But if you want to have it again—and again and again—you're going to have to learn to control yourself a lot better. Hysteria may be an exciting starter, but it's simply not sustainable."

He looked at me in astonishment.

"That's what she said."

"Who? The Swedish bit?"

"No. And don't call her that. Her name's Rekha. The other two are Priyanka and Malaiki—Americans. At least, they used to be. They were renamed, re-created, by Mahadevi, who turned them into apsaras and devatas—everyone calls her Mama Devi, or just Mama."

"The woman in the sari?"

"Yes, her. She's amazing. Totally cool like an Oxford professor, but does she deliver! Oh my God, does she deliver."

"Are you going to tell me about it?"

"I asked her exactly that question. 'Can I tell my friend Frank?' I said. Know what she said?"

"What?"

"That you already knew because you were hiding behind a tree and saw everything."

Now it was my turn to experience a jolt. Jeff saw from my face that it was true.

He said, "Oh my God," again, and sat on the bed.

Now we were two very bewildered, and excited, little Brits.

"I wanted to stay," he said. "I mean, forever."

"Stay where?"

"With them, of course. Wherever they went."

"After what I saw, I can't say I blame you. But tell me about that whole party. Who were they before Circe turned them into clones?"

He winced.

"You're wrong. It's the opposite. They're more themselves now than their Western culture ever would have permitted. I thought you would have approved. Anyway, Rekha is not exactly Swedish. She was born there, but her parents moved to the States when she was thirteen. That American guy is her gay traveling companion, and those Thais are his local lovers he picked up on Soi 4 near Patpong. They've gone, now that Rekha has her own party to play with. The two of them were backpacking around Southeast Asia when they—well, when what happened to me today happened to her. The other girls joined the group a couple of weeks ago. It's Mama Devi who you immediately want to stay with. Forever. It all comes from her."

"The sorcery?"

"Yes, the sorcery."

"So why did you come back? To say goodbye?"

He shook his head. "I wouldn't have come back at all. I didn't care about you because I—I no longer give a shit about anything else."

He squeezed my hand.

"Sorry, I'm telling it like it is. But she made me."

"Devi made you come back here? Why?"

"Exactly the reason you just gave. I'm too hysterical. I have to find a way to stay cool in the midst of the greatest ecstasy—that's how she put it. Look God straight in the eye without flinching. She said I had to get one whole lot stronger before the next initiation."

"Which is when?"

"Tomorrow."

"That's not a lot of time."

"She said I needed your coolness. Your skepticism. She said, 'This isn't some dumb little sex cult a cunning little Wog dreamed up to seduce the lost children of the West. This is the real thing.' She said I had to share with you, so I didn't start feeling so goddamn special, like a self-righteous Brit."

"She said 'goddamn'?"

"Yes." He smirked. "In that Oxford accent. She said 'self-righteous Brit' too. Just the sort of thing you would say."

Another question came to mind.

"But that middle-aged guy—you said he was American—he doesn't seem to fit at all."

Jeff smiled with just a lick of triumph.

"He's her zombie. I don't mean as in a Haitian half-wit. I mean he's so totally blown away by her, he's her spiritual slave."

"But that doesn't explain—"

"Why the girls seem to adore him? I don't know the answer to that. Yet."

He lay down next to me on the bed then, and I put my arm around him. I felt so strong, so solid—so much the other kind of Brit—and I realized how much I loved him. Me, the skeptic. I listened while he talked. I think he related, in perfect historical sequence, all of the major emotional events of his life. Then he fell asleep in my arms. After a while I disengaged myself and moved to the other bed so I could sleep. When I awoke the next morning he was already gone.

5.

I saw him for two more evenings after that. These encounters followed the same pattern. He would return at about 6 p.m., having experienced some form of ecstatic group sex-with-goddesses. He called each event an "initiation," and each one was deeper, fuller, more radical and inescapable. The word *hooked* didn't begin to describe what had happened to him. He told me less and less about the underlying philosophy, which he said was now "too deep to be defiled"—I presume by sharing with a philistine like me. The only good sign, if you can call it so, was that the hysteria diminished. It seemed he was growing in confidence in his new persona. But when I made this observation, he gave a patronizing smirk and said that his strength now came from having "no persona at all. That's all over, my friend, the delusion of self." He would sit down with his laptop and tap away furiously at the keys.

The next evening he returned only to tap away at his laptop for about an hour. Then he left me alone with instructions to check his computer diary if he did not return by morning. He scribbled his PIN access number on a scrap of paper.

By morning he had not returned, so I opened the laptop and entered Word. I was taken straight into the document he intended me to read:

> *The third day of any initiation is the most powerful. Mama Devi explained that to me before we started yesterday. Actually, the period is three and a half days. That's how long the subtle body takes to absorb the experiences fully into itself. I knew something even more bone shaking was about to occur, so that balance of extreme wonder and extreme terror reached such a pitch with me I had to force myself to concentrate simply in order to dress.*
>
> *They were waiting for me on the hill, as usual. They were further back from the temple, though, in deep jungle now. The girls were already naked. Devi, Rekha, Priyanka, and Malaiki were kneeling before the Shiva wheel that Mama Devi had brought. Devi explained yesterday the hidden meaning of the wheel: the god Shiva is dancing on a human form which is facing down, staring at earth. In such a state, man is simply a slave trampled on by a god. The only way out is to turn over to look at the god. That's what they were helping me to do, using sexual energy and the power of the kundalini, as modified for the modern world by Shiva himself, through Mahadevi.*
>
> *Mama Devi said: Your task today would be the envy of any young man. You must make love impeccably to each of the girls who are so generously making their bodies available for your salvation. There is a catch, though. These girls are themselves in a spiritual trance and will*

be very demanding. In normal circumstances it would be quite impossible for any man to satisfy all of them—or even just one of them. You must rely on the power of Shiva himself to enter your body and turn you into a god. There is simply no other option. If you fail, you risk death. I don't mean any of us would do you harm. We all hope you will succeed. But you must know that this force, which you have consented to take into you for three days now, reconfirming your free and unconditional commitment on each occasion, has reached a point where it could easily destroy your body one way or another. In other words, you are on your own with your god. With Shiva.

Priyanka was waiting for me. She was the first. She writhed like a snake with lust, called me to her with bloodshot eyes, caressing her breasts and cunt in a fever of sexual need. I felt a moment of fear, which I controlled just as Devi had taught. Instantly my body responded with a hard-on like a rock, except that it wasn't me, the horny, forked little human, who stood behind it, but Shiva himself who had entered me.

I went to her where she lay in the magic circle, on rough ground to which she was entirely indifferent, being possessed also by Shiva. I paid homage to her with my tongue until she could stand it no longer and dragged me up and onto her with incredible force. Shiva slid my erection into her with unbearable slowness, a millimeter a second it felt like, and she climaxed with each millimeter, groaning, gasping, and giving thanks to Shiva every time. Neither of us existed as a human personality at that moment. But Shiva forbade me to spill my sperm in her. When the tip of my cock reached the very limit of her vagina, she gave a great wail of surprise and burst into tears. They immediately pulled me off her at that moment. Devi explained that Shiva had used me to conquer the last hard remnants of her ego, and it would be dangerous for the health of her body to continue—the human form can only take so much reality.

They brought water and soap to wash me down like a horse. Devi herself took care of my penis, washing—almost scrubbing—it like a rough nurse in a military hospital. I think this was deliberate. Certainly the cleansing process brought me down to earth. Then Jack-the-Zombie brought a chillum for me to take a single toke from, and they led me into the jungle to take in the energy field in solitude.

About an hour later they came for me. Malaiki was there this time, naked and horny as hell at the center of the circle. I'd thought her personality was a good deal stronger than Priyanka's—and so it was. They had to hold her down while I licked her, because she wanted to take me into her right away. When finally Shiva took over me so that I would have the strength to enter her, and I penetrated through the first portal of her vagina, she gave a great shout, as if a devil had left her—and she climaxed like a tigress. So it went, and with each incremental penetration into the deeper mystery of her body, she yelled, groaned, moaned, and bucked like a bronco. Without Shiva I could never have managed. When it was over, my knees were bleeding and the area around my groin was bruised black from her bucking. This time they all gathered around to hug me, because my energy level was dangerously low after Shiva had left me.

Again they gave me just a single puff of cannabis to smoke and left me alone in the jungle, for more than three hours this time. I had to prepare for Rekha, the most enlightened of the three girls, the most perfected, the most dangerous. I knew that with her it would be quite *different. She is so advanced that Shiva would be able to use her to confront and enlighten me in subtle ways not available to the other two. I was not to go to her in daylight in the jungle, but at night in the holy central shrine of the sacred Citadel of Women itself, the holy of holies—to smash the last taboo with one almighty fuck! But Devi came to me where I was waiting and examined me carefully with eyes and hands, as if she were assessing the value of a bullock. Then she shook her head.*

"You're not ready, chela. If I let you go to her tonight, she'll kill you."

This news hit me in the solar plexus and caused me such grief that I fell to my knees, then to my stomach, so I could hold her feet and beg, the desire for the final consummation being so strong I would have much preferred to die than wait. But Mama Devi is hard as steel. She shook her head, and when I would not let go of her feet, kicked me in the face, then stamped on my hands and left. But I knew the rule: if a chela asks three times, the guru must consent. I called out three times: Tonight, Mama Devi. Tonight, Mama Devi. Tonight, Mama Devi.

She called back, already invisible in the thick bush. Her voice sounded almost mournful, muffled by the trees, creepers, and brush. "Very well. But you are on your own now. My job is done. My advice to you is to wait for at least a year—but that is only the view of a little human slave. Assess your relationship with the god. Be guided by him. Go back to your hotel now. Relax. Pray for guidance."

The document on the laptop ended there.

That was pretty heady stuff to absorb before my coffee and *pain au chocolat*. I took a tuk-tuk into the center of

Siam Reap, climbed the stairs to the café on the terrace, and ordered a beer. It was about an hour after dawn. My candy man, the waiter, had just started work. He waied me by putting his palms together and holding them to his lips. I did the same. Knowing from our previous transaction that I spoke Thai, he asked me in that language if I needed more ganja. After having breakfasted on Jeff's hallucinogenic journal, I wondered if what I really needed was a treble scotch, but I knew I'd want to smoke sooner or later that day, and my supply was running low, so I said, "*Toklong.*" Then I finished the beer in a couple of swallows. He brought the small zip-lock packet with the same grin, this time wrapped in the latest edition of the local English-language newspaper. I slipped the marijuana into my shorts pocket. Then, leaving the newspaper unread on the table while I finished my coffee, I gazed down on the street, which was slowly coming to life with tourists and traders, and the rising sun, which seemed to increase in heat and light at the rate of a degree a minute. The small quantity of alcohol, the pleasant, ever-increasing heat, the sane normality of the people on the street: all of these comforted me, and I began to see Jeff and his overwrought sex life in perspective. *What the hell, he'll get over it*, was a good summary of my mood. Then I flipped the newspaper over to look at the headlines.

There he was on the front page, his beautiful face now miserable, sagging and asymmetrical in death. "British Tourist Shot Trying to Enter Banteay Srey after Curfew," the headline ran. I froze in the morning heat.

I held myself together to beckon to the waiter and ask him in Thai to take all the dope he'd just given me and boil it in water. At first he refused, but I pointed to the photo and said, "*Pen puean*"—my friend. Then I started to sob and, like a good Buddhist, he went away and came back five minutes later with the ganja tea. By then I was pretty much a basket case, sobbing my heart out. Even the tea didn't have much effect.

6.

I saw from the start there was no point in forcing the issue at the British consulate in Phnom Penn, although I paid a duty visit. These were civil servants too far gone in Far Eastern decadence to be either, and anyway they were clearly afraid of everything Khmer, especially the government. I took a plane the same day back to Bangkok, spent a restless night in my condo, and made sure I was outside the British embassy in Wireless Road, along with the visa seekers and passport losers, half an hour before it opened.

Once through security, I asked to see someone I knew who worked there. Clare Smith was her name. I'd met her once at an embassy party for British expats. We'd shared enough beer and cheap wine to teeter on the verge of a good old drunken English hump, but I'd backed off as soon as the tropical night on the street hit me and I was reminded of how much more relaxed and, yes, civilized it would be to simply take a stroll down Soi Cowboy and pop into the Pink Pussy. That's exactly what I did, after agreeing with Clare that we must meet again soon—but without exchanging phone numbers. It was not merely her almost military insistence on being as tough about sex as any man—her version of liberation, I supposed—that ultimately had turned me off. It was her real job, the one she hadn't admitted to. The British Empire was once so vast that on it the sun never set, but I fancy then as now there were only two types who worked at our ten thousand embassies: the file shufflers and the spies. Clare Smith was too tough, too smart, too sharp, too aggressive to be a file shuffler. Now a spy was exactly what I needed. Was I the kind to prostitute himself for the sake of finding out how and why a good friend died? You bet.

She was thinner than I remembered, and better looking for it. That night I let her take me to the Sherlock Holmes, a trafficking point for the drug alcohol, located on lower Sukhumvit, and glugged draft ale while she ran the seduction, matching my consumption two to one. I was determined to make one condition, though, before she got into my knickers, and I put it to her when she was paying the bill.

"You're in Intelligence, MI6, right?"

Her pupils turned to pinheads. She hissed what I thought was the word *shit* and then jerked her head at the door.

Outside, she said, "Never, *never* do that in a public place. Especially not in a fucking English pub."

"So the answer's yes?"

She grunted. That it obviously had to be my place rather than hers—no one is more spied upon than the spies themselves—seemed to be an affirmative answer to my question, but I didn't press it. Her smarts, though, were good enough for her to realize that I was selecting her, in preference to all the other female services available in Krung Thep, for a reason. This was a transaction, in other words.

I guess I performed well enough to merit the payoff, for, after the regulation sweat-soaked twenty minutes, when we both lay back breathless and she asked if I minded if she smoked. Actually I did (I use tobacco only to keep a joint alight and would not object if they criminalized the carcinogenic poison), but of course I said, "No, go ahead."

She then said, "So, what did you want to know?"

"It's not drugs, women, children, terrorism, or human organs."

She took a long, slow toke.

"Then I'm not likely to be of any help, am I? Hope you haven't wasted your precious sperm, aye?"

She treated me to an elbow in the ribs. I do believe she was making a matey kind of joke.

I had already decided how to play it. I described the cult members—for that is how I now thought of them—without mentioning Jeff's violent death. As I spoke, touching in some detail on the woman in the sari, I watched her face while she frowned, inhaled, nodded, frowned, inhaled, then asked for somewhere to dump her ash.

"Yeah," she said, "I know about them. You're right about one thing: they're not kids, women, drugs, or any other trafficking. They've been watched by everyone. I'll find out for you."

"Watched by everyone?"

"CIA, feds, French, Dutch, German, Italian—half the secret world of the West is out here."

"Why?"

"Mostly because there's nowhere better. Forget James Bond and John le Carré. We're just a bunch of bums who like to get paid for being nosy. It's better than military or office work. Nobody wants Mexico or anywhere south of there, and Russia is Stone Age grim. So we find reasons to come out East—and watch. There are plenty of excuses, like you said: narcotics, women, children, terrorism. You've been watched lots, my friend. I even know you went down Soi Cowboy that night when you decided I wasn't sexy or submissive enough for you—'cos I checked with the bloke who was watching you at that time."

She turned to stare at me.

"I had quite a crush on you. I'm over it now. You're okay in bed, though. Anytime you're tired of brown sugar, let me know. I understand. If I was a bloke, I'd be the same. I know I would. For a while, anyway."

Then she looked at me in that way people do when they're delivering their personal philosophical punch line.

"Of course, one day you'll feel nostalgia for reality. Everyone does. I've been out here long enough to see that for certain. Who knows, I might still be available. Look me up when that day comes. Promise?"

"Sure," I said, and she dressed and was gone.

I was left in my big, empty condo, contemplating her last words. For a moment I saw it her way: I was an aging adolescent, like all the others, one of those Englishmen who waste their lives in a tropical fool's paradise, only to wake up one day and return like prodigal sons to the land of our mothers, where she, or someone like her—a no-nonsense adept of that mediocrity that the English in particular assert as the ultimate reality—would be waiting. Whereupon she would grunt, light a fag, drag me to the sack for a hump or two, then lead me triumphantly by the hand all the way to the pub, where she would introduce me to her drinking gang, and we would get sloshed and go home for another hump. After a few weeks the humping would diminish as the beer intake increased, and our little circle of alcoholics would grow ever more incestuous—and that would be it for the duration, until we all ended by coughing up our livers in a National Health hospital.

And I realized, looking out from my balcony at the dense black hammerhead cloud, visible thanks to the brilliant city lights, that she was wrong. Quite wrong. And that somehow poor Jeff, too, had had just that same realization. The intensity he died for was the reality, not the grim, gray, soggy nightmare to which Clare Smith paid her dues.

From that startling revelation it was but a short step to finally acknowledging to myself why I was pursuing Jeff's killers—if that was what they were—with such passionate intensity. It was their mystery, not their guilt, that I was after.

7.

Clare Smith was as good as her word. And of course the email was anonymous, without title or power of reply, so that I almost deleted it automatically, as I do with all spam. Fortunately, I was still slow from my herbal inhaling the night before (I had needed at least two joints to calm my nerves after the loveless romp with MI6) and absent-mindedly opened the attachment. Then I stared and stared. It was the address of some kind of philosophical society opposite the British Museum in Great Russell Street, WC1B, London, England. The Anglo-Asian Science of Thought Institute.

It was not the name that intrigued me, but the street. I happened to know that a certain building in Great Russell Street had been, perhaps still was, the headquarters of a well-known outfit dating back to the beginning of the twentieth century, which could honestly claim to be the first serious attempt by Westerners to come to terms with what is often called Oriental Wisdom. And what a hash they had made of their investigation, perverting the most sophisticated thought system devised by man into some kind of Victorian spiritualism, like an ape playing with a laptop. The Indian woman in the sari with the exaggerated Oxford dialect came to mind, and a shiver ran down my spine.

8.

I traveled cattle class on a certain British airline. The cabin crew were the usual graceless morons who made you feel you were shackled to the seat in a flying prison van, and the food would have been banned if offered as animal feed. It was November and raining when I arrived in the city of my birth. At first I was pleasantly surprised. Money had been thrown at it, albeit in uneven dollops, so that many downtown buildings I remembered as dirt gray now gleamed, and there was plenty of hip and cool. The facelift was hardly seamless, though, and did not seem to have affected the inhabitants, who struck me as the same weird mixture I remembered of self-righteous, self-pitying, and hard-boiled. I emerged from the Underground at Tottenham Court Road and walked to Great Russell Street.

I found the building and the first floor office apartment without difficulty. The front door bore the acronym AASTI in brass but was locked. There was no bell or knocker, so I rapped with my knuckles. There was stirring within and a sound so faint it could have been whispers or paper rustling under a fan. Then there were slow footsteps. A latch was unlocked. The door opened. The man whom Jeff had described as Devi's zombie stood

before me in jeans and a thick sweater with a quizzical expression. Behind him I glimpsed a woman in a sari.
"Who is it, Jack?"
The accent was high Oxford.
"Who are you?" Jack asked.
"Jeff's best friend," I said.

9.

"D.H. Lawrence was a reincarnate," Mama Devi said, touching her long gray hair. Her sari flowed from her shoulders like a many-colored river all the way to the floor, where she sat next to what must have been one of London's last genuine fireplaces. There was no fire, of course, merely a very old-fashioned two-bar electric heater. I sat on the other side of the heater, which kept me warmer than toast at the front of my body and shivering cold at the back. This was the London I remembered. Jack had disappeared somewhere into the depths of the eighteenth-century edifice.

"I'm using that word as a technical term borrowed from the Tibetans," she added.

"Meaning?"

"Meaning that without necessarily knowing it in that lifetime, that entity had been initiated into the Tantra, of which kundalini yoga is the most sophisticated expression, in a previous incarnation, and had elected to offer his wisdom to the West at a crucial moment. Everything good that has ever happened to Western civilization has come from the East, but we don't need to go into that. The point is that he was the clue. A very big, important sign the god sent to us that day, concerning your friend. It was he, not one of my party, who initiated the first contact by invoking that great reincarnate."

"He fancied the pants off of one of your acolytes," I said.

"Exactly. That was the other clue."

"But I fancied her as well. I would have screwed her standing on the top deck of a number nineteen bus in a rush hour if I'd had the chance."

Devi gave a mirthless smile.

"Let us stick to the point, shall we?"

"Which is what?"

"Which is that less than a couple of miles from the most spiritually charged space on earth, during the briefest possible window of time, your late friend contacted my most advanced chela by reference to a revered reincarnate. All we did was to accept his application and proceed to initiate him according to his talent, which was great in all respects except one."

I raised my eyebrows.

"He was too sensitive. Contrary to what laypeople believe, sensitivity is as much of a handicap as an advantage. True, he understood each of his levels of initiation without difficulty. But he lacked the resistance to withstand the onslaught from the god. I myself warned him, but he disregarded me. A spiritual master has no choice but to permit the karma of a chela to unfold at such times."

She looked at me curiously.

"Much better to be a skeptic of more robust build who approaches us after overcoming certain difficulties thrown in his path."

I didn't like the implication and looked away. When I looked back into her eyes, her mood had quite changed. Her voice rang like steel.

"Let us cut to the chase. The West is quickly discovering that the karma of five hundred years of genocide, mass murder, grand larceny, slavery, mutilation, narco empires, world wars, ruthless exploitation, barbarism, and ignorance inflicted on the whole of the rest of humanity is finally beginning to bite back. Anyone, anyone at all—you for example—born into a Western culture today has a choice: run for your life or spend the next hundred incarnations trying to clean up the mess in the most grindingly depressing conditions."

I stared at her.

"And by the way, sir, are you not being something of a hypocrite—or should I say schizophrenic?"

I had an inkling of what might be coming next, but I was too fascinated to stop her. There is no subject on earth more riveting than oneself.

"You pretend skepticism, but you know far too much about Angkor's secret meanings to be other than something of a minor reincarnate yourself."

I gasped.

"You, far more than your late friend, are the one who ran away—or should I say the one who *got* away?"

Her mood and expression changed in an instant. Now she was looking at me with benevolence, kindness, compassion, and wisdom.

"Come on, Frank, you must have thought the unthinkable at least once or twice since Jeff died."

"Huh?"

At this moment Jack returned. He was wearing a long yellow robe, with a necklace of dark wooden beads. Except it wasn't Jack. It's hard to explain, but it wasn't him. The body was the same, but the personality had altered radically. He radiated to melt stone. Devi saw that I saw.

"You see what the god can do when it wants to?"

"It?"

"All the gods are androgynous. Why stick to one sex when you have no biological body to limit your choices? But let us not digress. Face it, Frank. Look at the evidence, think it over, take your time. I have no interest in taking on another chela. To be honest, it is very difficult work, and I would be much happier retiring to an ashram in Poona, but I have to fulfill my karma of this life like everyone else."

"What do you mean?"

"That it was—is—*you* whom the god wants. You are the supremely qualified one. Jeff died for you, my friend. Without your knowing it consciously, he was the sacrifice you offered to the god. Yes, we are talking human sacrifice—I think you've been out of the padded playpen long enough to absorb that challenging truth. The god accepted the homage. Your deep, angry contempt for the West and the country of your birth is a symptom, a tell-tale sign of the raging thirst of your spirit."

She shrugged.

"Take it or leave it. But remember this. Jeff died attempting to enter Angkor at night against my advice. He took the risk with full knowledge of what he was doing."

"How do you mean?"

"There is no initiation without the presence of death. In the final initiation there has to be a clear and present risk of annihilation of the body—so has it been for ten thousand years, since the Aryan invasion."

She nodded to Jack, who approached us. I would never have believed that corrupt body was capable of such grace of movement, such elegance, such over-brimming love.

"See?" Devi said. "See what the god can do even with the most grotesque decadent if only he has the will—the desperation—to go all the way. Go now, and think about it."

I stood in automatic obedience to someone more powerful than I.

"But—"

"It's no good asking me for the details. I haven't the faintest idea. The god will arrange all things—or not, according to its will."

10.

A year has passed. It is 1 a.m. on the outskirts of the Citadel of Women. It is visible only as stupa shapes of a deeper darkness than the night itself. As at any Hindu temple, one is led progressively from outer squares to inner squares until one arrives at the womb where the god's linga is permanently impregnated. That is where Rekha is waiting for me, silently willing me to succeed where Jeff failed, her consciousness raised, like mine, to the highest pitch by the imminence of death.

I am dressed in black. My face, also, I have blackened with a mixture of grease and ashes. My shoes, too, are black—black as the moonless night, you might say. I've been searching for a way to get past the guards for over two hours. They are far more vigilant than I would have imagined and, like all Khmer, they shoot on sight without a moment's hesitation. I passed the other initiations after dark in the outer rings of the temple earlier this week. There were a few slips—nothing serious. Devi's tame guard arranged everything, but I am without his protection now.

Rekha's body is a source of unquenchable fever to me. Each time I licked her cunt I experienced the taste of nectar. When I took her breasts hungrily into my starving mouth, I knew the meaning of ambrosia. When I entered her hungry vagina I was taken up, up, far above the earth where I watched our writhing bodies while I merged with the cosmos. I've had no sex with anyone other than Devi's three female chelas since that squalid fuck with MI6 (the memory revolts me). My learning curve has been subtly different to Jeff's, for, as Devi says, I'm a tougher customer. But it comes to the same thing in the end. I must slip past the ring of fire if I am to achieve the final consummation. I've timed my break-in to the moment when the guard with his combat rifle makes his turn and a split-second window of opportunity arises. I am a single fragile flame in an ocean of annihilation that may close on me at any moment. This knowledge is making me horny as hell, but I've learned to control my libido. If I make it, I will literally enter the transformed body of the divine. Even if I fail, I'll never have to return to London, not in the next five hundred incarnations. It's a crack worth the *coup*.

John Burdett

John Burdett was brought up in North London and attended Warwick University where he read English and American Literature. This left him largely unemployable until he re-trained as a barrister and went to work in Hong Kong. He made enough money there to retire early to write novels. To date he has published seven novels, including the best selling Bangkok series: *Bangkok 8*, *Bangkok Tattoo*, *Bangkok Haunts*, *The Godfather of Kathmandu*, and *Vulture Peak*.

Reunion

Christopher G. Moore

I'd lost contact with Rith Samnang—his given name translated as Lucky in Khmer—after he was sent to prison in California. By that time he'd shortened and Americanized his name to Sam and used the American style of putting the family name after the given name. He was Sam Rith in America. Sam was never a regular correspondent. Dropping out of a person's mind and life takes time, aided by long periods of silence. It had been a long time since I'd heard from Rith Samnang. His old sponsor, George Anderson, had written me that Sam Rith had been deported to Cambodia after he'd served seven years in prison for armed robbery. After that I'd lost contact with the Andersons. If the truth be told, we may have agreed without saying anything that continuing to exchange emails about Sam was just too goddamn painful.

And the Andersons believed in God.

George and Laura Anderson felt that Sam's prison time and later deportation were their fault, that his failure to adjust to a new life in America had been caused by something they had done or said, or should have said or done. Guilt triggers shame, the feeling that we could have and should have done more. Feelings emerge that

Reunion

make us doubt ourselves as the kind of person who does the right thing.

The Andersons of Sacramento, California—good, religious people—had sponsored Rith Samnang in 1984. That year he had turned fifteen years old. I sometimes wonder whether, if Sam had gone to the States when he was ten, things might have turned out differently. It is difficult to know. I've known of other cases where the kid arrived in America at five years of age and his life crashed and burned very much like Sam's. The fact remains: although the teenage years are a troubled period filled with conflict wherever they are, a teenager who'd survived the Killing Fields, refugee camps, and relocation had to overcome things no ordinary teenager ever had to face. This isn't to condone Sam's robberies. He committed the crime, and he served the time. Isn't that what Americans say is the way things are in the United States of America?

I understood the Andersons' guilt over Sam's problems. In fact, I don't believe in any religion, but I've learned that you don't need to be religious to share in guilt. In fact, non-believer's guilt may be worse as there are no prayers, rituals, or priesthood to see you through the dark moments when guilt pulls you off the road and beats the shit out of you. What you do is find a way to deal with the guilt by some act of redemption. This story is a stab in the dark at that redemption target.

I am a career journalist at the tail end of a long ride, and before I lay down my pen (I still use a regular notebook and pen), I want to clear my conscience about the boy named Rith Samnang, who became the convicted felon named Sam Rith. Over the course of my career my edge didn't come from being a great wordsmith—I wasn't— but from being one of those people willing to go into a war zone and come back with what I had witnessed for a wire service. Fancy writing would have got me fired. But I was good at finding just the right detail that would tell the story, hit hard and low, and knock the readers off their chairs. That's enough for most editors. But you had to be a true believer in some cause, or crazy, to volunteer to go into places where people were being blown up, shot, cut up, tortured. You read the papers. You come across this stuff daily. But up close and in your face is a different experience from seeing the words in black and white in a newspaper.

Most journalists I knew from my time in Thailand, Burma, and Cambodia were not war-zone true believers; they were crazy, hard-drinking, hard-living, short-lived people who, if they stopped doing what they did, would fall off the edge. The adrenaline rush at the front is addictive. Ask anyone who's ever been there, and they'll tell you the same thing. Rith Samnang had the journo's battlefield junkie addiction from age nine or ten. Think about it. You're a veteran before your age hits double digits. What is laid down in the mind of such a person changes them into something few people can understand.

But I thought I understood Sam. Fools and romantics are always mistaking some wild hopes and dreams for an understanding of the world—until one day the evidence blasts their dreams into gecko-sized bits, like being on the wrong end of a double-barreled shotgun.

I had my press pass—a little green hardback book—my access card at the main gate to a large processing camp in Chon Buri province. In the early 1980s not many journalists covered the refugee camps. Editors said that their readers weren't interested. I went on spec. No assignment, just an instinct that I'd find a story. In a way

Reunion

I was a "camp follower" from 1979, when the refugees started pouring over the Cambodian border with the Vietnamese in hot pursuit. That was a story with drama, blood, and guts, the stuff that editors liked. Victims of the Vietnamese army who shot women and children as they sought to escape to Thailand made good copy—though a fair amount of the killing had been done by the Khmer themselves to discourage desertion. The rank and file saw the endgame and wanted out. I'd reported on that story, too. I first saw Rith Samnang in the early '80s.

What I remember most about him, as a fifteen-year-old kid who looked no older than twelve, was his goofy smile, lopsided on a skeleton of a body. He'd adjusted to camp culture, the lack of water, electricity, squalid huts, the muddy roads in the rainy season, the barbed wire fences that kept the refugees in. It was a glorified concentration camp without the deadly showers, but after the life Sam had escaped from, the camp was a slice of heaven on earth.

Perspective is something you learn in a war zone. Someone was always more physically and mentally fucked up than the person you interviewed the day before.

Sam. The boy. The operator. He offered to be my guide that first day.

"You speak Khmer?" he asked.

I shook my head.

That's when I saw his goofy smile, the one that was a reflex action to a chance to score.

"I translate for you. Free," he said. "You no pay Samnang. Good luck for you to meet me. And you can call me Sam."

Sam led the way through the sandy, dirty, hot camp, along a dirt road lined with shacks made from bamboo and tin, the roofs covered with grass. Inside this city of shacks lived thousands of Cambodian refugees, waiting to be relocated to other countries. Orphans, old people, people without legs or arms or eyes, couples with babies crying—all of them waiting for the next meal or the next scrap of information about their case. Sam guided me down a side lane to a bamboo structure that functioned as a makeshift restaurant, and we went straight to (what I later learned was) Sam's table. I bought him a plate of rice and pork. He inhaled the food. I bought him a second plate. It was as if an inexhaustible vacuum hovered over the plate, the food vanishing in moments.

He told me how the local police made their money from the rice and other food, but the big money came from smuggled cigarettes and whiskey. I made notes as Sam sipped a bottle of Coke. "They make money from this, too," he said, holding up the empty bottle, and the owner returned a moment later with another bottle and put it in front of Sam. Corruption, extortion, and violence weren't the words he used. But they figured into my report about the camp. Through Sam's help I found a number of refugees who had stories about how the camps were run.

True to his word, Sam never asked for any money. But he did okay on food and smokes and a bottle of whiskey—all of which I paid for. By the end of the day, six o'clock, tired from the heat and the flies, sick of the smell of sewage, and my head pounding, I looked around at the shacks on the dirt road and reminded myself of how few people understood how deep was the gutter of life that people on the run from a war zone fell into. Crawling back to ground level took all the courage and strength and faith such people could muster.

"I want to go to America," Sam said. "Can you help me?"

Reunion

That question must have been asked of reporters hundreds, if not thousands, of times as they walked through a refugee camp. But even the most battle-hardened correspondents felt something in the pit of their stomach when a kid like Sam begged for help. We weren't aid workers. We were journalists, and our mission was to help ourselves to the facts as we found them on the ground. The people who were part of those facts, they didn't fit into column inches. They weren't our business.

Or so I told myself.

"Kid, I'd like to help."

I looked around at the people along the road. Each of them wanted out. Tired of waiting, hoping, and merely existing. After a day in the camp you felt exhausted and couldn't wait to leave. Sam had been in one camp or another for five years. He'd spent endless days and nights trying to stay sane, waiting for his fortune to change. He'd suffered his fair share of disappointments and false starts, broken promises, and bullshit artists.

"It's okay," Sam said. "Some other time."

He offered me his hand. I shook it.

"Let me see what I can do. No promises. Everyone in the camp wants a shortcut to America. Your chances of cutting to the front of the line aren't great."

This was more than just covering my ass, which was the only way you survived in camps, war zones, or journalism; it was making certain Sam didn't get the idea that I was going to be his ticket to America. I don't believe in capital punishment except for one offense: fucking with people's dreams and hopes. Put those bastards against the nearest wall and shoot them.

I had interviewed aid workers for The Consortium of Save the Children, World Education, and The Experiment in International Living under the US State Department support. I'd done a favor for a woman from Oregon a few months earlier. She'd needed a letter delivered to the right person at the American embassy in Bangkok. I had delivered the letter and seen that she got the response she needed. It seemed trivial at the time: Sarah Cohen—yes, Jews worked for Christian relief agencies, too—had an inheritance issue once her father died, and the lawyers in America needed a document notarized.

"I'll see what I can do," said Sarah Cohen as she sat in her small office.

Six months later, Rith Samnang, aka Sam Rith, true to his Khmer name of Lucky, got his relocation papers to California. The Andersons agreed to sponsor him. When Sarah wrote me a letter to tell me about it, I thought the kid must be on a winning streak.

The truth was his luck gauge had registered empty long before the Americans deported him back to Cambodia. He was in glide mode, hoping for a tailwind to get him over the hump of life. After ten years in America his luck ran out. Ages fifteen to twenty-five are some of the best years of a man's life. When seven out of ten of those formative years are spent locked up inside an American prison, the man at twenty-five carries some damage. He's a walking bundle of wounds. In Sam's life, the damage had already been inflicted before his prison time. He'd already spent five years inside hardscrabble refugee camps along the Thai-Khmer border and in Chon Buri. An American prison was an easy ride.

To a refugee camp alumnus with the equivalent of a five-year degree in the art of survival, a California prison looked like an elite graduate school filled with small-time legacy students. Factor in his time lugging weapons through Khmer Rouge–controlled villages and

Reunion

fields, and you had a man who had gone through the worst of what life can dish up. Each stage of his life had brought him under the thumb of a new set of men with guns: the Khmer rouge, Thai cops in the camps, and American prison guards. He'd been handed from group to group, and after a while he had trouble imagining a life that wasn't lived under the shadow of uniformed men wielding guns and the power of life and death.

When you live abroad so long, you associate people from your past with the technology of the time. Sam emerged with graying hair from my rotary-phone and letter-writing past. When I received an email from him six months earlier, it seemed strange. That he had tracked me down on the Internet and written me was something remarkable. And he wanted to befriend me on Facebook. He asked if I'd like to renew our friendship.

"Sam, good to hear from you."

Next thing, we were talking on Skype. How the world had changed.

"I'm going to Phnom Penh to cover the UN war crime trial," I said.

"You can't get Cambodia out of your blood."

I saw him on the video feed, now a forty-three-year-old man with the same goofy fifteen-year-old boy's smile. He had a point. Some places and experiences, if they come to your life early enough, find a way of sticking with you. No matter what happens next in your life, you can't quite shake the emotional lice that have nested in your soul.

"I can be your translator," he said.

"I know, and I don't have to pay you."

"I didn't say that."

"But you were going to."

"Deal? Food for words, just like the old days."

"Deal."

"One more thing."

With Sam there was always one more thing.

"I have an invitation to talk at the Foreign Correspondents' Club in Bangkok."

The Foreign Correspondents' Club of Thailand had some of the best panel discussions in the country, bringing in experts, old hands, frontline witnesses from Burma, Cambodia, and Laos, as well as Thailand.

"How did they find you?"

"I found them. I said I could talk about the Khmer Rouge. And I could translate for them if that would help."

Bingo. A translator, storyteller, and Killing Fields survivor bundled together. That would have pushed the right buttons on the committee that arranged panel discussions. The sex industry, Burmese raping and pillaging, and the Khmer Rouge always made for big-draw nights at the club. People like Sam, who grew up in refugee camps, knew where to look for an angle. With the UN war crime tribunal about to get down to the serious business of trying the surviving leaders of the Khmer Rouge, Cambodia was a news item again.

"When are you talking at the club?"

"In two months."

"If you need a place to stay ..."

Before I could finish, he said, "I need a ticket."

The club wouldn't pay for his ticket. I should have seen that one coming. It was like being on the street and seeing someone lower their rifle at you. You don't ignore it; you don't smile and wave. You hit the ground, dust in your nose and mouth as you crawl for cover. That's the thing with getting old: your reflexes and instincts go dull.'

"But I don't have the money for a ticket."

I let a pause draw out a little too long.

Sam spoke next. "I can always borrow the money."

"I'll send you a ticket."

"You're a good man, Tony."

"I am a fucking idiot."

He laughed and that ended the call.

I wired him the money; Sam bought the ticket. He had bigger stakes in mind, the cynic in me said. He'd broken the hearts of the Andersons. Not by design—he wouldn't have intended to hurt the sponsors who'd gone to all the trouble to give him a new life in America. You can take the boy out of the refugee camp, but you can't take the camp out of the boy or man. The phrase is one you heard expats use when talking about bar girls. The fact—and journalism is founded on them like termites on a large mound—is that a tight subculture creates an identity that never quite goes away. When Sam Rith looked in the mirror, he saw the boy named Rith Samnang staring back, the kid who was the go-between with the cops and the restaurant owner, who supplied him with smuggled cigarettes and whiskey.

I was waiting at the airport to pick up Sam. His flight had arrived on time. I paced the small patch outside the arrivals area, just beyond the invisible line that separated arriving passengers who'd cleared immigration and customs from those waiting for them. Working an invisible border was something Sam and I had in common. We knew how close we could get to one, and how to navigate a perimeter without being too obvious. Those who survived that sort of thing were the ones who knew the dangers of getting stranded in no-man's-land. But to get through the minefields, they also had to have luck on their side.

Minefields made me concentrate, focus, and observe the finest of details. Waiting for Sam at the airport had that effect.

I recognized him immediately, even though Sam had become a middle-aged man dressed in a white shirt and dark trousers, and his hair was flecked with gray. I knew that it was Sam as soon as he emerged through the automatic doors. He pulled a case on a roller behind him, searching the crowd of airport limo touts looking for victims to fleece for limo service into Bangkok. His eyes lighted on me and then kept moving, only to return a moment later.

"Mr. Tony!" he shouted and ran through the gauntlet of touts.

"Sam."

That's all I could get out. It was an emotional reunion.

He wiped away a tear as he hugged me. That tear was for what? Not the old correspondent standing in the airport with a copy of the *Bangkok Post* folded under his arm. No, it was for the ten-year-old kid, then the fifteen-year-old kid, and the one who'd gone to prison. That's what reunions normally produce: memories of what we've been through, who we've been, what we've become, and how all those trails have suddenly merged together in an arrival hall in Bangkok.

"Hey, man, you look exactly the same," he said, sniffling.

That was a lie. But it was an okay one.

"You don't look fifteen years old, Sam."

"Was I ever fifteen?" he asked. "Was I?"

Good question, I thought, looking him over. We both knew it was the key to everything else we'd be talking about over the next couple of days.

"I can't ever remember being fifteen myself," I said.

"I remember things. Like every day I spent in the camps."

Being a fifteen-year-old running a smuggling and contraband operation out of a mom-and-pop shack of a restaurant, negotiating with the cops, watching his back for others who wanted what he had, which wasn't much—that background existed in a galaxy light years away from the one that modern kids lived in with their iPads, shopping malls, and video games.

Back at my place, I walked him to the spare bedroom, opened the door, and flipped on the light. Hanging from the ceiling were a couple dozen streamers that said, "Welcome back, Sam!"

He stood in the doorway frozen. He blinked back tears.

"I need a moment, Tony. If that's okay."

I left him to unpack his case, hang up a couple of shirts and a pair of trousers, and stuff his underwear and socks in the drawer. Afterwards he came out and joined me on the balcony. He found me sitting back with my legs crossed and resting on the iron railing.

"Take a seat. We have a little while before going to the club."

"I appreciate what you've done for me, Tony."

"I didn't do much, Sam. That's the truth. Have a beer and relax. That's the Chao Phraya River below. The River of Kings."

"'Cry Me a River'—you know that song?" he asked.

I nodded.

"I think I wrote that song a long time ago."

"That would make you a rich man."

We looked at the lights strung around the decks of a couple of tugboats. A large floating restaurant boat cruised past. A ferry crossed from one side of the river to the other—the Oriental Hotel ferry, taking guests to their restaurant on the opposite bank. Sam drank from a bottle of Tiger beer that I handed him, not taking his eyes off the Chao Phraya River.

"Nice place, Tony."

"Small but comfortable."

Small as in small talk. The two of us sat watching the river and trying to think of what to say that wasn't some fucking monster of a cliché. Having emptied a full sack of them at the airport had left us both a bit embarrassed and was now drawing us into silence.

"You nervous about tonight?" I asked him.

"I don't mind talking about what happened. Water under the bridge."

"People will want to know about Pol Pot, the Khmer fucking Rouge, and how the whole thing happened."

"They think I know that?"

Sam shrugged, took another long swig from his beer, rolled the beer around inside his mouth, and then swallowed.

"I thought you knew and were just holding back all these years."

"You're still the same as before. Why don't you tell them what happened? You saw more than me."

"The people at the club tonight don't want to hear what I have to say. They want to hear you. But the good news is, they'll be on your side. You won't be needing anyone to watch your back."

Reunion

. Sam took a moment to reflect on my words.

"An audience on my side? That will be a first," he said.

That was the first hint of bitterness I'd ever heard from Sam, and he saw the look of surprise on my face.

"I've been trying to come to terms with all the shit that happened."

He stopped to finish his beer. Another ferry crossed the river, and we both watched as it headed toward the lights of the dock near the Oriental Hotel.

"Talking about it helps," I said.

"That's the theory," he said. "Don't mind me, I'm a little edgy. I'm not used to talking to audiences who want to listen. Most of my audiences have been looking for some excuse to beat the shit out of me, kill me, or throw me in a camp or cell."

"Why don't you tell the audience that tonight?" I said.

The drive from my condo to the Foreign Correspondents' Club in Bangkok took over thirty minutes. We crossed the Sathorn Bridge. The traffic was backed up on a Wednesday with office commuters in their air-conditioned cars.

As my car inched along Sathorn Road, Sam rubbernecked at the high-rise office towers and condos. Chrome and glass buildings like giant spaceships. That fifteen-year-old kid I remembered from the Chon Buri refugee camp had broken out of his cage, trying to figure out where he was, what it meant, and how he could survive. For most people the first time in Bangkok, like many firsts in life, left a mixture of feelings. It wasn't what they expected. For someone who'd lived through the Killing Fields and the refugee camps, modern Bangkok registered the yawning gap between those who ran the refugee camps and those who were confined inside.

"Phnom Penh will look like this one day," I said. The whole world was headed down the same path.

"Hundreds of cities in China are already starting to look like this. In a few years all the cities will look the same."

Sam looked doubtful.

"Maybe in a hundred years," he said.

"You'll want to live on a higher floor," I said. "Once the ice caps melt, most of Bangkok will be underwater."

Trying to joke with Sam did little to lift his mood. I concentrated on my driving and left him to stare out the window.

The vast structures of cement, steel, and glass, lit against the night, reminded him of the poverty of his own life. Sam had never been to Bangkok. Like the first sexual experience, it was all thrills and awe as the surroundings pulled him outside what he'd previously thought about the world. The condos and office towers showed their best at night—cones of light, dark shadows, power and money—producing in Sam the desired wow factor.

He kept asking me, "Tony, who owns all of these buildings? How did they get so much money?"

"Rich people," I told him. "With connections and influence."

The kind of people who wouldn't attend a Foreign Correspondents' Club meeting to hear Sam talk about his experience at the hands of the Khmer Rouge. Refugee camp survivor stories didn't fit inside their bubble.

Once we'd stepped off the lift at the penthouse level of the Maneeya Building, Sam walked to the bank of windows that overlooked the city. He stood framed against the night sky outside, losing himself in the vastness of Bangkok below.

"With all of this, why do they want to listen to anything I have to say about the past?"

"They'd be interested in what you think about the possibility of justice being delivered by the war crimes tribunal."

At least I was interested in knowing Sam's view on the matter. He turned away from the window.

"Justice? Or peace?"

He repeated the words as if reciting a mantra as we walked through the club entrance. Sam was guided along the main floor to the table where the other speakers and club officers sat, while I slid onto a stool at the bar and ordered a beer. The room was packed.

Aside from Sam, other members of the Wednesday evening panel on the Khmer Rouge war crimes tribunal were a human rights lawyer and two more survivors of the Killing Fields. The middle-class audience of embassy workers, NGO staff, UN officials, and journalists listened in silence as each of the panelists told their story. But the thing about atrocities is after a while they blend into the skin, blood, bones, meat, and gristle of a vast abattoir. Describe one room in an abattoir, and you've described them all.

The human rights lawyer explained how the court had been created, the role of the judges, the politics of the charges, and the purpose of the exercise. His was a bloodless, intellectual account that eased the audience from the horror stories told by those who had witnessed the Khmer Rouge cannibalizing their own kind.

Massive state-organized violence runs on an assembly line, where efficiency and mindless repetition numb the torturer and remove the faces of the victims, even for those hearing the story years later. As with the ongoing parade of drowning victims or car crash victims, after a while, it's difficult to keep the individuals straight; they blend into an abstraction, one big Victim with a capital V who is indistinguishable from the next.

It would be wrong of me to leave the impression that members of the club were unmoved by what they heard that evening, or that somehow the speakers' individual stories came across as boring or pointless. The impact was the opposite. Stories by the two men and one woman who had survived were nugget-sized and easily consumed, if not easily digested. Each of the Khmers had been lucky. Each had come within a hair's breadth of being cut up as some product destined for soap, leather, steak loin, or candles; they had defied the odds and lived through the Khmer Rouge reign of terror. Each spoke without notes, drawing on personal experiences. The Khmer woman, Nuon, with hands folded, fingered a wedding ring as she spoke. She addressed the audience in Khmer—Sam translated for her—about how she'd been forced against her will into a marriage to a soldier.

The cadre in Nuon's work camp had chosen her husband. She'd had no choice. At first, she had resisted, but one night several members of the cadre came to Nuon's shack and raped her as her chosen husband stood nearby. He'd been ordered to watch. She'd had two children from the forced "marriage." Neither had survived. The father had had doubts about whether he was the father of the eldest boy. Nuon remembered her husband telling the son that he was the son of Angkar, the Communist Party. Sam carefully translated her words from Khmer into English as if he was watching a documentary of Nuon's life.

Another panelist, a slight man with a hint of a stutter named Kiri, spoke about hiding on the prison grounds of

Tuol Sleng and watching guards torture prisoners using garden tools, knives, ropes, chains ... anything sharp or with an edge that might inflict pain. The guards were teenagers who had absolute power.

But it was Sam's night. He told a story he'd told hundreds of times. I'd first heard it at the restaurant at the Chon Buri camp. But by the time of that night at the club, he'd had a lot more years to refine and polish the story until it shone like a hard, cruel blue diamond. Sam explained how the Khmer Rouge had kidnapped him and used him as a porter along the front line in Battambang. The unit he was attached to had overrun an enemy position, killing four soldiers. The Khmer Rouge hadn't eaten in some days. The unit leader was a man named Nimol. He was twenty years old, and his name translated as Flawless.

Nimol slowly pulled out his knife, the light of the campfire flames glimmering along the edge of the blade. He sat on his haunches and used the knife to cut away a dead soldier's uniform. Nimol tapped the dead man's belly with his thumb, moving his hand in a circular fashion as if tracing a line. With the tip of the knife he cut into the flesh. Happy as his work progressed, he looked over at his comrades and smiled. He appeared to know what he was doing. After a few minutes he held the dead soldier's liver in two bloody hands.

Nimol lifted himself away from the body, which he gave a kick. He turned toward the campfire and dropped the liver onto a small grill. He poked the soft, bloody meat with the tip of the knife. The other men sat around the fire watching the liver cook. Every couple of minutes, the Khmer with the knife jabbed at the meat. Then he slipped the blade underneath and flipped it over. Sam had stayed some distance away. The men didn't like him near the food or supplies. Like the others, Sam hadn't eaten for a couple of days.

Once Nimol judged that the liver was cooked, as chief butcher and chef, he slipped the sizzling meat onto a bamboo mat. He cut off a piece and popped it into his mouth, grinning and chewing. He had seen Sam sitting by himself off to the side, clinging to the shadows, hugging his knees, the blood drained from his face, hoping to make himself so small he'd disappear. Nimol called Sam over to the campfire.

"You ever eat a man's liver?"

Sam shook his head.

"How old are you, boy?"

"Almost ten."

The soldier nodded.

"You want to be a man?"

Sam nodded.

"You eat your enemy's liver. That makes you a man. You understand?"

Sam shivered from the sudden realization that he truly had no choice in the matter. When Nimol spoke, he spoke for Angkar. Everyone knew that it was extremely dangerous to question one of the cadre. The answer to a comrade always had the same form: "Yes, I understand."

The good soldier Nimol cut off a hunk of liver and extended his hand with the knife outstretched.

"Then eat."

The other soldiers watched, looking between the boy and their leader, holding the knife. They had learned to look scared; it was the expected way to show their respect to a senior comrade. Much older comrades had been afraid of Nimol, too. True believers of Angkar inspired fear. Nimol said they were doing this for Angkar. In truth, men like this comrade were tough not because they ate an enemy's liver but because they believed in something more powerful than all of the ghosts and restless spirits that had frightened their families.

Sam told his story in a flat, conversational voice as if he were talking about the plot of a movie he'd seen. One of the women in the audience fainted. Another left the room to vomit. Khmer Rouge stories had that effect on people whose lives had been sheltered inside the bubble of office complexes, shopping malls, condos, and international airports. Most of the people in the room had never been hungry, had never seen anyone die of starvation. This was the class of people that had maids and cooks who went to the markets and prepared their food. All they ever saw on a table was food someone else had cooked.

In the question-and-answer session that followed, Sam was asked by one of the NGO staff members if he ever had nightmares about that night.

Sam said: "It was only one night. Until I escaped over the border to Thailand, I had hundreds of nights with the Khmer Rouge. No one night of sleep has enough room for what I witnessed to haunt my dreams. A nightmare visits you in sleep because one bad thing happened when you were a child. But if a thousand evil things have happened to you, they cancel each other out. You are numb. That means no pain. It also means it was normal. Hunger, fear, anger were normal, too. It's only when I talk to a room of important people that I can see on your faces I've said something freakish."

Sam had been a hit at the club. They didn't get many smiling ex-cannibals on their panels.

I arranged for Sam to hire transportation in Phnom Penh, and he showed up at my hotel behind the wheel of a dented and faded fifteen-year-old white Toyota. An old NGO car he'd bought cheap. The night before opening day of the war crimes tribunal, I'd been invited to the wedding of a senior court official. All of the press, court personnel, and government officials had been invited. I figured Sam could gate-crash if he were with me. I thought that since Sam had been hired as a translator, he would fit in with the crowd and meet some people who might be useful down the road.

The wedding celebration was on Diamond Island—Koh Pich, as the Khmers called it—a finger of land extending into the Tonlé Sap River. After we crossed the bridge, the heavy traffic slowed to a crawl, Bangkok-style. An entire complex of buildings had been built on the island. A long row of buildings with numbers had signs out front announcing weddings, and as people flooded in, it seemed everyone in Phnom Penh was getting married that night and hiring one of the halls to throw a huge party.

Sam looked at the crowds.

"I want to show you something," he said.

He turned the car around, drove to a small footbridge connecting Diamond Island with Phnom Penh, and parked.

"That's Koh Pich Bridge," he said. "Three hundred and fifty people died in a stampede there a couple of years ago."

I remembered the incident. It happened during the annual Water Festival that stretched back to the twelfth century and King Jayavarman VII. Each year villages all over the country were emptied as four million Khmers streamed into Phnom Penh to celebrate.

"I covered the story," I said.

Thousands of people had become stranded on the bridge when the police turned on water cannons to get them to move along. They panicked. The bridge swayed. People jumped over the side. A number drowned that night. It was as if the Khmer Rouge had returned to clear the city again.

"Each family got $1,250 if their kid or relative got killed," Sam said.

He lit a cigarette and opened his window, and the thick, muggy air slowly seeped into the car.

"I never saw any money for the death of my mother and father or two sisters and brother. Not a nickel. People's lives when I was a kid weren't worth a dime."

"Whoever said life was fair, Sam?"

"You know what the prime minister said afterwards? 'No one will receive punishment. We will learn a lesson so the problem won't happen in the future.' How's that for a line of political bullshit?"

The next day, the UN war trial would start. Sam's detour to the bridge seemed to be a lesson he was trying to teach me about what to expect down the road. Punishment for the Killing Fields, a stampede fueled by a few Khmer Rouge leaders, most of them now too old to walk unassisted, was in the hands of a court that wasn't in the control of the prime minister. The question was whether the UN would learn the Khmer way of chalking up mass death as a lesson to keep in mind when thinking about the future.

"You want to interview someone who lost a son that night on the bridge?"

It was hard to explain to a civilian, even one as experienced as Sam, that as horrific as the stampede deaths were, it was an old story. No one was going to run a follow-up about a father who'd lost his son in Cambodia a couple of years before.

"We should get to the wedding," I said.

"The father was a Khmer Rouge. He got blood money for his son. Isn't that a story?"

It was an angle, and sometimes a story exploded like old ordnance on an abandoned battlefield; other times it left an editor thinking his reporter in the field was juicing up an old story to fill time and space.

Sam flicked the cigarette out the window and rolled it up.

"What if the father's name was Nimol?"

At first the name didn't register.

"You know him?"

"I once saw him cook a human liver."

That Nimol. Sam had hooked me as he likely knew that he would. I'd heard his liver-eating story enough times to wonder about the group of Khmer Rouge that had used Sam as a porter and made him eat human flesh. One of the men in a lineup of culprits who'd truly fucked up his life, Nimol would have every finger on the victim's side of the one-way glass pointed at him.

"Nimol lost his son?"

"I'll arrange the interview," said Sam.

He seemed both pleased and relieved as he pulled the Toyota back into the stream of traffic and headed back to the wedding hall, where several hundred people—about the same number who died on Koh Pich Bridge—drank, danced, and sang, and the bride and groom walked along a path strewn with rose petals.

My memories of Phnom Penh from the UNTAC days in the early 1990s needed some radical adjustment. A war-torn, battered slum hellhole of a city, crisscrossed with dirt side roads, with chickens and dogs and the odd pig foraging in the potholes, had been replaced with paved roads and modern buildings. Planning a city that had been ravaged by war had taken time. Politics had come into play. Building the courthouse for the UN war crimes tribunal had raised political temperatures and paranoia. The fear was that the old Khmer Rouge supporters, who numbered in the millions, might demonstrate in front of the courthouse and bring the city to a halt.

The problem was easily solved. Build a courthouse in the middle of nowhere, away from Phnom Penh. Make it inconvenient as hell, a royal pain in the ass to find. That's where the UN war crimes trial found itself. If the Koh Pich Bridge stampede was any indication, it would take the promise of a party, city lights, and food and drink, plus the possibility of throwing water on pretty girls, to bring the masses to the proceedings.

Watching judges behind a bulletproof window from cinema-like seats would play to a much smaller audience. The opening day drew a crowd of just four hundred spectators. Respectable, dressed in their best clothes, they sat in their seats for a glimpse of the Khmer Rouge top brass—the ones still alive and not totally crazy, that is—four old men who looked embalmed on the opposite side of the ceiling-to-floor bank of glass windows. Like grandfathers in a poker game.

All the bets had been made.

The outcome wasn't a gamble. But getting to the point of a final verdict and sentencing, the lengthy appeal process, had been a hot subject at the wedding the night before. Two or three years was the best guess.

I heard Sam's voice through my earphones. He translated an objection made by the lawyer of one of the old Khmer Rouge men. The old man had a back problem and wanted to be excused from the courtroom. We caught up during a break as Sam came down to the pressroom. He smoked a cigarette, arms folded, nodding as he answered a couple of questions from the *New York Times* correspondent about charges against three of the Khmer leaders. Sam translated from the officially released document.

I was standing next to Sam when Jamie, a former *Newsweek* bureau chief, came up and introduced himself. Jamie, who had heard Sam talk at the Foreign Correspondents' Club in Bangkok, said: "You said what you saw in the field seemed almost normal after a few months. But surely you'd acknowledge that what the Khmer Rouge did amounted to genocide and war crimes, and they should be brought to justice."

And Sam replied, "Justice, yes. That is good. But if I tell you that you must choose between peace and justice, what do you say? Knowing you choose only one and not the other, which one would you choose?"

"It's not for a foreigner to decide. It's your country. How do you call it, Sam?"

"How do we learn a lesson?" Sam asked. "Punishment ... or agreeing not to let something like the Killing Fields happen in the future?"

I smiled, thinking he'd paraphrased what the prime minister had said about assigning responsibility for the stampede deaths on Koh Pich Bridge.

"What I'm asking, Sam, is who is the trial for? Us, the international press and our audience, or for the victims of the Khmer Rouge?"

The recess ending saved Sam from having to reply. He returned upstairs, leaving the press to return to their laptops and stare at the screens that showed the courtroom still empty. Another correspondent who'd been listening to our conversation, a man from one of the Australian newspapers, came over and sat next to me.

"Sam's a slippery one. You heard how he got the job with the court?"

I confessed that I hadn't.

"He got a couple of letters of recommendation from members of the Foreign Correspondents' Club of Thailand, an NGO, and a third secretary from the Canadian embassy to support his application as translator. Clever bugger."

Later that evening we drove to a hole-in-the-wall restaurant that served Thai and Khmer food. Tables on the pavement were filled with travelers on a budget. Across the street were secondhand bookstores and a couple of guesthouses. I asked Sam about those letters from Bangkok. It occurred to me that Sam had set up the whole enterprise with that purpose and hooked me into financing his trip. I wasn't a happy camper, and Sam saw my look of disgust, which I made no effort to hide.

He laughed and tapped the press card hanging from a plastic strap around my neck.

"I was going to ask you but thought you'd already done enough."

"Lying is a sin, Sam," I said. "Especially to friends."

"Did I tell you that I was a monk until six months ago? I was in the monkhood for two years."

Another detail that he'd left out the night we'd done catch-up on the major changes in our lives. Going into the monkhood would rank as something you'd mention as one of those milestones on the road of life.

"*You* were a monk?"

I know the way I said it I came across as mocking. It was unfair to him and I immediately regretted my tone.

Sam smiled, but that didn't cover the hurt.

"Why shouldn't I be monk? Because I was in prison?"

"Sorry, man. I was an asshole to say that. It's just, after all that happened to you as a kid, how anyone can have faith in God or bibles or religion is beyond me. I don't get it."

"Buddhism isn't a religion. There is no god. Even an asshole if he works long and hard enough can find enlightenment."

No apology or explanation for why he'd kept the monkhood—a recent and important event—a secret from me.

"When did you disrobe?"

"A week after the Koh Pich Bridge stampede."

That event would have knocked anyone's faith, I thought. We had sat in his car on Diamond Island, looking at the bridge, and Sam had made a point about the money paid and the political decision to absolve anyone from responsibility.

"In Bangkok you said how the other prisoners in California had left you alone. You spooked them. No, it doesn't surprise me that you'd go into the monkhood. Or that the stampede fucked up your faith."

"The deaths on the bridge didn't make me into a non-believer," Sam said.

Something dark, pleading, and sad colored his voice.

"Why did you leave?"

Sam rubbed his right hand over his cropped hair and held out his glass, smiling as the waiter filled it. A moment later, a Khmer in a polo shirt and jeans came to the table. Though he dressed young, the man looked like the juice had been squeezed out of him and the skin had wrinkled and buckled, leaving the husk of what had once been a handsome man.

Reunion

"Let me introduce you to the owner of this restaurant. Nimol, this is my good friend Anthony Collins. He's a famous journalist. And I told him that you had stories from the old days."

His little speech was for my benefit. Once he'd finished, Sam switched into Khmer and translated it for Nimol.

"Not a problem," Nimol said.

He may have had more than a three-word English vocabulary, but as the evening wore on, it was clear his English words didn't run into double digits.

"You can ask him anything," said Sam.

"Is there a connection between Nimol and why you left the monkhood?" I asked.

Sam translated. Nimol nodded and said something in Khmer, and Sam replied to him in Khmer.

"He wants to know if you're a Buddhist."

"What did you tell him?"

"That you were waiting for the next life to decide."

Sam weaved and dodged questions like a professional fighter ducking punches. I was completely in Sam's hands for the translation. I'd used lots of translators over the years, and some of them were puppeteers, massaging the political prejudices and slanting answers so as to flatter the person who was being translated.

Nimol opened a bottle of whiskey and filled three water glasses. A waiter brought a bucket of ice. A second bottle of whiskey arrived thirty minutes later. Courage in a bottle wasn't just an old saying; it loosened tongues, allowed men to discuss things that sobriety repressed. Into the second bottle of rice whiskey, Nimol explained how he collected the government handout for the death of his son who'd been killed on Koh Pich Bridge, and how he'd ended up staying in Phnom Penh and opening the restaurant.

"The restaurant was Sam's idea," said Sam, translating the Khmer.

I looked around the premises and to the street they were located on and quickly concluded that the money paid as compensation for the dead son couldn't have financed it.

"Where'd he get the full nut to get into business? Ask him that, Sam."

Sam polished off his glass, locking eyes with Nimol that seem to communicate a signal for Nimol to leave the table.

When Nimol had gone, Sam said: "After Koh Pich Bridge, the newspapers were filled with pictures of the relatives of those who'd been killed. One morning, a couple of days after the bodies had been handed over to the relatives, I was walking on the street with my bowl, along with other monks, to receive food. We walked down a dirt road into the countryside spreading to the east. Women, old men, sometimes children would patiently wait as we received rice, vegetables, and maybe fruit.

"I knew it was Nimol standing at the end of a row. His clothes were dusty from the road, his sandals were worn and dirty, but it was his face. I'd never forgotten that look as he held out the knife with the liver on the end. How he watched my hand. I remember it was shaking. I tried to keep it from showing. I reached for the meat. He pulled the knife back a little as if to taunt me. He wasn't going to let me just have it. I had to want it. I had to demonstrate a desire. Only then would my hand stop shaking. Only then could I move to grab it from his knife, take it as mine. He smiled as I pushed the human liver into my mouth. He watched me chew, first on one side of my mouth, then the other, my teeth grinding the meat until I finally swallowed. He laughed, saying, 'Now you're a real man. You will follow Angkar. You've eaten his enemy.'"

Sam had read in a local newspaper that Nimol had lost his son on the bridge, but he'd been surprised to see him on his regular alms walk. Sam felt his heart pound as if it were still in the chest of a ten-year-old boy. Nimol searched the face of each of the monks. At first he showed no sign of recognizing Sam, who had gone from being a ten-year-old boy to a man in his forties. Looking at him, there was little trace of that slender boy in the grown man. But Nimol could tell from Sam's reaction that he'd found his man.

Nimol removed two thick wads of Khmer money from his shoulder bag and put them in Sam's alms bowl.

"Your son's blood money, brother?" Sam asked him.

"I make merit for him."

"You've traveled a long way from the old days, brother."

"A relative of my cousin told me you'd become a monk."

In Cambodia the old-fashioned "bamboo telegraph" stitched people into a fabric from which there was no escape. Nimol had traveled through the gate that converts making merit into peace of mind.

The morning sun filtered through the dust kicked off the road by passing bicycles and motorcycles. Sam had a thought running through his head as he watched Nimol *wai* him: "To survive you do what you have to do. Eat a dead man's liver? I've done that." The words were delivered in a banal and flat tone. Sam used them a couple of years later at the Foreign Correspondents' Club in Bangkok. They were the American equivalent of being a member of the "been there, done that" club.

He'd eaten human meat from the same hands that had *waied* him—showed him respect.

By midday Sam had seen the abbot with his request to be permitted to disrobe and leave the temple. He said there had been a family emergency. It was true in a tortured kind of way, the way the Khmer Rouge had tortured language, bodies, families, and monks. But there was no point in sharing the details of his plan with the abbot, who certainly would have disapproved and might well have denied him the permission to disrobe and return to civilian life.

By the time Nimol came back to the table, he was more than a little drunk. He carried a bowl with the steam rising. He set the bowl on the table, stumbled with the chair, and sat down heavily, reaching for the whiskey bottle to fill his glass.

"Nimol works for me," said Sam. "Don't you, buddy? If I need an errand run, Nimol climbs on his motorcycle, drives across town to pick up a package or deliver one, and at night he goes to the kitchen and cooks up a batch of his trademark soup."

Nimol slid the bowl across the table until it was in front of me.

"Eat, Tony. Be a man."

Noodles, the long, flat broad kind, lay below a flotilla of sprouts and tofu that bobbed around thumb-sized lumps of meat.

"Is this what I think it is?" I asked him.

"What might that be?"

"Something from here."

I slid my chair back, pulled up my shirt and touched the skin on my side.

"Tony, you never got it. That's okay. No one ever got it."

I pushed away the bowl of soup.

"Got what?"

"Nimol made me a man. And the circle of life was complete when I made him my man. What goes around comes around. I heard an Englishman say something like that once, and I thought it described Nimol and me very well."

Running contraband out of refugee camp restaurants had been the only trade Sam had ever had. A man with a hammer searched the world for nails. I had no idea what kind of business was being run out of the restaurant, but I would've made a bet that it involved paying off the local police and thugs.

Sam grabbed the bowl and spooned out a chunk of meat with some noodles attached.

"It's chicken, Tony. What kind of sick shit were you thinking?"

"The human liver story is a hard one to forget," I said.

"It was chicken. It always was just chicken. No human sacrifice or cutting out a dead man's liver. Good old Nimol had stumbled across a chicken. He shared it around the campfire that night. That's not the story people wanted to hear. Not the one reporters like you write down."

When I looked up, I saw a number of familiar faces from the courthouse. The tables had filled up with several correspondents I recognized from Bangkok, two tables of NGO types, and half a dozen court personnel seated with their families. They'd come for Nimol's famous chicken soup. Sam had handed out cards for the restaurant to everyone he'd met at the courthouse. Business was booming, and with a trial lasting two or three years, it looked like at long last Sam had found a way to reinvent himself.

There is justice in retribution, and there is also redemption in reinvention. With Nimol in the kitchen, Sam had come up with a way to ride both horses. Most people believe there are invisible forces that shape our lives, and those forces explain why we choose to walk down one street and not another, why the guy next to you catches a bullet and you don't, or why people cling to a version of events that shapes their identity and gives them a reason to explain why their lives are what they have become. Nimol was that force in Sam's life. Everything that had happened in Sam's life worked its way back to that core event.

Why, after all of these years, had Sam wanted out of the lie? I have a theory of sorts. Lies are always a dead end in the struggle to answer why things happened the way they did. When a whole society has been telling each other lies for years, no court can clear the history until the truth comes out. The only thing that can start the journey to understanding the past is to get beyond the lies, and I'd like to think that Sam had found enough confidence in himself to stand free of the lie and still make sense of his life so he could move ahead into the future.

After that night I saw Sam a couple of more times at the courthouse. He mostly avoided me. He had the look of a man who didn't want to look you in the eye. When I tried to talk to him, he found an excuse to slip away. Sam had a few other friends who were always going into and then leaving Phnom Penh. People who lived inside their minds and the memories of what they believed about Sam Rith. I wondered if Sam would tell them what he'd told me. Or had he passed that assignment along to me?

There were ways of leaving a place like Cambodia other than physically getting out. But leaving the past is much harder than we can ever imagine.

Reunion

As you get older you find all kinds of ways to leave behind a city, the past, a relationship, a brush with death. This leaving and returning is how life treats us. Equally. If we listen. If we reason. If we find enough whiskey or other triggers to open the sluice gate of truth to wash out the lies buried in memory, we return to a different past from the one we've lived with all of these years.

With a little help from our friends, as John Lennon used to say, we can leave and return and for the first time see it more clearly, see ourselves no longer cloaked with misinformation and lies. We don't need anything other than a nudge at the right time, from the right people, and the right moment to lift ourselves above dark shadows that we have failed to lose.

Phnom Penh brings back that giddy feeling of falling in love. When you're young, the romance of discovery gives you courage. Over time we lose those feelings to the gravity of life. The weight of old losses, grudges, hurts, and betrayals pulls us to the earth, as if they'd been waiting for the right time to take us to a bridge where the giddy romance of a water festival would turn into death. We learn our lessons the hard way. Or we don't learn them at all. Nothing brings back the dead. Not money, not justice, not prayer. Peace is that temporary space where the killing finds a lull. Cover enough wars and you conclude that coming to terms with past war crimes isn't a contest between justice and peace; it's the dead zone between what happened and what people tell each other happened.

Spit on your little hunk of reality, urinate on him, slice him open, and cut out his liver. Cook it and eat it for courage, strength, and dignity. And find out at the end of your days that it tastes pretty much like chicken.

Christopher G. Moore

Christopher G. Moore is a novelist and essayist who lives in Bangkok. Novels in his award-winning Vincent Calvino crime fiction series and Land of Smiles Trilogy have been published in 13 languages.

Broken Chains

Kosal Khiev

My name is Kosal Khiev. I am thirty-two years old. One year ago I was dropped off out here (Phnom Penh) like a parachute with nothing. No passport, no ID, nothing.

I want to take you back to 1980. That was the year I was born in a Thailand refugee camp. I didn't stick around long in the camp. In 1981, along with my family, I came to the United States.

There were eight of us: me, my grandmother, my three brothers, and my three sisters. We were living in this two-bedroom apartment out in Santa Ana. This was just after going through the war in Cambodia. We were dropped down in the States with nothing. We knew no one. Didn't speak the language. How did they suppose we were going to integrate? How was it that they thought we could adapt? So for me, I was left to my ways of getting by.

I grew up in the States. I didn't experience any of the trauma. All my stories from childhood are American stories. Jack and Jill, Humpty Dumpty, nursery rhymes. You can't get more American than that, right?

So I made poor choices, poor decisions. Drove forward, got locked up at sixteen, charged with attempted murder, gang-related, ended up doing fourteen years out of that. The thing is, though, I survived that fourteen. I'm not even going to tell you about my past. This is too much, you know. 'Cause it is the past. I tell you what's happening now, though. At age fourteen, instead of being paroled home after growing and learning and becoming a man, growing and becoming a man, right, I was placed in the hands of ICE—Immigration Custody and Enforcement—and I ended doing a year there. Heartbreak after heartbreak, thinking when will I come home? Or where would I call home?

A year ago on March 17th I was sent back. Now this is a piece I wrote called "Sound of Broken Chains." I hope you can literally hear the sound of broken chains.

> Let me break it down. I'm breaking down. Pound per pound. Break dance you around to the sound of broken chains. It's broken rage. Home broken set to the stage of memory scattered through a maze. A slave born free. Trapped in a day lost its way in poverty and graves, landmarks of moments stolen, now begs, plays reminiscent in moments frozen out, the film is rolling, the character is building, how was I stuck, how'm I feeling? I've been numb, it felt dumb.
>
> The legs and wings of cocked thumb, but I was caught with a gun. Come morning, knees broken crawling in crumbs, tear porno I was darn warm. Break free and just die, break free and just fly. Wanna ban a fight? I was sent up to the sky high on the motherland, land of my mother's mother, a father and his sons. My three brothers three sisters ten nephews six nieces . . . Look at my family picture broken into pieces. Look at my life broken in sequence, unedited. I was captive in secret. I was a refugee stripped of his rights, weakened. The horror just deepened. I was held captive, held in chains, and thrown

*into the deep end. Send the calm boy because this broken
boy's bleeding, hurled to the ground sleeping at night,
with the night I sleep.*

*Sleeping at night where the devil's keeping, all of
this where my love was deepened . . . sound of a little
boy sleeping, sound of a voice when the boy is weeping.
So let me break it down, break you down, pound for
pound, break dance you around to the sound of broken
chains, no breaks, feeling the way that the world shakes.
Now let the man take, what more do you want from me,
my heart still staked to the ground with the earthquake,
homemade . . . Listen to the sound of loneliness, its bone
breaks. Listen to the sound of me drowning in my own
lake, reflections of my father staring at my own face, one
love, one struggle, one race, take a sucker to listen, this is
my take, you follow the trail of my pace, so let me break
it down, break you down, pound for pound, break dance
you around to the sound of broken chains.*

I got shipped out here. Man, had this idea that Cambodia was all dirt piles, huts, rubbish. Fear coursed through me. I had so many doubts . . . but then Cambodia smiled during the night. She smiled during the night. I saw the beauty of it all. I saw the beauty of it all, man. Next piece here, this next piece here is written for all those that affected my life. Whether it be for the good or for the bad. I will love you unconditionally. That's Cambodia for you, man. It makes you do that. Makes you open up your own heart and it's all learning process, right?

*Fifteen years in a cage and all of a sudden, bam,
here you go world. Like being reborn. So I was soaring
with the butterflies. Her eyes remind me of sunlight . . .
reflecting moonbeams filled with dreams of sunshine,*

seeing such purpose that's worth not an eternity . . . hurt merges in dirt she's worthy of love. Pure joy. Certainly she hugs at love full of pure joy. Sublime noise . . . Her tongue caressed worse, I immersed myself, work. She's earth and I'm the dirt . . . curse the secret sore, that mentor . . . I arose and bloomed like days to the temple . . . men bores to the crack of a gag, cores that I am left in a field of the poor, now I'm uprooted. Suited in ashes, battle clashes spring, take me back, but I am looking forward to series of better passions.

Just let me ask you, our paths crossing weren't meant to happen. Don't clap and make my life trying to screaming out, what the hell happened, but even that the waves come crashing on the sea, back in a piece for action from my parents got me dreaming in those passions in business to be a winner.

As soon I seek redemption I question . . . those things in farthest directions to every word noticed quoted for you is a loan I mention, that's my words, get cut out by henchmen, so this is my extension my hot body and soul plus the spiritual dimension written through a pen, forgive me for my sin, my flaw, my pieces of my soul, collecting these pieces, this my thesis for the broken heart, so I hate callers . . . I'm free falling in hopes that I grow wings and blossom so from the bottom of my beast soul falling, catch my words I'm scrawling. I'm in a dream state kept in a box and slept until my jeans ached, wept till I'm sober till my jeans tasted like breaking waves still chasing for a warm embrace, now break your wave, still chasing for a warm embrace, see if you can trace the old gentlemen of hatred. Discovered the origin of love I pained with. Estranged until fate changes it. Now I'm pouring out my soul and painting it, go ahead and frame it, capture my essence. Realign my senses, love you are, love you where *the whole distance, catch my essence, allow my sentence. Love you are. Love you without condition.*

I know that I'm broken, so what's there to say? Me and Cambodia. It seems like we always had this journey all alone. We never parted. From my mother's womb trekking through the jungles to the camp . . . have I ever really left? I love Cambodia. I'm just trying to get back home, man. I'm just trying to get back to the arms of my mother, the arms of my brothers and sisters, nephews and nieces. I'm trying to get back to the abandoned one out there. The lost sons and daughters—hey, calling out—do you hear me? I haven't forgotten. I know where I came from, here's the beauty of it, the best of both world.

I'm the best of both world. Kosal Khiev, I'm a Khmer exile American and I salute my love, my respect to the dead, to the fallen and to those who are living in the struggle now and to anyone who has ever walked the line—call out—howl to the wind and I might howl back.

Kosal Khiev

Kosal Khiev is a Cambodian poet, singer, and performer jailed during his teens in the US prison system and returned to Cambodia after serving his sentence. He was born in a Thai refugee camp. His performance on TED secured his reputation as a fresh, important voice. He was chosen by the Cultural Olympiad in association with the 2012 Olympic Games in London to represent Cambodia along with poets from elsewhere around the world.

Darkness Is Faster Than the Speed of Light

Prabda Yoon

True, Wipa didn't much care where the tuk-tuk driver was taking her, but when she came out of a momentary daze and saw that the quaint vehicle was heading toward a vast, vacant, outlandish-looking lot, she couldn't help feeling surprised, and slightly alarmed. She had told the driver to take her "wherever tourists go," but this place just didn't seem to fit that description. Still not in the mood to speak, especially to someone who wouldn't understand her anyway, Wipa shifted nervously in her seat like a caged prey.

It was clear, though seen through the green lens of her red-framed Wayfarer shades, that they were approaching a concrete structure of monumental scale. Wipa was soon able to make out that it was a sports arena of some sort. The last time Wipa had found herself in a similar environment, she almost lost her virginity to a dumb soccer player, one of the heartthrob jocks at her high school in Bangkok, but definitely dumb, hence the "almost." That was a *million* years ago. Wipa had forgotten all about it until now. It was as if the tuk-tuk were taking her back in time. Certain unpleasant memories began to surface. And she was already up to her neck with unpleasant feelings. Not to mention images.

Strange day, Wipa thought. What does it all mean? Is someone trying to tell me something? Why would tourists come here?

Questions. There were going to be a lot more of those, Wipa was sure of that.

Maybe I should practice being innocent. Is that even possible? But the police aren't that smart, are they? I might be able to get away with it. I'm sure I can. It's only fair that I get away with it. I *am* innocent, in a way.

The driver brought his tuk-tuk to a stop by one side of the overwhelming structure. It didn't look particularly like a drop-off area. He turned around and put his smoked, crooked teeth on full display. It was an attempt at a smile. Wipa could tell he wanted to say something, perhaps to explain himself, but all he decided to do finally was nod and point at the stadium with sincere enthusiasm.

He wants me to enter the body of this sleeping giant, Wipa thought. She was right. He did, and proudly so. This was no ordinary sports stadium, at least not to the Khmers. It was completed in 1964, by a French-educated architect, for the big Southeast Asian Peninsular Games that never happened. They called it the Phnom Penh National Olympic Stadium, and to someone like Wipa's tuk-tuk driver this was definitely a must-see for all, a place tourists should go.

Giving the driver a questioning look, Wipa stepped down from the tuk-tuk and scanned the surroundings absentmindedly. She felt that she had no choice but to follow the driver's suggestion. Or perhaps it was more because she was at that moment in a state of mind too preoccupied with lingering anxiety and darkening thoughts to afford much thorough reasoning. Whatever, Wipa told herself. The guy wants me to tour the damn stadium, fine. At least it's going to be quiet. Come to think of it, maybe he knows what I'm going through and this is his way of helping, to offer me some peace. When that thought entered Wipa's mind, as she was making her way up the long concrete steps to enter the stadium, she turned around and found the tuk-tuk gone. The driver had moved it to the shade across the lot, against a concrete wall that was perhaps part of the gate. There were no other vehicles around, but Wipa could make out that it was a designated parking spot. The driver must have been watching Wipa because he immediately waved to her. How nice, Wipa thought. She didn't return the gesture.

It had been an overcast, humid morning but with no sign of obvious rain clouds until now. Just before she stepped under the roofed landing at the top of the stairway, Wipa looked up and felt tiny, gentle wet drops on her forehead. What if it poured uncontrollably for hours like yesterday? A good excuse to stay out, maybe? Or even to disappear? But the thought of being stuck inside the dreary stadium longer than necessary was almost too much for Wipa to bear. Where's my umbrella? Back at *his* hotel, of course. Wipa had brought nothing with her apart from some cash that was already in the back pocket of her jeans and the bright red shades she'd grabbed intuitively from the bedside table.

Is that blood on my shoe? A sudden chill shot through Wipa's spine as she glanced down and saw a small, barely noticeable red stain on the tip of her left canvas slip-on. It could also have been from the red wine she'd drunk at dinner the previous night.

The blood didn't reach me, she thought. It couldn't have. I'm sure of it.

I must be losing my mind. Wipa shook her head and tried to forget about the stain. She stopped moving and looked around. The gloomy weather outside and Wipa's sunglasses made the interior of the stadium appear even darker than it already was. Wipa took a few seconds to decide her next move. There were no recognizable signs, no suggested directions anywhere. What does one look for in a place like this? What would one *want* to see?

Wipa heard the sound of rain, followed by the distinct scent of moist ground. How fast that scent reached my nose! The speed of scent was something Wipa had never thought about. Now it fascinated her enough to make her stop and ponder.

But there was something else, a kind of murmur that seemed to be coming from the heart of the building. At first Wipa felt the urge to turn around and, despite the intensifying rhythm of rain, run back to the tuk-tuk, but the murmur grew strangely seductive, and the temptation to reach its source came over her as if the sound were composed with the notes of her name.

Still wearing the sunglasses, Wipa cautiously made her way up the dark tiled path ahead. On her left, Wipa saw an indoor court with nets, probably set up for volleyball or something else of similar arrangement; she couldn't tell for sure. Wipa and sports were worlds apart, though she could pretend to care and enjoy any type of televised crap if it pleased her clients.

The court was empty, but a small detail on it suggested possible foul play. Wipa saw pieces of cloth lying around right in the center of the court. She could make out a pair of pink panties and tiny white socks. Then, to Wipa's surprise, a skinny black dog ran onto the court, made its way straight to the socks, and stopped to sniff. The dog was completely dry. It had not come from outside.

Wipa looked for a way to get down to the court. It was on the ground floor while, Wipa had just realized, she was on the second. The murmur seemed to be coming from somewhere underneath her. Now there were also intervals of rumbling thunder above, making it more difficult to hear the murmur, but it was still audible to Wipa nonetheless.

Wipa saw a narrow set of stairs leading down to the court in the far right corner, a few yards away, but the entrance was blocked by a chained metal gate. However, the gate was only as high as her waist, so when Wipa got there she managed to climb over it quickly, effortlessly. At that moment Wipa heard another kind of sound, the sound of flapping wings. Families of pigeons living in the place, and probably some taking shelter from the storm, seemed to be welcoming the newest visitor. Some flew across overhead and landed on the other side, where they stood to watch Wipa make her way downward.

The murmur was coming from a cave-like opening Wipa could see on her left, beyond one corner of the court. More pieces of clothes were visible in front of the dark portal, but these seemed to belong to a grown man. Wipa's heart skipped a beat and her whole body turned cold, yet for some reason she was compelled by a strange and complex presentiment to rush closer to that darkness.

What Wipa saw and felt, for only a few seconds, she could never understand. But it was also something she would never forget. Sitting naked against a wall inside the portal were a middle-aged man and a girl of about seven or eight. The girl was in the man's lap, her front facing Wipa. The man had his arms wrapped around the girl's breast from behind. The girl had no arms. The man's face was pressed against the nape of the girl's neck. They were both sobbing. The girl was looking straight at Wipa as tears rolled down her cheeks, but it wasn't clear whether Wipa was actually *seen*. There was no change,

Darkness Is Faster Than the Speed of Light

no surprise, in the girl's expression. The man seemed too caught up in his sorrow to notice anything else in the world.

I'm *supposed* to look at this, but that's all, Wipa thought. She stepped back and out of the cave and then found a wall of light that led her out of the building.

Wipa's brief adventure inside Phnom Penh's National Olympic Stadium had lasted eight minutes, but to run from the stadium through fading curtains of rain to the faithful tuk-tuk took her only twenty seconds or so. That is about the same amount of time it takes light from the sun to reach the earth.

At first it was dark, Wipa thought, as her mind shifted from the most recent event in her life to what had happened in the hotel room earlier that morning, just before sunrise. There's going to be a lot of people with a lot of questions waiting for me. Yes, darkness was already there. That's what I'll tell 'em.

Some ancient creation myth makers would approve of Wipa's reasoning. Darkness had arrived first. Whatever there was before darkness happened, we would never know. Then after a while something else had occurred, something that seemed more important, more meaningful, more promising. Something that made life possible. And death ugly.

Whatever they'll say or think of me, I'll tell 'em. I'll have to them that it'll always be there, the darkness. It *won't* go away. That's what everyone should know, and I'll tell 'em.

Wipa told the smiling, half-wet tuk-tuk driver to take her back to the hotel.

"Hotel," she said.

"Hotel," he replied, nodding gleefully.

The vinyl passenger seat was only slightly wet at the front rim. The driver had covered his vehicle with a large green sheet of plastic. He'd just taken it down and put it away when he'd seen Wipa running toward him. Wipa sat back as the driver started the engine and saw that the little red stain on her shoe had been washed out by the rain.

Prabda Yoon

Prabda Yoon was born in Bangkok, left for the United States at 14 and returned at 26. He has since written almost everything, from short stories, novels, essays, film reviews, screenplays, to song lyrics. His 2002 story collection, *Kwam Na Ja Pen* (Probability), won the S.E.A. Write Award. He is also the founder of Typhoon Books, a small publishing house, and a cofounder of Bookmoby, a website for Thai ebooks and literary community.

Dark Truths
Bopha Phorn

Monday, 10 a.m., and the first rays of sunlight passed over Mark's face. One eye opened. He raised himself up to look out the window and then flopped back on the bed. The confusion of the previous day had fogged his mind, and a restless night had robbed him of sleep. He forced himself out of bed, crossed the room, and picked up yesterday's newspaper from the table where he'd left it. Read more times than he cared to count. Each time he'd read the story he'd hoped for a different ending, but the story, no matter how many times he read it, remained depressingly the same.

In the photo a German national, middle-aged, blond, blue-eyed, named Wolfgang Schultz, who had been convicted last Saturday, sat with a young girl wearing a blindfold. His right arm was swung possessively across her shoulders. The girl was eleven years old. Wolfgang had been convicted for having sex with four Cambodian children aged eleven to fifteen. The court had handed him an eight-year sentence and fined him $2,000. The money wasn't a problem for Wolfgang, but the same couldn't be said of the "time." Eight years was a big chunk to pull out of a man's life. But what he'd done to the kids had destroyed a lot more than eight years. The judge had said it had robbed them of a lifetime.

A life had ten cycles of eight years. An eight-year sentence had been light—so the NGOs covering the trial had said to the reporter. If only the frequency of pedo cases was one every eight years, life would be much easier. But in Cambodia, as he knew, there would always be more cases, more heartaches, and more reasons to wish he had a different job.

"Shit, I'm running late," he said, talking to himself as he walked naked into the bathroom. He looked in the mirror, stuck out his tongue, retracted it.

"Why do I feel like shit?"

He showered, dressed, and left for a coffee shop on the corner where he could sip his espresso, read the morning newspaper, and polish off a banana muffin.

As he reached for the muffin, his phone rang. There was the name of Raksa, his assignment editor, in digital letters running across the phone screen. Something's fucked up again, Mark thought.

"Hello, Mark. It's me, Raksa. How are you?"

"Do you really want to know?"

He waited for her to say something.

"Cheer up. Today is your lucky day. Remember that French pedo we talked about the other day?"

"Yeah, I have a vague memory of that conversation."

French, German, Australian, English … the list of nationalities involved in such cases had no end.

"I just got the message from Child Protection that that French guy was arrested yesterday," she said. "He's being held on suspicion of abusing some under-age boys. Sick, right? He appears in court this morning. Go straight to the courthouse, interview the cops and the country director of the NGO. I'll send Theary to translate for you."

"Just send Theary. She can handle it."
"Mark, I want you to handle it."
"I'm not feeling so well."
"Just do it."
The phone went dead.

Mark hated assignments to Cambodian courtrooms. He'd told her many times before that covering the crime beat wasn't his bag. Never mind that he'd graduated from law school in the UK, he'd told her; if he'd wanted to be in a courtroom, he'd have stayed in England and practiced law. Raksa disagreed. He should put his legal education to use, she said. Otherwise what was the point of studying law all of those years? Mark didn't have a good answer to that.

Mark had just finished his muffin when a second call came in. This time it was his editor-in-chief, Kim. Kim had a thing about pedophiles. He hated them. They made him crazy with rage. As a reporter, he had a record of hunting down pedophiles and exposing them in the press.

"Raksa told me you were playing hard to get. Get your ass down to the courthouse and find out what that Frenchman was doing with those kids. Am I making myself clear?"

"You've got a hang-up. That's not my problem," said Mark.

That was not the sort of thing that an editor-in-chief wants to hear from a reporter.

Kim exploded: "For God's sake! These monsters come to Cambodia and abuse children, and I'm supposed to think that's acceptable? Just let it go? Fuck that! I want you to find out what the cops are doing in this case. Ask the cops what they are doing to stop men like this from ruining the lives of kids. Unless, of course, you don't see pedophiles as a problem."

"Okay, I'm on my way."

Mark waited at the courthouse until 2 p.m. The Frenchman, named Christian, was brought into the court, and the charges of soliciting a child for prostitution were read out. NGOs were in the back of court, taking notes. Mark heard them whispering among themselves, asking whether the Frenchman would pay his way out or whether the authorities would nail him.

Back in his office at the newspaper, Mark checked his email. Kim had left a note: "Mark, send me a story about the French guy and the charges against him. And I want you to collect all the data on convicted and suspected pedophiles in 2011. I want a big-picture story. This guy is just one of many. Get to the bottom of the problem. That's what reporters do when they do their job. Do your job."

Mark sat back at his desk. Do I really want to do this? he asked himself. He logged on to the newspaper's database and cross-searched for pedophile stories and Christian's name. He scrolled through the data.

Item one: Christian was known as a ruthless and powerful person. He had an interest in a big-time casino along the Thai-Cambodian border that was frequented by powerful people connected to the government.

Then things got interesting. The Frenchman had a record.

Item two: Christian Duvel, age seventy-one, had been questioned by German police three times regarding the alleged offense of indecent acts with minors in 1995, 2002, and 2007 in Berlin and Frankfurt, after they had received complaints from five victims years earlier. No charges had been laid because the German statute of limitations barred prosecution.

The Frenchman had left a trail in Thailand, too.

Item three: In 1998 and 2000 in Pattaya, Christian Duvel had been arrested twice for allegedly abusing three boys of ages twelve to fifteen. In the end he wasn't charged because the victims and their families refused to cooperate with the authorities.

That smelled of money changing hands.

When it seemed that things couldn't get worse, Mark found Duvel's latest Cambodian brush with the law.

Item four: In 2006 in Cambodia, Christian Duvel had been arrested by the Phnom Penh Anti-Human Trafficking and Juvenile Protection Unit on suspicion of abusing four young boys. He'd been charged and detained pending trial but released after three months in jail. Later he'd been found not guilty in a Phnom Penh municipal court.

Mark read between the lines. The smart money bet Duvel had paid the court for his acquittal.

Item five: In 2007 in Cambodia, Christian Duvel had been busted in Siem Reap province for allegedly abusing two boys. He'd been granted bail and told to stay in town as he was being charged with the purchase of sex from an under-aged prostitute. On May 5, 2009, the Siem Reap provincial court heard the case and acquitted him.

The old standby had come into play, allowing Christian Duvel to walk: lack of evidence.

The guy was slippery as an eel. He played the system, knew how to game it to perfection. Child Protection had been after him, but he'd always been one step ahead of them.

Mark hammered out a 400-word story about the case with just enough detail to satisfy his editor. He hit the send key and stared at his computer screen. Like a lot of foreigners, Mark had his own bag of black secrets. It was hard to find a foreigner in Phnom Penh who didn't have a skeleton or two rattling in the closet. Mark's bag of old bones stretched back to England. He'd shared a flat with a fellow student named Bryan. There'd been things about Bryan that he should have picked up on sooner. You live with someone, and you learn to look the other way. And by looking the other way, that says something about you. It never worked, looking the other way. He'd thought about that the day the police had showed up at their flat.

"We received a complaint that both of you have abused children," said the police. "We'd like you to come with us to the station."

"I have no idea what you're talking about," he'd said.

He'd looked over at Bryan, who just stood there with his jaw clenched, and waited for him to say something to the cops.

"Bryan, what's going on?"

"Just shut up, Mark. We don't have to say anything."

"What are you saying? I didn't do anything wrong. Why are the cops charging you and me with screwing around with kids?"

"We want our lawyer," said Bryan.

Mark looked away from the computer screen, sweat dripping down his face, his heart pounding. From that moment his life would change in ways that would follow him to the ends of the earth.

The following morning the case, like a bad penny, turned up on his desk once again as he sat at his desk. It was 8:30 a.m., and the reporters who hadn't gone out to cover a press conference or one of the many protests huddled in the office to plan their day.

Before he'd had his second sip of coffee, Mark found himself under pressure.

"Hey, Mark, Christian goes on trial on April 25. Can you come with me?" asked Theary.

Mark pretended to read. He knew he couldn't avoid an answer but was going to take his sweet time.

"No, I can't."

"You are working here, right?" she asked.

"I'm busy that day, okay?"

She stood with her hands on her hips, shaking her head. She wasn't buying his line.

"Busy with what? Reading the newspaper you're supposed to be reporting for?"

"I'm working on something that I can't tell you about."

"Mr. Mystery Man has a secret story. It's always good to have a reporter like that on staff."

Theary was about to call him an asshole but stopped herself. Instead she clicked her tongue and walked back to her desk.

Raksa had been listening in. She waited until the printer had spit out a document sent from the fax machine. With Theary back at her desk, Raksa pulled up a chair and sat beside Mark.

"We need to talk. Whatever your secret story is, shelve it. You are the only expat here at the moment. I need you to cover the Frenchman's story."

"I'm the wrong guy for this story. Can't you find somebody else?"

"There's no one else. You know that, don't you?"

Mark rolled his eyes and gritted his teeth.

"All right, I'll go."

"I don't get you sometimes. Do you think reporters only go out to cover stories that interest them? Does it work that way in England? I don't think so. All anyone is asking you for is to do your fucking job."

On the day of Christian Duvel's trial, the courtroom was packed with journalists, NGO staff, and victims' families. Three judges sat on the bench with the prosecutor on their right and the clerk on their left. Duvel's lawyer and the lawyer representing the victims occupied the front-row seats. Mark found an empty seat behind Duvel's lawyer. He took out his notebook and drew in a deep breath. He'd been to law school, but he hated courtrooms. Once a man had been on the wrong side of a courtroom, he never wanted to enter one again.

Mark leaned forward to get a look at the victims, who were seated directly in front of the judges but hidden behind a screen that blocked the view of them from the public gallery and the witness stand. He also noted that officials from the French embassy were sitting two seats away from him in the second row. Friends and relatives of the victims talked together behind him in the third row. Other journalists and NGO workers occupied other rows, talking in low tones among themselves. Everyone had an opinion. Everyone, thought Mark, was eager to play judge.

Four prison guards in their blue shirts and dark pants, handcuffs hanging from their belts and pistols strapped to their sides, came into view. Two guards escorted Duvel, and the other two walked a short distance behind.

Christian Duvel arrived in court wearing a milky-colored T-shirt with the words "I love Cambodia" across the front and baggy army-green shorts. His black flip-flops made him look like a tourist. Duvel looked his age. All those years had ground his face into a webby grimace, turned his skin into a web of wrinkles, with liver spots on his neck and cheeks, and long, greasy gray hair. He was led to the witness stand by the guards. The court interpreter stood next to him.

"This guy's older than the Eiffel Tower," a local journalist said to a colleague from another newspaper. "Why does a guy like that hit on kids?"

"In prison an inmate will cut off his balls."

"Slowly," said the other journalist.

"Foreigners like him think money buys anything."

"Doesn't it?"

"We're about to find out."

This conversation, overheard by Mark, left him feeling irritated and annoyed.

Theary, who sat on Mark's left, thought the trial had the makings of a great drama, and she would have a first-rate article to file. She nudged Mark.

"Stand up," she said, as the judges filed in.

They took their places on the bench.

The senior judge, in the middle, adjusted his round glasses. He took a long, hard look at Christian Duvel, like a zoologist who had been presented with a new species of a scorpion. The judge showed no emotion as he opened his file and flipped through the papers.

The judge read the complaint, asking Christian Duvel for some basic information before moving to the heart of the case.

"Where were you on Sunday?" asked the judge—*bunthy* in the Khmer language. The interpreter then interpreted the question into English.

"I was in my room."

"Were the kids with you in your room?"

"Yes, they were."

"What were they doing in your room?"

"Playing games."

"What kind of games?"

"Many games."

"How long were they with you for?"

"Two days."
"What are you doing in your room?"
"Nothing."
"Nothing?"
"Did you ask them to masturbate you?"

Duvel went stone still in the witness stand, his cloudy eyes blinking at the judge.

"No."
"Did you touch their sexual organs?"
"No."
"What were you doing with the kids?"
"Reading a book to them."
"Where did you read your book?"
"In my bed."
"What kind of book?"
"A novel."
"Were they in the bed with you?"

Duvel nodded. The clerk wrote down an affirmative answer.

The judge continued his examination.

"What time of day did you read to them?"
"Sometimes morning. Sometimes afternoon or at night."
"You read to them all day?"
"I love reading to kids."
"Were you reading to them from pornographic books?"

Duvel looked offended.

"I don't have pornographic books. I find them disgusting."

"But the police found pornographic books in your room. How did they get into your room, Mr. Duvel, if you hate them?"

Duvel appeared to have found himself backed into a corner by the questioning. Mark saw how Duvel became confused, his confidence drained away, as his face turned a ghoulish white. Mark felt his gut turn. Theary had been translating.

"Mark, write that down, about the books. It should be in the story. Duvel's losing it."

The judge turned his attention to the prosecutor.

"Do you have any questions?" asked the judge.

"Yes, I do."

"Did you touch the boy's penis when he was with you?" the prosecutor asked him.

Duvel sat still, thinking, and then said, "I already said that I did not."

"But did you ask the children in the bed with you if you could touch their penises?"

"No."

"Vutha has said that you did touch his. Are you saying that he has lied to the court?"

"I don't know what he was talking about," said Duvel through the translator.

"But you admit that you gave him twenty dollars the night before?"

"Yes, I did."

"Why did you give him money?"

"To buy stuff. He was hungry and broke. I gave him some money to buy food or whatever he wanted."

Mark couldn't take his eyes off Duvel or the judge. He'd been listening to every word but hadn't made a note. It was as if his writing hand wouldn't work. He couldn't lift the pen to write a word.

The judge called upon Duvel's lawyer.

"Yes, I have questions to ask my client," said the lawyer, a man named Vandy.

Vandy had a reputation around town for taking pedophile cases and getting big up-front retainers from the clients. He fought for his clients, but the word was he was a hired gun; he fought only because he'd been paid to fight. He trained his biggest guns on the NGOs. He accused them of plotting trumped-up cases against foreigners, calling them pedophiles because it helped them keep their funding. Vandy was a hard man. There was no love lost between him and the NGOs. Between them, they did a strange money dance. But only one partner in that dance had a human heart and face, and it wasn't Vandy.

"What is your job, Mr. Duvel?" he asked.

"I am a teacher. I teach children English."

"What else are you doing besides teaching?"

"I volunteer my services as a photographer to NGOs."

"What kind of photos have you taken?"

"All kinds."

"Do you have adopted kids?"

"No. I wanted one, but I couldn't get one."

"Do you love kids?"

"Yes, I do, very much."

After finishing this round of questions from his lawyer, Duvel looked over his shoulder with a crooked smile. People in the court looked back with hatred and disgust.

"I don't have any more questions," said the prosecutor, lifting up the long sleeve of his lawyer's robe.

All the judges left the courtroom and returned ten minutes later.

"The trial is finished for today," announced the clerk. "The verdict will be announced on the eighth of May."

The judges filed out of the courtroom and the proceedings were over. People were on their feet, fighting to get a look at Duvel as the guards took him from the room.

Duvel didn't say anything on the way out. He brushed off questions from reporters with a defiant look, his monster eyes hot with fury.

Once the accused had disappeared into the police van, the journalists gathered around Davuth, country director of Child Protection, seeking an interview. After he'd answered the reporters' questions, Davuth walked over to Mark.

"Your editor said you were covering this trial," he said. "She said you studied law, so you will know that Duvel is a very dangerous guy. He's been caught and released too many times. I hope this time we can bring him to justice. We hope your article will help bring justice to all those kids. Please let me know if I can give you any background information."

Davuth handed Mark a business card.

Mark looked at the card, saying, "Law school teaches you there are two sides to every case."

"Some cases only have one side," said Davuth.

As Mark made his way back to the office, Theary kept asking him, "You don't think they had enough evidence?"

At first he said nothing. Finally, he said, "Courts and cops make mistakes."

"Did they make a mistake with Duvel?"

When the day of the verdict came, the court convicted Duvel for buying sexual services from a child. He was sentenced to a period of ten to twenty years in prison and fined $10,000. The court granted Duvel the right to appeal.

Duvel erupted after the verdict: "Fuck all of you! Don't you know anything about kids? You don't even look after the kids in your own country. I look after them. I feed them. I buy them new clothes."

Three policemen in blue uniforms surrounded him and escorted him out, still shouting.

As Davuth left the courthouse, he ran after Mark.

"Mark, remember me?"

Mark turned around.

"Yeah, Davuth."

"That's right. I thought you should know that Duvel is the son of a rich French tycoon. He was up on charges back home many times. But his father always found a way to get them dropped. Then Duvel shows up in Cambodia. Can't help himself. Same old thing. I thought you ought to have this background. This guy's not just bad; he's evil."

Mark returned to his office and sat in front of his computer, brushing his hair back from his eyes. He kept hearing Davuth's voice say that word, "evil." Mark hated that sound of that word. He'd heard it before. He'd heard it said about him. Like a stain that would never fade away, evil, once someone was charged with it, lurked for an eternity.

He had an idea. He would balance his story with some quotes from Duvel's lawyer.

"Hi, Vandy. This is Mark from the Cambodia Press. I have a couple of questions regarding Christian Duvel's case. What do you think about the court's decision?"

"I think there was no justice for my client, and I will appeal."

"Why do you think there is no justice, while the NGOs think the sentence is light? One of the NGOs has called your client evil. How do you respond to that allegation?"

"My client loves children. He gave the money to the children because he wanted them to have money to buy food. What's wrong with that?"

"What do you plan next for Duvel's case?"

"I'll appeal and ask the court for bail. I think my client has been framed."

"What makes you think that Duvel was framed?"

"Evidence was planted on him. Without the pornographic books, they had nothing."

Mark started to write the story about how Duvel's lawyer was going to ask the court for bail and appeal on the basis that his client had been set up by the cops. His editor wanted a story, Mark thought, and he'd give him one.

Mark finished writing his story and left the office early. He couldn't stop thinking of Bryan. The court proceedings in England. The judge, the people in the courtroom. And the word "evil."

It was a Thursday night, and most of the journalists were on their way to the pub along the riverside, where they'd hang out until late in the morning. He needed a drink. Some laughter and a crowd of people to help him forget.

On the way to the river, Mark answered a call from Kim. His boss was worked up right from the first words he shouted through the phone.

"Mark, what's wrong with you?"

"What's the problem?"

"Your report. There's no story. You talk to Duvel's lawyer and not to the country director. Why would you do something like that?" shouted Kim.

"I talked to Davuth."

"You did? Did he decline to comment?"

"No."

"Where are his quotes, then?"

"He was talking insane shit about evil."

"If he talked insane shit, that is what makes a story. You put it in. Tell me what else he said."

"He said ..." Mark paused, thinking about some of the quotes he knew should have gone into the story. "He said that all the pedos have the disease, and this disease is hard to cure."

"That's a goddamn good quote. What were you thinking of, Mark? Did you use your brain? What else did he say?"

"He said that pedos have different ideas from other people in the world, and they think people are wrong about them and the kids."

"This is fucking great stuff. It's a fucking front page story. Rewrite it with those quotes. Understand, Mark? Put the quotes in."

Mark decided not to go to the restaurant. He needed to be alone, to think. Kim had been right. He'd left the guts out of the story. The breeze coming off the river felt good. It was the only good thing about the long walk. He walked down a street where all the houses were colonial mansions built in the French style. In law school, he dreamed of having a house with a sloping driveway and large gardens. What lies and secrets lay beyond those walls?

He asked himself why people like Duvel and his old roommate Bryan were attracted to children. Was pedophilia a disease? Could it be cured? Or were these people lost causes, evil to the core?

In their London flat, he'd had a showdown with his roommate.

"Bryan, stop messing with kids. It's going to end badly."

"It's none of your business. Leave me alone. You can do whatever you want. I'm not bothering you with your business, so stop badgering me."

"Bryan, if you keep on, I'm going to the cops."

"Go ahead, roomie. I'll be waiting right here for you, if you dare."

It had been a threat, though Mark hadn't recognized it at the time. He should have phoned the police that day. When the police pressured him to testify against Bryan, he refused. You stand by your friends. To have testified against his friend would have been evil and against everything he believed was right. He should have done a lot of things. If he wrote a story now that went to the heart of the matter, it might not be redemption for what had happened in London, but it was a start in the right direction.

A week later Mark's big piece on pedophile cases was featured in the paper. He'd gone out to the prison and interviewed Duvel.

"I just want one true thing from you, your idea about the world and kids," he said to Duvel.

"These people want to do and experience stuff just like old people," said Duvel. "And they enjoy having things that old people enjoy. What's wrong with that? The world is so cruel to them. People just treat them unfairly. Old people try to get the advantage over the young kids who don't have much idea about life. Why can't I make them happy? Why can't I give them money? What's wrong with that? If they're stingy, you can stay at the corner. Let us do it. We're happy to."

The fully whine of self-pity exploded from Duvel. Mark looked at him with utter hatred.

"Pedophile?" Duvel said. "They accuse me of being a pedophile? And do you believe that? Let me tell you. They cooperate when the NGOs accuse us of being pedophiles and get us into jail, then release us after we pay them a big ransom. If you don't have money, you're gonna end up here the rest of your life."

The next day, Mark's feature was the talk of the town. Duvel was out of jail and seen inside a new SUV. He'd been granted bail.

Davuth was the one to break Duvel's bail news to him.

"My source at the prison tells me that people have seen Christian outside in his SUV. The court gave him bail. You have to work on this. Someone is helping him out. Find out who."

Mark had finished the call with Davuth when Raksa flagged him with a wave.

"Mark, you've got to talk. I've heard that Christian Duvel is out on bail," said Raksa.

"Yeah? I hadn't heard," said Mark.

"There's the follow-up story to your feature. Go to it."

"I've done the story to death. Assign someone else."

Raksa's jaw dropped.

"You're not serious."

"I'm drained out."

"No, Mark. Not drained out. Down the drain."

Mark stared at Raksa. After she left his desk, he wrote a front-page article about a guy working at the ministry of justice who'd been arrested for taking a $5,000 bribe to facilitate the bail application.

Mark had never understood the reason for his close friend's addiction to children. Why had Bryan become a pedophile? There were many opinions. You stand by your friends. That was what he'd been taught. You don't abandon them when they're in trouble. He'd stood by Bryan, and it had led to him standing next to Bryan in court.

Friday morning, Mark walked across the office to his desk, and along the way, he saw that Raksa was happy. Happier than he remembered ever seeing her. Once he'd settled in, Raksa bounced over and sat on the edge of his desk.

"Did you win the lottery?" he asked.

"Better than a lottery win. Call your source at Child Protection. I heard they are following a Cambodian pedophile, and this will be the first case like that they've worked on."

"And that's why you're jumping up and down?"

"It's a huge step, Mark. Don't tell me that you don't want to work on this case."

"You need to put a Cambodian reporter on a Cambodian pedo case. Doesn't that make more sense?"

"You're our resident expert. That feature got lots of people talking. They want to hear from you. I want to hear from you."

Mark dialed Davuth's office and got his assistant, named Thy.

"I heard you're investigating a new case, and it's a Cambodian pedo," said Mark.

"The police arrested him last night, and he goes to court today. And they have another guy who was sharing his room. Birds of a feather, as they say."

"Oh, really? You guys are fast."

"I'll send you the press release once I'm done."

"Okay, thanks. I'll look forward to reading that."

Mark opened his email and started reading the message.

"On June 20th," it read, "the Phnom Penh anti-human trafficking and juvenile protection police arrested a Cambodian national, Mr. Ken Sam, aged thirty, for allegedly having sexual intercourse with three boys of ages eleven to fourteen years. His accomplice was a twenty-six-year-old Cambodian national named Lim Sonith, who was found in their apartment along with pornographic videos.

"According to the police, a thirteen-year-old boy was lured by Sam to his house in Daun Penh district. Sonith was also in the house at the time. Both men were arrested. According to the police, Sonith, who claims to be innocent, admitted that he knew his friend was bringing young boys to the house. But he refused to give evidence."

Mark looked up from the press release and sat back in his chair. His past was reeling through his mind. He understood the panic that Sonith must have felt when the police had come into the house and arrested Sam and him.

He forced himself to read the rest of the press release.

"Child Protection has been following Sam for two years. They saw him with the kids along the river many times. Sonith had to know. He had a duty to turn Sam in. He didn't."

By the time he'd finished reading, Mark felt that life had made a choice for him, just as it had in England. Sooner or later, his story would come out. Sonith's case was a warning. It was only a matter of time. There was no one he could turn to who would support him, stand beside him.

"Mark, have you read the press release from Child Protection yet?" asked Raksa. "It's dynamite. Another story for you."

Mark didn't respond.

"Mark! Do you hear me?" she asked again.

"Can I not work on the story today?" Mark asked his assignment editor in a murmur.

"Mark, what is wrong with you? You're acting weird. This is your beat."

He could come up with another lie to reject the assignment, but he couldn't find the courage to tell the truth. Seeing his pale face and dim spirits, Kim took pity on him.

"You've been working too hard on this. Take two days off."

Raksa turned to another reporter two desks down from Mark.

"Rollo, can you go to the court with Theary?"

"Sure, can do," said Rollo, immediately walking to his desk to prepare his things before leaving.

"That's what I like to hear. The can-do spirit. Take over Mark's story," said the editor.

Mark left the office twenty minutes later, having cleaned out his desk. No one took much notice. He was glad they'd been too busy to ask questions.

"I don't hate these people. But they would hate me if they knew," he muttered to himself.

After the third day, people at the office started to ask questions about Mark. Where was he? Wasn't he supposed to take only two days? It was Rollo who got the information from an Internet search.

"Our friend Mark has quite the history back in England."

The office had gathered around him.

"It seems he was convicted for luring a twelve-year-old boy in Britain in 2010, and was sentenced to two years in jail and given a fine. He got the sentence overturned on appeal. Mark had refused to testify against his friend, Bryan. So the police charged him as an accessory. A smart lawyer convinced the court that the cops had tried to sweat a confession out of him. His friend wasn't so lucky. He got eight years."

Raksa, mouth open, shook her head. "Unbelievable."

"It gets better," said Rollo. "Mark's friend Bryan was a real piece of work. His uncle, Mr. John Lee, 80, was arrested and sentenced to five years in jail in 2000 after the police in London found that he'd been abusing his own nephew for three years."

In the days that followed, Mark's history floated like a black cloud over the office. Raksa briefed the office to give a standard reply to any inquiries about him.

"No, we have no knowledge of his whereabouts," she said. "He no longer works for this newspaper. We have a new reporter to cover pedophile stories now. We do a thorough background check on everyone working at this paper. There are no other Marks in this office."

"Do you know where Mark has gone?"

"No idea. We have no forwarding address or contact. He's vanished."

Davuth felt sure now that Mark must have been guilty and got off in England on a legal loophole. He'd been a law student. He was smart.

Evidence or no evidence, Mark had been tainted. The foul acts of some also stick to the people around them, who can't scrub them away any more than the offenders can. Mark would never be clean. He would carry the stigma of silence from one place to another, and any shelter he might find within the humble room of friendship would never convince man, woman, or child that a man with such knowledge could ever lay claim to innocence.

Bopha Phorn

Bopha Phorn is an investigative reporter for the *Cambodian Daily*. This is her first published short story.

Play with Fire
A Sergio Biancardi Mystery

Giancarlo Narciso

You don't have to be smart to stay out of trouble. It's getting into it that takes talent. The moment I stumbled upon the corpse lying on the floor, I knew I'd walked into a monumental trap. Whoever had set me up, it hadn't taken him much effort. I did it all by myself.

Right, being caught uninvited in the middle of the night on someone else's property might not be such a terrible crime. Things tend to get complicated, though, when that someone is spread face down on the floor, with his skull cracked open. They get even more complicated if, not much earlier, in front of a dozen reliable witnesses, you've sworn to break the guy's neck.

Well, so far just bad news. The good news was that it couldn't possibly get worse than that, right?

Wrong.

I was still musing over my chances of not ending up in a Cambodian jail when a roaring wall of flame burst up from the floor, telling me the situation had just taken a sharp turn toward catastrophe.

Great. I now had an alternative to being framed for murder: turn into a sizzling steak. It wasn't what I'd had in mind when I'd accepted that nice job offer. I remember well; it was only a few days earlier.

The fat guy who had introduced himself as Salvatore Curzi placed an oval dish in front of me.

"Today's special: *Spaghetti Fabiana*," he announced proudly. "Avocado, garlic, olive oil, lime, and shrimps. Oh, and black pepper, of course. I named it after my wife. It's her recipe."

I glanced at the food. It reminded me of tiny snakes swimming in a greasy, greenish sauce. I brought some to my mouth. It tasted of burned oil.

"Delicious," I mumbled.

Curzi picked up a bottle of Barbera d'Alba and opened it. He poured some into a goblet, raised it up, stuck his beaked nose into it, and sniffed with an inspired look. Then he sipped the wine and held it in his mouth. He seemed to ponder for a while before nodding appreciatively. Finally he gulped it down and filled both our glasses.

"We make the best spaghetti in Southeast Asia," he boasted.

He was more or less my age, tall, with a receding hairline and small eyes that were too close to each other, and he spoke with a curious mix of Neapolitan and American accents. He'd called earlier that afternoon, saying he'd got my name from people I didn't remember having met. He wanted to talk business and would I terribly mind dropping by at his place? Like most days back then, I'd nothing better to do, so I got onto my old Yamaha and rode to his restaurant by the riverside, in Toul Sangke.

The building was a crossover between modern minimalism and traditional, with bare wooden walls and a pagoda-shaped thatched roof. The compound, which included a large parking lot and a lush garden dotted by casuarina, coconut, and banana trees, was completely surrounded by a tall stone wall.

It was located in a quiet area, far from the crowds that fill the riverbank in Sisowath Quay, farther south, after the bridge. Sparse, low one-storey houses, a few food stalls, and not much else. A light westward wind was rippling the surface of the Tonlé Sap. Far out across the river, lights blinking on its final approach, a twin-jet aircraft came in low over the Chruoy Changvar peninsula, where I lived in a furnished room.

"This will turn into one of the most fashionable spots in Phnom Penh," said Sal. "All they have to do is finish the damned new bridge."

I felt no need to point out that although rumors about building a second bridge across the Tonlé Sap had been coming and going for years, no actual work had started yet.

Sal lowered his eyes and started eating. I lit a Camel and sipped my wine, waiting. He finished his spaghetti, raised his head, and glanced at me, then at my plate. A dash of disbelief filled his watery eyes.

"You don't like it? It's homemade, you know."

"What?"

It took me a moment to understand what he meant. I don't particularly miss Italian food. I've been away from home for too long, and besides, local fare is good enough for me. In any case, I never liked pasta.

"Oh, the spaghetti. Yeah, like I said, it's delicious but I'm not hungry. Had a late lunch. Sorry about that."

He shrugged and said nothing.

I killed my cigarette and looked at him.

"Mister Curzi, what—"

"Just call me Sal."

"All right. Sal, then. What do you want from me?"

He wiped his lips with the back of his hand and drank a sip of wine.

"Heard you used to be a cop," he said presently.

I nodded.

"How long were you in the service?"

I paused, long enough to show that I did not enjoy the subject.

"Sixteen years," I murmured.

"Why did you quit?"

"Grew tired of it," I lied, letting my irritation transpire and not giving a damn whether he believed me or not. Probably not. "Has this got anything to do with what you expect me to do here?"

He seemed to think it over for a while, then let his lips curl into a smile.

"You are exactly the kind of person I was looking for."

Oddly enough, only a few hours earlier, when we still had not met, he'd said exactly the same words.

"That's not what I asked."

Suppressing a chuckle, he shook his head and then turned serious.

"I was threatened, you see? About a week ago. Then again, day before yesterday."

"Who was it?"

"A guy on the phone who didn't bother to introduce himself. But I have a general idea."

I kept silent, and he drank some more. Then he looked at me again.

"See this place?" he said, tracing a wide arc with his hand. "Ain't too bad, right?"

I pretended to look at the fake colonial furniture and the Khmer paintings on the walls.

"Not bad."

"Problem is, when I built it five years ago, I had to borrow heavily. At outrageous rates. You know Chinese moneylenders . . ."

His voice trailed off and I nodded wisely, as though I knew. Then he resumed talking in a somber voice.

"I felt confident business would thrive and money start rolling in soon, enabling me to repay my debt in due time. What I didn't foresee was the global recession. Fewer tourists, and most of those few end up in the downtown joints. I'm sure things are gonna improve in six months, a year, but those bastards want the money now."

"Why don't you sell?"

"Giving up is not in my DNA," he said proudly. "Besides, this land isn't worth half of what I paid. As for the buildings, furniture, and equipment, I'd be lucky to get much, much less. If I find a buyer, that is. You see? Even if I sold, I still couldn't settle my debt."

He fished a cigarette out of a green pack of menthol Marlboros and lit it. Then, as an afterthought, he offered me one. I shook my head.

"So, what do you want from me? Protection?"

He didn't answer, and after a while I continued.

"I'm getting a bit too old for this sort of thing. Why don't you hire a local?"

He snorted, blowing out smoke.

"I'm not looking for muscles. No one has threatened me physically, yet, and I don't expect anyone ever will. You know how these people deal with foreigners. They do not resort to physical violence. They have better alternatives."

"Like?"

"How about burning down the whole place? Or poisoning the food? How would you like that?"

I nodded and thought it over for a while, then sighed.

"What should I do, then?"

"Just stay here and keep your eyes open. I already have a night watchman. What I need is somebody to check out the staff. I'm sure they planted a spy among them. I will give you a hundred thousand kips a day ..."

"That's less than twenty euros," I objected.

"This is Cambodia, not Europe. And I'm not finished yet. There's more. You're having immigration problems, right?"

He seemed to know too much about me. Last August I'd been caught working with a tourist visa, which is something you're not supposed to do. The fact that even the tourist visa had expired ages before didn't help. They fined me but I didn't have money to pay the fine, so the police took away my passport, placing me in a limbo. I couldn't leave, but officially I couldn't stay either.

Sal winked and continued without waiting for an answer: "The chief of immigration is a good friend of mine. He can handle this and it won't cost you a cent. I'll get the fine cancelled and your passport back with a two-year extension. What do you think? Frankly, you don't seem in a position to say no."

I wasn't, in fact. But I didn't appreciate being reminded.

"Deal," I whispered, suppressing my pride. "When do I begin?"

"When can you?"

There was no point in pretending I was busy elsewhere. He'd obviously checked me out before contacting me. I sighed in a quick surrender.

"How about tomorrow?"

He seemed relieved. "Great." Then smiled. "Ah, I nearly forgot ..."

"What?"

"Look at it as a fringe. Come tomorrow, you won't have to worry about lunch or dinner. You can have all the pasta you can eat. Free of charge."

As I entered the compound the next morning, Sal was loading a carton box onto a white Toyota pickup.
"Morning, Sergio. You're early."
I shrugged, parking my bike beside the truck.
"I don't like staying in bed late."
"This is Abu," he said, pointing at a little old man squatting on the grass near a banana tree. "Gardener and night-watchman. Plus other stuff. Running errands, fixing things . . ."
The little man got up, holding a brown and yellow snake by its neck, tail wiggling in the air.
"And catching Russell's vipers," concluded Sal. "They're pretty nasty. We got plenty in this area, on account of we have also plenty of rats, which they like. Thanks God we have Abu. He's quite good at handling snakes."
"What does he do with them? Keep them as pets?"
"I think he makes some extra bucks selling them to the snake farm."
Sal laughed, then spoke to the gardener: "Hey, Abu. This is Sergio."
The little man turned and looked at me with narrow eyes. The snake had gone still.
"Hi," I said.
He nodded imperceptibly.
"Abu doesn't speak much English," said Sal. "Hell, he doesn't speak much, period. But he's a good fellow. He's a Cham Muslim from Kompong Speu, been with me since I first came to this country, thirteen years ago. He'll

show you to your room. Sorry, got to split now. Catch you before sunset. Meanwhile, have a look around."

I followed Abu, keeping at a distance from the snake till we reached a small concrete bungalow in the backyard. It wasn't much, just a room with a double bed and a simple bathroom with blue tiles; outside was a veranda, with two bamboo chairs flanking a small table with a thermos on it. All very basic and simple, but clean.

I threw my bag onto the bed and went out into the compound. It was my first day of work. I thought I might just as well start straight away.

The weather was fine—for the tropics. It being January, we were in dry season, but the sky was gray, with plenty of clouds to give us shelter from the sun. You could walk without sweating.

Half an hour later I had covered the whole compound. There wasn't much to see. At the back of the wooden restaurant were a concrete kitchen and a storeroom, and beyond that, conveniently set aside, Sal's house and a round swimming pool. The wall surrounding the property was rather tall, but any idiot with a bamboo ladder could go over it in a blitz.

I walked up the stairs and entered the restaurant. Three waiters were readying the tables for lunch. A pretty girl sat in a corner, folding napkins. They were all young, like most people in a country where nearly a whole generation had been erased.

They all smiled and said hello as I walked by. I nodded back, without being too friendly. You never know whom you'll have to go against when you do a job like mine.

I checked the kitchen. Cooks and helpers were busy cutting onions and peeling potatoes. The one who looked like the chef had a face I didn't like. I talked at length with him, mentally noting points I might want to follow up on

later, then went back to the garden. Abu was squatting on the lawn, cutting grass with a small sickle.
"*Sua s'dei,*" I said with a smile. He ignored me.
I shrugged and kept walking toward the swimming pool.
A woman in a turquoise one-piece bathing suit was lying on her back over the yellow limestone tiles. Good, lean body with well-shaped muscles, brown hair, and an attractive, slightly aggressive face with wide cheekbones and full lips. Sunglasses with mirrored lenses. Must have been Sal's wife. She was still, as though she was asleep. But I felt her eyes studying me from behind the lenses.
I turned back and caught Abu watching me. Or perhaps the woman. He turned his head fast, but not fast enough to hide the hatred burning in his eyes.
I made another round and then sat at a table in the restaurant, watching the waiters going back and fro. I was not looking for anything in particular. Not yet. I was just trying to absorb the energy of the place. There was something in the air that I could not identify. All I knew was I did not like it.

Next day, shortly before noon, I was walking through the parking lot when a yellow Mazda Spider came in, tires screeching on the polished concrete. Nice car. But the woman who got out was even better. It took me a while to realize she was the same one I'd seen yesterday by the swimming pool.
She walked around the car and opened the trunk. Abu rushed to help her. He tried picking up a large box but it nearly fell. He managed to catch it before it hit the ground, but by then she was already screaming like hell.
"Not that way, idiot! Oh! Put it down and get lost before you do more damage."

Abu lowered his head and went away. She looked after him with an expression of scorn, then shook her head and sighed.

"Same old story. The more you try to teach them, the less they understand."

She looked at me, exasperated, and then nodded.

"Come on, help me. And be careful. It's delicate stuff."

I grabbed the box and lifted it. It was heavy.

"Wait," she said, then picked up two paper bags full of clothes and placed them over the box, slammed the trunk closed, recovered her handbag from the passenger seat, and started toward the backyard.

"Come," she said without turning.

We entered the house and she had me put the box on a teak table.

"Right. At least you're better than that imbecile. Fuck him and his snakes. I hope he gets bitten and drops dead one day."

She stopped suddenly and studied me for several seconds.

"So you're Sal's new henchman."

"I'm nobody's henchman."

"Oh, but of course. You are the fourth so far. Nobody is good enough for him, ever. I guess he's just looking for somebody who's willing to do what he hasn't got the guts to do himself."

She turned and started to unbutton her shirt. Then raised her eyes and met mine in the mirror.

"You still here? Get out."

I went back to the garden and resumed my tour of the premises.

That night the restaurant was reasonably crowded. Waiters ran from one table to the next, trying to cope with requests. Sal looked happy but nervous.

"Need help?" I asked.

"No, just do your job. And keep your eyes open. Nights like this, anything can happen."

I resumed my surveillance, wondering what he'd meant by that. Around nine o'clock the chestnut-haired woman came in, wearing a black mini-dress that ended one inch below her buttocks. She sat at a corner table, not far from where I was, and lit a cigarette. She seemed to see me for the first time and snapped her fingers.

"Bring me a gin tonic. Quick."

I had a feeling she was testing me. I stopped one of the waiters who was passing by.

"The lady wants to order," I said.

He went to her table and bowed. "Madam?"

She looked him up and down and repeated the order, and he ran away.

I started to move, but before I could take a step, her face softened.

"Won't you sit down with me?"

I hesitated, and she was fast to seize the moment to her advantage.

"Come on. I don't bite," she whispered in a husky voice, then smiled, pointing at the empty chair at her side. I sat.

"My name is Fabiana," she said. "And you are ..."

"Sergio. Sergio Biancardi."

"Italian?"

I nodded. "From Milan."

"Been here long?"

On average, three personal questions in a row were as much as I could take without exploding.

"In Phnom Penh, you mean? Couple of years." I tried to smooth out the edge in my voice. "You must be Sal's wife."

A trace of pain flickered in her eyes.

"Yeah, I'm his wife. So what?"

The waiter brought the gin tonic and asked me whether I wanted to order too. I shook my head and he went away, walking backwards. The hurt look in Fabiana's eyes had grown in intensity.

"Something wrong?" I asked.

She said nothing for an instant, then drilled her eyes into mine.

"My husband wants to kill me," she said softly. "Is that wrong enough for you?"

I watched her for a long while, and all I thought I saw was a bored, spoiled, fairly attractive young woman toying with persecutory delusions. I looked around, and my eyes met Sal's at the opposite end of the hall.

I got up.

"Please excuse me," I said, and left.

Much later, after the staff had gone home, Sal and I sat on the terrace, each with a can of Tiger, watching the Tonlé Sap. It was that time of the year when it flows south, into the Mekong.

"You didn't eat tonight," said Sal.

"I started feeling hungry at five and had something at a stall, outside."

His jaw fell.

"At a stall? Are you out of your mind? You could get sick. Next time ask the kitchen to cook you something. Today we had *orecchiette e broccoli*."

"It's all right," I said. "I felt like having soup. I had *chhnang dei*. Like I said, I quite like the local fare."

He gave me an uncertain look, then shook his head.

"I sometimes think expats who don't like their home food have unsolved issues with their past. It's, you know, like they're running away from something."

I felt a dash of irritation rising up in my throat, but then again, he might have had a point. We both said nothing for a while, just sat there, eyes lost in the darkness. The splutter of a diesel engine came and went as a narrow boat sailed upriver.

A shooting star lit up in the sky. Sal looked at it and then turned to me.

"Did you make a wish?"

"A what?"

"A wish," he said. "My wife says, make a wish when you see a shooting star, and it will come true."

For a second I thought the guy was a useless idiot.

"No," said I at last. "No wish."

"Well, I did. I wished this problem with the moneylender would be fixed soon. I don't mind your being here, but when I go to bed at the end of the day, I'd like to relax. Have you found out anything interesting so far?"

I'd already told him how I felt about the cook, but he'd dismissed my fears. That cook, he said, had been with him for seven years. He paid him well and knew his family. Besides, he was a very good cook, one of the best they could find, so I'd better forget about him, okay? Other than the cook, I had no other names on my short list of suspects.

"Not really, no," I answered. "Two days is a bit too early."

He nodded and again kept silent for a few moments.

"So you met Fabiana," he said.

"Right."

"She's much younger than I am, as you must have noticed."

I thought she was much younger than me, too, but didn't comment on it. Sal placed the beer can on the floor and stared at me.

"You're not thinking of taking her to bed, are you?"

"What?"

He kept on transfixing me with his dark eyes, then suddenly burst out laughing.

"Just kidding. Christ, man, you should have seen your face."

Nice little joke. I gulped down some more beer and tried laughing too.

Third day of work and still no results. I was beginning to think there was nothing to find out. Sal went downtown to attend to some business. I did one more tour of the compound, passing by the swimming pool. I caught no sight of Fabiana and did not know whether I was relieved or disappointed. I kept on walking, still convinced I was wasting my time, but I had to earn my hundred thousand kips a day. And more importantly, get my passport back, stamped with a new visa. I crossed paths with Abu.

"*Salam aleikum*," I said.

His face seemed to register a trace of surprise.

"*Aleikum assalam*," he whispered, barely audible but clear.

Perhaps I'd found a tiny breach to his heart. Right or wrong, a Muslim in a country where ninety-nine per cent of the population is Buddhist tends to feel he's being discriminated against. Treat him well and you've won a friend.

I left the garden and went to the wall to complete my tour, keeping close to Sal's home. I was turning behind the corner when I heard her voice.

"Sergio?"

I raised my eyes. She was at the window upstairs, smiling.

"Good morning," I said.

"Hold on, I'm coming down."

She withdrew her face and reappeared at the door at ground level a few seconds later.

"Come inside. Have a drink."

She was all smiles, fluttering of eyes, languid glances. Somewhere inside a voice started whispering, telling me not to stay, to get out of there fast, while I still could.

I knew I was playing with fire. But I also knew I wasn't going to heed my own warning. I was curious. And not just that.

I felt something tickling my spine. Something that made me shiver.

We were facing each other on two huge rattan chairs. I'd already drained a can of Angkor and started a second. She was sipping a Coke without much interest.

"He wants to kill me," she murmured in a tired voice.

"Why should he?"

"Jealousy."

"And has he got, um ... reasons for this?"

I was sure she would be outraged.

"Yes."

"Huh?"

She'd caught me off guard.

"What do you mean, yes?"

"Listen, there's no need to deny the truth. It's my fault, and he's right. Only thing I can say, I told him since the very beginning I wasn't in love with him. But he wanted to marry me anyway. And in all honesty, I did my best to be faithful to him. Most of the time I succeeded."

"Most of the time ain't enough for most men. And for most women, too, now that I think of it."

"Sergio, I'm twenty-six, okay?"

"And your husband is nearly twice your age, I know."

"That's not what I mean. Some men are old at twenty, others can still be very attractive at sixty . . ."

Her eyes surfed over me for a second and then she glanced away, as though fearing she was revealing too much.

"What I mean is that at twenty-six, a woman doesn't want to feel ignored, as though she's not a woman anymore. And no matter how hard you try to steer away from temptation, to keep your eyes downcast, there always comes a moment when you're not so strong. And if the right person happens to be around at the wrong time . . ." She shrugged, meekly. "I know it's wrong, but I'm not used to faking being better than what I am, like so many women do. And I never lied to Sal. I always told him I didn't love him."

She gave me another glance, sad, lips parted, then again lowered her eyes. A blast of hot air from the door blew over my skin.

I didn't believe her. I mean, yeah, she looked sincere, but it was a story I'd heard too many times already.

"Mrs. Curzi, if your husband is really planning to kill you—"

"Please, I'm Fabiana."

I ignored her.

"Why don't you leave him? Why don't you ask for a divorce?"

"Because I have no other place to go. I no longer have a family in Italy. And all my savings went into this damn restaurant."

"But ... but the restaurant was financed by other people. That's why Sal asked me to—"

She laughed.

"This is what he told you, right? Same damn fairy tale he tells everybody. You see, he ... oh, just forget it, Sergio, will you? It's a long story, and I'm not sure you wanna hear it."

"Try me."

Again she looked at me, but this time there was a different light in her eyes, more like a plea.

"My husband lost a hell of a lot of money recently," she said.

"You mean with the restaurant?"

"No. Gambling. It's true that the restaurant isn't doing well, but the real reason we're nearly broke is that Sal likes gambling. Which wouldn't be too bad if he won. But he loses. A lot."

"This doesn't explain why he should want you dead," I said. "People don't kill without a motive."

"And what if I told you that Sal bought an insurance policy? Should I die before him, he will cash in a fat prize. There's your motive. And in his mind, you're the one who's going to carry out his plan. That's the only reason you were hired."

I stared without speaking. She had me mesmerized.

"Like I said, you are not the first," she went on. "For the moment, Sal is just testing you. Once he's sure you can be trusted, he will ask you to kill me. It will be worth it, no worries. Your fee will be generous."

"So how come you're still alive? Why did he turn down those who came before me?"

"I guess because they didn't pass the test. You can't go around asking the first person you meet to kill your wife, can you? First, you must be absolutely sure he has the guts to do it, won't crack under interrogation, won't turn you in, won't attempt to blackmail you . . . Sal is a very patient man. He'll approach you very gradually, and not before he's absolutely sure you're the right man."

I stared hard at her.

"How do you know all this?"

She smiled a bit and sighed.

"Among all those men who came before you, there was one who was decent. He sort of . . . well, liked me."

"Did he and you . . . ?"

She raised her hand to silence me.

"Not *that* kind of liking. He was good and stayed here long, passing nearly all the tests, or so we guessed."

"Why didn't you go to the police, then?"

"Because Sal never went so far as to make a clear proposal. He started with some vague hints, slowly moving closer to the subject. But Pierre—this guy, a Canadian—he wasn't stupid. When he realized where Sal was heading, he resigned. Before leaving, though, he came to me and let me know what my lovely husband had in store for me. So, to answer your question, I didn't have enough evidence to go to the police. But after that, I started keeping my eyes open and soon realized Pierre was right: Sal wants to have me murdered."

I said nothing. Her logic was impeccable, the facts were consistent with her tale, and she behaved and spoke like a normal person. Perhaps a bit too normal. I hadn't entirely changed my idea that Fabiana was used to crossing the border that separates reality from delusion a bit too easily.

She was silent too, staring at me with a glance I knew far too well. The glance of a woman who is aware you like her and wants to make it clear to you that she would not mind feeling your hands over her body. Which I would not have minded, except she was twenty-six, spoiled, and far too attractive, while I was nearly a quarter of a century older and a hobo who lived in a hovel, struggling to gather enough money to survive until next week.

I finished my beer and got up. It was hot and I felt a bit dizzy, like I was drifting in the sweltering room.

She got up too.

A moment later we were kissing, and I wasn't sure who had taken the first step.

It was a hot and humid kiss that took away my breath and sped up my heart. My hand slid under her shirt, down her back, to caress her buttocks. It took me a minute to fully realize what I was doing. I stepped back and went out without saying a word.

The restaurant was even more crowded than it had been the night before. Despite Sal's complaints, business seemed to be thriving. Still, he looked nervous, like something was troubling him. He kept on running from one side of the hall to the other, getting in and out of the kitchen, barking orders to the staff. I went to him, thinking he might need help. He had just finished taking the order from a table of nine noisy Italians.

"Is there anything I can do?"

"What? Oh, yes," he said and glanced at the Italians. "They all want *linguine al pesto*. While I go get the wine, pass the order to the kitchen and tell the cook this has priority and he should take extra care. I'll let him have the order slip in a minute. Please make sure everything goes smoothly. These people are with a big tour operator and this is the first time I've worked with them."

There was something strange in his voice and manner. And his eyes were elusive. I decided he was just stressed, discarded the thought, and ran to the kitchen.

"The boss said nine *linguine al pesto* for table sixteen," I told the chef. "Give them top priority."

"Where's the slip?"

"It will come. The boss said it's an important group. Please don't keep them waiting too long."

The chef snorted and muttered something to a couple of helpers, who rushed to the freezer and pulled out green cubes of frozen pesto sauce. Minutes later I was helping a waiter carry out the spaghetti. One of them, a woman in her forties, said loudly in Italian, "Who ordered *linguine al pesto*?"

Before I could answer, Sal showed up with four bottles of Valpolicella. He placed them on the cart and looked at me with a horrified expression.

"What are you doing?"

"The *linguine al pesto* ..." I started saying, suddenly feeling stupid.

"I can see what they are. What I can't see is why you brought them here. They ordered *spaghetti alla carbonara*."

His expression had turned to pure rage. I didn't understand what was going on.

"You said nine *linguine al pesto*."

"Oh, get away, you poor, dumb idiot. How come I can never trust you to do anything right?"

"But ..."

"There's no but." His hand sprang forward, grabbing my forearm. "You're a bloody idiot. You manage to fuck up even the simplest thing."

I felt the blood leaving my cheeks.

"Take your hand off me."

He tightened his grip and placed his other hand over my breast, pushing hard.

"Get the hell out of here. Go do what I pay you to do instead of meddling with our work."

This time I reacted. I wriggled free of his grip and grabbed his wrist.

"You touch me once more, I'll break your fucking neck, you dig?" I hissed, still holding his wrist.

Then I let him go.

He stared at me for a few seconds as though he wanted to skin me alive, then stepped back and spat out his answer.

"You're fired. Pick up you rags and get out of here. Now."

The whole restaurant had turned silent as the inside of a cloister. Everybody was looking at me. One of the Italians whispered something in her companion's ear, looking utterly terrified. I knew I was losing control. I let the air escape from my lungs in a long breath, then turned on my heels and left.

I was lying on the bed in my room in Chruoy Changvar, well into my second bottle of Golden Muscle, which I drank mixed with Coke. Best, cheapest, and fastest way to get drunk in this country. It was past two in the morning, and my anger was barely starting to abate.

Then my mobile rang.

The scared voice sounded familiar.

"Sergio, it's me . . ."

"You, who?"

"Fabiana."

"What do you want?"

"He's trying to kill me, I beg you ..."

"Oh, knock this shit off. Nobody wants to kill you."

"Please, help me," she pleaded. "I barricaded myself in my bedroom. He went away but said he would be back to break down the door. He beat me up. I've got a broken arm. Said he knows you and I have a relationship ..."

"The fuck you say, a relationship? All we did was kiss for half a minute."

"Abu must have told him. That bastard hates me. Hates all women. He worships Sal, said he saved his life once, so now he's his watchdog. He's always been trying to turn Sal against me."

"Sorry, lady, no business of mine. Call the police."

I was trying to sound convincing but knew I was doing a very poor job of it.

"The police? In this country? For a woman who's being beaten up? They wouldn't lift a finger. They don't move for their own women, let alone a foreign one. They might drop by tomorrow, when it will be too late. I beg you, Sergio, I'm scared, I can't hold out much longer."

I swallowed another sip of Golden Muscle and got up.

"I'll see what I can do," I said, then cut the line.

A minute later I was on the Yamaha, racing toward the bridge that connected the peninsula with downtown Phnom Penh.

The main gate was ajar. I got off the bike and entered the compound.

Lights out, not a soul, not a sound. A westward breeze was blowing.

The door to the restaurant was wide open. I rushed up the steps and peered inside.

Nothing moved in the dark hall. I walked in, among empty tables, floor planks squeaking under my feet. A smell of kerosene lingered in the air.

I hadn't taken more than a few steps when my left foot hit something soft and I stumbled, struggling to regain balance. I turned and looked down, angst already pushing up my throat.

The man lay on his stomach and chest, arms out to either side. I kneeled and turned him over. His front and left eye were covered by a dark, thick fluid I felt no wish to touch, and I knew at once it was Sal. A few steps away was a hammer.

I touched his throat. No pulse, no breathing, nothing. He'd been dead long enough to stop bleeding.

What had happened? There were only two scenarios I could think of.

In the first one, a shocked Fabiana sneaks out of her bedroom and crosses the restaurant, in an attempt to get out of the compound and to safety. Little does she known that fiendish Sal is lurking in the dark with heinous intent. With a ravaging jolt he seizes his unsuspecting prey, they have a brawl, she gets hold of the hammer, and with all the strength she can summon hits Sal, who drops dead on the gore-splattered floor.

Possible, but quite unlikely. What was the hammer doing there? How could she overcome a heavy man like Sal? The answers were beyond my imagination.

In the second, far less evocative scenario, Sal had been killed by unnamed thugs sent by those folks who lent him money.

Even more unlikely. Murdering a debtor is not a smart credit collection tactic. The dead are not good at paying debts.

Then, the awareness that I had just become a likely candidate for the role of number-one suspect in a murder case hit me with the impact of a high-speed train. Hadn't I, earlier that very night, uttered reckless threats against the victim in the presence of several bystanders? Er, yes, Your Honor, but...

That was my last rational thought as my attention was drawn to a few minor details, such as, a) the kerosene smell had grown much, much stronger, and b) black smoke had begun creeping up between the floor planks.

Then, in a sudden eruption, flames surged through the floor, quickly engulfing the whole hall, although technically, that didn't strictly qualify as a minor detail.

Fed by the wind, the fire spread to the wooden walls and the stairs leading up to the terrace, threatening to reach the thatched roof. Everything blazed with raging fury.

Flames started lapping Sal's feet. Black smoke snaked around me. My eyes filled with tears. Over the roaring flames I heard the cracking sound of a beam splintering and leapt instinctively aside, without looking. It fell a couple of meters away.

I had to make a move fast.

Fire was already threatening me on three sides, sparing only the northern wall that separated the dining hall from the kitchen and the food store, which, unlike the rest of the building, was made of concrete. There I could last longer.

I bent over, grabbed Sal's wrist and hauled him up over my shoulder, then pushed through the wall of heat and smoke toward the kitchen door.

I wasn't motivated by pity. I was simply hoping that the police could run forensic tests on the victim's body. The more data they had, the better their chances of identifying the real murderer.

Staggering, I reached the door to the kitchen and tried it.

It was open.

I entered the kitchen. I knew there was also a rear door that gave access to the garden. The staff always locked it from the inside at night before exiting through the restaurant's main door.

I went straight to it, unlocked it, and pushed.

It didn't budge. It was bolted from the outside.

I looked around, searching for some tool to knock it open, and found nothing suitable. It was a heavy door, built to keep thieves out, not to use as a safety exit.

Next to the door there was a barred window, and the bars were large bamboo canes rooted in concrete. No way to break them either.

I was on the verge of panic. I thought about wrapping myself in a few wet tablecloths and rushing back to the restaurant and across the fire, trying to reach the front door, but the flames were too high already, and I could feel the heat over my cheeks. It was then that I completely understood why people chose to jump out of the Twin Towers windows on September 11th.

Then something moved outside, in the garden. An instant later Fabiana's face peered in through the window bars.

"Fabiana! Thank God. Open the door and let me out of here."

She looked like she hadn't heard.

"He's dead," she whispered, eyes looking at something far away.

"Yes, I know. Please, let me out, now!"

"He gave me no chance," she mumbled. "Broke into my room. I managed to run to the restaurant, but he caught up with me and started beating me up again, harder than before."

I didn't like the sound of her voice. And the more I looked, the less I liked her face. It was flawless. No cuts, no trace of bruises. And certainly, no broken arm.

"Enough of that, Fabiana. Sal didn't even touch you. It's pure fantasy. You killed him because you're nuts."

She stared at me for a while, and then her eyes went blank again. I had a feeling she had no intention of opening that door any time soon. I quickly reviewed my options once more and concluded I had run out of them. Smoke was already filling up the kitchen, and soon the flames would reach us. I could only hope the firemen arrived in time, but that's not the way things work in Phnom Penh.

"Open the fucking door, Fabiana! There's no time."

She seemed slowly to realize where and who I was. A thin smile danced briefly over her lips.

"I didn't kill him," she said and something in her voice sent a shiver down my spine.

"No, of course not. Don't worry, we'll take care of that later. Now help me out."

"You did."

Nutty as a fruitcake.

"Fabiana …"

"For revenge. For what happened between you two. Everybody saw you threatening him."

I sighed. She had spoken in a quiet and controlled voice, but a borderline can be very deceptive and look perfectly normal. She had a point, though. I was the perfect scapegoat. Even if I managed to survive the fire, proving my innocence wasn't going to be easy.

"I did not kill your husband," I said slowly.

Dark reflections shone briefly in her eyes, then she smirked scornfully.

"Go tell it to a jury. Think they'll believe you?"

"But you . . . you'll tell them, right? You'll tell them your husband was beating you?"

"So what?"

"Sal was already dead when I arrived," I shouted. "I did not kill him!"

"You see, problem is, I find it hard to believe. And I have a feeling the police won't, either."

"You asked me to come here."

"Now, did I, really?"

I was voiceless for a few seconds, then the fog in my mind started to clear.

"You set me up, didn't you?" I said slowly. "When you called me, you had already killed Sal. After the quarrel you realized you could get rid of him and pin the murder on me."

She shrugged. "Is this what you think, then?"

The door to the dining hall caught fire. I was speechless for quite a while.

"You know what?" I said. "I'm starting to feel sorry for Sal."

"Save your sorrow for a better cause. It's admirable of you, but I don't think Sal did much to deserve your pity. He was part of this since the beginning."

I looked at her for some seconds.

"What?"

"He was in on it, although the plan was mine, of course. And I chose you, not Sal. Someone mentioned your name, I checked you out, and when I realized you were the right man, I told my husband to hire you."

The door disappeared and the flames invaded the kitchen and started licking the roof beams. I was losing hope that the firemen could get me out in time. Over the roaring flames I heard screams coming from the streets. People from the neighborhood must have gathered outside the compound's walls, but there wasn't much they could do. You can't put out a massive fire with a couple of buckets.

"It's true we had money problems," continued Fabiana as though she was totally unaware of the commotion outside. "This stupid restaurant has never turned a profit, so we had the idea of burning it down and cashing the insurance. Only problem was, Sal would have been the first suspect. At this point, I had the idea of hiring somebody, laying him off for no fair reason, and *then* setting fire to the place. It was a perfect setup. Disgruntled employee burns to death in arson attempt. I was to make sure you didn't have an alibi."

She seemed delighted to tell me how smart she had been.

A beam snapped with a thunderous sound and several tiles fell onto the concrete floor. Fabiana startled, then laughed. I had a feeling she was thrilled by the whole thing. She was even crazier than I thought.

"What Sal didn't know was that I had in mind a slightly different ending," she said. "You see, the insurance works both ways. Whoever dies first, the surviving spouse gets the money. You get it now?"

I said nothing. Her eyes were full of contempt.

"Of course I killed him. It wasn't hard. Sal never suspected a thing."

A cabinet caught fire. Smoke was everywhere, and I had to press my face against the window bars to breathe.

"Let me out, Fabiana," I said, coughing. "I'll run away and never come back. And even if I'm caught, I won't tell them anything, I swear. I will confirm your story."

She pretended to think it over carefully, but the amused look in her eyes gave her away. She sighed and shook her head sadly.

"Even if you didn't, it wouldn't change anything. I will testify that you came here looking for revenge, Sal tried to stop you and you killed him, then you started the fire. It will be my word against yours. Who do you think they'll believe? A respectable businesswoman or a bum who overstayed his visa? When we did the casting, you were perfect for the part."

The fire was now inches away. I tried to adhere as much as I could to the window.

"You're right, nobody will believe me. So open the door and let me out. I'll run to Laos."

Again she shook her head.

"I don't think I will. It's easier if you burn to death. Less complication."

"Fabiana!" I pleaded.

"Goodbye, loser. *Lia suhn hau-y.* I'm done talking. Now I'll run out to the street, screaming for help. Such serious crimes have been committed tonight in my home. Arson and mur—"

Abruptly something made her start. She turned.

"Who the hell ..."

She stepped back, looking at something outside my field of vision, then sighed heavily in relief.

"Oh, it's you. Get lost, you stupid imbecile. Don't you see there's a—"

Then, terror was in her eyes. She cowered, raising one arm to her face, in a protective gesture.

"No!" she shouted.

Something flew in the air.

Fabiana's hand gripped her shoulder as she ran away, screaming. The cry died out, and for a moment there was only the roar of the fire. Then I heard the outside bolt slide. A second later the door opened.

I grabbed Sal's body by his wrists and pulled him out into the garden. Abu was standing there. He didn't say anything but turned and walked away, alongside Sal's home, disappearing behind the corner. I went after him.

Fabiana was lying on the edge of the swimming pool, quivering. A yellow and brown snake was crawling away over the tiles, toward the coconut trees. Abu leaned forward and grabbed it by its tail. I went close to Fabiana. She had lost consciousness but was alive, though her breathing was labored. Two red dots, rather close to each other, spoiled the white of her bare shoulder.

"Mistah Sal—he dead," said Abu, sliding his other hand along the reptile body till it reached its neck. "Madame kill Mistah. Snake kill Madame."

"The police will think …"

He looked at me, face expressionless.

"I speak police," he said. "You no problem."

The restaurant roof collapsed all of a sudden, filling the sky with red sparkles. When I turned back to Abu, he was gone.

Fabiana was still alive when the first fire truck arrived. She was taken to the hospital and treated. After a few days she was recovering well. She never ended up in jail, though. She was still at the hospital a week later, when her condition worsened suddenly. She slipped into a coma and died the next day. That's often the case with Russell's vipers. Once they bite you, there's not much you can do.

Me, I spent the whole day at the police station but was let out at sunset with the recommendation not to leave town.

The cops showed up again a couple of weeks later. They came to my home, had me pack my stuff, and threw me in jail for two days. On the third day I was dragged to the desk of an immigration officer who held my passport under my nose and told me I was being deported for violating Cambodian immigration laws. Two cops took me to the airport, put me on a plane bound for Bangkok, and told me never to set foot in Cambodia again. Or else.

But that was later. A few days before then, I had run into Abu near Hotel Cambodiana. We had *samlor chapek* together at a food stall, and a couple of Tiger beers. We didn't talk much.

"Why did you save me?" was all I managed to ask him, moments before parting ways.

He shrugged, looking at the boats on the Mekong. "Why not?"

Then, lips turning into something that, with a great deal of imagination, might have been taken for a smile, he got up, gave me a last glance, and started down the road.

Barely avoiding being run over by a tuk-tuk, he passed under the branches of a huge banyan tree and melted into the crowd of passersby.

Giancarlo Narciso

Born and grown up in Milano, Giancarlo Narciso fell in love with Southeast Asia in the mid seventies. He lived in Indonesia, India, Singapore, Japan, and Mexico, before settling down in the Italian Alps in 1993. Giancarlo keeps on returning to the island of Lombok, Indonesia, which is the only place he calls home.

He is the author of twelve novels, mostly set in South East Asia, among which are award-winning *Incontro a Daunanda*, *Otherside* and *Singapore Sling*.

Orders

Christopher West

Inspector Khin Sovann sorted the pens in front of him and tapped a cigarette out of its red packet. He lit up and sat back in his wooden chair, settling himself for the day's work. Outside the window of his office was a frangipani plant, now covered in a delicate tracery of yellow and white blooms. Beyond that were the streets of Phnom Penh: motorbikes, horns, tuk-tuks, lorries, cars, and—someone always seemed to have one blaring—radios. Right now, at least, those streets were a reasonable temperature. But by eleven o'clock ...

Not my problem, he mused, glancing at the fan on his ceiling. A knock at the door announced the arrival of Jorani with the usual cup of *tai*. She smiled at Khin as she put the cup down, though their eyes didn't meet.

"Smoking cigarettes is bad for the health," said the WPC. "It encourages the buildup of noxious substances in the body, for example, tar in the lungs and fat in the arteries."

"I'll give up one day," said Khin.

Jorani gave that smile again and walked out. Khin couldn't help watching her as she did so (and she knew he was watching). Then he shrugged, reminding himself that he was a married man. He glanced up at the old black-and-white photograph on the wall: his father, in his jacket and *sampot chang kben*, and those spectacles. Bang Khin had always followed the Path, and he should do the same. It wasn't always easy, though.

Right now he had a report to finish. The shooting on the Strip was just another gangland thing: one stupid, greedy young man confronting another stupid, greedy young man and the whole business getting out of hand. Still, the formalities had to be gone through.

The inspector's desk phone was ringing.

"Khin, it's Chey here. I need you right now."

It sounded genuinely urgent—not urgent enough for Khin to gulp down the rest of his *tai*, but urgent enough for him to hurry to his superior's office once he had drunk properly.

Chey was younger than Khin but had moved up the promotion ladder speedily because he was good at politics. This included long lunches and dinners with superiors, and the effects of all this eating were clear in his appearance. However, Jorani never lectured Chey about his weight the way she talked to Khin; to his subordinates, "the chief" was a distant man. Even Khin, naturally curious, knew little about him. But Chey was fair-minded and valued old hands like Khin, who in return appreciated that.

"Senator Pach Vicheayin," he said, the moment Khin entered the room. "You're familiar with him?"

"I'm afraid not," Khin replied. His curiosity did not extend to national politics, a subject he found depressing.

"He's important. And he's been receiving death threats."

"Who from?"

"That's what I want you to find out."

"And leave the shooting? The gangs are still threatening one another ..."

"Pach is important."

Khin nodded.

"I want you to go and meet him," Chey continued. "We must be seen to be reacting. This is serious, Khin. That's why I'm putting an experienced officer on the case."

Khin smiled. Politics.

"Now, here's one of the notes."

Chey handed over a tatty piece of paper, with "You will die in a way that fits your crimes" typed onto it.

"What crimes?" asked Khin.

"It's not for officials at our level to go around accusing senators of crimes," said Chey, as Khin held the paper up to the light. "Though of course it might be a way of finding out who is behind these notes."

Khin nodded. "No prints, obviously."

"Obviously."

"Fair quality paper."

"Hard to trace, I'd have thought—but you're welcome to try."

"And the typing, of course. That letter prints strangely."

Chey smiled.

"It does. I'd like you to go and see the Senator first, though. I'll get the Commissioner to make an appointment."

Khin even got use of a car. He gave the Senator's address to the driver, Duong, who began punching details into a sat nav.

"You know every street in Phnom Penh, Duong!"

"Orders, sir. We have to use these things."

Orders

Khin nodded in acceptance.

The inspector had printed out a few details about Pach, which he read as the car made its way through the crowded streets. Pach's career went all the way back to 1976, when he had been a young Khmer Rouge cadre but had quickly defected to Vietnam, apparently horrified by the excesses of Angkar. Since January 7, 1979, the date the Vietnamese army had ended the madness, Pach had skillfully ridden the waves of Cambodian politics, enjoying a sudden conversion from socialism to the ideals of the market economy at exactly the right time.

"Politics ..." Khin muttered to himself, glancing up from his printout. "Hey, why are we going this way?"

"That's what the sat nav says, sir."

"But we don't need to go down Pochentong Boulevard."

"Orders, sir."

Khin went back to his papers. There was no hurry.

Khin had to push a bell and wait for electronic gates to open before Duong could drive up to the Senator's house. As they got out of the car, a large dog in a cage barked and hurled itself at the bars, as if half-mad.

The Senator answered the door himself and made a perfect *sampeah* salute (of the most condescending variety, of course, the hands held as low as possible).

"Thank you so much for coming, Inspector. Would you care for refreshment of some kind?"

He showed him into a sitting room about as large as Khin's entire apartment and pointed to a bar, stocked liberally with whiskeys.

"I'm fine, thank you, Senator."

Pach nodded his head in the direction of a seat, which Khin took and sank into.

"These threats are most disturbing, Inspector."

"I'm sure. Do you have any idea who they may be from?"

"None at all."

"Politics can be a rough business."

"Not that rough, Inspector."

"And your personal life?"

Pach frowned.

"I'm sorry to have to ask such a question, Senator," Khin continued quickly, "but to protect you as effectively as possible, we do need all the information we can get."

"Well, there's nothing for me to fear there. The world knows I am a devoted family man."

Khin nodded. "A family is the greatest blessing. Now, I believe you also have business interests. Very wise—but, again, a possible source of enmity."

"Inspector, I have always carried out my business in a clear, honorable way."

"I am not questioning that, Senator. But even the most honorable businessman can make enemies."

Pach shrugged. "Not to that level. Inspector, I think the source of these threats is obvious. A madman. What I require from the police is not questions but protection. Around the clock, till this person is apprehended. How many people can you provide, and how soon?"

"The Security Services will surely provide adequate—"

"Teenage boys with big guns and fast cars. I want professionals. Men of experience," he added, nodding at Khin.

Politics. Khin gave a bow of his head in response.

"Sadly, I am not trained in such work. But I shall ensure that a team with suitable experience is provided as soon as possible. You may have to put up with a little, er, proximity."

"I have nothing to hide," Pach said testily.

Khin smiled. "A close surveillance team will be with you by this evening. They are all trained officers and know how to be discreet. I shall also give you my personal number: my mobile. It is never switched off."

"Thank you," said Pach. "I shall expect these men by 3 p.m., after which I have an appointment." And he raised his hands in the *sampeah* again and said goodbye.

Khin did not expect to find any records of misdemeanors by the Senator in easily accessible police files. Instead it was best to ask around. Thirty years in the force had given him an unrivaled set of contacts. In Vice, for example.

Officer Chhith was a tall, thin man with a perpetually gloomy expression, which Khin assumed came from the kinds of cases he had to deal with. Back in 1984 he had been a cheerful young police cadet with a passion for football. (He'd kept goal, and done it well, in a team where Khin had played right back, less well. Khin had always dreamt of being a forward.) Chhith shook his head when his old teammate raised the subject over an Angkor beer in the police canteen.

"I don't recall any involvement, Vann," he said. "But I'll have a look through some files for you. You never know what might turn up."

Corruption looked a more promising field. Nhek Phirun had shared a beat with Khin in the early 1990s. He'd been a sharp observer of street criminals then and now kept as acute an eye on the upper echelons of big business. Sometimes this meant the same people.

"Pach is part of a syndicate developing land around Boeung Kak," said Nhek.

Khin nodded. The old lake in the center of town was gradually being filled in. People from its shores were being moved, often forcibly, out of their homes to make way for development.

"So there are people out there who don't exactly love him," Nhek went on. "But he's not one of the really big wheels. Just along for the ride, really. If I wanted to threaten developers, there are other people I'd target rather than Pach."

"Perhaps somebody wants him out of the syndicate."

"Then why just issue anonymous threats?"

Khin nodded. He wondered why Nhek had not progressed further in the force. Not good enough at politics, no doubt.

Khin walked down to the cyclo stand at the foot of the road. He knew most of the drivers, having done favors for most of them at some time. Such behavior was not calculated to create career success, but Khin found it made his job easier and more pleasant.

"Kao, take me to Lang's Coffee House."

"*Baat*, Lok Khin."

Once they were moving, Khin asked Kao what he knew about Senator Pach.

"Not much. He's pretty clean, I think. Why do you ask?"

"I'll tell you when I can. He's involved with Boeung Kak, isn't he?"

"Ah!" Kao, who liked nothing more than to learn something other people didn't know, grinned. The cyclo swung around a corner, nearly sending a fat matron on a black bike into the pavement.

"So tell me about the evictions," said Khin. "Some people are angry, I guess."

Orders

"Wouldn't you be?"

"People have been promised new homes."

"New shacks, twenty miles out of town."

"So there is anger."

"Of course. A couple of weeks ago, a bulldozer was set alight. Nobody knows who by."

"Nobody?"

"Ly"—Kao didn't know his first name—lived in a wooden shanty with a corrugated tin roof, in a little enclave of such buildings near a huge building site. Scrawny chickens strutted around the entrance. Inside, however, the shack was full of electronic gear, with which, no doubt, Ly coordinated the fight against further development. A large, thuggish-looking man stood uneasily with Khin until Ly appeared. Khin gave the *sampeah*.

Ly looked surprised.

"We don't often get respect from the police."

"I'm sorry to hear that," Khin replied.

"What do you want?"

"To talk. About your organization."

"Our protests are legal and intended to be peaceful. Violence only occurs when our people are subjected to it, in which case they fight back. We are not monks, officer, we are men and women fighting for our homes. Our homes, and those of our children."

Khin thought for a moment of his own childhood home in the suburbs of Phnom Penh, and the day in 1975 when he was forced out of it.

"That is understandable. I'm not here to judge. If I were in your situation, maybe I'd do the same. But I wonder if everyone reacts as you do?"

"You mean the greedy ones who sell out?"

"No, I mean the ones who resort to, let's say, less public methods. I imagine you sometimes find yourself criticized from within your own movement for staying within the law."

"No," Ly said firmly. "We are united."

"There have been incidents of sabotage."

"Oh, that. My belief is that it was the work of the developers. The machine was old; maybe it was of no further use. It was probably also insured for a healthy sum. And by having it go up in flames, that means more propaganda against us."

Ly glared at Khin, then relaxed.

"Or maybe it was just vandals. Young men with no work and nothing better to do. There are plenty of those, amidst all this wealth we see being created around us."

Khin sat at his desk, pondering. That "no" had been too firm. But Ly had not given any ground—the people of his neighborhood were innocent victims, none of whom would initiate violence. The inspector had, of course, requisitioned the file on the bulldozer, but no leads had been found, and the case was in the process of being dropped. As Ly had guessed, an insurance payment had been made, and the developers had got mileage out of the incident. But that did not mean that Ly's insistence on universal harmony among the protesters was right.

So should he bring Ly in for further questioning? That would create more fuss, no doubt—all those electronic gadgets would be spreading more anti-police (and thus anti-patriotic) propaganda on the Internet. But if it had to be done.

Khin was by nature a waiter—his old coach had probably been right to play him as a back. He'd get Kao asking around and come back to this angle later. In the

Orders

meantime, there was Pach's security to arrange. One man patrolling the grounds of the house, plus one on duty inside: that should be enough. Plus, for when the Senator went outside, two plainclothes men on bikes—extra because the men on the site needed to be permanent.

The phone was ringing. It was Chhith.

"Your senator. There was an incident, a number of years ago ..."

The "incident" had of course never happened, officially. An accusation of rape. Nothing had come before the public prosecutor. But the woman had been insistent, though she had finally dropped the charges, for no official reason. Chhith, "Safe Hands," had looked into this, and had now found a name.

Mu Kateka had once been beautiful. Or maybe it was the serenity in her expression, as she sat untangling the hair of a little girl. The serenity left when she saw Khin.

"What do you want?"

Khin gave the *sampeah*.

"Don't be afraid. I'm not bringing any trouble."

"Cops always bring trouble."

"That is not kind," said Khin.

"It is my experience ... Champay, go and play with your sisters. I'll finish your hair later."

Khin watched the girl scoot cheerfully off into the next room. He also noticed that in that room was a typewriter.

"She is beautiful," said Khin.

Mu smiled, despite herself.

"So what do you want?"

"It's about an incident many years ago ..."

"Ah, I knew it. You make one mistake in life ... I have nothing to say on the subject."

"But it still pains you, I see."

"No, it pains me that a policeman is coming round here discussing it, which means that someone somewhere wants to use it, and thus me, in some political game. The sort of game where ordinary people like me always lose. I am not playing. I have nothing to say."

Khin was impressed by her sincerity.

"Actually, I am not interested in the incident itself. Or whatever it was that made you retract your claim. I'm interested in what Pach was like at that time, whether there were others like you."

Mu shook her head.

"I don't know. Maybe not after my complaint. Not out of remorse, of course, but out of fear. You cannot lose face in politics."

"But before?"

"I know nothing of that time."

Silence fell. Often the questioner's most powerful weapon. Khin sat back and let his attention rest on the whirring of a fan and the street noise from outside.

"Why are you asking these questions?" Mu said finally.

"I've been asked to."

"Who by?"

"It's part of an investigation—" Khin began, then paused.

A cold, official line would yield nothing.

"Someone has been threatening him. I'm trying to find out who."

Mu looked horrified.

"You think it's me?"

"No, but I think you might know who the person is. Or know someone who might know."

"I don't. Sorry."

Orders

"You seem suddenly pleased," said Khin.

"I can't help it. Someone out there has a sense of justice. But I'm glad I have no idea who."

Silence fell again. This time it was Khin who broke it.

"I'd like to have a look at that typewriter of yours."

Mu looked more puzzled than horrified. But maybe she was just a good actor.

"I have nothing to do with these threats, Inspector."

"Then you've nothing to hide. Hand it over, please."

The next evening, another machine on the building site was vandalized. This time a young man was caught while running away, his hands smelling of petrol. His story was that he had done it for a dare. Khin asked to interview him.

"I need to see a lawyer," the young man said.

"You will."

"Now. Soon. It's my right."

"In theory," Khin replied. "In practice, these things take time."

"That is illegal. You are corrupt."

"And you have been lying to us. Start telling the truth, and we'll look at your case more favorably."

"I've told you what happened."

"And I don't believe you. I think your act was political. And as such, rather more admirable than just stupid vandalism. Your home is going to be knocked down, isn't it?"

"Yes, but ..."

"You think something should be done to stop that. You don't trust people like Ly. They just post words on the Internet. That won't stop the developers, will it? Words. This needs action."

The young man grimaced, Khin was sure with the effort of hiding his real feelings of assent to what he was hearing.

"It was just a dare."

"It might have been a dare—but not just fueled by cheap beer. Maybe your colleagues thought you were weak, that you wouldn't really fight."

The young man glared at the inspector and then hid his head in his hands.

"We have the name of an organization. We don't know if they've been threatening people like Pach—yet. But we're working on it."

Khin was reporting progress to Chey, who was sweating more than ever after yet another lunch with someone important.

"And what about that other lead, the woman?" said Chey.

"The typewriter was not used to make the threatening notes."

"Does she know that?"

"Not yet."

"And you think she knows more than she's telling us?"

"Yes."

"Lie to her about the typewriter."

Khin looked doubtful.

"That's an order."

Mu looked scared. Khin felt sorry for her. Lying to people to pressure them for information was not his way. But orders are orders.

"I don't know who could have had access to that typewriter," Mu said. "Maybe someone broke in."

"It's more likely to be someone in your family."

"No!"

Khin tried to look cold. "If you could give us more information about Pach, maybe other lines of enquiry would open."

"You cops are all the same," said Mu.

Khin nodded. Maybe she was right. Such is karma.

"Pach ... was not always Pach," she finally said. "When I first met him, some people still called him Deng."

"He's Chinese?"

"No, it was just an alias. From ... that time. When many people had such names."

Khin nodded. He already knew Pach had once been a Khmer Rouge cadre.

"When did you meet him?"

"In the summer of '79. When he was lording it over those he had 'liberated.' He was telling everyone how he had fled Cambodia the moment he saw what the Khmer Rouge were really like. But it was a lie, I know."

"How do you know?"

"He had a place in the center of town. If he'd defected in 1977 it would have been requisitioned. Instead, it was as if he'd never left. I think he just changed sides, right at the end. He did some deal with the *yuon* when they arrived ..."

"Can you prove any of this?"

"No. And I won't repeat these allegations in any public arena."

Khin took a sip of *tai*.

"Do you know what he did during those years he was supposed to be across the border?"

"I don't know. But I once heard someone say he was a guard in one of those prisons."

"Tuol Sleng?"

"I don't know. Maybe. Didn't they keep records?"

You don't spend thirty years in the police without seeing terrible things. But Khin still loathed having to look through Khmer Rouge prison records. The mixture of depravity and orderliness, the petty accountancy of mass murder—and the anger he felt, that the man in charge of it all, Khang Khek Ieu, was still alive.

But there was work to be done. Leafing through the haunted, thin-faced photographs—most, though not all, victims had mug shots taken before they died—he found the faces oddly familiar, though he could not place them. They were, he felt, a kind of family.

"Comrade Deng" had joined the prison staff in early 1978, and following the path of many such people, Deng had ended up on the receiving end of the barbarity in the last days of that year. However, there was no photograph of this man. Just another of those meaningless confessions, which could have been written by anyone.

The Senator greeted Khin in the same room as before, made the same *sampeah* and the same offer of whiskey. But his tone was suspicious.

"You say you've come to check on your men. Do you need to speak to me to do that?"

"I need to know if you feel comfortable with them. Nobody else can tell me that."

"I suppose not ... Well, they're doing fine. Any progress on finding the madmen sending these threats? There was another one yesterday, by the way."

"May I see it?"

Pach went to fetch it. While he did so, Khin gazed about the room he was in, noting details. A desk looked tempting. Khin walked over to it and tugged gently at the top. It opened ... but he heard feet approaching. Pach was back.

"Here. Same idiocy."

Khin took the note. Same paper, same typewriter. He handed it back.

"Madmen," Pach repeated.

"Maybe ... maybe not. Senator Pach, you have not been honest with me, have you? I don't know who those notes come from. But I do know why they were sent."

The Senator's face registered disbelief.

"Oh, yes?"

"Yes, Comrade Deng."

The Senator's calm vanished in an instant. Khin reckoned his first look was one of fear, but anger replaced it almost at once.

"Those are lies! Who have you been talking to?"

"Nobody. I've just been doing research."

"No, it's not possible."

"Why not?"

"Because ... it's not true."

"What's not true?"

"The lies."

"Lies that say what?" asked Khin.

"All sorts of things ..."

"Such as that you became an interrogator at Tuol Sleng prison on April 25, 1978? Such as that you were responsible for the death of over two hundred people? Death by torture, 'smashing,' as you called it? Such as that two weeks before the Vietnamese reached Phnom Penh, you apparently went the way of so many of your colleagues, confessing to treachery and being smashed in turn. But that last one *is* a lie, isn't it? You never became a prisoner. You did, no doubt, find a way of escaping your workplace. And shortly after January 7, 1979, you were a key figure in the National United Front for National Salvation. I shan't even ask what you did to make yourself so welcome to the invaders ..."

The Senator fixed Khin with a glare.

"You have no proof that I am this man. Not a shred."

His anger turned to laughter.

"Your police career has just ended, Inspector Khin."

Khin allowed himself a smile.

"I doubt it. Remember, I am in charge of protecting you. A junior police official is not going to walk into a Senator's house and accuse him of treachery—unless he's very confident the Senator will do nothing. Such an unimportant figure probably assumes the Senator will be grateful—for it is only by knowing the truth that the junior and unimportant policeman can really protect the Senator from his real enemies. If you tell me the truth, Senator Pach, we know where to start looking. If you deny the truth, all we can do is sit and wait for the attacker to show his hand."

"I never ..." Pach began, but his voice died away.

Silence followed—a rare commodity in Phnom Penh.

"I didn't enjoy what I did. I was obeying orders," he said finally.

Khin felt rage rising in himself but fought it back. To get angry is to lose face, and he had a job to do.

So, where to begin? There were numerous groups that had protested the leniency of the sentence on Khang Khek Ieu. The governor of Tuol Sleng had originally been given nineteen years: less than a day per victim, as objectors pointed out. Maybe some of these groups had

Orders

militant splinters, just as the orderly, "legal" Ly had his young machine-wrecker. Khin began compiling a list—but then another hoodlum was shot on the Strip, and he found himself having to balance the two investigations. ("We just don't have the manpower," said Chey.)

A few days later, Khin was at his desk when his mobile rang.

"It's Pach." The voice sounded nervous. "Your men are not here."

"Oh. They should be. I'll have a check and—"

"I think there's an intruder in the grounds."

"Your guard dog—"

"It's not barking. But I saw something in the garden."

"Are you alone?"

"Yes."

"I'll send a car."

"You will come. At once."

"Yes, of course."

Khin put the phone down.

"Jorani, tell Chey I've been called away on urgent business. And get me transport ..."

Driver Duong was waiting by the vehicle.

"Same destination as last time," Khin told him.

Duong got in and turned on the sat nav.

"The machine is so clever. It remembers the address."

"Yes, but not the best route. Override it."

"Orders are to use it, Inspector."

"Yes, but this is ..."

Khin's voice fell away. In his mind he saw those photographs again. *Like family.*

"Very well. We must follow orders."

Nobody answered when Khin rang the bell.

"We must climb the gate," said Khin. "Duong, help me up."

"Watch out for the dog, sir."

"I have a gun."

Khin kept himself fit, and he was over the gate in a moment. No dog. Or any other sign of movement. He ran up to the front door and beat on it. No reply. Duong joined him.

"You go right. I'll go left. Meet you around the back."

Khin's route took him past the dog cage. The animal was lying motionless on its side.

"Anything?" he asked Duong, when they met up in the back.

"There's a window open."

The two men ran around to the window, and Khin shouted through it. No reply.

"Duong, guard this exit. If anyone tries to get out, stop them. Shoot if necessary."

Khin scrambled in through the window.

"Police!" he called out. "If you've got the Senator, let him go, and there'll be no shooting."

Nobody replied. So was the intruder still in the house? Khin edged into the next room, following his gun as he'd been taught.

Nobody.

The same maneuver into the next room.

Senator Pach was lying on the floor. There was blood all around him. Khin checked that the room was empty and then went over to the prostrate form. The Senator's face had been smashed in. The way the Khmer Rouge had killed.

Orders

Khin went into Chey's office clutching his report. He felt a range of emotions. Shame, above all, at having arrived too late to protect Pach. He knew he should have overridden the sat nav order, but at that moment his emotions about the Senator's past had got in the way of his professional duty. The Path is indeed hard to follow.

There was a more general feeling of shame, too, at having let down the force of which he was so proud. And fear for his future career? Very possibly. It was at times like this that he regretted not having played politics; there were no allies in high places to protect him. He was, he realized, the perfect scapegoat.

And Chief Inspector Chey was the perfect scapegoater.

Chey looked up at Khin as he came in. His face revealed no emotion. Khin handed him the report. Chey said a quiet thank you ... Maybe this was this essentially mysterious man's prelude to some vicious personal attack. Chey must have lost an enormous amount of face among his superiors for this mistake.

Chey glanced through the report and then looked up.

"A most unfortunate business," he said.

"Unfortunate ..."

"It is generally agreed that there is little that could have been done. And the murderer left no clues ..."

He put the report in a tray.

"You have cases to be getting on with, Inspector Khin."

And that was it.

Back at his desk, Khin lit an Ara and sat watching the smoke vanish into whorls beneath the ceiling fan. Then he glanced at the picture of his father again. Would he have lived if he'd not relied on those spectacles? Probably not: the Khmer Rouge would have found out his middle-class origins some other way ... And then the inspector's mind ran on to more pictures from the past, rows and rows of them this time, from the death-roll of Tuol Sleng. One, suddenly, stood out, strained by hunger and suffering. Take it from that place, and fill it with official dinners instead.

He got up and went back to the chief's office.

"Sir, I have a question."

"Ask it."

"You knew this would happen, didn't you?"

Chey smiled. "Not at the start of things. I knew very little. Later ..." He gave a shrug. "What happened, happened."

"Did you type the notes?"

"No."

"But you know who did?"

Chey said nothing.

"Your father died in Tuol Sleng, didn't he?" said Khin.

Chey nodded.

"In mid-1978?"

"June. My mother followed him in August."

For a moment, the inspector did nothing. Then he gave a nod and a *sampeah*, more to the dead than the living.

"Those gangland shootings need investigation," Khin said, turning to the door.

Christopher West

Christopher West studied philosophy at the London School of Economics, and since leaving university has earned a living as a writer—of anything, from novels to brochures for ice-cream machines. He lives in Britain but has written extensively about the East. His first published work *Journey to the Middle Kingdom* was an account of a journey to China in 1985. His later novels include four crime novels set in contemporary China: *Death of a Blue Lantern*, *Death on Black Dragon River*, *Red Mandarin*, and *The Third Messiah*.

Sabbatical Term

Richard Rubenstein

Art Pfeffer flew from Beijing to Phnom Penh with a small suitcase containing three changes of clothing, two pairs of sandals, a tattered Khmer-English dictionary, *The Selected Works of Mao Tse-tung* in paperback, and a mostly empty Moleskine notebook. He had hesitated over whether to include condoms in his toilet kit and had finally thrown in half a dozen Trojans, muttering "Why not?" but feeling foolish all the same. Like many American men, Pfeffer found Asian women smokily intriguing, but he was not heading to Cambodia to realize some Oriental sex fantasy. The upsurges he dreamed about were political, not personal.

Pfeffer's travel alarm also made the cut, but not his Leica. He left the camera in Beijing at the insistence of his Chinese host, an amiable junior diplomat named Wang Gao, who now sat beside him in the airplane. "No camera, Professor Art," Wang had insisted. "Cambodians are very suspicious of foreigners taking pictures. Especially Americans. If you suffered as they did, you would be suspicious also."

Pfeffer thought he knew a great deal about this suffering. He was one of a group of Asian Studies scholars sharply critical of US intervention in Indochina and sympathetic to the region's leftist rebels. But it was only near the end of the six-hour trip, when the plane descended low enough to reveal the cratered landscape of Cambodia's central plain, that he began to grasp what it meant to be bombed for five years running by the world's most fearsome air power.

"Jesus!" he announced to no one in particular. "Looks like the fucking moon!"

Wang leaned over from his seat to share the view. "Without the B-52s, Khmer Rouge would have taken power three years ago instead of last year," he said quietly. "By then they controlled almost all of the countryside. So B-52s erased the countryside."

"What's your estimate of the casualties?"

"Nobody knows."

Pfeffer took out his Moleskine and made a few notes on "the violence of lost causes." Then he flipped through the first few pages of the notebook, studying the cryptic phrases that indicated the main goals of his trip.

"1. Research KR Organization? Leaders? Program?"

His first task was to find out what was going on in Cambodia under Khmer Rouge rule. Who, exactly, were the country's secretive new leaders, and what were their intentions? Although they had now ruled Cambodia for more than a year, the answers remained unclear. Bizarre reports suggested that they were planning to abolish money, ban religion, and destroy the traditional family, but nobody knew whether to credit them or not. Western journalists were banned from entering the country, and the few French scholars still in residence had not published anything about the regime worth reading.

Pfeffer was the first American scholar to visit Phnom Penh since the KR takeover. His trip could never have happened without Chinese intervention. He arrived with a letter of introduction to Cambodia's Minister of Social Affairs from the Chinese Foreign Minister, Qiao Guanhua. He silently thanked his mentors at Berkeley, who had managed to get him invited to China and had given him a sabbatical to do research on Cambodia.

Pfeffer figured he'd get a book out of it. An important book.

That had led him to make a second entry in his notebook: "2. Research IRC and begin writing." IRC stood for his working title, *Inside Red Cambodia: The Khmer Rouge and the Future of Asian Communism*. The third entry read, "KR rule: Next stage in the evolution of communism?"

Could the Khmer Rouge be planning to outdo the Maoists in order to create a genuinely egalitarian society? *That* was the question. In China, Chairman Mao's Cultural Revolution was in trouble, but Pfeffer's political intuition told him that this would not discourage the Khmer Rouge from trying to pick up the ball the Chinese were in the process of dropping . . .

The sound of the airplane's engines changed and the plane started to lose altitude, beginning its descent to Phnom Penh. Pfeffer turned briefly to glance at his seatmate. Wang Gao had tagged along as a "minder." He was an up-and-coming official with a good degree from the Foreign Affairs University and had his own mission. When he'd asked Wang Gao about the new regime's political philosophy and intentions, Wang had replied with a smile and silence. Either he didn't know or wasn't about to share what he knew.

"Gao."

Pfeffer nudged him.

"Yes?" he yawned.

"I've been thinking about Lenin's concept, 'the advantages of backwardness.'"

Sabbatical Term

"This will be in your book?"

"I'm thinking about it."

Fatigue made the young diplomat slightly less polite than usual.

"Professor Art, we have discussed this before. Backwardness is seldom an advantage. Cambodia is primitive—more than Old China. Tribes living in the forest. Feudal relations govern the people. Warlords. Revenge killings. No industry to speak of. The bombing ruined the agriculture. You saw the craters. People are hungry, so they pray to the spirits of the land. No schools above the elementary level. Not much to make a socialist future."

"Chairman Mao warned the KRs about being too ambitious."

Wang said nothing. The plane banked sharply, and he pointed out the window.

"See how charming Phnom Penh still is? The Khmer Rouge shelled it. Most of the shells fell in the northern suburbs, where the refugees lived. Now no more shells—and, since the evacuation, no more refugees either."

Glancing down, Pfeffer saw the three rivers merging. Fishing boats were moored along the banks of the Mekong River. To the north, the setting sun outlined a hilltop shrine near the Tonlé Sap. A minute later, the green-gold roof of the Royal Palace flashed into view.

"During the evacuation," Pfeffer said. "More than two million people were sent to the countryside."

"It was a difficult time," Wang replied. "Many died."

Pfeffer opened his notebook, stared into space momentarily, and began a new page labeled "Revolutionary Puritanism."

"Professor Pfeffer?"

He looked up, blinking, to discover a woman in uniform—an army officer, he guessed, although her khaki shirt bore no insignia.

"I am Art Pfeffer."

He rose to greet her, more than a little startled by her unadorned beauty and the direct way that she returned his glance. She was clearly what they called a "Khmer Klem," her Indian-like features reflecting centuries of intermarriage with the peoples of South Asia. She spoke reasonably good French.

"You can call me Koy Devi, professor. I serve as an assistant to Comrade Minister Khieu Thirith. The minister wishes to see you at your earliest convenience."

"Wonderful! When? And where?"

"Now. At her office. I will take you there."

"But..." He felt his open shirt collar, ran a hand through tousled hair. "I am not properly dressed for an interview."

Devi smiled. "We are not so formal here, professor. Your costume is perfectly acceptable."

When Pfeffer continued to hesitate, she spoke more forcefully: "The minister does not have a great deal of time. She will be leaving shortly to tour the provinces. Please come with me."

At the ministry he was led into an expansive office. A pleasant looking, bespectacled matron in her forties, Minister Khieu Thirith sat behind a large desk on the top floor of the easternmost Bank Building, signing a sheaf of documents. After Devi had ushered him into the office, the minister looked up briefly and nodded at the chair in front of her desk.

She left him hanging as she leafed through papers, stopping to sign a page before turning to the next set of documents.

"I beg your pardon," she said in French-accented English, "but my duties require me to sign many decrees."

He nodded. Khieu was the highest-ranked woman in the KR hierarchy, responsible for administering all the regime's welfare programs. Parliament had convened months earlier, passed a few laws, adjourned, and vanished, apparently permanently. Ministers like Khieu were now legislating for the nation. Finally she put down the pen and looked at him, smiling.

"Welcome to Phnom Penh, professor. I hope that you have enjoyed seeing our city, as empty as it must seem to you."

"Yes, very much."

"Your visit is most opportune," she continued.

Pfeffer raised his eyebrows questioningly.

"We have read your writings on the Chinese Cultural Revolution. Your article in the *Journal of Asian Studies* was of great interest. And we appreciated your letter on Cambodia in *The Bulletin of Concerned Asian Scholars* even more."

Pfeffer must have gaped with surprise, for Devi giggled softly, and the minister smiled. "We are a young revolution, professor. We understand that what the outside world thinks of us is important. As the Master wrote, '"Tis better to be vile than vile esteemed, when not to be receives reproach of being ...'"

Pfeffer guessed the source. "Shakespeare?"

"Sonnet 121. I studied him at the Sorbonne. I earned my degree there in English literature and married my husband at the Hotel de Ville."

"Minister Ieng Sary."

"Yes."

Pfeffer knew the minister was married to the formidable foreign affairs chief, perhaps the best-known leader of the new regime. Her sister was also married to an important official—an engineer, he recalled, with a reputation for theoretical brilliance. He frowned as he thought about these marriages. Patronage based on family ties was one of the great curses of old-style Cambodian politics. The new regime had promised to eliminate "familism" as a malignant source of corruption. But even among communists, it seemed, politics in Phnom Penh was still a family affair.

"Madame Minister..."

"Call me Comrade Thirith." Then, to Devi: "Comrade, please bring us some tea."

"Comrade Thirith, I do not mean to be rude, but there is one question that has been bothering me. It has to do with your family's role in Cambodian politics..."

"Ah! You want to know whether our leadership is an incestuous elite, a communist version of the old patronage system."

Pfeffer could not help smiling at her quickness.

"We are an elite, of course. What poor nation has made a revolution without such leadership? Sary and I were from families wealthy enough to send us to France for our higher education. We were members of the Cercle Marxiste at university, along with many others now in the government. There is practically nothing that we have done since taking power that we did not talk about over a café on the Boul' Mich.

"But we are not incestuous," she continued. "I married Sary, and my sister Ponnary married another comrade who now serves in the cabinet, but we are the only high officials with such family ties. We are passionately opposed to familism. The old custom of putting one's relatives first has become a serious threat to our nation's survival. We are not starving en masse—not yet. But this could easily happen if each family works to feed itself rather than the collective. That is why we tell our people, 'The Khmer nation is your family.'"

Pfeffer answered slowly. "But how do you stamp out this sort of thinking? Its roots go very deep. We also tend to put our own relatives ahead of everyone else."

"But this is exactly the right question!" she replied animatedly. "Familism is only one expression of individualism. The same impulse that leads people to say 'This is *my* family' leads them to say 'This is *my* land' and 'This is *my* corporation.' Do you know Pascal? '*Ce chien est à moi*' . . ."

"'This dog is mine, say the poor children,'" Pfeffer recited. "'This is my place in the sun. Thus begins the usurpation of the entire world.'"

"Bravo!" Khieu clapped her hands. "But *regardez*, my dear Professor, if 'This dog is mine' usurps what should belong to everyone, what about 'This invention is mine'? Or even 'This thought is mine'? This is where the Cultural Revolution has fallen short. Chairman Mao's instinct was to try to stop the bureaucrats from saying 'This office is mine' and the intellectuals from saying 'This expertise is mine.' But in China the usurpation has been going on for twenty years. In Russia, it happened even more quickly. Here, we are determined to prevent it from ever starting."

"Yes, I see," Pfeffer said with growing excitement. "The first truly radical revolution! But how do you hope to succeed where the others failed?"

"I think that you already know the answer," Khieu replied. "Russia and China were societies disrupted by war but still intact. Here we lost everything, and we start from zero. People who have been fighting as long as we have do not have much individualism left to protect. They understand that the collective—the Khmer nation—will rise or fall together."

Pfeffer sipped his tea, took a breath, and ventured a final question. He was conscious, as he spoke, that other people had slipped into the room and quietly joined them, listening intently.

"And the evacuations?" he asked nervously. "Will you repopulate the cities now that the economy is reviving?"

"Cities!" she almost spat. "For us," she declared, "they are a useless expense. Worse yet, they are cesspools of crime, profiteering, vice, disease, corruption. The evacuation has certain economic purposes, of course. But its most important goal is to create communist men and women. Later on, perhaps in another generation, we will have the human material needed to create decent cities."

"Ah! The advantages of backwardness."

"Just so!" Khieu rose from her chair and paced the floor, speaking with growing intensity. "My brother-in-law has put it very clearly:

"*Un:* Backward societies have little private property. Our people lost almost all their property in the war. Therefore, we will proceed to construct the socialist future without private property.

"*Deux:* Backward societies are not burdened by elaborate bureaucracies and hordes of office-holders. The war destroyed Lon Nol's corrupt state. Therefore, we will proceed to construct the socialist future without a bureaucratic state.

"*Trois:* Backward societies have very little money. In the war our money lost almost all of its value. Therefore, we will proceed to construct the socialist future without money."

"No money?" Pfeffer felt compelled to object. "No money at all? But, Comrade Thirith, every society needs a medium of exchange . . ."

"Barter," she replied, wagging a finger at him. "For now, barter will do quite nicely. And, don't forget, we are not a regime that worships private property. We have already requisitioned supplies, paid people in kind what they are worth, and distributed surplus goods to the poor. But I want to make one last point."

"Please, comrade."

"*Quatre:* Backwardness has one undeniable *disadvantage.* Fatalism. Resignation. Superstition. People need to imagine a better life in some form of existence after death—in short, religion, which in this country means Buddhism, with its temples, schools, priests, and hordes of useless monks. The war seriously disrupted the *sangha*, the Buddhist establishment in Cambodia. Therefore, we will proceed to construct the socialist future without Buddhism."

Clapping filled the room, punctuated by a few cheers.

"We need to get this comrade out of the office and onto a speaking platform, where everyone can hear her!"

The speaker was a handsome, brown-skinned, serious-looking man several years older than the minister. Pfeffer recognized him from photos as Khieu's husband, Ieng Sary.

"I see that you have had a good conversation, Professor," Ieng said, turning to Pfeffer.

"Yes, Mr. Foreign Minister. I am learning a great deal. But I have many more questions to ask."

Ieng contemplated him thoughtfully.

"Of course you have. We want to answer all your questions..."

Seconds later, a melodious voice broke the brief silence.

"Pardon me, but I believe that the answers you seek will not be found in this building, or, indeed, in the city of Phnom Penh."

Pfeffer turned to find a small, compact man gazing at him, a figure with a broad Khmer brow, intelligent eyes, and hair beginning to gray. Suddenly, the man smiled. Despite himself, Pfeffer recalled the old cliché about smiles lighting up a room. He extended his hand, and the Cambodian grasped it firmly.

"Professor, if you wish to tell our story, you must go where it is being written. Go to the countryside. Experience what the people of this city experienced when they left behind the comforts and temptations of urban life. You will find the truth about revolutionary Cambodia in the rural districts. And you will discover what it feels like to rely on your hands and those of your comrades, not just on your brain and your books.

"My impression of you is that you are a man who wants to help build the Revolution, not just write about it. Am I right?"

Pfeffer found it difficult to catch his breath. The speaker emanated a remarkable aura of charm and authority.

"Yes," he said, nodding. "Yes, no doubt you are right, Comrade...?"

The short man was silent.

Thirith Khieu spoke: "Professor Pfeffer, permit me to introduce my brother-in-law, our prime minister, Comrade Saloth Sar."

"No, Thirith," the Cambodian said. "Let us use my new name. Professor, I am called Pol Pot."

Devi drove with confidence. Pfeffer watched as she twisted the wheel of the jeep, guiding it around the ubiquitous detritus and potholes that made National Highway 1 a back-jarring obstacle course. His hosts were sending him to see the Revolution in action in Prey Veng province, about sixty miles southeast of the capital. There, Devi said that a number of agricultural communes struggled to meet Pol Pot's command to triple their annual output of rice. Pfeffer would be welcome to participate in the work, but he would be treated for the most part like any other worker.

"Fair enough," Pfeffer replied. "I don't expect special treatment."

"The comrades in the ministry discussed this. Some felt that you should be allowed to function as a scholar and given the time and facilities to conduct interviews and to read and write. But others said, no, let him be one of the people. Then he will have something true to write about. This was the view that prevailed. But they also ordered me to accompany you and to stay here with you. There have been . . . excesses on the part of some overly zealous managers. The comrades do not want your health or welfare to suffer."

"So you will watch over me?"

Pfeffer could not help smiling at the idea of being looked after by such an attractive minder.

"Yes," she replied forthrightly, "I will. During the day I will work, too. And after work and at the evening meetings, we will stay in the same *p'theh*—the same house—and you will tell me how you are getting on and what else you would like to see. There is a major irrigation project under way not far from here. You should see that as well."

During the day, he would be part of the Revolution, and at night . . . the enchanting Devi, so self-possessed, so tough and appealing, might become more than a mere comrade. His spirits remained high even when two truculent guards at the commune gate inspected his belongings roughly and confiscated several items, including his extra pair of sandals and (with sarcastic comments that were not translated for his own good) the condoms. He half expected to lose his notebook and pens as well, but when one guard handled the plastic bag containing his writing materials, Devi uttered a few sharp words and he tossed it nonchalantly back in the suitcase.

Nor did his enthusiasm flag the next day and the days following that, when he worked harder than he had ever done, stooped over, his hands in the muck, transplanting rice shoots one at a time, while officials representing the commune exhorted him to work faster. The pressure of discipline was tangible and inexorable. His aching back and thighs slowed him, and he saw that other workers, less well fed or older, were close to collapse. Hard measures, Pfeffer told himself, were needed to get soft people to work at this pace. He put himself in the soft category, although he was not driven nearly as hard as the "new people" evacuated from the cities. The commune managers treated them with contemptuous harshness while clearly favoring the "base people" who had long lived in the countryside.

One evening, as he and Devi sat on the veranda of the communal house, Pfeffer related an incident that had disturbed him during the day.

"A woman came down a dirt road near the paddy," he reported. "She had a little cloth bag, and she was picking berries by the side of the road. Suddenly, two men ran up to her. They picked her up roughly, threw her berries away, and carried her back toward the headquarters building. She shouted something—I couldn't make out the words—and then sort of slumped against them without saying anything."

"She was foraging for food," said Devi.

"So?"

"Foraging is one of the major offenses against the collective. The leaders say we must work for each other, not for ourselves, and not for our families. They say that if some are allowed to forage, everyone must be allowed, and if everyone forages, we return to the old system of each person working for himself."

Pfeffer took note of her language: "the leaders say," not "I say." He decided to press the matter further.

"Aren't they foraging because they're so hungry? I'm not a glutton—I don't eat that much ordinarily—but here I am hungry all the time. And many people look emaciated and ill. I asked one tottering old man how he was feeling, and he said, 'I am a bit weak, but at least here we have something to eat. In other provinces thousands are starving to death.'"

Devi surprised him by agreeing with this bleak comparison.

"Yes," she replied, "there are serious differences from region to region. The soil conditions are different, the weather is different, and so are the cadres. The Organization is trying to make things more uniform, but we have never really been a unified nation. Conditions are terrible in some places, terrible! But overall, they say, we are making progress. I hope they are right. If we don't move forward . . ."

She stopped, staring into the growing darkness as if viewing some age-old scene of backwardness and degradation. Then she shuddered visibly.

Pfeffer felt impelled to reach out and put an arm around her shoulders.

He muttered, "Devi. It's okay."

She pulled away instinctively but then let herself relax against him. Pfeffer kept his arm in place, lowered his head until his lips were touching her hair, and sighed, as an unexpected wave of affection and desire washed through him.

Devi felt something for him as well. Before going to her sleeping room, she kissed his cheek lightly and whispered, "I think that Comrade Mek is wrong."

Mek was the chair of the commune committee.

"What does he say?" he whispered back, savoring the faintly spicy scent of her skin.

"He says you are CIA."

Over the next few nights Pfeffer succeeded in getting Devi to tell her own story. Her father was a stone carver—a member of an ancient middle class created a millennium earlier at the time when the Angkorean Empire ruled most of Indochina and native stone was used to create brilliant statues, monuments, and temples. By modern times few carvers remained and their work was limited to replacing damaged pieces of ancient temples. Her father cultivated good relationships with the Buddhist hierarchs and sometimes received commissions to create new pieces. He and his wife, who was skilled in textile crafts, were successful enough to send Devi off to school—still a rarity among Cambodian girls. After graduating from the French-language *lycée* in

Sabbatical Term

Phnom Penh, she joined the urban cadres of the KR, who met regularly to study "MLM"—Marx, Lenin, and Mao—and who ran supplies to the insurgents in the countryside. She therefore escaped the general purge directed against "bourgeois intellectuals" when the rebels took power. Instead she became an officer in the militia and a protégée of Minister Khieu. At some point after this, Pfeffer suspected, she had also become a person with hopes, fears, and ideas of her own.

"And that is how I ended up here, talking on the veranda with an American professor," she concluded, laughing warmly.

He shared the laughter. In a place where laughter was rare, the pulse of intimacy surged. When she fled to her bedroom, stripping off her clothes on the way, he did the same. She slid under her sheet, giggling, and crooked a welcoming finger at him. He slid in beside her, grinning like a man possessed. At the height of her orgasm she cried out and shuddered, then smiled beatifically.

Laughter was not on the agenda several nights later, however, when Pfeffer attended his first Lifestyle Meeting. He had read about the Chinese Communist practice of "criticism and self-criticism," but nothing prepared him for the passionate intensity of the Cambodian version. As the evening progressed, members of the commune rose one by one to describe their activities over the past few days, criticize their own motivations and behavior, and describe how they intended to change. The stories were a strange mixture of stylized recitation and agonizing personal revelation. The meetings had a cult-like atmosphere. But each speaker's sincerity in trying to convey transformation was deeply moving. In an interval of silence following one performance, he surprised himself and astonished Devi by rising to speak.

"Comrades, I have spent the past two weeks here transplanting rice, spreading compost, and cleaning farm equipment," he declared. "I work twelve hours a day, like you. Like you, I eat two meals of watery rice and go to bed hungry every night. I am a soft man, and for the first week every bone in my body ached from this work. Now, the aches have gone away, but there is still an ache in my heart. That is what I want to tell you about.

"Comrades, I have to confess that I sometimes feel that this work is beneath me. I feel that a person like me, an educated man from a bourgeois family, should not be digging in the dirt and shoveling manure. I should be sitting in an office, teaching students, and writing books. And eating meat every day! I often feel that I am too special, too much of an individual, to do manual labor for the collective when I might be producing great ideas and advancing my own career instead."

Ignoring the murmur in the room, he plunged ahead.

"I thought when I came to Cambodia that I was a communist. Now, I see that I have a long distance to travel before I can call myself a man of the people. I am a teacher, but I am learning from you what it means to put the people first and one's own self-interest second. I am learning how capitalist societies degrade difficult work and exploit the people who do it, even as they glorify easier, more interesting work and reward those who do it. I am going to dedicate my own life to ending this unjust system in my own country and replacing it with something better, as you are doing here.

"Thank you for this education, comrades! Long live the Revolution! Long live Democratic Kampuchea!"

The room erupted. The committee leaders were on their feet, applauding with the others. Mek came up and embraced Pfeffer, kissing him on each cheek. Pfeffer looked to the side, where Devi had been seated, hoping for a congratulatory smile. Then he searched the back of the hall, but she was nowhere to be seen. The leaders soon bundled him off to a smaller room where they drank to his health with cups of rice wine.

After the fourth or fifth toast, pleading fatigue, he returned to the house to find Devi sitting alone on the veranda. She looked out of sorts. He went immediately to her side.

"What is it?"

She looked away.

"I don't know. No . . . I do know, but it's hard to talk about."

"Go ahead, talk."

"I understand that this experience has been important for you, but that's what your speech was about—*you*. 'The Education of Professor Art Pfeffer.' There is so much you don't understand . . ."

"What?" Pfeffer was visibly irritated. "What don't I understand?"

"You have been here for a few weeks. You see what you want to see. You don't see what you don't want to see."

"Explain!" he demanded impatiently.

She gestured with her hands as if to say that there was too much to explain.

Pfeffer glowered, and she continued in a softer voice.

"Art, I have been a communist since I was in school. Longer than you have, I imagine. I still believe that this may be Cambodia's last chance to become a decent, modern country. But our troubles are increasing. One *must* understand what is really happening here in order to evaluate it properly. In order to decide what to do next."

He began to reply, but Devi held up a hand.

"Tomorrow, I will take you further east, to see the irrigation works in Svay Rieng. We will meet a friend of mine there. And you will learn what you need to learn in order to write your book . . . unless, of course, you have decided that book-writing is too bourgeois an occupation for a revolutionary militant like yourself."

Pfeffer did not know what to say. But Devi had already turned her back to him and was soon asleep.

The sheer scale of the irrigation project overwhelmed him. Thousands of workers toiled in the damp heat, digging ditches that disappeared to the horizon, embedding logs along the banks to keep them from collapsing, or shoveling mountainous piles of removed earth into a line of dirt-smeared trucks. From his perch on a hill overlooking the valley, he felt as if he were watching a D.W. Griffith movie about pharaonic Egypt or Assyria, with a horde of extras slaving to build some imperial city.

"Trucks supplied by China," said Nuong Vet, Devi's friend and a local KR committee member. "We requested earth-moving equipment, but so far, no response. So we do it by hand. This is happening all over the country. Irrigation is the only way to increase rice production, since people can't work any harder than they do now. But, of course, the price is very high. Many have already died to build this project. And we will not know until the dry season whether it will work."

"Vet," said Devi, "there are rumors about new arrests."

Nuong nodded, and gestured toward a wooden table with bench seats placed under a nearby tree. The three sat there, sipping sweet iced coffee out of a thermos, while he spoke in the shadowed tones of a man mourning a close friend.

"Professor Pfeffer, the Revolution is not going well. Perhaps you already sensed this. People are starting to die in large numbers from overwork and disease. The leaders will not accept aid from the Americans, even though they are offering to support them for their own strategic reasons. Our great experiment is in danger of failing.

"While you and Devi were working on the commune," he continued, "her boss went on a fact-finding tour of the country. She came back to Phnom Penh and reported that people were starving in the provinces because of bad management, corruption, and feuds among the local leaders. Of course, there is some truth to this. We all know that some cadres refuse to share the suffering of the people and enrich themselves disgustingly. There have been protests, even a few violent incidents, directed against them. But Pol Pot has reacted ferociously. Since he cannot admit that there is anything wrong with his program, he says that all these problems are the result of deliberate plots against the Revolution. The arrests have already begun."

"That's disturbing," Pfeffer replied. "How many arrests?"

"So far, hundreds. It will soon be thousands. They are being sent to a place called S-21, a deserted high school in Phnom Penh. The place is also called Tuol Sleng. Those who go into it do not come out. I am told that they all confess to treasonous crimes and accuse others of helping them. Then the others are arrested, and they also confess and implicate more people. Of course, they are all tortured."

Pfeffer had gone pale. Devi's face was like stone.

"Thank you, Vet," she said. "Now, please tell him about Vietnam. He knows nothing about that."

"Of course." Nuong's grief seemed to deepen as he continued. "Professor Art, look at me, please. What do you see?"

Pfeffer was perplexed but managed an answer.

"I see a Cambodian man of average build with a light brown complexion and a very intelligent face."

Nuong smiled. "No. 'Cambodian' includes all sorts of groups. Even 'Khmer' is more or less meaningless because of our great diversity. We are Sino-Khmer, Malay-Khmer, Khmer Klem, and so on. When you look at me, what *ethnicity* do you see?"

"Ah!"

Pfeffer understood the question but was still unable to respond. Finally, Nuong answered it himself.

"My mother's family is Vietnamese. My father and mother met when he went to Vietnam in 1950 to learn to become a revolutionary fighter. I am Viet-Khmer. And, because of that, I am in great danger."

Pfeffer frowned. He knew something about the traditional Cambodian hatred of Vietnam, born of centuries of conflict with the powerful neighbor. He had heard folklorish tales about cruel and deceitful Vietnamese, and Devi had told him about the KR chiefs' fierce determination to avoid becoming part of a Vietnam-dominated "Socialist Republic of Indochina." Even so, the KRs were Khmer nationalists, and Nuong Vet was clearly a Khmer.

"I still don't get it, Vet," he told Nuong. "Why are the Viet-Khmers in danger?"

"You know, the border is only thirty miles from here," Nuong replied. "While we speak, the Vietnamese are concentrating troops on their side. Heavy weapons are being brought in. There is talk of an invasion, although I do not think it will happen quite yet."

"Why would they invade Cambodia?" Pfeffer was plainly shocked. "I thought there was a peace treaty!"

"Yes, Pol Pot signed a treaty in Hanoi earlier this year," Nuong answered. "'Our great socialist ally,' and so forth. But the KR loathe and fear the Vietnamese. And Hanoi considers us too primitive and crazy to remain independent. By the time Pol Pot returned from his trip, Vietnamese troops were already raiding our border villages. Since then he has been arresting his own army officers by the hundreds and charging them with being Vietnamese agents. They, also, disappear into S-21."

Nuong took a sip of iced coffee. Pfeffer found himself unable to speak. He had the sickening sensation that everything that had seemed hard and real to him had become sticky-soft and illusory.

"Now the two so-called plots are merging," said Nuong with new intensity. "Anyone accused of hindering production is considered a Vietnamese spy. Anyone considered pro-Vietnam becomes a candidate for S-21. Pol Pot has denounced those who have 'Khmer bodies but Vietnamese minds.' Art, my wife is from a Vietnamese family that used to live near here. I have a Viet-Khmer body and a Vietnamese wife. And I have openly criticized the government's irrigation schemes."

He turned to Devi, his face in shadow.

"Dear comrade, I am sorry that I agreed to meet you today. You must not come here any more. Fairly soon, I will decide what to do. You must decide, too. Don't delay!"

Pfeffer and Devi embraced Nuong and left the project, driving west. By unspoken agreement, they did not turn off the highway at the road to the commune but continued on toward the capital. For more than an hour, they thought their own thoughts. Then, not far from the city line, Devi pulled the jeep well off the road, extracted the key, and held out her arms, tears flooding her dark eyes. Pfeffer came into her embrace, and they held each other wordlessly. Then she pulled back and observed him gravely.

"What will you do now, Professor? Your sabbatical term has another month to go."

Pfeffer hesitated.

"I don't know, Devi. I came here with a hypothesis about your revolution creating a new type of society. What I've found has given me second thoughts. But there's a great deal of uncertainty. What if Pol Pot realizes that he can't keep driving people so hard? What if he decides to accept American aid? The Vietnamese could still pull their troops back from the border. Despite everything, the Revolution could still succeed . . ."

"You are not a very good listener, are you?" she replied sharply, turning back to the wheel.

They drove the rest of the way in silence. Pfeffer got out of the jeep at the entrance to his apartment building.

"Will you come up for a while?" he asked, his eyes pleading.

"No."

"Devi . . . I didn't mean . . ."

He could read from her face that to continue wouldn't change her decision.

"We will speak about this again," she said.

Pfeffer walked into the lobby and saw an envelope protruding from his mailbox. He opened it and read the capitalized message: "URGENT THAT YOU COME TO MY EMBASSY IMMEDIATELY. DO NOT DELAY. COME ALONE. BRING NOTHING WITH YOU. GAO."

His shock made the atmosphere echo. Stunned, he glanced at the stairway, wondering whether to go up to his apartment. Then, shaking his head, he walked back into the street, hailed a jitney cab, and said, "Embassy of China, quickly please." As the cab turned the corner, he noticed two uniformed men leaving the lobby and staring in his direction.

Wang was standing directly behind the iron fence enclosing the Chinese embassy. When the gate swung open, he grasped Pfeffer's arm firmly and walked him quickly to an interior office. Several Chinese officials were seated there. They remained silent while Wang did the talking.

"Professor Pfeffer, I am happy to see you again."

"Same here, Mr. Wang."

"Art, are you CIA?"

"What?" Pfeffer registered genuine astonishment. "Of course not, Gao. I am probably on their enemy list."

"That may be, Professor, but the Cambodian leaders have announced that you are CIA and that you have participated in a plot with Vietnamese agents to assassinate Prime Minister Pol Pot and overthrow the state."

"That's crazy," Pfeffer said.

"Indeed," said Wang. "Since the regime does not want to alienate your government entirely, they would probably just deport you. But there might be a trial first. And before that, perhaps, an interrogation . . . We have been in contact with the US State Department. Everyone agrees that it is best for you to leave the country immediately."

Pfeffer sat still, trying to absorb the news. Then he jumped from his chair, causing two security officers to leap to their feet as well.

"Devi!" He almost shouted. "If they think I'm CIA, what will they think of Devi?"

"This is your friend, the protégée of Minister Thieu?"

"Yes."

"She will probably be all right. The minister will continue to protect her. In this country, everything depends upon this sort of friendship . . ."

"Yes," Pfeffer broke in. "I know about the Cambodian patronage system. Comrade Thirith assured me that it no longer exists."

"For your friend's sake, let us hope it does," replied Wang.

Several hours later, an embassy car with blackened windows drove Pfeffer, Wang, and the security men to the airport. The professor's protectors whisked him past airport security and onto the tarmac, where he spoke briefly to Wang.

"Goodbye, Gao. You've been a very good friend. Thank you!"

"Goodbye, Professor Art. I hope that you write your book."

"I have one more favor to ask, Gao."

"I know," he replied. "Check up on your friend, Devi."

"Yes, please. Explain my sudden departure. And tell her . . ."

"I will give her your warmest, most respectful regards," said Wang.

About one month after arriving in Berkeley, Pfeffer received a short letter from Gao. After the initial greeting, it read:

> *I have seen your friend, who is still employed at the Ministry of Social Affairs. Apparently, her employer*

portrayed her as the innocent victim of an unscrupulous CIA seducer. She asked me to send you her very best wishes, and to let you know that although she is safe, her parents have been charged with profiteering and spying for the Vietnamese. They have been sent to S-21. She hopes that you have become a good listener and asks you to remember her kindly.

Richard Rubenstein

Richard Rubenstein is the author of eight books on violent conflicts and their resolution, including the best-selling *When Jesus Became God* and the more recent *Reasons to Kill: Why Americans Choose War*. A graduate of Harvard College, Oxford University, and Harvard Law School, he is University Professor of Conflict Resolution at George Mason University and teaches at the GMU School for Conflict Analysis and Resolution. He lives in Washington, D.C. and blogs at www.rich-rubenstein.com.

Hell in the City
Suong Mak

First Day: Sunday, May 13, 2012

It was nine o'clock at night, not so late in the capital city. In particular the area was noted for containing Cambodia's leading department stores. But next to the luxury stores with their little crowds of people were wilderness areas, dozens of buildings built after waiting for the lease purchase but now abandoned following the sudden economic collapse. The collapse had not only destroyed the riel currency but also pricked the bubble economy, filling the city with such buildings.

The sky was dark but the streetlights, the vehicle headlights, and the foggy glow leaking from the mall combined to make the street bright enough to see. A little deeper into the group of buildings that could not be sold, however, these awesome structures obscured the light from all sides. Their combined shadow as they leaned over each other created a large cave in the middle of the city.

In the shadow of one dark apartment building small white dots loomed gradually larger. Something stepped out into the bright lights of the capital. A little man in a white T-shirt was leaving hastily. He turned left and then right before starting to walk quickly across the grass and through the decayed gate of the project. One step further and he stood on the pavement, two to three meters from the bus stop. The motorcycle taxis that usually parked there were gone.

He went quickly past the bus stop. People began to look at his white shirt. He ignored these eyes full of questions. Once past the bus stop he relaxed again. He stopped a rare taxi and asked, with some urgency, to be taken away from that area.

The odor of alcohol made the taxi driver open the window a little. He glanced at the new passenger suspiciously. A man who took a seat in the back was nothing unusual, but the driver's experienced eyes saw something suspicious. The red marks contrasting with the white shirt—was it blood?

The taxi driver compared the passenger's body shape with his own and then asked some questions.

"What's going on? Did you hit something?"

Through the rearview mirror the driver knew that the man's expression changed a little, eyes moving to look at him through the mirror. Then the passenger answered with an accent.

"I drank some wine and got into a fight."

The driver stopped the conversation there and glanced at his passenger once more before driving on quietly.

From somewhere in the dark a panting voice mingled with the cry of a woman, emerging through the soft whisper of vehicles on the road. Light from the backs of buildings flashed through the area's wrought iron fencing and staircases, fading in brightness over a narrow band of blue and white floor where the maker of these noises sat.

The magic trick of the darkness allayed her shock and helped her ignore what had just happened.

Shy even when alone in the dark, the girl pulled the tattered remnants of her clothing around her body in an attempt to conceal it. Blood flowed from long and deep wounds to her left temple.

It spilled from these lesions for hours. Though she was exhausted, her instinct for survival summoned her to the present, reminding her that she could not sit there forever. The young girl forced herself to stand up. The muddy color of blood seeped through her T-shirt, and the skin of her face and trunk were sticky with blood from her body. Unable to continue standing on her own, she grasped a railing. She had no idea how long she'd been curled up, or how much blood she had lost.

She looked at the ground again and tears flowed, mixing with the blood on her face. She remembered the events exactly. The horrible shock, as though she had been beaten by an iron pole. She had gone blank. He had used something on her, one of those electric shock guns that they sold at Olympic Market. And then she remembered the smell of the alcohol. She remembered the man's accent, as he whispered in her ear, "See you here again tomorrow!" She dragged herself down the stairs of the abandoned apartment.

At the foot of the stairs a fraction of light illuminated a piece of wood. It was stained with blood, barely visible in the dim light. She felt a low whine rise up inside her. Black hands, dirty and stained, raised to touch the wound on her head. Her memory now replayed the nervous cry she had made, as she begged the little man in front of her. However, each time it was followed by the sound of the wood hitting the head, again and again, until the sixth time, when she realized that if she didn't stop crying, the man clutching the wood would also not stop.

She saw the light outside, not too far away. She tried her feet again and managed to reach the entrance door of the abandoned building. She remembered the overgrown grass along the trail. She had cried nonstop when the man dragged her from the sidewalk. He had struck her with an iron rod to the neck. The pain of that blow emanated from her neck and temples, but she still felt it all through her body. And now she could not break through the darkness to the light outside. Again her hands pulled the clothes around her beaten body. She was too shy to walk outside.

Nine o'clock was also not too late for selling noodles in a residential community. A woman, sixty years old perhaps, was cooking, but her eyes strayed often up the street, looking for someone. Her withered and thin hands, ugly from hard work, tossed the noodles almost automatically as all the while she was thinking about her twenty-two-year-old daughter, who had asked her that morning if she could hang out with friends on holiday.

Her daughter had told her she'd be home no later than eight o'clock, but it was past nine and still there was no sign of her. The noodle seller was angry, but she was worried, too, because her daughter was not a clever child. Obedient and kind, but silly all her life—some were born that way. On the surface she looked normal, but after talking with her for a while, people guessed that she had some kind of problem. She didn't recognize words or items of current interest. Her poor academic performance had forced her into jobs of no significance in small companies, at small salaries. But the two of them got by. They were simply an unremarkable Khmer-

Vietnamese family who accepted fate with no conditions and no claims, and lived this life relying on their own strengths.

The girl had also been born slightly malformed, another shortcoming and another punishment of karma. As she tossed her noodles, the mother considered these problems, and her aging heart grew more and more restless.

Quickly answering the hard knocking on the door, the young woman let the little man into the house. She looked at his bloody white shirt, at the wounds on her husband's body. He pushed past her, taking up the *krama* scarf in the bathroom and beginning to clean himself. But he could not avoid his wife's fearful questioning.

"What's going on? Why is there blood on your shirt?"

He frowned, annoyed, and then answered with the same single sentence he had given the taxi driver. But it was not enough for his wife.

"So, are you OK? Should we go see the doctor?"

The little man sighed while taking off his bloody white shirt.

"Stop nagging! I told you already I'm OK!"

"Why is there blood on your shirt?"

"My friend was punched! Understand?"

His shout ended the conversation. The woman looked back at the television.

The little man began to scrub at his bloody shirt and shorts, but the blood was not easy to get rid of, its stain unremovable. Bloody clothes are not different from bloody hands; they can never be the same.

He began to splash water from a plastic tub over his naked body and thought back over the last few hours.

Hell in the City

Mostly he remembered the soft body of a strange woman. How he forced her to touch his cock. Her hands were not soft enough; they were hard and calloused, destroyed by work. He was a little disappointed, but it had been better than nothing. White skin like a Chinese or Vietnamese, the square face shape.

He whistled happily as he remembered the death threats against her should she inform the police. He imagined she was hardly a model of virtue. There no way she would go to the police, that half-simple girl. How could she run to the police? He smiled a little as he bathed his body. Then he took the *krama* to wrap around his waist without wiping himself dry. A new idea ... maybe they would meet again tomorrow? He smiled again before opening the bathroom door.

His wife looked at his thin but hard and strong chest, at the water that still sparkled on his body. He was not interested in his wife's gaze and flicked the shirt to dry on the rack near the window. Now the bloody color left only a pale brown. He fell down on the mattress bed, exhausted. The television went silent, and then the lights were dim and he was conscious of a soft plump body next to his.

In the darkness, with the body and mischievous hands of his wife, he forgot all about the events of earlier that night.

It was ten at night but there were still plenty of people on the busy street. Many of them, particularly store employees on their way home, took a shortcut through the abandoned buildings near the mall. There was lighting along the sidewalk. However, when looking through the decayed gate onto the shortcut, some were fearful of the empty buildings, with their torn-off doors and long grass.

At night the three-storey building was entirely dark, and the workers gossiped that it was a den of drug addicts.

It was a Sunday night, so there were fewer people than usual, but the street was still not deserted when a second person emerged from the abandoned building. This figure crept out, not rushing like the first. Bloody red paint seemed to be splashed all over the person's upper body, running down onto her pants. The figure half crawled and half walked, exhausted, finally moving right into the bright light on the pavement.

She looked left and right in confusion. People were around, and she did not want to die yet. She was conscious that she had lost so much blood that she was almost out of strength. But the will to crawl away from death remained within her, and she knew that her best hope lay at the end of the street.

As she stumbled, she was not alone. She was faintly conscious of exclamations, of people changing their paths to avoid her, accelerating their pace when she stuck out her hands to ask for help. Now she was the same age her mother had been when her father had walked out, leaving her mother with nothing to live on but the determination to survive. She reached the other side of the street and saw the white light of a clinic, just down the street a little.

A heavy rock sits in the heart of a mother when her daughter does not return home. Having no phone, the noodle seller walked to one of the ubiquitous "pay phones" on the street, old ladies like her sitting in plastic chairs lending out their cell phones for a fee. She had the number of her daughter's friend, but there was no good news. Her friend said that she had left her at eight. Now it was ten already, with no sign of her daughter. The old woman's heart twisted as she returned to her noodle stall, still serving bowls to customers. But finally she decided to sit down for a moment. She asked herself, Where is my daughter? Where did she go?

The young girl slowly dragged her body, limping down the street to a small private hospital on the ground floor of an apartment building. Behind her as she entered, the glass door was stained with her hand prints and blood. She cried out loudly that she had been assaulted and raped. She sobbed, and the wounds and blood on her body clarified the seriousness of her attack.

The nurse called the doctor out, and he quickly took in her torn clothes and the blood.

"Doctor, please help me! I've been raped!" she cried.

Her speech was artless, but opaque with a terrible pain, both physical and mental.

"I was beaten. Help me, doctor!"

The doctor provided first-aid care immediately. Blood was removed from her face and her cuts were cleaned, revealing abrasions on her limbs, a swollen mouth, and a bruise on the left side of her neck.

"I was shocked!" she cried. "He used one of those guns, the ones from the market. He used electricity on me!"

The staffs were no longer listening to her raving.

"He hit me so hard, he hit me so hard, . . ." she repeated, over and over again.

The doctor, having seen to her injuries and seeing the blood loss, was incredulous.

"How did you get to the hospital? Who brought you here?"

But the girl only shook her head.

"Myself."

The answer surprised the doctor. He had assumed that a good citizen brought her there and then left to avoid the hassle.

"You are very strong to lose so much blood and then get here on your own."

The medical team assumed her memory had been damaged by the trauma of the rape and beating. She descended into a coma.

Second Day: Monday, May 14, 2012

In the morning almost all the newspapers shared the headline "Rape Using Electro-Shock Device Near Abandoned Buildings." Hot news like this spread quickly through the media. The news was all over the television. The use of an electric shock device in particular tantalized the reporters and commentators, as well as the public following the progress of the case. The intense interest forced the opening of a full-scale investigation, starting with the crime scene.

It was still morning, but the sun was already powerful enough to scatter light throughout the building. The investigators assessed the decayed low fence, the overgrown grass. Throughout the building they could see dust, dirt, and stains from the rain that had leaked in for years, turning the building into a range of colors.

When entering the building, No. 13/10, the dust, the dirt, and the spider's webs all assaulted the nose and eyes. The floors of the building were littered with plastic trash, glue cans, various drug paraphernalia, and a range of deeply unpleasant smells, some all too familiar. The investigation team leader ventured downstairs via a rusty old ladder. The accompanying TV crew were repelled by all that they saw, but the program director, who was a woman, looked resolutely around this dirty, rusty steel cage. From inside the neglect they could dimly make out the neighboring occupied buildings and homes. Up several steps was a mezzanine.

The conditions on the mezzanine during the day were very different from at night. Maybe that poor young woman had only seen the dark, the news director thought as she gazed at the dust and coarse dirt around her. The concrete that had not been cleaned for years, and the place was full of garbage. Some patches of the floor were blood-stained, the stains relatively new in one place. Any woman dragged in here would be terrified, day or night. The director couldn't believe that anyone, even a rapist, would willingly have sex in this environment.

A career that requires imagination can sometimes be a curse, and the TV news director found herself depressed and ashamed as she imagined herself as that poor, simple young woman. She quickened her pace. She wanted to get away from the scene now. The air inside the building was stifling. The bustle of traffic noise outside loosened the silent tension for a moment. She turned back toward the main street, observing the crossing to the hospital that the victim must have taken. It wasn't until the young woman had reached the hospital that the police were finally informed. Calculating the distance to the hospital, she decided to walk there with a photographer to interview the doctor on duty.

The girl had been sent to a public hospital with the financial assistance of the foundation of a female politician. Waiting for news from her daughter had been hell for the mother, but the truth had been equally horrifying. She panicked and cried when she heard from the police. Now she was standing looking down at her sleeping daughter, still suffering from the injuries and trauma. The eyes of the mother pierced into the heart of her daughter. Her eyes became her daughter's eyes, which were empty but for the pain of her body and the hallucinations of her mind. The gaunt and rough hands, their beauty destroyed by years of hard work, caressed the daughter's messy hair as she lay in the bed.

"Don't think so much! Forget it! Come back home when you're better."

The daughter looked at her mother's face for a moment, and her tears began to flow again. She closed her eyes, exhausted, not having the strength to say anything. As soon as she saw her mother's face, everything had begun to come back to her. She remembered more than what she had reported to the police earlier. Her instincts told her that her mother was ready to listen and take those cruel memories from her.

The door opened, and two women from the welfare foundation entered. Both mother and daughter raised their hands to salute. The newcomers asked polite questions about the daughter's health but quickly turned to address the mother.

"If we can catch this man, what will you do? Will you want a revenge?"

The old woman shook her head. "No. Up to the police and law to punish him."

"But why, seeing your daughter like this, why don't you ask for vengeance?"

The mother still continued to shake her head, her answers based on her truest feelings.

"No, I don't want that. I'm afraid it might come to hurt us again."

The women from the foundation looked at each other. Many victims said the same thing. They all feared continued disgrace. They knew only of inequality, exploitation, and assault—the things they felt belonged to the poor. The mother and daughter lived in a world without opportunity, and fear stalked them in a way that may seem unreasonable to those in better circumstances. And the power they feared was more than physical. They had no rank, no title, and no position. They were simply an old woman abandoned by her husband and a malformed, half-stupid daughter.

The women from the foundation left and a moment later were replaced by a TV crew. The mother looked on with confusion while the young girl in the bed turned her face away. The TV reporters assured them that they would interview the girl with her face concealed. And the mother didn't know that she could refuse.

The TV news director was sweating as she pushed the glass door open. It had been cleaned by now, and no traces of blood remained from the night before. The cool air of the clinic refreshed her. She introduced herself to the nurse at the counter and told her what she wanted, and the doctor in charge was found.

"When I saw her, she said she was raped, and some of the people present thought she may have received an electric shock." The doctor was excited by his own story. "She was beaten with a piece of wood, too. She said so. I gave her a brief physical examination, but then another doctor came and took over."

The use of an electrical shock device was the most sensational part of the case, the thing that caused such widespread interest in the media and made the incident a hot item on Facebook.

"About that electric shock, did you find any evidence of it on her body?"

"Umm ... the wounds were not consistent with electric shock."

The doctor's answer disappointed her.

He continued, "But if she was shocked in a non-fatal manner, there would be very little in the way of wounds to see. If some kind of shock device was used on her, there might be no way of us proving it."

There was enough uncertainty now in the doctor's answer to pique the TV news director's curiosity. She would need to find out more about this. She asked about several other details.

"I heard that the police came because you informed them. Why did you decide to report the incident?"

"After seeing the patient in this state, I knew she'd been injured quite severely," the medical director said after thinking for a while. "And the obvious rape made the case so serious I needed to inform the police. We decided that it must be reported immediately. It was a hideous crime. I would like to see the perpetrator caught as soon as possible."

Or perhaps you feared providing medical treatment to someone with no money to pay for it, she thought to herself.

Apparently reading her thoughts, the young doctor was smiling now.

"We would not refuse first aid to any patient, in particular an emergency patient. I would always provide first aid. It's not a lot of money, and I believe that if we help, if we contribute to society, it will not cause the hospital financial damage. But there should be some government-funded unit to respond with this sort of assistance. It could help the patients with no money and perhaps provide some funding for the hospital, something like that. This would help to solve the problem, I think."

Hell in the City

Leaving the hospital, the TV news director looked at her watch. It was getting late. She produced a show listing the crimes of the week. It was not live, but she believed it provided valuable information to its audience. And this week they were going to hear about electric shock devices.

The TV reporters had left, and the mother watched her daughter as she slept. She then stood up and quietly left the room, taking the lift out of the hospital. She intended to return home to prepare things for tomorrow's noodles. Of course, the condition of her only daughter worried her terribly, but she could not stop selling noodles because it was her only means to live on, to pay for rent, food, and everything else. She remembered the time before she had that money, and a life filled with problems and bad people—an undue share.

She walked through the hall on the hospital's ground floor. A television was on for the patients awaiting treatment, and the current news story was about her daughter. The old woman collapsed on a chair and watched. The journalist who interviewed her daughter was speaking with the police and many other people the mother didn't know. Other issues were introduced, and suit-wearing men and beautifully dressed women spoke, telling people that the electric shock devices sold to women as protection were turning out to be a public safety disaster. There were criticisms of urban decay. This was all being said in the newspapers, too. In a strange way the mother felt glad, happy that if anything said or written about the rape could help other girls, then her daughter's bad luck might mean something.

The old woman stood up even though the news was not over. Her brain was now listing the noodle seasonings that she needed to buy for tomorrow. Life for her was day-to-day, and she did not have the luxury to dwell on the past for long.

Fourth Day: Wednesday, May 16, 2012

A TV news van drove toward the police station. The program director and also the script writer reviewed the circumstances of the case again and considered other aspects presented in the media, looking for a new angle.

New people had been found to comment on the case, though a suffering young victim of rape still lay in her hospital bed. But the program director had lost interest in the victim. The young woman had been all over the media already; others had interviewed her. The electric shock devices, though, remained news, were criticized both in the newspapers and on television. But apart from this there was nothing to "play" with anymore. Perhaps she could interview more doctors, but that would not be enough. She suspected that the police station they were headed to would have something new for her.

The team met with the police lieutenant in charge of the rape case. The lieutenant was a big, dark-skinned man who looked more like a gangster than a cop. There were other investigations at this station, he reminded them. He agreed that it was a very difficult case in which to find the culprit. The abandoned buildings were filled with junkies—everyone knew it. There were no suspects, no one to be charged, and only minimal, circumstantial evidence. Hardly any progress. It was unlikely the villain would be caught.

As a TV news program was required to explore the various aspects of any story, the program director thought of the crime scene and then questioned the lieutenant about the abandoned buildings. The area was a notorious haunt for junkies, she noted, constantly associated with criminal activities such as robbery and bag-snatching. Someone must be ultimately responsible for the problems associated with these locations.

"This is private property, and we cannot interfere," the lieutenant commented. "The scene of the crime has an owner. Shall we make the owner responsible? But how can we? He cannot be there twenty-four hours a day."

The lieutenant expanded further: "If we can prove any negligence, then both civil and criminal charges can be made. I have also ordered the owner to act in every way to assist the police in their investigations."

The lieutenant added. "I want to tell people that if there is anyone who saw something happen or who took part in this event, or can provide any clue, they have a duty to share this information with the police. We simply do not have the resources to check every square inch of the city. There is someone out there closer to the criminal than us."

The police lieutenant then said that the real news was the use of an electric shock device.

"We must prevent the use of this type of equipment. These devices are commonly available but are not helpful to any parties."

The interview with the police lieutenant was drawing to an end. But his closing comment caught the attention of the TV news director: "The victim's mother was devastated and couldn't understand why nobody saw or helped her daughter while it was still early in the night and there were people everywhere."

A flash of inspiration—the mother of the victim had not given any interview yet. There had previously been no reference to her mother. She asked the police officers where the mother could be found, but they refused to tell her because people in the area did not know yet who the victim was. But after pledges were made to guarantee anonymity, they relented.

A thirty-something man sat reading a newspaper in a café shop near a garage, waiting for a car lease in the early morning. He had seen the news the day before—rape, electric shock, beating. Details of the assault were horrible and depressing. The police sought the public's assistance in identifying a suspect. Details were released of the specific time and place of the crime. Special phone numbers were created to collect information.

The young man read all of this aimlessly. He recalled a small man with a bloodstained shirt who'd got into his taxi a couple of nights before. Relevant or not? Should he tell the police or not? He thought not. He folded his newspaper and paid for his coffee. Then he walked through the alley to the garage, where he hired his taxi, the same one he hired every day. The young man couldn't afford the luxury of reflection. He drove the streets of Phnom Penh and tried to limit his thoughts to the work of the day.

The mother's home was not easy to find. The police information lacked detail. The TV news director and her crew had to park at the nearby temple and then continue on foot. There was no other word for the area but slum. She had been told only to look for a woman who sells noodles. It wouldn't be hard, they promised, because she was well-known in the area, having lived there so long. After walking along a narrow corridor between rooming houses, she arrived at an old house that loomed up before them. The owner had divided it into small rooms to rent separately. Each room was ten square meters or less. Fortunately for the TV team, the mother was at home preparing the noodles for the evening.

She was a Khmer-Vietnamese woman, about fifty years old, though she looked much older. She was thin, with sunken cheekbones and small hands bulging with veins. Her hair was curly, permed for free by students at the nearby beauty school. In fact, she was paid a little to let them experiment on her. She was dressed in pale polyester clothes that were pilled and faded.

The team introduced themselves, but the woman did not want to be interviewed because the people around there still didn't know that it was her daughter with the "bad news" on the TV. The news director promised that her face would be obscured, and that they would not tell anyone who it was or where the interview took place. She accepted their promises and their inherent authority.

She led the team to see the room she rented for thirty dollars a month that housed both mother and daughter. It was a very small room for the price, and the crew imagined that if one rolled over while sleeping the other would know it.

Interviewing the mother, it was clear that she was not well educated. She could read and write only a little. No surprise. People like her worked hard all their lives with no opportunity to learn anything else. Her whole life had been spent eking out a living.

The news director tried to steer the long small talk to the real reasons for the visit. She asked questions and the mother answered with all of the unnecessary and questionable detail.

"The criminal told her to 'shut up'. Then he took a piece of wood and hit her head until her skull was cracked."

"Did he say anything else?"

"He told her, 'Don't tell the police!'" Her dialogue became more Vietnamese accented. "He said if she didn't die then he would see her again tomorrow. You see how bad he is? Sunday he did evil, and then wants more on Monday. What kind of human is he?"

"When did he say this, aunt?"

"It was when he was attacking her. Attacking and threatening together!"

The news director frowned. She was not sure what the woman meant by the word "attacked."

"You mean when he hit her?"

"No. I mean when he did it... when he raped her."

To hear a mother say this cut right into her heart. In fact, she had understood the mother's meaning from the start but could see no other way of getting her reaction to the story.

She was lost for a moment and couldn't think of further questions. The mother bowed her head and continued speaking with a soft voice.

"She is not smart," the woman said. "But she knows the limits of modesty well enough. That's why she almost didn't dare to leave that place. If she hadn't, she would have died from the loss of blood. She would have died if she'd waited there till morning."

The news director looked at the mother. Her simple words, spoken in a blunt accent, clearly relayed her conversation with her daughter. The director began to imagine the time when the old woman had heard the story from her daughter's lips, and how her daughter's heart had felt when she expressed her pain to her mother.

"She dragged herself out. No one helped her. She crawled alone to hospital. The doctor asked who took her there. The doctor said how strong she must have been."

Now the mother seemed to be venting and couldn't stop telling her story. Maybe, the director thought, telling these things to strangers was easier than sharing them with the people she knew.

"Did she say the criminal was drunk or smelled of sniffing glue?" the interviewer asked.

"Of course." The thin woman spoke slowly and hesitantly. "People around there said the criminal was sniffing glue and drinking."

"People around there, not your daughter?" the news director repeated. She had to try at least to distinguish between rumor and fact.

"She said the criminal smelled of alcohol and thinner. This stuff is common. Especially in those abandoned buildings—it happens all the time! But some people were afraid to report it."

The news director felt uncomfortable with the words. The vulnerability of both mother and daughter was painful. The woman had exhausted her life selling bowls of noodles for a few thousand riels. She was like so many others, the old women the news director saw every day, the ones who cleaned her clothes until their hands became deathly pale and the skin flaked off because of laundry soap. The horrible permed hair, like that of so many other kind-faced old women on the street, styled with no consideration for the shape of her face. If the doctor had not reported it to the police, if the politician's foundation had not intervened to help pay the hospital fees, if the news channels hadn't urged people to look at this case, how would this family have seemed any different?

The news director ended the conversation by asking the woman if she had any message she'd like to give the public. She replied immediately without thinking.

"If people helped, these bad things would not happen. Many people were around that night who could have stopped it, but no one helped."

The TV crew left the house. The news director returned to the van parked by the temple. While the cameraman and photographer were busy taking pictures of the community, she was in deep thought. She instructed them not to take any more images of the surrounding area, for fear the woman might be recognized. Even shots of the bedroom she wanted excluded.

Fifth Day: Thursday, May 17, 2012

At the police station the case was now being treated much more seriously because of its growing notoriety. Supervisors demanded to see progress, to hear news of the investigation. But there was nothing to report—no suspect, no trace of evidence.

Because it was a famous case, the public began to ring the hotline with all kinds of crazy "clues." However, none of the information received, after being checked thoroughly, was useful to the case. The histories of criminals arrested but not convicted were examined. Prisoners just released were also checked. But still no real leads emerged.

It was eight o' clock but several police officers were still in the station working on the case. The phone rang again. Another lead, this time a taxi driver. On the night of the accident, at approximately ten, he'd had a passenger wearing a bloody shirt who'd asked him to drive him home. The man had claimed to be fighting with friends. The police asked for a description of the passenger, and they heard about a small man, with hollow cheeks. He

Hell in the City

look liked a Vietnamese but spoke Khmer fluently. He was wearing a white T-shirt and jeans and had long ruffled hair. The description matched the testimony of the victim exactly.

The young man hung up and walked away from the pay phone to his taxi, throwing some newspapers on the front seat. He was relieved for the first time since he'd heard the news of the crime. After his discussion with the police, he thought that the man might well be the wanted criminal. He had done the right thing, and now his heart was at peace. His conscience had been soothed. He had done his part for society, and the police would now arrest the criminal or not—it was up to them. The young man smiled to himself for the first time in days.

Sixth Day: Friday, May 18, 2012

In the early morning the police brought in a woman from a house in the slums for questioning. Following the clues from a report by a taxi driver, they had finally found the home of the suspect. Inside was a plump young woman in her early twenties who admitted that on the night of the accident her husband had returned home with bloodstains on his shirt and pants. But neither the husband nor the clothes were anywhere to be found. He had absconded to his first wife's house, where he remained. The husband, the police learned, was a pedi-cab driver who always waited for passengers in front of a particular shopping mall.

Working on the wife for some time, the police were confident that they had the right person. An officer was dispatched to observe the driver near the mall, and the suspect was brought in at about four o'clock that day. A search of his first wife's house found a shirt and pants wrapped in plastic. The bloodstains remained on the jeans. Upon the suspect's return to the police station with the evidence, a second interview was conducted and, based on the evidence, the suspect finally confessed.

Fifteenth Day: Sunday, May 27, 2012

That afternoon at the abandoned building, which had still not been closed up, people gathered after hearing about the arrest of the accused in the electric-shock rape case. A large crowd of people, including reporters from the newspapers and television channels, was waiting for the confession of the accused at the site of the crime. The TV news director was standing at a door of the building, watching people—many of them women of different ages—jammed together as if waiting for an important person. The facial expressions and words of the mother still haunted her: *If people helped, these bad things would not happen. Many people were around that night who could have stopped it, but no one helped.*

She asked the people nearby, "If you had been there that night, would you have helped the girl who was raped?"

There was enthusiastic response and the woman nearest, wearing a floral shirt and a dark-colored sarong, answered loudly: "Of course I would have helped! At the risk of my own life."

The director smiled sadly and thought how different these people were from the ones who had been there that night. How unfortunate that the girl had not encountered this crowd on that day! Or, she wondered, were they all just full of it?

A police truck drove into the property. The press squeezed in as the crowd reacted. Some police had to

Hell in the City

control the people, keeping them away from the suspect when he was brought down from the truck. He looked pale and wary. The police officials were themselves a little nervous—they could not be responsible for releasing him to this crowd to be lynched. But still some people attempted to land a slap on the suspect's head. Police officers surrounded him and jostled him into a section of the building that had been roped off and guarded all morning. It was time for him to show them just how he had committed the crime.

A police director shouted through a megaphone, begging people to remain calm and not hinder the work of the police. The crowd began to quiet down. The police led the accused to the various points of the crime. The TV crew followed him every step of the way.

The event had started at the sidewalk, the man explained. Returning from her friend's home, the girl had gone to the toilet in the shopping mall. Leaving there, she had met her attacker by chance. He had dragged her from the sidewalk in front of a motorcycle taxi driver waiting for customer. The girl had cried out for his help, but the accused told him that they were husband and wife so that the taxi driver would not interfere. The man had been quick to believe the story and seemed indifferent to what he saw.

The girl had resisted and begun to cry more and more loudly, so the accused had grabbed a steel pipe he found nearby and beat her around her neck. She cried for mercy, invoking her old mother who was not well. He had answered her by dragging her into one of the abandoned buildings. Here it had been almost completely dark. The girl had continued to cry for help and did not stop screaming. So the accused had grabbed a piece of wood at the scene and beaten her on the head six times, causing deep wounds to the skull. Thick blood had begun to spill from the wound. The pain having become unbearable, the cries of the girl stopped. The accused had dragged her up to the mezzanine where he forced her to lean against the balustrade and attempted to rape her but was unsuccessful. Drawing her to the floor, he had used his own shirt to wipe the blood off the face of the girl. Forcing her to lie on the ground, he took her clothes off and then pulled down his own pants but found the sexual act difficult and unpleasant.

During this time he constantly threatened the victim. When leaving he took her purse. Then he had left. The deed was ended.

The TV news director was still standing on the mezzanine. When the police and journalists walked by with the accused, she looked down from above and wanted to find something to throw at the head of the man in handcuffs. She felt miserable with nausea. While standing up there on the mezzanine, she had overheard two newspaper photographers joking about the best way to photograph the accused. "Up here will make a cool shot," one of them said. She could barely understand this indifference and coldness in the face of all they had seen and heard.

The accused had been brought back to the police station, but most of the journalists had not followed. Remaining from the crowd were only the TV news director's team and two newspaper journalists. All of them were allowed to interview the accused with the inspector, the lieutenant, and the detective sitting by his side. The TV news director let the newspaper journalists interview him first because they were on a tighter deadline. She found what they were choosing to discuss inconceivable.

The newspaper journalists asked some preliminary questions about the background of the accused. But they quickly moved on to the detailed activities of indecency and rape. Why at the foot of the stairs? Why try to rape her while standing? The accused looked nervous at first, but soon he started to enjoy the telling. His expression became elated, and he seemed to become heroic, even proud. There was whispering and laughter. She looked at the police in charge, but it was very hard to guess their feelings. She was approaching the breaking point.

Finally, she burst out: "Don't you feel anything?"

But the three policemen in charge quickly turned the interview over to her.

She asked the suspect what he had been doing before he had met the girl.

"Drinking with friends. After they all were gone, I waited for her there," he said, referring to the scene.

But she still did not understand why he needed to rape a girl if he had two wives already. He answered that when he was drunk he always felt this urge.

Her job as a news director ended there. She wondered why she could see no trace of his humanity, his feelings. On a drunken whim, he had hurt a young girl, and because she had resisted he had wounded her seriously. How could he do that?

The accused sat with a self-satisfied expression and glanced in fear at the three police officers who were sitting by him. She couldn't avoid the thought that, were she alone with him, she might have been tempted to slap him.

The accused was forced to answer her further questions.

"There was no blood when you hit her neck. But then you hit her six more times?"

Why had he hit so savagely? Why had he had to inflict so much harm?

"I was afraid because she was shouting. I hit her to stop her crying, not to knock her out or kill her. I beat her to hurt her so I could control her more easily."

Was he claiming to be kind because he hadn't inflicted more serious damage? She asked the last question: How could he have had an erection when he knew the girl was in such pain?

The accused glowered at her and his jaws cracked as he answered, simply, "Drunk!"

She stood up. Perhaps what she had asked had not been the most important questions about the case. The police lieutenant, who had been following her reaction carefully, actually invited her to slap the face of the accused. She turned to look at the rapist but could not do it. She said thank you and goodbye to the police officers and glanced at the accused again. He cast back at her a look of hateful self-importance. He felt no guilt about what had happened.

One day this man would walk the streets again. Although he would be punished according to the law, the chains on him would eventually be removed. But the wound in a heart of the young woman would never heal.

Both mother and daughter were together again. They were no longer a news item, and neither was the accused. Soon there were other stories that caught the public's interest. Peaceful again, the women's normal lives began to be restored. They felt satisfied. A life in which grueling work was a necessity rarely gave the opportunity to reflect on the sadness felt by others. But even while working, occasionally they could not resist the pain at the depths of their hearts. They could not forget. The mother couldn't afford to carry the pain and trauma at the surface. But at night she no longer allowed her child to leave the house. She could never be replaced.

Suong Mak

Suong Mak is a Cambodian writer. His novel *Boyfriend*, the first contemporary Khmer novel about a gay-male couple, is being translated into English. His short story in this anthology is his first work to appear in the English language. He is 26 years old.

Khmer Riche

Andrew Nette

Despite the sea of bodies and machines that jammed Sihanouk Boulevard, Eng Huot was easy to find.

Hammond approached the building where their meeting was to take place, a six-storey monolith of concrete and reflective glass. The crowd parted to reveal an expanse of footpath taken up by two black Lexus four-wheel drives. Next to them four large Cambodian men in bodyguard chic: dark safari suits, walkie-talkies, stone-cold stares, bulges on their hips.

The nearest guard tensed as the middle-aged white man peeled off from the crowd and walked toward them. Hammond looked directly into the bodyguard's eyes, two black slits in a slab of muscle and scar tissue.

"He's expecting me."

The bodyguard kept his eyes on Hammond as he spoke into his walkie-talkie, rapid-fire Khmer interspersed with bursts of static, then nodded at a colleague, a short, thick-necked man who opened the plate-glass front door.

The air inside was frigid. A woman in traditional Khmer dress sat behind the marble reception desk, ignoring Hammond as he stepped into the elevator and pressed the button for level six.

The lift opened onto a rooftop restaurant. Fine dining on the menu, gangsta rap from the speakers. A tall Cambodian in a dark blue suit, white shirt open at the neck—a leaner, fiercer version of the men downstairs—blocked Hammond's path.

"Stay here," he said.

Without waiting for a reply he maneuvered between the tables to the one with the best view of the festivities below, bowed slightly, and spoke to the Cambodian sitting there.

The Cambodian waved the suited bodyguard away, said something to a red-haired Westerner next to him. Hammond knew his name was Somerset, Huot's British business partner. The two men laughed.

Hammond was suddenly aware of how disheveled he must appear. Sweat clung to his shirt. His light gray suit was creased after the flight from Singapore. Once, a long time ago, he'd found the games played by people like Huot amusing, mysterious. Now, after what felt like a lifetime of problem solving for the super rich, they came across as petty and tiresome.

To control his irritation, Hammond focused on the crowd below, snaking its way down Sihanouk Boulevard past the Independence Monument to the Tonlé Sap River. Some of the million or so people the inflight magazine said descended on Phnom Penh at this time every year to celebrate Bon Om Tuk, Cambodia's water festival.

Huot speared something with his fork and put it in his mouth, then nodded for Hammond to approach.

Huot took off his Ray-Bans as Hammond sat. Somerset kept his dark glasses on.

"Would you like anything to drink?" Huot said in perfect American-accented English.

Hammond glanced at the champagne bottle in an ice bucket, green glass beaded with moisture, shook his head despite his thirst. He knew it wasn't a genuine offer. The meeting wouldn't last long enough.

Huot's hair was still growing back after the monastery stint following his father's funeral. Apart from that, with his tailored shirt and mild-mannered, light-skinned features, the thirty-three-year-old looked like an IT technician dressed for Casual Friday at the office. All traces of the hardship of Cambodia's past had been bred out of him.

Hammond mentally ticked off what he knew about Huot's father, Eng Lim: ex-Khmer Rouge, ex-government military, made a fortune from illegal logging in the '90s, stashed it in a Singaporean bank until the crackdown on money laundering after 9/11. Repatriated the funds back to Cambodia, invested in real estate built on stolen land. The classic bandit capitalist that half of Asia's economic might was founded on. No formal education. First time he used a laptop, he thought it was a typewriter, threw it against a wall when it didn't work. But a legend across the region for his business prowess. Even greater things ahead, had it not been for the helicopter crash three weeks ago.

"How was your flight?"

"Fine, thank you."

Huot smiled, lit a cigarette from a gold lighter, exhaled a stream of smoke, leaned back in his chair, a signal to Somerset. Pleasantries over, time for business.

"Thank you for coming at such short notice." Somerset's voice was soft, plummy. "People speak very highly of you. Which is just as well because Chancellor's been missing a month, just vanished off the face of the earth, taking with him some property of ours."

Somerset shot Huot a sideways glance and shifted in his chair.

"We've had our best people searching for him. Not a fucking peep. It's almost as if he knows our every move before we do."

"What makes you think I can find him? Missing persons isn't my usual line of work."

"That's not what I hear. I've heard everything is in your line of work, if the money's right."

Hammond saw himself reflected in the dark lenses of Somerset's sunglasses, his thinning salt and pepper hair, water-blue eyes, small mouth, high forehead etched with deep frown lines.

"The task requires an eye for detail and a degree of subtlety not possessed by our friends downstairs," said Somerset. "There's a good chance our people have missed something that will not escape a man with your forensic skills."

"Whatever it is Chancellor has stolen—"

"Is extremely valuable, and it would be disastrous if it fell into anyone else's hands," Somerset said. "That's all you need to know. The story we've spread around town is Chancellor's returned home indefinitely to visit a sick relative. But we're not sure how much longer that will hold. Just find out what you can, report back to us."

"What with the ..." Somerset peered into his champagne flute as he searched for the right word, "accident, it's a delicate time. We start construction of our new project down in Sihanoukville in a few weeks and don't want any more trouble."

Hammond had read about the Sihanoukville project in the newspapers, a luxury resort for Asian tourists. Eng senior had hired local military police to forcibly evict villagers from the site. They'd killed two, hospitalized several more.

"I'll take your silence as consent."

Somerset slid a plain envelope across the white tablecloth.

"The basics of the task are in the dossier we've already emailed you. There's some additional information in this envelope."

"This is the last time we'll meet. From now on Klar here will be your liaison with us."

The Englishman pointed what there was of his chin at the blue-suited Cambodian now standing over Hammond's right shoulder.

"I prefer to work alone," said Hammond.

"Not this time. Cambodia can be a dangerous place. Klar could come in handy."

Hammond opened his mouth to protest, thought better of it, and got up to leave. Klar followed.

Bagman, dealmaker, problem solver, investigator, mediator, adviser, contractor, fixer, pimp. Hammond had been referred to as many things, but his preferred title was corporate consultant. It had an anonymity he found comforting and useful. A bland catch-all designed to hide the multitude of sins he might be required to commit.

A lot of big businesses in Asia had someone on the payroll, an ex-cop or a soldier, whose job it was to sort out problems before they ended up in the hands of the police, the courts, or the media. When that didn't work, they hired someone like Frank Hammond. He was an expert at navigating the gray zone between legality and illegality, which in Cambodia was big enough to drive a freight train through.

The sun was setting as he left the building, the sky magnetic blue streaked with pink.

Klar stepped toward one of the four-wheel drives parked on the footpath.

"Do you want to take one of the cars, Mr. Hammond?"

Hammond watched the sea of people flow past them, old people, young, well-dressed Phnom Penh families, darker-skinned, shabbily dressed people from the provinces.

"No, I'll walk."

Hammond took off his suit jacket, held it against his chest, and joined the crowd. He found a thin seam of people heading away from the riverfront and mined it slowly toward the city. Klar followed several people behind.

Gradually the crowd began to dissipate, and the lights of the city came on. Hammond walked past a row of Chinese shop-houses, their steel accordion doors opened to reveal families eating dinner, the flash of a welding torch from a machine shop, a secondhand clothes market, large squares of fabric spread across the pavement piled with multicolored clothes and mounds of odd shoes and sandals.

Hammond paused in front of an old Soviet-style building, now a casino, just as the neon roulette wheel attached to the front of the building flickered into life. He fingered the BlackBerry in his pocket and thought about calling some of the names in the dossier Somerset had emailed. Suddenly, though, he felt tired and hungry. He turned to Klar a few meters away.

"You going to follow me all night?"

The Cambodian shrugged. "You have your job. I have mine."

Klar's accent was a lazier version of his boss's. It reminded Hammond of an American reality television show where the cops are always arresting black people.

"Spend a lot of time in the States?"

"You could say that."

"Studying?"

"Not quite."

Hammond decided not to push it.

"Your name, Klar, what's it mean?"

"Tiger."

Hammond smiled. "Original."

"Has its uses."

"Not your real name, then?"

The Cambodian hesitated, unsure where Hammond was headed.

"Come on, you're supposed to do what I say, and I want to know what your name is."

"My parents called me Dara."

"Well, Dara, I don't know about you, but I'm starving. Want to eat?"

"Up to you, man."

They found a busy restaurant. People sat in groups eating large bowls of noodle soup, the floor strewn with chicken bones, beer cans, and shreds of pink paper napkins.

A young girl, still in her blue and white school uniform, took Hammond's order, relayed it to a much older woman who slaved over two steaming vats. The schoolgirl returned a few moments later with Hammond's noodle soup, a beer for Dara, resumed her position at the counter. The wall behind her was plastered with photoshopped pictures of her and another child standing in front of the Sydney Opera House, the Eiffel Tower, and other international landmarks.

305

Hammond thought about the job as he ate. He hadn't talked money with his new employer. He seldom did. All the broker had told him was that the job would be short and well-paid. A bonus if he got results.

Nor did he know what Chancellor had stolen. Money, drugs, documents? Hammond didn't particularly care. He needed the work, his finances shot to hell by the global financial crisis and his second divorce.

Hammond had worked in Cambodia once before, in the early '90s. He'd been brought in to negotiate the release of the son of a Filipino tycoon who'd been kidnapped by a rogue detachment of the Cambodian military. Back then, the entire country had seemed out of control. Now it was just the elite. They'd turned the entire government into a giant tribute system, each level kicking up to the one above. So much money concentrated in the hands of so few. Cambodia had swapped the Khmer Rouge for the Khmer Riche.

Hammond pushed his bowl aside, fished out the envelope Somerset had given him, tore it open. He smoothed out a folded A4 page, took out his reading glasses, examined the page under the lemon tint of the fluorescent lighting. It was a photocopy of a single-column newspaper cutting in Khmer. He picked the envelope off the floor, checked inside. Nothing else.

He handed the page to Dara.

"Tell me what this says."

Dara swigged his beer, took the piece of paper, mouthed the words as he spoke. Hammond could tell he did not read Khmer fluently.

"It's a report about a murder, some old woman killed during a robbery."

"That's it?"

"Pretty much."

Dara handed the page back to Hammond.

"Says she was a fortune-teller or something. Someone broke into her hut, killed her with an ax, stole, shit. Happens all the time."

Hammond took off his reading glasses, pinched the bridge of his nose. The article obviously had something to do with the job, but what?

"Let's get out of here."

Hammond had booked himself into a guesthouse, a tiny backstreet place, the type favored by tourists on a budget and men paying for sex by the hour.

The Cambodian looked from Hammond to the hotel's entrance and back again.

"Man, I don't understand you," he said, his syntax becoming more drawn out. "Eng offered to put you up at the Cambodiana. Why the fuck you staying in a no-name shit-hole like this?"

"I like my anonymity," said Hammond over his shoulder as he walked up the stairs.

Chancellor had lived in Toul Kork, a suburb in Phnom Penh's north. In the early '90s it had been the largest red light district in Phnom Penh. Now it was the preferred residential location of the city's rich, government ministers, local businessmen, and their expatriate partners. Hammond remembered it as a stretch of uneven dirt road lit only by fairy lights, lined on either side by wooden shacks with groups of heavily made-up young Vietnamese and Cambodian girls sitting out front.

Chancellor's residence was typical of the now gentrified neighborhood, a two-storey brick villa, reflective glass windows, Doric columns, surrounded by lush garden. Inside, floors of marble, plaster walls inlaid with polished timber.

Out of the corner of his eye Hammond saw Dara scan the place with undisguised envy.

"Help me find Chancellor, Huot might let you have this place as a present," Hammond said as he wandered into the lounge room. "You can make someone of yourself."

"Mr. Hammond, in Cambodia it's not possible to make someone of yourself," replied Dara, deadpan. "You can only be born someone."

Hammond looked directly into the Cambodian's dark eyes.

"I take it you weren't?"

"I hope my boss is paying you to come up with a lot smarter shit than that. Yeah, my parents were farmers, fled the Khmer Rouge, eventually got to the US when I was young after a four-year stretch in some shit-hole refugee camp on the Cambodian-Thai border. They live in Philadelphia and are still poor."

"What did you do there?"

"Sold drugs to rich white people, before Uncle Sam caught me, put me in jail, and six years later deported my ass back here."

Dara had arrived at Hammond's guesthouse that morning on a Honda Dream motorcycle, wearing jeans and a white T-shirt. Anonymous, as Hammond had told him. Only the tattoos on his muscular arms stood out. Not the usual faded blue spidery script and astrological drawings. Dara's were dark, swirly, almost medieval looking. Gang tattoos.

"Arrived here with the shirt on my back, nothing else. No documentation, nothing. Lucky for me, I came to the attention of old man Huot's son. Otherwise I'd be in the same situation as a lot of the other Cambodian returnees."

"And what's that?"

"Dead or in prison."

Hammond walked into the next room, a large kitchen, opened one of the cupboards.

"Did you know Chancellor?"

"I met him once or twice."

"What was he like?"

"Thought he was a player, like most of the foreigners my boss deals with." Dara leaned against the kitchen doorway. "This place hasn't been touched since Chancellor's disappearance."

It only took Hammond a few minutes of searching to confirm otherwise. The place had already been given a thorough going over. All money and personal valuables had been removed—that was no surprise—but someone had also taken every scrap of paper. Nothing—no bills, no files, not even a shopping list.

All Hammond knew about Chancellor after an hour of methodical searching was that he had a drinking problem, judging from the number of liquor bottles in the house, and an interest in black and white photography. Framed shots peppered the walls of the house, pictures of colonial Cambodia, combat shots from various stages of the country's bloody past, old temples and other buildings abandoned in the jungle.

Only one picture featured Chancellor himself, nearly the same age as Hammond but in much better shape, tanned skin, a shoulder-length mane of white hair, dark, intense eyes that peered directly into the camera. He was standing in front of a gutted villa.

Half of Cambodia was in ruins. Buildings destroyed by the Khmer Rouge then ransacked by the locals for building materials. What was left was being finished off by real estate speculation and land prices. There was no telling where the photo was taken.

Khmer Riche

Hammond spent the afternoon in an upmarket café making calls on his BlackBerry and surfing the Internet on his laptop in search of anything that might help him get a fix on Chancellor. All he came away with was a trickle of information and a disembodied feeling. Air-con, espresso coffee, Wi-Fi ... If it hadn't been for the staff hovering around the edges of the room, Hammond would have forgotten this was Cambodia.

As for getting a clearer picture of Chancellor, the excessive secrecy of Phnom Penh's business world, combined with the tendency of locals and expats alike to treat gossip and innuendo as fact, meant reliable information was scarce. The place was a continuous, 24/7 Chinese whisper.

Chancellor was typical of many long-term expatriate males in Asia: single, work-obsessed, childless, successful. Prior to his disappearance he'd been one half of a local legal firm nicknamed "the Rottweilers." The other half was an American called Richard Fink. The two had met in Bangkok, shifted to Phnom Penh in the mid-'90s, proven themselves useful to big shots in the Cambodian People's Party—at that stage locked in a furious struggle with opposition politicians allied to the country's king, Norodom Sihanouk.

As it turned out, they'd backed the winning horse, and it had paid off big-time. The Rottweilers became the go-to people for foreign businessmen seeking entrée into Cambodia, and they milked it for all it was worth. Like Dara said, Chancellor fancied himself a player.

Through a personal assistant, Fink agreed to meet Hammond that afternoon at the Elephant Bar in the Hotel Le Royal, the oldest, most prestigious hotel in Phnom Penh. The Khmer Rouge had used it to accommodate visiting delegations. Now the bar was full of exhausted

European tourists recovering after a day's sightseeing at the water festival. It was a bright room with high ceilings, a piano version of Whitney Houston's "Greatest Love of All" wafting through the air.

Fink occupied a two-person alcove toward the back of the bar. He was medium-height, skinny, almost completely bald, his beady eyes set back in his skull, surrounded by dark circles. He was drinking whiskey neat. Judging by his demeanor, it wasn't his first.

Fink didn't get up as Hammond approached. The lawyer reached out a hand in what Hammond thought was the start of a handshake, grabbed a handful of cocktail nuts, scooped them into his mouth.

The moment Hammond sat, a petite Cambodian woman materialized to take his order. He reached for the drinks menu, but before he could say anything, Fink barked something in Khmer. The woman nodded and left.

"So, Eng Huot's got you looking for George," Fink said, as he reached for another handful of nuts.

"Do you know where your partner is?"

"Ex-fucking-partner." Fink raised a bony index finger, waggled it in Hammond's face. "And I got the paperwork to prove it. And no, I don't know where he is or what it is he's stolen that Huot wants back so badly."

The waitress reappeared, placed a large whiskey next to Hammond and another before Fink. Fink finished the drink in his hand, gave the glass to the waitress, picked up the fresh one.

"When did you last see him?"

Hammond sipped his whiskey, a single malt.

"A week before the 'copter crash that killed Eng Lim."

Fink moved to the edge of his seat.

"Look Mr. Hammond, let's get a few things straight. Maintaining face matters in Cambodia, so for appearances' sake and out of respect for Lim, who I met when I first came to Cambodia, I agreed to meet with you. But don't act like I'm some patsy you can shake down, 'cause I know people in this town, too. People with a lot more juice than Huot.

"Way I hear it, his days are numbered now that Daddy's out of the way. Hasn't got the smarts or the stomach for business, not like his old man." Fink chuckled, took another handful of nuts. "Won't be long now, they'll be picking the flesh off his bones, Eng and that stuck-up little faggot British partner of his."

Hammond took another sip of his scotch.

"I accept that you've no longer got any connection to Chancellor and don't know where he is. I've done my homework on you. I know you're not a man to be trifled with. If you're half the businessman I think you are, you'll have done yours, too. You've found out enough about me to know I've been doing what I do for a long time. I know a lot of people, people who could be very useful to you. Level with me, I'd consider it a personal favor."

Fink drained half his drink, sighed. His belligerent exterior gave way to a tired expression.

"All I've heard is superstitious nonsense."

"Such as?"

"I lived in Bangkok for several years before coming here, thought the Thais were obsessed with ghosts. They got nothing on the Khmers. These guys could turn a simple head cold into a major paranormal event.

"Take the helicopter crash. The old man decides to visit his favorite casino on the Vietnamese border. There's a crash. Some say there was a bad storm; others, the night was as clear as a bell. Maybe it was mechanical error, maybe sabotage by a business rival. Hell, some people even think Eng Huot did it because he was impatient the old man wouldn't hand over the reins of the family business sooner. Not that you could do a fucking investigation because the local villagers stole all the wreckage, and even a few bits of Eng Lim, for good luck charms.

"Whatever happened, Eng Junior's spooked big-time. After the funeral he stages a massive exorcism at the family villa. For three days and nights he and the family make food offerings to the spirits, play loud music. Half the monks in Phnom Penh are hired to perform special chants to appease the spirits, persuade them to leave the house. Way I hear it, whatever scared them is connected to this thing George supposedly stole from Huot."

"Any idea what that is?"

"Don't know." Fink drained the rest of his drink. "Don't want to know."

"Did Chancellor give any indication that he was going to—"

"Pull a fucking disappearing act?" Fink shook his head. "I worked with George for years, thought I knew him. I mean, he'd been distracted, making mistakes he normally would never make. I put it down to all the hours he was clocking up working on that Sihanoukville resort the Eng family were trying to get off the ground.

"He took off once or twice without telling anyone at the firm, somewhere down south, didn't come back for a few days. We all thought he just wanted a bit of time out with that brunette from the NGO he was fucking."

Hammond sat up straight. There'd been no mention of a girlfriend in the dossier Huot had sent him.

The day guard at the NGO had given Hammond the woman's address for twenty dollars. He and Dara had spent two hours waiting outside the block of apartments where she lived when she left just after 4 p.m., hailing a motorcycle taxi. Hammond tailed her, perched on the back of Dara's motorbike. She got off at the entrance to the water festival. Hammond followed her into the crowd, while Dara checked his ride into the public parking space.

The promenade along the Tonlé Sap was packed, extended families sitting on rattan mats watching the races. The long boats, ornately decorated vessels, low in the water, were manned by teams of men in color-coded shirts. Vendors walked among the crowd selling toys, food, cigarettes, and fake designer sunglasses. Hammond noticed knots of grimy, bare-footed street kids on the lookout for any opportunity that presented itself—a dropped piece of food, an unattended bag.

Dara caught up with him just as the woman disappeared up the stairs of a bar overlooking the river. She reappeared moments later on the balcony amidst a group of Westerners watching the races.

Brigid Moreau was tall with long, dark hair and a slim, boyish figure. According to Fink, she'd done stints with various NGOs in Iraq and Somalia. She'd been seeing Chancellor for at least three months before he disappeared. Hammond and Dara found seats at the back of the bar, watched Brigid drink the early evening away.

"Don't look like she's missing Chancellor much," Dara said as the woman ran her hand up and down the back of the male on the neighboring bar stool, another older man, academic looking with thick-framed glasses and a goatee.

Hammond took his chance when the man headed to the toilet.

"Brigid, isn't it?"

The woman turned, swayed drunkenly on her bar stool as she looked at Hammond. She was younger than Chancellor by at least two decades, but already her looks were fading from too much alcohol and exposure to the sun.

"Do I know you?"

Slight European accent, though Hammond couldn't place it.

"It's Ted, George's friend. Remember? We met when I was in Phnom Penh on business a couple of months ago."

"Teddy, sure, yeah," she said without enthusiasm. "How are you?"

"Good. Yourself?"

She nodded. "Okay."

"How's George? I haven't managed to catch up with him so far on this trip."

"Don't know, haven't seen him for a while."

"That's a pity."

"It is. He was the only interesting thing in this place."

"He still in Phnom Penh?"

She shrugged drunkenly. "Last I heard he'd gone back to Australia to visit an ill relative."

"I hope it's nothing serious." Hammond sipped his drink, smiled. "Do you know when he'll be back?"

"No, but it doesn't matter. I'm not going to be here for long either. Got a job in Kabul."

"Sounds interesting."

"Yeah, I've got to get out of this place."

She drained the dregs of her beer.

"Phnom Penh's nice but boring, not like it was in the old days."

"I hear Kabul's pretty hairy, security-wise. You're not worried?"

"No, I'm a conflict girl. I know it's not PC. It's just the way I am. Besides, it won't be my first war zone. Iraq, Somalia ... I always seem to be around the corner when the bomb goes off."

Out of the corner of his eye, Hammond saw her male companion returning.

"Pity, you made a good couple."

"Really? George was good in bed for an old guy, no offense, and it's not like a European girl can be choosy in this city. But he went weird on me, started hanging out with this strange old Cambodian woman."

Hammond remembered the newspaper clipping in his pocket that Somerset had given him. Without thinking, he grabbed her by the wrist.

"What old woman?"

She twisted against his grip, squealed loudly. "Hey, you're hurting me!"

Heads turned in their direction. Hammond let go.

Her partner, noticing the commotion, hurried toward them only to be intercepted by Dara. A split second's altercation left the academic unconscious on the floor. Hammond turned back to the woman, oblivious to the embarrassed silence that had engulfed the bar.

"Sorry, Brigid, but this is very important. What old woman are you talking about?"

"I don't know, just some old Cambodian woman. George claimed she was a witch or something. He was obsessed with her, started to believe all that hocus-pocus shit she spouted. Gave me the creeps."

Hammond stared at the copy of the newspaper cutting, willing the Khmer script to re-form into letters he could understand.

"The old woman lived in slum area near the old port of Phnom Penh." Dara snapped his mobile phone shut. "I have the address, the easiest way to get there is to walk."

It was the last night of the water festival—Bandet Pratib, the fire parade. Huge barges cruised up and down the Tonlé Sap, each lit up with hundreds of lights. Their glow made the river look like it was burning. Lights were everywhere—strobe lights, neon lights, fairy lights, fluoro lights, lights draped from trees, tracing the outline of the royal palace.

The riverfront was still crowded, but the demographic and feel had changed, becoming more male, more aggressive. People collided and pulled at him. He swerved to avoid piles of garbage. A median strip had been turned into a tent city. A patchwork of faded canvas and plastic tarpaulins covered the ground, festival-goers already sleeping it off. They passed a stage. Women in pink miniskirts, ear-splitting Cambodian pop music interspersed with the DJ patter.

The light and noise faded when Hammond followed Dara down a narrow side alley. The Cambodian paused.

"Should be somewhere around here."

Hammond leaned into the shadows while he waited for Dara to get his bearings, wiped the sweat from his forehead, the blood pounding in his temples.

A weak light came on in a nearby building. A door opened, and the head of an old man slowly poked out, followed by the rest of him. He blinked several times, mumbled something, and pointed at them with his walking stick, a length of blue PVC piping.

"He wants to know what we're doing," said Dara.

"Ask him if he knows where the old woman's house is."

The old man nodded as Dara spoke.

"He knows, but he wants money."

Hammond reached into his pocket, withdrew a wad of American money, peeled off a fifty-dollar bill. The old man took it, hobbled crab-like along the alley, stopped outside a small wooden shack.

Hammond and Dara exchanged glances.

"You the boss. You first, man," said Dara.

Hammond pushed on the front door. It swung open, releasing a musty odor from within. He slowly reached a hand into the darkness, felt the wall for a light switch. A globe hanging from the ceiling illuminated a single room.

As he stepped inside, Hammond noticed a low-pitched buzz in his ears. It was too far away to come from the festival. He shook his head, but it continued.

First thing he saw was a rattan sleeping mat laid out on the hard-packed dirt floor, a large rust-colored stain at its center. He forced himself to look around the room. An old wooden wardrobe, a small table covered in stained metal bowls, amulets, trinkets, different sized jars filled with herbs and powders.

In the corner was a makeshift shrine, surrounded by candle wax, strings of beads, what looked like children's toys, a small car, a collection of headless dolls. Tin cans full of incense sticks flanked the empty space where whatever had been worshipped once rested. It had been moved recently, leaving an outline in the wood about the size of a dessert plate surrounded by wax and incense dust.

Dara appeared next to him.

"Man, this place gives me the creeps."

"The old woman's been dead all this time, but nothing's been moved," whispered Hammond. "It's like people are too scared to touch anything."

The Cambodian produced a pack of cigarettes, lit one, exhaled a stream of smoke, and offered one to Hammond. Hammond accepted, his first for three months. They smoked in silence. The nicotine calmed Hammond's nerves. He sensed the old man hovering outside.

"Dara, ask the old man what happened here."

The two Cambodians spoke for a long time before Dara translated.

"Like the papers said, a murder."

"What else?"

"He says the woman, Samouth, was a powerful *kru khmae*."

"A what?"

"I don't know how to translate it for you." Dara glanced nervously at the old man as he spoke. "She cured sick people, prepared charms to keep away evil spirits. Powerful people came to see her, to ask for her advice. One man came a lot, a powerful businessman. Sometimes he brought his son. They would park their car, leave their bodyguards at the entrance to the alley and walk in to see her."

Hammond looked at Dara.

"You know who he means."

"I got me an idea, yeah."

Hammond drew on the last of his cigarette, flicked the butt away.

"Did she ever get visited by foreigners?"

"Yeah, one man, long white hair that made him look like a ghost."

"Jesus Christ! Chancellor."

Dara nodded weakly.

"Any idea who murdered her?"

Dara hesitated.

"Dara, ask him the fucking question."

The old man chuckled, leaned forward on his cane, and looked knowingly at Hammond as he spoke. When he'd finished, he walked back down the alley and was soon enveloped in shadow.

Hammond looked at Dara impatiently.

"He said, ask the businessman. He and his son were the first ones here when the old woman was killed, even before the police."

Dara scratched his scalp nervously.

"Man, I'm scared. Let's get the fuck outta here."

Hammond stared at the vacant spot on the altar. The buzzing in his ears grew louder.

"Not before we search the place for anything that might help us find Chancellor."

They ran their hands over the old woman's possessions, trying to make as little contact with the surfaces as possible. After several minutes, Dara grunted, pulled out a plastic folder from the bottom of the wardrobe, handed it to Hammond.

It contained a sheaf of pages covered in hand-drawn charts and spidery Khmer script, a bundle of photographs, most color, some black and white, stained with age and eaten away at the sides. They were portrait shots, Cambodians of different ages and backgrounds, including Eng Lim and his son.

The hairs on the back of Hammond's neck bristled. He took a deep breath, slowly turned to Dara and showed him the picture of Chancellor. It was the same picture Hammond had seen on the wall of the lawyer's villa, the lawyer standing in front of the ruined villa.

"Do you have any idea where this was taken?"

"Nah. It's just another ruin."

"Come on, think."

"I dunno, maybe Kep, a town down south." Dara peered hard at the photograph as he spoke. "It was a high roller resort in the '60s. Lots of buildings like the one in the picture were built, all destroyed by the Khmer Rouge. The ruins are still there. I went there once as part of the boss's security detail. Huot was looking at buying some of those old places."

Hammond couldn't explain it, but the photos were too much of a coincidence. Added to this was Fink's statement about Chancellor taking off for periods of time down south. Hammond's gut told him that if they found the building in the photograph, they'd find Chancellor.

"Do you think we could find it, if we went down there?"

With a shrug, Dara said, "There's only so many of them."

Dara hardly said a word the entire trip. Hammond put it down to fatigue and the effort required to concentrate on driving. It was just after midnight, but already the traffic was heavy, vehicles ferrying festival-goers back to their villages in the countryside.

Hammond tried to stay awake, succumbing to sleep several hours out of Phnom Penh. When he woke, he saw daylight through the tinted windows of the Lexus and heard the sea. He got out of the car, stretched, the sun already warm on his skin.

The car was parked by a small café overlooking the beach. Hammond walked across the white sand to the surf line. He watched men haul bamboo baskets full of crabs from boats moored in the shallows and carry them to the beach, where groups of women waited to sort and weigh the catch. Some of the crabs were thrown straight into large cauldrons that sat on open fires.

He walked back toward the car, found Dara drinking a coke and eating a plate of crab and fried rice, ordered the same. Next to the café stood a large double-storey villa similar to the one in the photo of Chancellor, the ochre-colored plaster cracked and covered in vines from the surrounding jungle.

After breakfast they drove into the center of Kep, a collection of houses and hotels along a stretch of beachfront road running around a small cape. Jungle-covered hills overlooked the town, ruined buildings visible above the foliage.

It took them an hour to find the building in the photograph, perched on a hill overlooking a deserted stretch of beach on the outskirts of town. It had been completely fenced off by green corrugated iron. Hammond had seen numerous buildings surrounded by the material in Phnom Penh, the tell-tale sign the property was slated for either reconstruction or demolition.

When he was sure there was no one else around, Dara produced a crowbar from the boot of the Lexus, found a join in the corrugated iron, prised a gap big enough for him and Hammond to climb through.

The ground around the building was overgrown with weeds, covered in rubble and garbage. The walls were pockmarked with bullet holes and covered in graffiti. There was no door at the entrance. Inside, plants sprouted from cracks in the tiled floor, and mottled sunlight streamed in from holes in the ceiling.

A fire smoldered in the far corner of the second room they entered. Cooking utensils lay on the ground around it. In the next, someone was sleeping on a portable camp bed, screened by mosquito netting. Hammond could tell from the shock of white hair protruding from the top of the sheet that it was Chancellor. The ground was strewn with dirty clothes. An upturned wooden crate doubled as a bedside table. On it sat a cylindrical shape draped in a square of black fabric.

Hammond stepped closer. A chunk of masonry snapped under his shoe. Chancellor grunted, sat up. He had a beard to match his mane of white hair. His eyes were open and looked wild.

Without a word, Dara pulled a small black pistol from inside his denim jacket and shot Chancellor in the forehead. Blood sprayed on the netting.

The sound of the gunshot lingered in the empty building, smoke from the barrel twisting in a beam of light through the ceiling. Chancellor was still for a moment, as if unsure what to do, and then fell backwards onto the bed.

Hammond reached out to grab the Cambodian.

"Christ, man, what the bloody hell do you think you're doing?"

Dara wheeled, wide-eyed, shot Hammond in the stomach. He crumpled to the ground, watched the blood seep through his white shirt. When he looked up, Dara was sliding the black fabric off the object on the wooden crate. The Cambodian gently picked it up. It was a large glass jar full of liquid. Floating in it was something dark, the size of an outstretched adult hand. It took Hammond a moment to recognize what it was.

Hammond grunted, the pain like hell.

"A dead baby in a jar?"

"No, old man, this ain't any baby. It's special. That old witch, Samouth, she cut this one out of its mother's tummy before it was born, smoked it, put it in this jar so she could use its power. My mom and dad used to tell me stories about these things, said they can speak to you through your dreams. Protect you, make you rich."

Dara held the jar at eye level, a look of awe on his face.

"When that old man back in Phnom Penh told me this had been stolen from Samouth, I didn't believe him."

Hammond forced himself to sit upright. The pain was getting worse.

"All this for a fucking dead baby?"

He coughed, tasted blood in his mouth.

"I never thought I'd ever see one, much less own one," Dara continued as if Hammond hadn't spoken. "This little baby is why Eng Lim was so powerful, why Chancellor murdered the old woman and stole it, why Eng Huot wants it back so bad. Now it's mine, I ain't never gonna be poor again."

"But, Eng, he's knows we're here, he's expecting us to come back—"

"He don't know shit, old man."

Dara turned the jar, the piss-colored liquid catching the mottled sunlight. He looked at Hammond.

"I never called him. He doesn't know we're down here, what we're doing."

Hammond closed his eyes at the pain, opened them again.

"Oh, Jesus," he moaned.

Dara paused in the doorway.

"Sorry, old man, he ain't gonna help you now. Ain't no one gonna to help you."

Hammond lay on the ground. Closed his eyes. Heard what might have been the sound of an approaching helicopter, might have been the roar of the sea. Then nothing.

Andrew Nette

Andrew Nette is a writer based in Melbourne, Australia. He is one of the editors of the on-line magazine Crime Factory (www.thecrimefactory.com). His short fiction has appeared in a number of print and on-line publications. His debut novel *Ghost Money*, a crime story set in Cambodia in the mid-nineties, was recently published by Snubnose Press. His blog, www.pulpcurry.com explores crime film and literature, particularly from Asia and Australia. He tweets at @Pulpcurry.

A Coven of Snakes
Bob Bergin

When I was a kid, I had a job cutting grass. It was sort of a country club. My parents didn't belong, so I didn't know much about it, except that it had fields and fields of grass. In the summer they would hire a half dozen kids every Saturday to cut it. We didn't have any power mowers then, just the push jobs.

The big guys pushed the mowers. I was younger than they were, and my job was to trim around the edges. You had to stay bent over, crawl along the grass, and keep squeezing these tight old shears. I thought that was tougher than pushing a mower.

One morning I was trimming along a driveway, right at the base of this little hill. I was going snip, snip, snip, and crawling along through the grass. Suddenly, down on the ground, two or three things went shooting right by me, too quick for me to see what they were. From the corner of my eye, I saw something else going by.

Without thinking, I reached out and grabbed. My reflexes were really good then. It was a snake. I had a hold of this damn snake. I had him by his tail. He wasn't thrashing or anything, just pulling straight ahead, wanting to get the hell out of there. He was a big guy, the color of a new penny with dark brown bands, sort of pretty looking. Here I was, down at his level, hanging on to his tail. What the hell was I going to do? I didn't think I was afraid of snakes, but I had never been so close to one before.

"Jesus, that's a copperhead you got there, kid. Let him go!"

And I did. He shot off straight ahead.

It was our supervisor, a guy who worked for this place full-time. He was a lot older than us.

"Get out of the grass," he said. "Step back to the driveway. Wait there."

He jogged off. A couple of the mower guys ran over.

"What happened? What happened?" they wanted to know.

"Snakes," I said. "Copperheads. I grabbed one by the tail."

I don't think they believed me.

The supervisor came back, running this time, carrying a big double-barreled shotgun.

"Show me where those snakes went."

We walked back into the grass, watching where we stepped.

"It's right up ahead," I said, "where the hill starts going up."

The grass was taller there and hid what was behind it. One of the mower guys brought a stick. The supervisor used it to push the grass around.

"There, you see that?" he said.

I wasn't sure what we were looking at. A small heap of rocks, a piece of an old wall, maybe. The supervisor poked at it. A half dozen rocks fell away. We could see them then. I don't know how many there were—it looked like dozens—dozens of copperheads, tangled together, intertwined, wrapped around each other. A pulsating ball of squirming snakes. It made me shiver. But I couldn't look away.

"Get back on the driveway," the supervisor said.

At first I thought the snakes had scared him off, but he was just trying to get a clear field of fire.

Blaam! Blaam!

He gave those snakes both barrels. I don't know how many he got. When we dared to go look, there were maybe six of them lying there in pieces. A couple were still thrashing around on the side. The supervisor finished them with a shovel.

That image of those snakes all tangled up together was something I thought I would never forget, but I did. After a while I never thought of it again—until one night many years later.

I was in Thailand, working as a civilian analyst for this US Army unit. It was the kind of unit you don't hear much about. Not because what we were doing was so secret, but because it was so dull: political analysis, and even more dull, political analysis of local communist movements. The good thing about it, it got me a tour in Thailand; the bad thing, I thought I would die of boredom before I could finish my tour. So when the boss walked in and said, "I want you to go to Cambodia for a couple of weeks," I was overjoyed. For about a minute.

I was a civilian, but I had put in my time in the army. You learn quickly there never to volunteer for anything. I wasn't volunteering now, but I felt like I was being volunteered. We had no mission in Cambodia; we had no reason to be there.

"Boss," I said, "why am I going to Cambodia?"

"You're going to help catch a murderer."

"Murderer?" I said. "Hey, boss, I catch communists. I don't know nothing about catching murderers."

"You'll learn," he said. "They need a guy who knows about the KR."

I knew about the KR all right. That was what we called the Khmer Rouge, the Cambodian communists. Everybody knew about the Killing Fields. The Khmer Rouge were responsible for millions of deaths, for cruelty on a scale beyond human comprehension. They weren't running Cambodia anymore, but the KR were still around. Even the Vietnamese Army that invaded and took over the country couldn't root them out.

"Murder in Cambodia," I said to the boss. "Tell me about it."

"It's murders, multiple. Ten, maybe more. Foreigners, maybe Cambodians too. Nobody's sure."

"In Phnom Penh?"

"Yeah, Phnom Penh, other places too. They have a new one up near Siam Reap now. It's the third one they've had there. That's where they want you to go."

"They think the KR did it?"

Could be anybody, I thought, gang of kids, bunch of soldiers. The police even. The Cambodians made our old Wild West look like a playground. Their economy was a shambles; their society had been turned upside down.

The boss shrugged. "There's a special unit working with the Cambodian cops. They're out of ideas. They don't want another criminal expert. They want somebody who knows recent Cambodian history."

"And that must be me," I said.

"And that's you," the boss said.

I got a flight to Siam Reap. There was a runway with tufts of long grass growing out of cracks, and a couple of old wooden sheds. I was met by a Frenchman in a battered green Land Rover. His name was Marc. He looked like an American, sounded like one. He was the lead investigator, on loan to the Cambodian cops. We got acquainted as we drove to his office.

"I lived in the US for almost ten years," he explained when I asked him. "I grew up there. My father was at the embassy in Washington. I finished high school there, then went back to France."

"And now you're a French cop."

"Interpol," he said. "I'm not much of a gendarme. Almost all the police work I've done has been international."

"How long have you been on this case?"

"Six months. I came to Cambodia to give some training. Then some clever soul detected a pattern among the foreigners being killed. The embassies got involved. Someone decided my talents would be better used finding killers."

"So what do you think is going on?"

"I don't know. At first, I thought it would be a simple thing—you know, young guys preying on tourists. A tourist gets killed and it's almost like an accident. Turned out it wasn't that simple. The killings are brutal, cruel. We found two victims together. One was forced to kill the other—with a shovel. And there's always mutilation."

"Sounds sort of like the Khmer Rouge."

"Maybe," he said. "For now, we don't have any motive. The bodies we're finding are not in KR areas, not even close."

"Well, that doesn't mean that the KR can't—"

He answered before I could finish: "You're right, of course. But what's left of the KR is being hunted. They have their hands full just surviving. And while the KR may be evil, and capable of anything, they're also very ideological. The victims are tourists, of no significance to the KR. We can't find a link to the KR."

I kept quiet. He had a point, just not a very good one, I thought. Maybe political theoreticians were running the KR, but the rank and file were thugs. Thugs don't consider a rich tourist in Marxist terms when they bash his head in.

We drove through a small town, came to a military compound, a Cambodian flag fluttering in a small breeze. The guards saluted us as we drove through the gate.

"The office we use is in here. It's temporary," Marc said.

Then he gave me a quick realities briefing.

"We are here as advisers, and only as that. The Cambodians run the investigation, and we tell them what we think. We do not criticize—ever—regardless of how much we disagree with what we see. If you have a problem, you bring it to me. I take it up with their chief. When we need to, we do our own thing—to the degree we can get away with it. We'll talk more later."

The office was a small wooden building that looked like a leftover barracks from French colonial times. There were two rooms, enough for the staff: Freddy, an American of uncertain affiliation, and Wan, a Thai. Marc introduced me.

Freddy said hi and shook hands.

Wan, sitting at a desk, stood up.

"You come from Thailand, my home," he said.

"His name, 'Wan,' means sweet," Freddy advised me.

"Yeah, I know," I said. "'*Wan*,' as used in '*paak wan*'—sweet mouth, or bullshitter."

"Hey, you very smart," Wan said. "You speak my language."

"Enough to survive in Bangkok," I said.

I liked the Thai, and Wan looked as laid-back as the best of them—which was deceptive. The casual Thai way of dealing with the world often hid great stores of determination.

Marc and I sat down at a desk, across from each other. There was an old French map on the wall.

Marc saw me looking at it and said: "I guess you know we're only a few miles from Angkor Wat. That's why we set up an office here. Tourists are not coming back in great numbers yet, but they're coming. The last body was found not far from here, and we think there may be others—killings over the last two or three years that didn't seem linked before."

"Why do they seem linked now?"

"Everything is being looked at more carefully now. Not so long ago, violent death in Cambodia was commonplace. It was the way things were. No one ever looked for motives. There was hatred and violence. That was enough."

Wan brought us coffee. Once we were alone again, Marc gave me my marching orders. He pointed at a filing cabinet.

"The files are duplicates of everything we have in Phnom Penh. They contain all we know about the killings—the three here and another six or seven in Phnom Penh. Photos, reports, interviews, even think pieces by smart people in embassies. Everything is translated into English. I would like you to read it all. Talk with Freddy, talk with Wan, get a sense of how things are done. I have to go to Phnom Penh this afternoon. I'll be back in two days. Then we can talk. Hopefully, you'll have found something that will point us in a new direction."

I started on the files after lunch—rice and chicken from the Cambodian army kitchen. I never did get used to the way Cambodians made chicken dishes—chunks chopped off the bird, bone and meat all together. You bit very carefully, or risked a bone splinter going through your gum.

The files were grim, but I saved the photos for last. I didn't want to look at them with the taste of lunch still in my mouth. The written descriptions of the victims were bad enough, even as bureaucratic reports. Then there were the interviews of the first witnesses on the murder scene—with their expressions of horror. And then the interviews of Cambodians who had been in contact with the victims—with their expressions of disbelief. There were also interviews of foreigners who might have met the victims, but of those there were only a few.

In each case the victim had been in Cambodia for only a couple of days, or a couple of weeks. All of the known victims were tourists, and with one exception all were men. All—again, with one exception—were traveling alone. Their contacts were almost exclusively with Cambodians: hotel staff, tour guides, waiters, motorbike taxi drivers, money changers, bar girls, a few whores. Mostly bar girls. That was what tourism was then.

The exception was a woman traveling with her boyfriend. Both were French. Their bodies were found together. Based on the way they were found, and the woman's wounds, the report concluded that she was killed first, by her boyfriend. It appeared that he was forced to do it and did it with a shovel, chopping at her neck until he severed it. He was not a handyman, apparently, and his aim was not good. The report estimated that he drove the edge of the shovel into her neck, shoulders, and chest at least a dozen times before he succeeded in severing the head from the body. When he finally succeeded, he was killed. As in the other cases, both bodies were mutilated.

I didn't spend much time looking at the photos—they were too awful. And after the first one, they didn't really tell me anything. All showed the horrible things one person can do to another. There was incredible mutilation: missing genitals, gaps in bellies, gaps in throats, ripped anuses, torn mouths, pulpy masses where an eye had been, or a nose. The faces were disfigured beyond recognition and yet somehow still retained expressions of horror. By the end of that day I was emotionally drained.

Freddy and Wan took me to a local bar that evening and got me home afterwards. I don't know how much I drank that night, or even what it was. A room was reserved for me at the camp, in the Cambodian officers' quarters. I woke up in my clothes looking up at a lizard walking across the ceiling and wondering where I was.

It was mid-morning when I finally got to the office. Freddy looked at me with curiosity; Wan with concern.

"You survived, apparently," Freddy said.

"I'm not sure yet," I said.

I got myself a coffee and sat down across from Freddy.

"I read the files yesterday," I said. "What do I do today?"

"We could drive out to our local killing scenes," he said, "but there's nothing to see there now. Right after lunch, the Cambodian cops are going to do an interview, a local tour guide who took the latest victim to some temples. Why don't you sit in on that?"

I looked at my watch.

"Sounds good. I'll have time to sober up."

Freddy laughed. But I wasn't kidding. As we walked to the office where the Cambodian cops were going to do their interview, Freddy said, "Ah, before we go in there, you should know, ah ... they use things here. You know, to secure cooperation."

"Shit," I said. "Like electrodes?"

"No, not electrodes, but maybe electrodes would be better. They use traditional methods. You know, like things that squeeze."

"Wonderful," I said. "Let's go in."

They had this guy, a young Cambodian, good-looking kid. He was sitting in a sort of wooden armchair, just one piece of rope cinching him in. He didn't look too unhappy.

The man watching him, the cop interrogator, I guess, nodded to us as we came in and then turned to the kid and started asking questions. It was all in Cambodian. Freddy would translate if we got to anything interesting.

I watched the back and forth for a while, the cop asking, the kid responding. Freddy hadn't said a word.

"What the hell's happening?" I finally asked. "Is the cop getting anything?"

"Nah, not a goddamn thing. It's all bullshit so far."

About this time the cop slapped the kid, hard. In the small room we were in, it was like a shot going off. Then the cop picked up something from the small table at his side. It looked sort of like a nutcracker. With one quick move, he had the kid by one of his thumbs, and the kid let out a hell of a yowl.

"What the hell is that thing?" I said.

"It's like what you squeeze lemons with."

The kid's yowl brought in another two cops. One matter-of-factly pulled the kid's shorts down, while the other held him down in the chair.

"He's going to do his balls now," Freddy said.
I stood up.
"Come on," I said. "We can read their report later."
When we were outside, I said to Freddy: "How do you put up with that?"
"I have to," he said. "I work here."

The next day, Marc was back.
"You read all the files," he said. "What do you think?"
"There's a hell of a lot of paper," I said, "but not much real information. Somebody gets killed, and the Cambodian cops talk to everybody. They just don't seem to get any answers."
"It's difficult. This is a society where facts are relative. What a fact means and how it's handled depend on the circumstances. The circumstances are related to how much trouble a fact can get you into."
"Great," I said. "I understand the concept, but it doesn't help the investigation. Another thing, after seeing how some witnesses are interviewed, I understand where the misleading information and false leads come from."
Marc shrugged.
"Yes, well ... if you put a witness under great stress, that happens. Unfortunately, that's the traditional way it's done."
"The photos ..." I said. "Look, I'm not a cop. I haven't seen anything like those photos before. Genitals are cut off, anuses torn open, mouths ripped apart. Is this sexual assault? Everything is disfigured. The mutilation hides what really happened. But what does it mean? Is it sexual assault?"
"It's a good point. I can't answer it. It's a definition you need to get from a psychologist. The Cambodian

investigators went on a gay tack for a while. It led them nowhere. They decided the mutilation was too gross for sexual attack."

I just nodded. There was nothing to say, but maybe something to follow up later.

"Okay," Marc said, "looking at the files from your exalted Western perspective, what did you learn about the cases themselves?"

"Well, I found that the victims were all tourists. There's not a businessman or a researcher in the bunch. The victims are all men—with one exception, the French lady who was found with her boyfriend. And you're dealing with not ten cases, but a dozen, or maybe thirteen or fourteen. Here, in the Siam Reap area, you have the French couple and two others linked to the same perpetrator, but there are two or three other possibles."

There was something else that bothered me.

"There's one point I wasn't certain about. In several files it appeared that the Cambodian cops suspected the victims were abusers of children. Two of the Americans, in fact, had child abuse on their records that were obtained through the embassy. But that line of inquiry was never strongly followed. I wondered why."

"Yes, you touch on something that bothered me as well. A lot of the tourism in Cambodia right now is sex-driven. Children are a part of that. The cases you mention were of great interest to the Cambodians. They thought they would lead to a breakthrough, but that line of inquiry didn't lead anywhere. They interviewed procurers—they have a good list. They interviewed everyone where these two guests stayed; they looked at taxis, at hangouts, they went everywhere a man might take a child. What they found proved, emphatically, that these two were not abusers of children."

I started to say something. Marc held up his hand and continued.

"Those two were sex tourists, there's no question of that. But the sex was with adults, always. And the adults were women. It doesn't mean that they could not have engaged with children at some point, but they seemed almost too busy with the ladies for that."

I was quiet for a while, trying to think.

"You know," I finally said to Marc, "there's something nagging at me—but I don't know what the hell it is."

"It will come to you later. So, what are your conclusions up to now? Do you have recommendations?"

"I have one recommendation."

Marc smiled at that.

"Just one? I hope it's an important one."

"One thing that struck me from the start: the Cambodians that all the victims met were primarily women. They met very few men, some motorbike riders, some touts, a money changer or two, not much else. It's the way things are. In the hotels, guest houses, restaurants, and of course, the bars, women do the jobs that put them in contact with the tourists. For every man a victim met, he must have met twenty women."

Marc nodded. "Yes, that's the way it is."

"Yes, but ... when I look at the Cambodian police reports, I see that the police disregard all this. When the policeman questions these women, it's as if this is a job below the dignity of the police. It is as if the woman is not worth questioning. Needless to say, the questioning does not get very substantive."

"Sometimes these women are just girls. But I see your point."

"The cops are missing a lot. It means the investigation is not thorough, not complete."

Marc nodded, looked at his watch.

"It's getting late," he said. "Let me ask my most important question, and then we can adjourn until this evening. Do you see the Khmer Rouge linked to all this?"

When I'd started my investigation, I'd thought that was going to be the hardest question to answer. It was not.

"No. I can't see a link to the KR. The killings are brutal. It feels like it should be the KR, but it's not. I can't explain beyond that."

"I understand. You studied the KR, you have a good sense of what they're responsible for. What you feel is valid—I can accept that. Look, let's stop for now. I will show you a nice place for dinner tonight. We can talk about your recommendation then."

That night Marc took me to a wonderful place, an old French hotel. Once it must have been grand; now it was just shabby, or at least most of it was. A small section had been renovated, restored to what it once had been. That included a small lobby, a restaurant, and the terrace. It was an experiment, the beginning of what in time would return the hotel to its days of glory under the French colonialists.

We sat on a terrace overlooking a lotus pond. It could have been the 1930s. The dozen guests around us might have been French planters, but they were actually tourists, and not French. There were waiters in white shirts and black bow ties, and drinks in long glasses.

"Ah, you see, the tourists are coming back," Marc said. "They will spend just one night here and go back to Phnom Penh. Perhaps in two weeks, another group will come. "Tonight," he went on, "we can talk about the killings, but only briefly, and only about your recommendation. For the rest of the evening we will discuss the glories of Angkor Wat. You haven't been there yet, have you?"

"I haven't," I said, "and I'm looking forward to going there. As for my recommendation, I think you know what it is. Someone must talk to the ladies again. That's all I have."

"It's a good recommendation. But, you know, it's very difficult for the Cambodian cops. If they interview the ladies again, it will have exactly the same result. It's their culture. I have thought about this since we talked this afternoon. Having the Cambodian police question the women again will not be effective. And I can't do it because of my position."

He paused, took a drink of wine.

"Up here, would you be willing to give it a try?"

I was more than a little surprised. I was an analyst, not a cop. It took me a few moments to find my voice.

"Bar girls and sex workers, that would be something new," I said. "Yeah, I'll give it a try."

Marc smiled. "Get yourself a guide. A working girl from one of the bars would be good. I don't think you'll learn much, but you'll get a sense of what goes on here, and maybe some insight into what we could be missing."

When I got into the office the next morning, I went directly to Wan.

"Wan," I said, "I need a girl, a girl from one of the bars, a whore."

That was a bit direct, but "working girl" could have been misunderstood. It brought Wan right out of his chair, speechless, but only for a moment.

A Coven of Snakes

"Sure, boss. What kind of whore you want: big, small, fat, skinny? You want young girl, or girl much experience?"

"I guess what I want is a smart whore."

"Oh," he said. "All whore smart. Not smart, not good in whore business."

"I want a whore who is smart in business, smart with tourists. I want a whore who knows everything and knows everybody—Americans, French, Cambodians, even UN people."

"Hmm," Wan said, screwing up his face to think about it. "You want very smart whore. Maybe I know one. Must be beautiful?"

"Beautiful is okay. Must speak good English."

"Ah ..."

He thought a bit more.

Finally: "I know good one for you. Nice lady! Speak very good English. You meet me tonight, Victory Bar. You come early, come when sun go down."

"I meet you at the Victory," I said. "I'll see you at sundown."

The bar's name was an echo of a faraway past. Wan being there made it an irony. Siam Reap meant "Defeat Siam." The town had been named during an ancient war between Cambodia and Thailand, when Thailand was still Siam.

When I walked into the Victory that night, Wan was at a table by himself. The place was an oversized wood and tin shed, open at the front and down half of one side. It was maybe too early. There were no other customers I could see, only a half dozen girls sitting around a table at the back.

I sat down across from Wan.

"No girl?" I asked.

He gave me a welcoming smile, then put his serious look on.

"Listen, boss," he said. "Girl is in the back, nice lady. Her name is Dominique, but you and I must talk first, then I call her."

"Sure."

"I already talk with Dominique. I tell her you researcher, not cop."

I nodded. It was what we had agreed to earlier that day.

"Your name is 'Mr. White,' but I think you should be 'Doctor White.' More impressive for girl."

I laughed.

"As long as she doesn't expect me to take out her appendix."

Wan didn't seem to find that funny.

"You must be careful, boss. Many bad people in sex business."

"I understand that," I said, "but I'm just looking. I don't plan to piss anybody off."

Wan shrugged. "Okay, just so you know. Dominique, she is okay and very smart. She speaks very good English. I call her now."

Dominique was in her mid-twenties, and not at all bad looking. In jeans and a blouse on a tight little body, she looked like she could have belonged to a troupe of Apsaras, the celestial dancing maidens of ancient Cambodia. She stood in front of me, brought her hands together gracefully in front of her face, and waied me as a Thai would. Wan introduced me with my Doctor title. I can't say she seemed impressed.

"Nice name, Dominique. Something nice the French left behind."

"French?" she said, and went on quite seriously. "Oh, no, Dominique is a Cambodian name. My mother was Dominique, and her mother before her."

What could I say? It was like that in all the old colonies. Over time, the master's ways became the ways of the subjugated. The origins of words and names and habits were often forgotten, or disregarded.

Wan briefed her: I was a researcher looking at foreign participation in the local sex scene for an academic paper. He gave her our program. Tonight we would look at the bars in our neighborhood, tomorrow an introduction to sex shows. When he finished, he asked if she understood. She said she did.

"Dominique," I said then, "let's go bar-crawling."

We had no information that even remotely suggested that the victims had visited any of the local bars. With Wan and Freddy's help, I selected nine bars that fit our criteria—bars where a tourist might go. We excluded any that catered only to the locals, which presumably held no attraction for a foreign tourist. Two on the list were "legitimate," more restaurant than bar, run by older Frenchmen with Cambodian wives. We would check out just one.

The evening was a bust, a bore. The bars were clones of the Victory. Even at prime drinking time there were few customers, only girls. I gave Dominique photos of the four who were the local victims. I told her to show them only to the girls she felt comfortable with, and to the management mamas she knew. She got big shrugs for her trouble. Nobody knew them; nobody had seen them.

We went to the French bar, talked with the old Frenchman. He shrugged.

"When you get to my age, everyone looks familiar," he said. "But these were not here."

I was starting to feel like a Cambodian cop.

In the bars I also kept an eye out for obvious villains, the touts and toughs you expect to hang around. There were none. Oh, there was the occasional teenage boy washing glasses in the kitchen, or the old guy with quivering hands and dementia who cleaned up, but the male of the species was rare.

If anything positive came out of the evening, it was that by the end of it, Dominique and I were working as a team. She may or may not have suspected what I was doing; it didn't show either way. I was quite taken with her. She was bright, good with people, and fun to be with. It was easy to forget her usual line of work. It was almost like being on a date.

It was after midnight when we finished. I dropped her back at the Victory, where she would join friends for the ride home. When she said she would be available any time the next day, from early morning on, it gave me an idea.

"There's nothing going on until mid-afternoon," I said. "I've been thinking about going over to Angkor Wat in the morning. How about joining me? I can write it off to local orientation."

She laughed and said okay.

We met at about 10 a.m. and set off for the temple, a short ride in a pickup truck. We pulled into a dirt lot under some trees. I got out and turned, and there, across a 600-foot-wide moat, was Angkor Wat, the stone temple that had been at the center of Khmer civilization for 600 years—and the largest religious structure ever built by man. It was breathtaking.

A Coven of Snakes

We crossed the causeway and entered through an imposing gateway in the wall that surrounds the temple. Inside are long galleries and courtyards, and at the center is the group of five towers that constitute the sanctuary.

We walked the enclosed galleries that seemed to go on forever, their sandstone walls covered with intricate carvings of warriors and elephants and horses, scenes of battles, portrayals of hell's punishments and heaven's rewards—and everywhere the Apsaras, the lovely celestial dancing girls.

Once we came to a courtyard where dozens of Apsaras looked down on us, and we stayed to admire them. Dominique pointed out that each of them was an individual; each one had her own smile, her own hairdo, and a sarong different from the others.

"These girls are the favorites of the Lord Shiva," she said. "They dance for him. One day I will take you to Banteay Srei, the palace of women. It is smaller than this, but very beautiful."

By then I was ready to go with her anywhere.

We had a quick lunch and then went back to the job. After the wonders of the morning it was like being dropped into a tepid pool of dung. Dominique had arranged a sex show matinee. It was held in a tacky bedroom of a small wooden house, and featured three girls that did things to each other that made me glad that Dominique stayed downstairs. I doubted their show would be the big hit of the tourist season.

The rest of the day looked more promising—from a research standpoint. Dominique took me to a village where children were available. When she made the arrangements, she asked if I wanted to meet them as the tourists did or just wanted to see the children as they

346

were. "As they are as children," I said, "not as objects." We would not have been allowed there had Dominique not known the right people.

There were easily a dozen boys and girls, from perhaps eight years old to twelve. As we were just visitors, they were like the children they were supposed to be. They came from this village and were kept in a house inside a walled compound just off the main road. When we arrived in mid-afternoon, they were napping, playing games, or riding bicycles around the compound. We might have been visiting a village school at recess time. Dominique explained how it worked when the clients came, how the children were taught to meet them. It was not nice.

For that evening Dominique scheduled a couple of brothels to look at. I called it off. What had started as a nice day had left me depressed after our visit with the children. Dominique picked up on my mood.

"Maybe tomorrow we should take a break, go to Banteay Srei?" she suggested.

She arranged for a pickup truck to take us there. It was a long ride on a deeply rutted dirt road. As we bumped through rice fields and past tiny villages, it struck me that we must be in the area where three of the bodies had been found. All the locals knew about it, so I asked Dominique.

"Yes," she said, "three dead foreigners were found not far from here. I will show you when we are there."

Not much later, as we passed some wood and thatch shacks at the edge of the rice fields, Dominique told me that two bodies, those of a man and a woman, had been found just beyond the shacks. The Phnom Penh newspaper had pictures of the murder scene, she said. All I saw were dried out rice fields.

A Coven of Snakes

Compared with Angkor Wat, Banteay Srei was a jewel box. The structures are built on a very human scale, with nothing massive about them; even the towers are no higher than about twenty feet. The figures carved in the stone were very finely cut and highly detailed. The Apsaras were small compared with those we had seen at Angkor, but even more voluptuous. All had sweet smiles. Dominique called it "the place of the women."

We walked into a large open area, where three stone shrines stood side by side on a low platform. Dominique took me to the one she said was dedicated to Shiva, and then to a building nearby that had been a library, which was adorned with scenes from the story of Shiva. As we stood there, admiring this place, Dominique told me a story about a dance that enthralled me as I listened to her tell it, but later left me very disturbed.

"There is an old dance," she said, "about how men are fascinated by women's bodies. Once they see a woman's body, they cannot take their eyes from it. There are six female dancers, and a man watches. The only music is a flute that is played by a girl sitting in the shadows. The music is very sweet at first—simple, lonely notes that a shepherd would play, and the dancers move slowly. Then the music from the flute changes, gets faster, becomes more like the sound of a village festival. The dancers move quickly now, express their emotions with their hands. The veils covering their breasts vanish.

"As the music goes on, it brings one dancer closer and closer to the watching man. He sees her sarong slip down her belly, slowly—until it drops completely away. Nothing covers her. Her body is white like milk.

"The man is entranced. His eyes follow along the curve of her belly. He can't help but look. His eyes become fixed on her moving body. It is all he sees. He cannot see the lone dancer who comes from behind. That dancer carries the sword of Shiva.

"The man sees only the first dancer. He leans out toward her, reaches out to touch her—and the dancer behind him thrusts the thin blade of Shiva into his back, drives it through his spine.

"The man drops, his body sprawls across the floor. He is helpless—like a dog with his backbone snapped.

"The flute brings the other dancers closer and closer, until the music suddenly stops. The dancers drop, fall on the man's body. They bring out hidden knives ..."

"Ouch," I said.

"It is a sacrifice to honor Shiva."

"It's a hell of an ending."

The ending snapped me back to the here and now. I had been mesmerized listening to Dominique. The lovely stone Apsaras around us seemed to move to the sound of a distant flute. It was an ending I had not expected.

"I'm no expert on ancient Cambodia," I said, "or on dance, or religion, but I've done a lot of reading. I've never come across that story. It's very cruel."

"It's a story," she said. "It's only a story."

"It's a killing! How does that honor the Lord Shiva?"

She looked uncertain. Had I offended her religious sensibilities? I felt a twinge of remorse.

"The Lord Shiva is the god of creation," she finally said, "and the god of destruction."

"It still sounds like a nasty dance."

"It's only a dance," she said. "If you see it, you will understand."

Well, maybe, I thought, but we left it there. It was no big thing, not something to argue about. I told her I would like to see the dance, although I thought it unlikely I would have the chance. Even if there was a local dance troupe that catered to tourists—and there probably was—it was unlikely that their repertoire would include a dance that ended in human sacrifice. We didn't talk about it again, and I thought that was the end of it.

On the long drive back to town I had a lot of time to think, and the dance kept nagging at me. By the time we reached Siam Reap, I had made up my mind.

"Look," I said to Dominique, "I have things I need to do this afternoon, so let's call it a day. If I have time tonight, I'll come by the Victory."

I went over to the office to telephone Marc, who was still in Phnom Penh. After an hour or so, I finally reached him. I told him I had a question, but I didn't tell him it was based on a story about a dance.

"With all the damage to the bodies," I told him, "I can't make it out on the autopsy reports. I wondered if you could have somebody check if any of the victims had their spines severed—down near their base."

"Wait," he said. "Let me make a note of that. I'll get back to you."

As I expected, Marc was too preoccupied to ask where my idea had come from. I just hoped he would later remember to look at the notes he'd made. I wasn't expecting to hear from him for days.

I hung around the office the rest of the afternoon. As I was about to leave, Marc called me back.

"Listen," he said, "this is preliminary, but we found that three of the four victims in Siam Reap had severed spines. The fourth victim, the French woman who was killed with a shovel, had an intact spine. Where the hell did you get this information?"

"It's not information," I said. "It's just speculation for now."

I went on to tell him about Dominique's story of the dance.

"I'll be damned," he said when I finished.

"Have you ever heard of this dance?"

"No," he said, "but that means nothing. There are many Cambodian dances I've never heard of. I have a friend here, a retired Cambodian cop. He knows crime and he knows religion. I'll talk with him. Incidentally, I was able to get you a quick answer on the Siam Reap cases because of all the international attention they drew. The autopsies were carefully done and documented. I'm not sure that holds true for the earlier cases."

I didn't see Dominique that night or the next day, but I did drop by the Victory the next evening. She sat with me and had a drink. After what I had learned from Marc, I was a little unsure with her. I didn't mention our visit to Banteay Srei or the dance—but she did.

"My friend said there is a group that does the dance of Shiva, and it's scheduled for Friday night ... if you want to go."

"Friday," I said. "That's tomorrow."

She shrugged. "If you can't make it ..."

"No," I said, "I want to make it."

"Then I will make the arrangements," she said. "We must go out of town a short way."

"Not all the way to Banteay Srei, I hope."

I hadn't thought about that. I'd assumed the show would be somewhere in town.

"It's not far, just a few kilometers from town. It's a small temple where the dancers practice."

"Okay," I said, "let's do it."

When I got into the office the next morning, I was surprised to find Marc already there. He had come up from Phnom Penh early.

"You're on to something," he said. "We need to talk."

He told me what he had learned since we'd last spoken.

"Two of the Phnon Penh cases had severed spines, just like the ones here. We don't know about the others yet. Because the bodies had so many wounds that might have caused death, no one was paying much attention to severed spines."

He raised the topic of the dance: "I talked with my friend, the expert on the local religion. He doesn't know the dance either. But he said that we need to keep in mind that there have always been cults, and the cults have rituals, and the rituals sometimes call for sacrifice—could be of humans. So what you're looking at is not outlandish."

Something else bothered me.

"But why were these particular victims chosen?" I asked.

"My friend had an answer for that too—because they were available. And because of why they came here, particularly if they came to abuse children. That made them unclean, not fit to live, and therefore worthy subjects for a sacrifice. The French woman was not a suitable sacrifice because she was not a man. So they forced her boyfriend to kill her first. The scenario in that case had to be very different from the others. My friend suggested that at some stage we try to have your friend arrange a performance. He believes that will bring things out in the open."

"I'm ahead of the schedule. The performance is arranged—for tonight."

"Oh, my goodness," Marc said. "I had hoped for more time. There are things we need to do."

Those things included alerting the Cambodian police, including a special paramilitary unit, and getting them involved—"to deal with the possibility of violence," as Marc put it. I told Marc that I didn't know exactly where the dance would be held, except that it was a temple where the dancers practiced.

"Not a problem," Marc said. "The cops know the lay of the land. They'll sort it out."

As Dominique told me, the temple was not far out of town, just a bit remote. We left the main road and drove down a hidden lane that led nowhere. In the fading light the temple was mostly just shadows of ruined structures and mounds of rubble. We went through a broken wall into a small courtyard. Dominique had me sit on a stone block at the end of a low platform to wait for the show to begin.

"Stay here. I'll have them light the lanterns. The dancers will come from over there," she said, indicating the far end of the platform.

Over the next few minutes lanterns were lit around me, not close by but back among the trees and the buildings. As there was no direct light, the platform stayed covered in shadows that swayed with the soft evening breeze. It was quite a romantic setting, really. I had to remind myself why I was there.

The flute was so low at first that I thought the sound was only in my mind. When I realized that I was actually hearing it, I looked for the girl who was playing it, but she was well-hidden somewhere among the shadows.

And then the dancers were on the platform. I had not seen them come—six of them. They were just moving shadows at first. As they came closer and moved into a pool of pale light, I could make them out, lithe young figures in sarongs with veils that covered their breasts. They swayed to the music, which was slow and languorous for a time, but then the tempo picked up and they started to move more quickly.

One of the dancers separated from the others and moved toward me. For a moment I thought it was Dominique, but it was not. It was some young creature with long limbs. Her breasts were bare. Around her waist was some filmy material that left her belly and the tops of her legs showing, and hid only a bit of what was between. And then that fell away. I remembered Dominique's description—"and her body was white like milk." This body wasn't; it was golden, and beautiful, and as in Dominique's script, I couldn't take my eyes from it. The dancer came closer and closer. My God, she was so beautiful—I had to touch her. I reached out ...

That was what my own script would have me do. In fact, I was totally conscious of what could happen to me. When nothing immediately did, I couldn't help but turn to see what was going on behind me—and that saved me. The sword of Shiva slid across my body, just above my hipbone, instead of being thrust through my back. My sudden turn had ruined her aim. Dominique gasped as she realized she had missed. I felt no pain then, just a warm wetness down my side. I managed to avoid the blade and grab her wrist. I twisted as hard as I could—I felt no mercy now—and heard the sword of Shiva clatter on the stone. It was only later I realized I was bleeding like a stuck pig.

It didn't matter. Dominique and the dancers vanished. Bright lights lit up the scene. Marc stood before me.

"You're bleeding very badly," he said.

I must have blacked out at some point.

"Where did they go?" I asked.

"Into a building, probably. There's nowhere else."

One of the Cambodian cops was a medic, and he bandaged up my side where I had been sliced.

"That should hold you together until we get into town," Marc said.

A young Cambodian cop ran up.

"Sir, sir!" he said to Marc. "They've found the women."

"I'll come with you," Marc said to the cop. They spoke briefly, and then Marc turned to me. "You stay here," he said. "There's a police van coming. They'll get you to the hospital."

"It's just a scratch," I said.

Marc just shook his head.

"I need to see this to the finish," I said.

That got me another long look from Marc.

Finally he said: "Well, come on, then. We can drive most of the way in a jeep."

I was really starting to hurt, much more than I wanted to admit to anyone. It was stiff upper lip as I climbed slowly into the jeep. That took me longer than our drive across the compound.

We passed small buildings, some partially collapsed, others just piles of rubble. Our headlights picked out one with police standing around it. It seemed largely intact. Part of the covered gateway in the front had collapsed and blocked the way in. We drove around the side, where there were more police and soldiers. Headlights of a dozen jeeps and pickup trucks lit up the scene.

"You called in the army," I said.

"The cops did. It's a political thing. Come on. The women are all in this building. They got in through the hole in the wall. It's blocked now, but the troops will have it cleared shortly."

A Coven of Snakes

The soldiers were using a thick wooden pole as a battering ram. The ladies inside had pushed stone blocks into the opening. There was no other way in or out. The cops had checked.

Marc said, "At least we know where they are. It's a matter of time."

A cheer came from the troops when the stones blocking the hole were pushed aside. Marc walked over to where the officer in charge stood, for a quick conference. He came back looking disturbed.

"They want to go in and bring them out," he said. "I told then to wait, to tire the women out, but they won't agree."

Nothing happened for a time; everybody stood around. Finally, an army officer walked over to speak with Marc. When he finished, Marc turned to me.

"He wants us to help, to go inside and try talking with the women. Are you up to going in there?"

I really wasn't, but I said yes, I was quite up to it.

"Their team will go in first. We'll go in right behind."

We had to duck under an overhanging stone block and step over broken stone on the floor. Inside the wall we were able to stand up straight. The soldiers brought flashlights and electric lanterns. Marc made room so I could see. The soldiers turned on the bright lights.

The women were all huddled together against the far wall. Ten of them, as we found out later. They clung to each other, frightened. I guess I was light-headed from the loss of blood. As I looked at them, everything around me suddenly started to revolve. The scene in front of me turned into a quivering ball of snakes among the fallen rocks of a ruined wall.

Blaam! Blaam!

It was an accident, I suppose. A young, poorly trained soldier, frightened by the screaming woman who came running at him, waving long knives.

The girls all had knives. Dominique held the Sword of Shiva, as she called it, a long, thin, finely honed blade. The others had what you might call daggers, not as long, but nasty looking and just as sharp. It was Dominique and two of the dancers who suddenly ran toward us with their knives. They would have done us harm—but the frightened young soldier jerked back the trigger of his shotgun before they could reach us.

Dominique took the first blast full in her face. The second caught this very lovely young girl in her chest. It spared her face but practically chopped her in half. Fragments caught some of the other girls, left them writhing on the ground. It was the snakes I saw again.

Thanks to an infection, it was a week before I got out of the hospital. All of the excitement was over by then. Marc visited me there, and we talked about what had happened and why.

"You were right," he said, "about the women not being properly questioned. The victims did come here for the children. The women misled us, told the cops that all the sex was between adults. The women had decided to deal with the problem themselves. It is a cult. We were dealing with the local chapter here. There are others in Phnom Penh and other parts of Cambodia. There will be more victims as time goes on." Marc sighed then. "Just another problem for this poor country."

The morning I was released from the hospital, Marc drove me to the airport. After I was checked in, he reached over and touched my shoulder.

"I'm really sorry about how things ended," he said. "I shouldn't have let you get into a situation where you could get hurt."

Lying in my hospital bed I had tried not to think about some things, but I thought back to Dominique now, and how I had enjoyed her in those few days. I remembered the moving shadows in the temple that night and how beautiful the dancers were. It was something I would never forget.

"There's nothing to feel bad about," I said. "Who could know that there are things like that—things so beautiful, that can be so evil."

Marc shrugged like a Frenchman. "Yes," he said, "there is so much beauty here ..."

He paused, as if looking for a word.

"You know, I was about to say that maybe it was the Khmer Rouge who poisoned the land. But the evil is more ancient than that. It's been here from the beginning. And the women ... they were trying to destroy the evil they saw around them, the evil others bring here."

"She tried to kill me, for God's sake," I said. "Why did Dominique want to do that?"

"Perhaps she sensed that you were beginning to understand what was happening. Or maybe evil corrupts those who come too near it."

We shook hands then, and Marc walked off.

I watched from the window as the aircraft climbed out of Siam Reap. I could see all of the ancient city below, and Angkor Wat, the gem that crowns it. From high above, it was all so beautiful.

Bob Bergin

Bob Bergin, a former U.S. Foreign Service officer and a dealer in Southeast Asian antiques, writes on the history of aviation in Southeast Asia and China, and on OSS and military operations in the China-Burma-India World War II theater. He has published three novels set in Southeast Asia, and a collection of short stories: *A Delicate Beauty from Phetburi: Tales of Intrigue in Asia, Africa and Other Exotic Places*.

Rebirth

Neil Wilford

She was trapped.

"I need your help. You must come now. Please ..."

Then she hung up.

That kind of call only ever meant money or trouble, usually both. But of course he went, his memories of their last tryst in a five-dollar room still flashing fresh and raw.

Two hours later, at the back of the darkened hole-in-the-wall bar where Chanta worked through the night, every night, he'd agreed.

"All right," he said, "meet me tomorrow at my apartment. I'll have the money. Get it done at a clean place, OK? I don't want you bleeding to death in an alley in Stung Meanchey."

Pay in, pay out, then live to enjoy another night free from responsibility. In this town the edges of possibility were bordered only by the imagination.

"Scott good man."

Her tears wetting his neck almost made him feel complete. In control, for once in his life.

"Where is she? Where?!"

The third crystal glass of the morning shattered against

the wall. The tension around the team of bodyguards swallowed the sound whole.

"General, no one's seen her for two days already."

"I didn't ask who hadn't seen her! I asked who had and where!"

The General knew how to project fear. Cuban heels, toe tips just visible on a straight sight down the chin across a frame of stone. Shining mahogany skin, gold Rolex face displaying three portraits, platinum diamond chunked wedding ring, and a Pailin ruby the size of a grape on the index finger. Symbols of loyalty and longevity. Advertisements of access, power.

The eyes gave him away. Hard onyx beads set in deeply pockmarked cheeks reflected a lifetime immersed in the unspeakable. The pencil-thin tattoo tracing the jawline ear to ear the only concession to the unnatural.

But he was worried. Where was Chanta? And where was his baby?

Scott had made it home just in time. Black cloud walls were marching across the sunshine announcing the afternoon monsoon. In minutes the streets were reduced to deep rivers of filth. He was glad to be back. It felt good to get one over on the season.

He'd scooped her up through his front door without a second thought after finding her squatting, pale and shaking, in the corridor. After he'd laid her gently on his bed, she'd groaned then smiled and slept so hard he'd worried she was dead.

"It's gone. They look for me now," she said, after eating. "You must go."

A hero host and now being told to go? He usually told girls it was time for them to leave so he could avoid the walk of shame in the harsh morning light. They never looked the same then, especially at the ATM.

"Who's looking? Go where? What are you talking about Chanta? You need to rest, relax."

"You don't understand. You barang," she said, shaking her head sadly, "never understand Khmer culture."

They'd divided the city into search areas. Mao, the General's most loyal lieutenant, had taken the forty blocks behind the riverside stretching toward the central market. Security for the seemingly endless array of bars, restaurants, guesthouses, and karaoke parlors was run by the military. Mostly protecting their own assets.

What was Chanta thinking? She knew the consequences. And now here he was, driving around town in the rain on the sharp end of the General's rage.

Everywhere he'd gone had drawn blanks. People weren't in the habit of lying to him, so he'd trusted their solemn denials. What choice did they have? Faced with this quiet monster of a man, violence glowing in his skin.

His radio bleeped and crackled.

"Nothing here boss."

Each of his teams reported the same. Fuck. He shivered at the thought of the General's response. His Chinese Glock copy felt suddenly hot against his side.

On his knees, the General trembled. Eyes closed.

"I don't have it. Not yet."

"*Soon?*"

"Yes."

He lifted his hand and left the candlelit wooden room, sweating.

Rebirth

The rain had finally let up, the city sparkling after its dousing. Dark slime and trash backed up around the useless drains. A gentle rotting stink rose into the midday sky.

Out through his barred apartment windows the skyline was changing daily. Endless hammering and grinding conducting an insidious soundscape impossible to avoid. A city trying its best to erase its memory and succeeding fast.

She hadn't said a word, curled fetus-like, facing the wall. Rolled in a duvet, she seemed somehow immune to the humidity.

Scott needed to get out, get some air. Some time to think. Drink.

"I'll be back soon. I've got some things to do."

He took her barely perceptible movement as agreement.

"General, we are close. We'll find her. Believe me."

"I'm certain you will. Just keep going. I trust you."

Nothing terrified Mao as much as his General, calm and softly spoken, in times of stress.

Scott took his usual circuit around town. Relieved to be away from the melancholy at home. Happy hour lasted four, sometimes twelve, hours here where the bars outnumbered the customers. An endless choice of good-value mediocrity when there was no pussy in the equation.

He drank with acquaintances. Few foreigners had real friends here, or a history. Most came for a new life, an escape, a chance for reinvention. To be something they never were or could be at home. Or to hide from it.

Easily found in the Penh but not as easily abandoned, as so many could testify.

Golf ball-sized raindrops killed the sunset with no warning. Trapped where they were at the bar, the drinks were in again as the celestial faucet poured loose and wild.

"Getting in is easy. Getting out is a whole different ball game."

That was the best advice he'd got for the problem now sleeping at his apartment after steadily drinking his way through the night with the old expat hands he considered his closest associates.

He'd had to drag her by the hair into the back for her lies. Mamasan had told him Chanta had disappeared but had said nothing about the barang who'd come to meet her. The tall young American who'd reduced the girl to tears before getting fall-down drunk.

Mao smiled. Re-education at his school held to simple rules.

Late now, the neon-lit strip illuminating desire for the night's final options. Scott took his time, meandering from one bar to the next, each slightly more similar than the last. Food stalls lined the street with greasy Western fare for the drunks and noodle soups for their paramours. A familiar moto-taxi driver shouted across the street that he knew where Scott lived. He stumbled onto the back of the decaying rectangular Dailim seat, bracing himself on the one remaining footpeg.

The driver slowed at the crowd gathered on the pavement, the few police present not even trying to keep

Rebirth

them back. Typical roadkill gawp mob, Scott thought while poking the driver on. Had he stopped and looked, he might have recognized the mamasan.

Scott stood rooted in his doorway. Consumed by the sight of her.

Naked. Face pistol-whipped swollen, the resignation still lingering in her eyes. Her stomach sliced clean across below the naval. Peeled back. The mess of a gunshot between her legs a vicious afterthought, a cold-blooded frustration.

Frozen. His every instinct battling his gut reaction. Decision made, he moved fast. Get the essentials and get out now. When he realized he was missing the keys to his life, he ran faster.

"She was without it, General."

Mao didn't flinch when his gun was pulled by the General. He shot the second oldest of his guard team in the head before handing Mao back his weapon and walking out.

Scott kept running. It was 6:00 a.m., the streets boiling with activity. He'd tried the riverbank but the monsoon-bloated Tonle Sap flowed high and brown. No hiding to be had there.

He checked his wallet. Fifty dollars to get him out of the country and avoid a life in Prey Sar prison. Shit. Think!

"Yes, nephew?"

"Aunty, I've lost Chanta. I need another."

"Don't worry. I have a perfect one. A good girl, strong and dark. She will be ready for you. I will bring her from Kompong Thom province tomorrow."

The General hung up and relaxed. Allowed vengeance to gently occupy his mind.

He had to get off the street. Who knew who was looking for him? Everyone seemed to be staring and whispering. A thousand eyes boring into his soul from every corner. Scott bought a bottle of whiskey to straighten his nerves and then checked into an anonymous downtown hotel. The stairs up to his room were sticky, the walls grimed with handprints. No one would find him here, at least not until he'd made some kind of plan.

"General, we have him."

Mao hung up, settled back, and waited.

The General had chosen the blacked-out, fully loaded Range Rover HSE for the night's business. It gave the right impression. Garnered the demanded respect. The high whistle of quarter-million-dollar wheels was a familiar sound in this new time. Traffic was a precise social barometer masquerading as anarchy. For most, the risk of being totaled by the impatient, the fearless, or the untouchable ran very real.

His driver never slowed, never stopped for the whole journey before pulling to a halt across the pavement outside one of the General's many hotels.

As he strode into the mildewed lobby the staff fell over themselves, scrambling up from their prone relaxation. The manager jittered to the front.

"General, if we had known you'd be coming ..."

"I'm here on separate business. I'll deal with everything else later."

"Is there anything we can provide for you?"

Rebirth

"No. Stay here, all of you."

The safari-suited bodyguards stationed on the fourth floor parted immediately on his appearance. They opened the door of number 44 and closed it gently behind him.

Scott lay naked, tied to the bed by thick strands of Khmer checkered cloth. A bundle of the same was knotted into his mouth. No sound, no bruises. His fear had already soiled the sheets. Mao stood like a statue, silent in the corner.

"You are nothing but a guest in my country who has long outstayed his welcome," the General hissed into Scott's ear before placing his passport, credit cards, and a half-empty bag of white powder on the bedside table. Chanta's bloodied panties hung off the bathroom door. The General surveyed the scene with satisfaction before nodding to Mao and leaving.

Scott's eyes bulged as Mao slid across the room, hypodermic needle in hand.

His surprise at the ease of his death passed across his face as the edges folded in.

The English language rags ran small paragraphs. Yet another foreigner who'd underestimated the China white. The stench had forced the management to break down the door after complaints. The Khmer papers led with color photos of Chanta's body. The drug-addicted barang found dead yesterday in a cheap hotel room had desecrated this young flower of the Kingdom.

"I have it."

On his knees, the General laid the tiny mummified body on the mat in the candlelit wooden room. Seven other fetus mummies rested on the gold-sprayed plinth, shimmering behind the incense smoke.

Eyes clenched shut, sweating, he laid his hand on his first. The power surged through him as he felt it speak.

"*Good. We can continue.*"

Balance had been restored.

Neil Wilford

Neil Wilford hails from a small seaside town slightly famous for having been an occasional home to Charles Dickens and Wilkie Collins. After studying history and literature at Manchester, UK and Illinois, USA, he swopped Southeast England for Southeast Asia and has been resident in Phnom Penh since 2001. *Rebirth* is his first published work of fiction.

KROM
Songs from the Noir
Christopher Minko

The lyrics below were authored by Christopher Minko and performed by KROM, a Cambodian band in album titled: *Songs from the Noir* released in 2012.

Buckets of Blood

I walked the line
So many times
I walked the line
A line so bloody fine

That's why there's buckets of blood
And I'm-a-laying in bed
Thinking it over
With a rock in my head

I walked the line
So many times
I walked the line
A line so bloody fine
I walked the line
With many a bottle of wine
And when I crossed that line
You were no longer mine

That's why there's buckets of blood
And I'm-a-laying in bed

KROM: Songs from the Noir

Thinking it over
With a rock in my head

But baby
All I really want to do
Yeah baby
All I really want to do
Yeah baby
All I really want to do
Is baby
Sing a love song for you

Prison of Sobriety

And I called out your name
But my call was in vain
From the prison of sobriety
Locked in a cell of notoriety
Yeah in that prison of sobriety
They throw away the key to reality

And I weep
I cannot sleep
Your pain I keep
In the prison of sobriety
There aint no room for vanity
In the prison of sobriety
You won't find a high society

So I cut all my emotions loose
And just end up in the hangman's noose
In the prisons of sobriety

Christopher Minko

No such thing as normality
In the prison of sobriety
Yo is gonna lose your sanity

And I weep
I cannot sleep
Your pain I do keep
In the prison of sobriety
Locked in a cell of notoriety
In that prison of sobriety
They throw away the key to reality
In that prison of sobriety
Yo is gonna lose your sanity

The Ying

No like but she do
No eat, no money
Love you like monkey
I not lie you, I talk true

No like but she do
No eat, no money
Love you like monkey
I not lie you, I talk true

Oh yeah, that Ying
She's a beautiful thing
Those oriental eyes
Seduction is the prize
She's an artist, a gallery,
A painter of lies

KROM: Songs from the Noir

In the soi of delusion
No logic applies

No like but she do
No eat, no money
Love you like monkey
I not lie you, I talk true

I turn 16 today
She tells old white men at play
They're lost in a jukebox of time
Years of sagging flesh and grime
Breaking tiny oriental hearts
Into fractured butterfly parts
On a smudged chrome chair
Covered in sexual crime

No like but she do
No eat, no money
Love you like monkey
I not lie you, I talk true

An arc of morning Mekong
That's her mournful song
Yeah, something's not right
Yeah, something's fucking wrong
In the enclosure of glass
Number on pearl shaped arse
On the semen stained floor
Curl the naked raped broken poor

No like but she do
No eat, no money

Christopher Minko

Love you like monkey
I not lie you, I talk true

In the soi of delusion
22 for the illusion
Merchants of sex without name
Lean from alleys in a serpent's lane
But no matter
How hard she tries
She can never hide the pain
In those cold Sukhumvit eyes

Oh yeah, that Ying
She's a beautiful thing
Those oriental eyes
Seduction is the prize
Oh yeah, that Ying
She's a beautiful thing
Her soft silk skin
The lure of original sin

No like but she do,
No eat, no money
Love you like monkey
I not lie you, I talk true

No like but she do
No eat no money
Love you like monkey
I not lie you, I talk true

Bangkok Tattoo

My Bangkok Tattoo
She's lookin' at you
My Bangkok Tattoo
I'll always love you

It's the original sin
Gets under your skin
The darkness of
An ink bled view

My Bangkok Tattoo
She's lookin' at you
My Bangkok Tattoo
Your love got me through

Sanskrit verse on every curve
On skin, so fine, once mine
It was you who soothed
My sacred nerve

My Bangkok Tattoo
My words were too few
My Bangkok Tattoo
(Oh) what did I do?

My Bangkok Tattoo
I'm alone without you
A tear shed true
You never knew

My Bangkok Tattoo
She's lookin' at you

Christopher Minko

My Bangkok Tattoo
I'll always love you

My Bangkok Tattoo
(Oh) Mam I love you

My Bangkok Tattoo
She's lookin' at you

Don't Go Away

Don't go away
Just stay another day
Don't go away
I've got so much to say
Don't leave me now
Cause love I don't know how
Don't leave me now
Gotta find that love somehow
So don't go away
Just stay another day
Don't leave me now
Cause love I don't know how

Bangkok nights
A birth ignites
Phnom Penh lights
A couple fights
Violence erupts
They are torn apart
Both of them now
With a broken heart

So don't go away
Just stay another day
So don't leave me now
Cause love I don't know how

And when they reached out
Was far too late
Cause someone had opened
The pearly gate
So she passed away
'N' what more could I say
Then please just stay
For another day

So don't go away
Just stay another day
So don't leave me now
Cause love I don't know how

So don't go away
Just stay another day
So don't leave me now
Cause love I don't know how

Mango Madness / Monsoon Sadness

Mango madness
'n' monsoon sadness
In the heat of the night
There's whole lotta badness
Yeah mango madness
'n' monsoon sadness

Christopher Minko

In the heat of the night
There's a whole lotta badness

White trash
Hole in the wall
Buying young girls
The oriental call
Yeah in the heat of the night
There's a whole lotta badness
It's mango madness
'n' monsoon sadness

Yeah a whole lotta madness

The click of high heels
The crack of a gun
A dark alleyway
A man on the run
Yeah in the heat of the night
There's a whole lotta badness
Yeah mango madness
'n' monsoon sadness

Yeah a whole lotta badness
Yeah a whole lotta sadness

A torn dress
A breast exposed
Those cold eyes
Of a body sold
Yeah in the heat of the night
There's a whole lotta badness
It's mango madness
'n' monsoon sadness

KROM: Songs from the Noir

Mango madness
'n' monsoon sadness
In the heat of the night
There's whole lotta badness
Yeah mango madness
'n' monsoon sadness
In the heat of the night
There's a whole lotta badness

Yeah, in the heat of the night

It's mango madness
'n' monsoon sadness
It's mango madness
'n' monsoon sadness
It's mango madness
'n' monsoon sadness

Where'd Ya Go

Oh where'd ya go
I wanna know
Cause ah miss you so

Oh where'd ya go
Seven Buddhas in a row
Lost in a dragon's inferno

An oriental ghost
Sends out a searching probe
Just looking for that angel
In a saffron robe

Christopher Minko

Oh where'd ya go
You're no Jane Doe
This isn't the last picture show

Called the soi of delusion
You didn't answer
Was then I knew I was alone
On my own

Oh where'd ya go
Your lantern glows
Rest assured, the naga knows

Through haunted crossroads
Of compassion and depravity
Comes a precious moment in time
Of simple clarity

So now I know
Where you did go
And I still miss you so

How do I know
Where you did go
Cause your love taught me so

Phnom Penh

An oriental twist
A legend exposed
The curl of a wrist
Year Zero dissolved
Yeah, that's Phnom Penh

The city we've grown to love
Phnom Penh
The city we've grown to love

Khmer language verse x 2

Pearl of the orient
Let the silk unfold
An apsara smile
A problem resolved
Yeah, that's Phnom Penh
The city we've grown to love
Phnom Penh
The city we've grown to love

Khmer Language verse x 2

Yeah, that's Phnom Penh
The city we've grown to love
Phnom Penh
The city we've grown to love
Yeah, that's Phnom Penh
The city we've grown to love
Phnom Penh
The city we've grown to love
Yeah, that's Phnom Penh
The city we've grown to love
Phnom Penh
The city we've grown to love

Christopher Minko

Tango Traffic Tango

The cattle class
Of ancient men
Are greeted with open arms
Welcome to our daughters
We breed them on our farms
Ripe for human trafficking
We sell their innocent charm

Yeah, air traffic
Rail traffic
Road traffic
People traffic
And human trafficking
Where money and sex are king
Yeah, human trafficking
Where money and sex are king

So welcome to our daughters
We breed them on our farms
Open up and take them
In your ageing sagging arms
Yeah, welcome to our daughters
We breed them on our farms

Yeah, air traffic
Rail traffic
Road traffic
People traffic
And human trafficking
Where money and sex are king
Yeah, human trafficking
Where money and sex are king

KROM: Songs from the Noir

Yeah, welcome to our daughters
We breed them on our farms
Fresh and lush for picking
A bargain price for trafficking
Yeah, welcome to our daughters
We breed them on our farms
Y'can grope them all over
With your wrinkled sweaty palms
Yeah, welcome to our daughters
We breed them on our farms
Yeah, welcome to our daughters
We breed them on our farms